Central Park Collision

NICOLE SANCHEZ

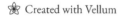

For me, for proving that I could

Author Note

First, thank you so much for picking up a copy of my debut book!

This book features detailed steamy scenes, which if you can't read between the lines, I mean there is a lot of sex. If this makes you uncomfortable or we're related please feel free to stop here! I appreciate you giving me a chance. This book also has themes of memory loss and scenes of abuse. If these are triggering topics for you, please go in aware.

Prologue

CHARLIE - OCTOBER

I DON'T REALIZE how still I've been sitting until the office lights hum above me before blinking out. I glare up at them, tired of the constant need to get up and wave my arms around like a mad man. Whoever created motion sensor lights without the ability to set them to 'on' should be shot.

I stand and stretch my arms overhead before turning to look out the floor-to-ceiling window of my office. My reflection in the privacy glass shows my surprise. I run my hand through my hair, realizing I need a haircut. I usually keep it short and neat, but I've been running myself into the ground. I should have gotten married this month, but I didn't. The engagement ended when my fiancée walked out on me because, in her words, "If you're married to your job, you can't be married to me."

At some point, it had not only become night, but it started raining. Not just raining, pouring. A vague memory surfaces of my assistant, Ashley, telling me she was leaving because of a hurricane. Usually, she would tough out the night, stay until I left, but she wanted to get home before the storm got bad and created the potential to shut down trains. Manhattan doesn't see many hurricanes, so I seldom have to worry about them.

I look at my watch with a heavy sigh; that was nearly six hours ago. Well after a reasonable time to end the day, but truth be told, had she asked earlier, I would have let her go then. Most days, I don't leave my office and it might make me pathetic, but I do rely on Ashley telling me that shit weather is here. So, you know, I don't miss things like a hurricane skirting the city. I pull out my phone, and see that my taxi app, PickMeUp!, has surge pricing due to the storm, but I order a black car anyway. I pack up my laptop, grateful that there are even cars available at two-thirty in the morning.

I'm still managing my emails when the car pulls up, honking immediately. They're just as desperate to get off the road as I am to get home.

"You crazy, man?" the driver asks after verifying my identity.

I don't answer him, choosing to focus on my draft email to one of the Asia offices I'm working with. I finish the email and look up.

"Crazy rain," I agree, having only half heard him. The streets of the Financial District are nearly bare, only a handful of cars and pedestrians are braving the storm.

"Rain? This is from a genuine hurricane! I know that doesn't seem like much after Sandy, but it's still a nasty storm out there. I was working during Sandy, you know. It was a superstorm, nothing like it. A hundred-year storm they call it. You must work in finance. All you Wall Street guys are the same, working until the sun comes up, only to go home and shower and go right back at it. You all have so much money, but what's the use if all you do is work?"

I'm only catching every other word out of his mouth as I keep working. The driver shoots up the West Side Highway, taking the exit for 96th Street. Usually, they would take the FDR, but I wonder if this driver knows something I don't.

I'm not paying much attention anyway. My father sent an email telling me not to fuck up the deal, as if I need another reminder. The company we're looking to buy is a Japanese medical device manufacturer, and my dad is already talking about me taking a trip to Tokyo to discuss the deal in person.

This email, telling me I need to brush up on Japanese business customs, is unnecessary. I've already been to visit them when we first started looking, but now he wants me to go to close the deal.

It's no wonder Ainsley ended things. I try not to think about her, about how we should have been married already, fucking our way through a month in Seychelles. It was excessive, taking a month, but I thought she deserved it; a month of my undivided attention. Though, the way this deal was shaking up, I probably would have been working while my new wife swam naked in the private pool overlooking the ocean.

I have no right to know, but I wonder how she's doing. My life has felt emptier, filled only with work since she ended things. It was like I abruptly lost a limb the way she cut herself out of my life so completely. There were events I would have seen her at: the January charity gala and other Dartmouth Alumni events I knew had been on her calendar. Our mutual friend, Taryn, let me know that Ainsley wasn't going to attend those things; she needed space from me. I respect that, but damn it, I want my friend back.

The car slows, and I glance up to see that we're entering Central Park on the 97th Street transverse. The sheets of rain seem to be falling harder, killing any visibility. Another email chimes on my phone, and I fight the urge to groan. My best friend and coworker, Jack, is emailing me now, annoyed about the thought of having to go to Japan, but wondering if he could swing bringing his girlfriend. Proposing in Japan might outweigh any other engagement plans he was making. I switch from my email to text Jack about his upcoming proposal and ask if he's serious.

As we near the exit of the park, the driver shouts in surprise, jerking the wheel.

"Oh fuck!"

The impact of the car colliding with something makes my

heart twist, my brain already trying to rationalize what we hit. Maybe a trash can blown into the street? The driver slams on his brakes, the car skidding to a complete stop. I don't think, dropping my phone and climbing out as the driver sits stunned, gripping the steering wheel. He doesn't let it go, a stricken look plastered on his face.

"Hey!" I shout, snapping at him, trying to startle him back into movement. I know in my heart that it wasn't trash he hit. I move toward the front of the car, surprised by the rain all over again, but I don't hesitate, looking out where the headlights shine.

Crushed under the tires is a bicycle and my heart seizes all over again. Lying in the street is a woman, her shattered helmet inches from her head. I rush to her, terrified at the way her leg is splayed to the side, bone sticking out of her skin just above her ankle. I'm shocked by how white it is against the red of her blood. Even in the dark I can see it glowing. Her arm is twisted under her torso, head turned away, eyes closed. Her blonde hair is splayed on the street in a grim halo.

"Oh God," I mutter, dropping to my knees beside her.

The driver has finally emerged from the car, his eyes wide and panicked. "I didn't see her! She came out of nowhere!"

I reach my hand gingerly to turn her head. There are scratches down the side of her face, blood seeping from them. For just a moment, she opens her eyes and looks at me, hazel eyes dark with pain.

"Call 9-1-1!" I shout, pulling off my drenched jacket. It's not much, but it's something I can use to protect her from the elements. I can't tell if it's a tear or just the rain, but she's wet around the eyes, gritting her teeth. I did this. I wasn't driving the car, but if I had left work at a normal time with a storm like this coming through, she wouldn't be lying on the pavement, broken. This is an image I will never get out of my head. The vision of this shattered, dying woman in the street will be something that stays with me for the rest of my life.

I did this.

"You're going to be okay," I tell her, trying to sound confident. I hope it's a promise that I can keep. "Just keep looking at me. What's your name?" I ask, trying to keep her awake and alert. I wish I had paid closer attention to those stupid medical dramas that Ainsley watched. I don't know what to do right now besides shield her. I feel like I should be putting pressure on a wound, but everywhere I might try looks like I would do more harm than good.

"El-" She groans and tries to shift her arm. I know enough that she shouldn't be moved much. I probably fucked up moving her head, but I needed to see if she was still alive.

"Don't move. You can't move." I want to reach for her and hold her still. Distantly, I can hear the sounds of the sirens as they come for us, come for El. I regret asking her her name. It's clear she's in pain.

"I...get...home."

I brush her hair back as blood and water plaster it to her face. "We will get you home, I promise." She tries to close her eyes but I pat her cheek; lightly at first, then with a little more force. "You need to keep your eyes open. I don't know much, but I know that."

"So..." Her pause here is so long, I'm afraid she's stopped breathing, stopped living in front of me. "Tired," she finishes, the word more a sigh than actual speech. Her eyes linger on mine, desperately looking for something. She's fighting to keep her eyes open, but each blink is getting longer and longer.

"Well, it's three in the morning, I would expect nothing less."

She tries to laugh, but it turns into a groan of pain and I panic. What if she has internal bleeding that I'm making worse? The ambulance sirens are closer now, so much closer I can see the lights as they turn the corner. The vehicle comes to a screeching halt before us along with a cop car, there to collect statements.

The paramedics throw questions at me, demanding answers

about what happened. I tell them what I can, what I remember. This woman, El, slips away again, closing her eyes, but the paramedics are monitoring her vitals. While they put the C-collar on her, straightening her leg and arm, I turn to the driver.

"Give me my phone and bag," I order, using my work voice. The driver jumps into action, glad to have something to do other than talk to the police. He hands it to me as the paramedics are transferring the woman onto a backboard and then the stretcher. I reach under the car, salvaging her purse, which is pinned in the front basket. It's not a habit of mine to rummage around ladies' purses, but I check to make sure that I have her wallet. Her phone is wedged under the tire of the car, unlikely to see another day.

The paramedics are efficient at their job and are already preparing to load her into the cab of the ambulance and I follow them.

"I'm sorry, sir, you can't come," a tall, lanky kid who can't be over twenty-one says.

The longer we stand in the rain arguing, the more annoyed I get. "I appreciate that, but I have to object. Please, she needs someone there when she wakes up."

The two paramedics exchange a look and the female finally nods, if for no other reason than to get El to the hospital more quickly. I climb into the back, beside the kid, who continues to work on El. I thumb through her purse, pulling out her wallet.

"Her name is Elia Daniels," I say, looking at the license photo. No one takes a good picture, but she looks particularly unhappy. I run my hand over my mouth, glancing at this woman who is unresponsive on the bed.

There is a hellish weight that settles over my shoulders knowing that it was my decision-making that put her there. If I had listened, if I had left earlier, if I had taken the subway instead... Any number of decisions I could have done differently to spare her this painful fate. If she survives, I know I'll do anything to fix this.

Now I know her name. Now, I can try to make things right.

One

~✦~

ELIA - ONE WEEK LATER

THE BRIGHT SKY is what wakes me up from my dream. The dream isn't particularly memorable. It's the kind of dream that seems fantastical while your eyes are closed, but once you open them and let your consciousness through the dream door, it starts to fade away a little at a time, then more quickly the harder you try to hold onto it. Sort of like trying to hold water in your hands, slowly slipping away until you have just a little there, just a concept, until even that is gone.

I'm usually good about keeping my blinds closed, not because of the sun, but because my bedroom window faces another building, and I've seen a little too much of my neighbor's dick to keep them open. The sound of beeping is unusual, so maybe it was my alarm that woke me. Or maybe I'm not even in my own place? My eyes fly open at the thought, wondering if I went home with someone last night, but I can't even really hold on to what I did last night. Was I out with Vivian?

Opening my eyes clues me in immediately. I'm not in my bed or a stranger's. I'm in a hospital room. Folded uncomfortably in one of those wooden chairs is a handsome man I don't recognize. I take a minute to study him in his own slumber. He has sandy

7

blond hair that's straight and hangs like a curtain over his eyes. There is a trail of hair along his jaw, not a maintained beard, more like the beginning of one, less intentional, more from a lack of shaving. He has full lips that are lightly parted. It looks like it's a restless sleep, from the way he fidgets, and I don't blame him. I've sat in those chairs before, during college. It's not the place to get a goodnight's sleep.

Other than the strange man, I'm alone in the room and the door is slightly ajar. Now that I'm really taking stock of the room and myself, the pain I'm in settles in, resonating from my leg up, and I gasp, wanting it to stop. I look down and see that my left leg is elevated by a sling that holds my casted appendage. My right wrist is also tightly wrapped in a hard cast.

The computer resting on the table in front of the man chimes and his eyes open. They go to me first before checking the laptop. His warm brown eyes brighten with surprise when he sees me.

"Hello?" I rasp, my voice sounding sore from disuse.

The man jumps to his feet, sending the table sliding across the floor.

"You're awake." His voice is smooth, quiet, trying to not startle me. I cough and look around for water. The man walks toward me, quickly, but reaches around me, pressing a button.

"Water?" I croak since my mouth is parched. My tongue feels heavy and keeps sticking to my mouth. I can't question him properly without something to drink.

"Of course." He chuckles to himself, pouring water from a bottle on the table into a small pink cup. My unencumbered arm feels weak as I lift it to take the cup from him, but he doesn't let it go, helping me tip it toward my mouth.

"We were worried about you," he says, his voice still quiet. His face is so perfectly chiseled but with deep lines around his eyes.

I hate that I can't figure out who he is because for him to be here with me must mean I matter to him.

Suddenly, footsteps echo throughout the room. "Ah, Miss

Daniels. Lovely to see some life in your eyes," a doctor says. He's older, probably in his fifties; whereas, the water boy who was folded in the corner of my room looks to be in his late twenties or early thirties.

"What happened?" I ask, more than a little confused.

"What do you remember?" the doctor asks.

The unknown man watches with confusion, but when he opens his mouth to answer my question, he notices the doctor is staring at me, patiently awaiting my answer.

"That I hate people who answer a question with a question," I say, finding strength in my voice.

The doctor indulgently smiles at me. "Okay, can you tell me how old you are?"

"I just turned twenty-four," I answer and both men exchange a look.

They run me through several more questions; my doctor is able to keep his face passive, but the strange man flinches at a few of my answers. During all this questioning, a nurse has been taking my vitals, her mouth tipping downward with each answer.

I get tired after a dozen questions and I snap. "Can someone please tell me what is going on?" I ask, looking from one man to the other.

The mystery man steps further away so he can lean against the windowsill.

"Elia, there was a car accident last week that you were involved in," the doctor says gently. "You tore ligaments in your knee, broke your tibia and fibula, and broke your wrist. You also had a minor brain bleed, which I think led to your amnesia. Based on how old you think you are, you've lost a few years." The doctor is trying to not overload my system with too much information at once. One injury at a time, but it feels like high school all over again; sitting on the outside of an inside joke everyone else knows.

I scoff at the insinuation. It's easier to hold on to the thought of having amnesia instead of that I was in a car accident and unconscious for a week. It's easier to think about that than the giant gap in my memory.

"Amnesia? What is this? *Days of Our Lives*?" I look over at the guy, my voice shaking just a little when I talk. "Who are you, even?"

"Charles Breckenridge. I was in the car that hit you." Charles sounds uncertain about revealing this information.

"You hit me with a car?" I sputter, turning on him.

Charles straightens up, running his hand down his chest. I track the movement, my mind picking this asinine detail to focus on as he explains further.

"Technically it was my PickMeUp! car, but I am still so sorry for this." He keeps talking, but his words turn into static.

I've lost years of my life because of the carelessness of some car. *Years*.

I look away from him, thinking about healing and growing that I would have done as a person in those years, and it's all gone, the board wiped clean of the person I became. I want to get out of this bed and go to Viv or call her and find out what the hell is going on. Before I can take the next logical step, I give into my anger.

I consider the cup in my hand then I hurl it at him with my insignificant strength. Even doing that exhausts me. Charles catches the cup with ease, some water falling to the floor.

"Charles isn't all to blame. Car versus bike often ends poorly for the bike. He has been here since your accident," the doctor says.

"Whose side are you on anyway?" I scowl. I'm suddenly so exhausted and I just want to go back to sleep even though I just woke up. I fight the urge to slip back into unconsciousness, but I can't hold off forever.

The next time I wake up, Charles is there, but it's dark in the room. His face is only illuminated by his computer screen. Above him, the muted TV is showing the late night news reports from the day. A segment on hurricane clean up in North Carolina is airing, and I try to dredge up a memory of it, a warning on the news or on social media, but all I get is a headache for my efforts. I can remember Sandy, but that was ages ago and not when I was living in the city.

I realize that Charles is talking quietly on the phone while his hands breeze across his keyboard. The cellphone is tucked against his ear and he's talking so low, I think I might be imagining it. He must be talking about me, because his eyes flick up to me while he is talking.

"I gotta go, Jack." Charles doesn't wait for the person on the other end of the phone to answer before he lets it slide off his shoulder into his hand, ending the call.

"Busy man," I say, just to make conversation.

"Yes well, I've been sitting in a hospital room for a week now. I do have to do my job." He's surprisingly not angry, even after my sarcastic tone and my throwing a cup at him.

I want to find it in me to be grateful for this stranger being here with me, but when I look, all I find is pain and anger and hurt. Where are my friends? Why am I stuck depending on a strange man to be here so I'm not alone?

"Job." I roll the word over in my mouth for a minute, trying to remember where I work. I'm a receptionist at a law firm, mostly doing some menial tasks like filing correspondence and answering phones. Do I still work there? Am I fired for missing work? I remember the conversation from earlier and the way that amnesia was thrown around. Each grasp I make for information comes away without results, making me grind my teeth. Everyone had subtle frowns on their faces, even the nurse, when I gave my answers. "How much amnesia do I have?"

"I think amnesia is more of a lack of something."

I don't give Charles a smile for his comment.

He rises, walking over to me. "Do you want me to get the doctor?"

"I want some fucking answers," I snap, not sure where this rage is coming from. I'm not an angry person, I don't like to fight with people or raise my voice. I try to keep things calm generally. I can feel tears well in my eyes, and I blink them away furiously.

Charles looks taken aback by my outburst but only briefly. I think he expects, to some extent, anger from me.

If I would take a moment to think about it, really think about it, I don't have to wonder where these emotions are coming from. They're from the helplessness that is trying to crawl its way out of my chest in the form of a scream. I don't want this stranger by my side. I want Vivian. I want my mom. I want my mom so badly it hurts. I want her to just tell me that this will be okay and that it will all work out. But she's dead. She and my father have been dead for two years. But it must be more now.

"Okay, I mean, HIPAA really prevents the doctor from telling me too much about your condition, but just sitting here? It's about five years. You're twenty-nine, not twenty-four. I can't tell you specifically though." He pulls the chair he's been occupying over, rubbing at his neck.

"Where is my phone? I have to call Viv."

Charles rises without complaint, grabbing my purse from the closet. I can glimpse my personal effects in a nondescript plastic bag on the top shelf. He holds up my phone in a plastic bag. The screen is obliterated, so is everything about the phone, cracked and spiderwebbed and broken beyond repair.

"It was crushed under the wheel of the car. I was able to get the SIM card from it and put it in a new phone, but you didn't have any contacts for me to call. I mean, I could have called Lotus House, but all that would have gotten me was your usual order." He slides a new sleek phone into my hand. It's warm from being in his pocket and I wonder if he was waiting to see if someone would call me.

"I didn't have your password to log you into your emails or anything, so I'm not sure what else could be there. There was no home number or mom or dad or aunts, and I didn't see a number for a 'Viv' in your phone either," Charles continues.

"My parents are dead," I rasp, a fresh wave of grief hitting me. This grief isn't just that they're gone; it's that I don't have them here to reassure me I'll get through this. I scroll through my phone to see that he's right; there are few contacts, none of which I recognize. I'm truly alone in this accident if I don't even have Vivian's number. I don't have it memorized so it's not even like I can call her.

"I'm sorry." The weight of his words implies he's sorry for more than just hitting me with his car. I look at my leg, where it hangs elevated.

"Where was the accident?" I glance at him and see pain in Charles' eyes.

"In Central Park. There was a hurricane, or part of one, anyway." He gestures over his shoulder at the TV. "We were just getting a lot of rain and heavy winds. The driver didn't see you until it was too late. The cops said you were lucky you had a helmet on, even if it didn't stay on. They said you probably would have died. As it was, I didn't think you would wake up."

"Then why were you here when I was?"

His brown eyes meet mine. "I didn't think you should have to be alone when you did. The doctor wants to run a few more tests, then get you started with some light physical therapy. They can't work on your bad foot, but they want to keep the other muscles around it strong."

"I can't afford that," I say immediately. Assuming I'm still at my job, my take home pay is less than twenty thousand dollars, and my health insurance plan was trash when I got it. The rent I split with Vivian is more than that. Another piece slides into place: she was moving in with a boyfriend. I don't know my rent anymore; I don't know if I can afford that. I don't even know where I live.

"I'm handling it. Anything you need, I'll have you covered."

"I can't accept that," I say automatically.

Charles shakes his head. "Look at it this way: insurance should be paying for your treatment; either yours or the car insurance. Rather than fuck everything up and potentially delay treatment, it's just getting billed to me."

His words make sense, but I still can't figure out why this stranger is doing this for me. He's studying me closely, watching for any sort of response, but other than that flood of anger I felt toward him when I woke up, my emotions feel muted. It's like listening to music underwater; I know I have feelings about all of this, grief and anger and shock and, somewhere deep inside, gratitude, but they're all out of reach for me to really get a hold on. I just hope that my emotions aren't locked away with my memories.

I look out the window of my hospital room where I can see lower Manhattan lit up in the distance. The city that never sleeps is still wide awake. I realize for the first time I'm in a private room.

"Insurance would never pay for this." I gesture with my good arm at the space I have. "This is *actually* larger than my first apartment. What am I supposed to do when I leave here? You can't pay for me forever."

"Let's get you cleared to leave and then we can worry about what we're going to do about the seventh floor, pre-war apartment in Washington Heights that doesn't have an elevator."

"I'm sorry, what?" Last I remember, I lived on the second floor in a rented condo in Hell's Kitchen.

"I didn't go into your apartment. I went to see if any of your neighbors might know who I could call. All it got me was hit with an umbrella by this surprisingly strong old woman who didn't like me asking questions."

I'm surprised again by just how far Charles has gone for me without even knowing me.

"Don't dismiss me out of hand; let's see how it goes. You've been unconscious for a week. Save your strength; you can fight with me later."

I can't help but track his tongue as he wets his lips before biting the lower one.

I don't get a chance to answer because a male nurse walks in, frowning at Charles. "Mr. Breckenridge, you might be able to convince other people to turn a blind eye, but I'm not someone you can charm. Visiting hours ended at six," the nurse says, starting to take my vitals and check on me.

"I hear you, I hear you, Carlos. I'll see you again tomorrow, Elia." Charles packs up his computer.

I sit up quickly, wincing, not wanting to see him go. I may not know him well, but at this point, he's all I have until I can sort out what to do about Vivian.

Charles sees me jerk up and catches the flash of pain on my face. He's across the room in two easy strides, like just my thoughts have pulled him to me. His attention on me is so complete that my cheeks flush.

Rather than tell him the real reason I sat up, I grab the remote that was easily in my reach and wave it at him in explanation. "I'll see you tomorrow I guess," I say, trying to keep my voice cool.

My answer seems to please Charles because a faint smile graces his lips, possibly the first I've seen. I can't help but smile in response. I want to make him do it again.

Carlos watches Charles pack up and leave and waits till he's out the door to start talking. "You really put a spell on him, Miss Daniels. He refused to leave your side unless it was to go home and shower," Carlos says, with a little chuckle.

When I'm alone in my room, I decide to Google the man

who's footing this bill. Charles Breckenridge yields several results. After diving in further I see that there are two of them, father and son. They work at the same company; from their ultra sleek website, it looks like they do something in finance. I skim the news articles that mention him, mostly staring at the polished pictures of him in a tuxedo beside beautiful women. Somehow a man that looks like he could be James Bond has become my ruin and my saving grace.

True to his word, Charles shows up the next day, and the day after that, and the day after that. At first, I'm weirded out by his constant attention, but then I start to look forward to his visits after just two days. It's lonely in the hospital when he's focused on work, so even having him there to chat with between meetings makes me feel a little less alone. He's usually working, but he brings me the paper and a tablet to entertain myself like I'm a small child on a flight.

"I'm not a kid," I say waving the tablet at him as it boots up.

"No, you're not," he agrees, glancing up from his computer. The hospital sheet is gathered around my hips while I sit up, so I can't miss how his eyes dip over my body. The look isn't hungry, but a reminder that he's well aware that I'm not a child. I feel my cheeks burn in response, and I zip up the hoodie, another gift from Charles, giving my body a more shapeless look. He has the good grace to be embarrassed for being caught.

"Then why do you insist on treating me like one?" I snap. At my best moments, I'm able to feel guilty about being so short with him. Charles truly is doing everything in his power to make me more comfortable, but moments like this, where I'm itching to get out of this bed, suffocate those feelings in favor of taking out my frustration on the only person not being paid to put up with my bad attitude day after day. Most nights, when I try to apologize for my numerous transgressions during the day, Charles waves me off, using my mental, physical and emotional exhaustion as excuses for how I've battered him.

I feel like I'm tired all the time, but the docs tell me that's to be expected. My physical condition, outside of being run over, was apparently not great to begin with. Whatever that means.

"I'm not. I just wanted you to have something larger to look at while surfing the web and trying to catch up on all the things you missed. If you woke up in the middle of the night, I wanted you to not feel so alone."

My fingers dig into the box in my hands, and a quick glance at Charles confirms he's back to setting up his workspace for the day. How he manages to have a level tone and put up with my bullshit, I don't understand. I want to reach out and touch him and thank him profusely for being so thoughtful, but he's across the room and I'm stuck in bed.

"Is that why you programmed your number into my new phone?" I ask, opting for a cheeky response.

I swear, the man blushes, and I want to make him do it again. "I wanted you to have someone you could reach out to even when we go our separate ways."

When. I want to frown at the word, but I don't. "Well thank you. You're really too generous."

He shrugs, unsure of how to respond to my gratitude.

Emotions are different, of course, when I come back from physical therapy in a wheelchair and I hurl the water bottle in my hand at him. Unlike with the cup this catches him off guard and it hits his arm. My muscles are aching so deeply and I'm in so much pain from my leg to my arm that I'm crying.

"I hate you," I grit out, not wanting him to see my tears. The nurse pushing my wheelchair isn't on my floor, she's from the physical therapy department, and she doesn't know what to do.

She doesn't know who Charles is to me, but right now I don't care. I don't want him to see my pain, I don't want him to see my tears. I want him to leave me alone. I wish that he had just left me alone, left me on the street.

Charles looks at the nurse, then at me, looking lost, unsure of what to do to make this better, unsure of how to help me.

"She's getting discharged tomorrow," the nurse explains.

I don't want her help getting from the chair into bed, even if my unbroken leg is screaming, even if every bone in my body feels brittle and likely to break. I'm supposed to keep my other muscles strong so I'm not at such a deficit when my cast comes off.

"And then what? I live in a walk-up. Seven floors up, you said. I'm independent. I don't need a man to swoop in and save the day. You've ruined me and my life," I choke out, as a sob finally breaks through. I'm almost at the bed when my good knee gives out, exhausted from having to bear my weight alone.

Charles jumps to me, catching me around the middle, which only makes me snarl in rage. He and the nurse help me into bed, setting my pillows because I can't even reach behind my back.

When the nurse walks out of the room, Charles speaks. "I know you probably don't want to, but I want you to stay with me."

I turn to look at him, aghast. "Stay with you?"

"Is there an echo in this room? Yes. I have the space."

"This is New York City, no one has space." I'm still furious but his earnestness is thawing my rage.

"I do. I have a spare room you can use. I have an elevator in my building and we can have your physical therapist come to you. I also live by Central Park and I have a gym and I'm not far from here, actually. Think about it, Let me do this for you."

I scowl, looking away from him.

"You've done enough, don't you think?" There is more of a bite to my words than I intend. I really meant that he's already been here for two weeks straight, sitting by my side while I was unconscious, going to my apartment to try to find out more about me, getting me a tablet and a brand new phone.

He has to fight the urge to physically recoil from my words and I want to pull them back immediately. I want him to smile again.

"No, I don't." He stands up straighter, pulling away from me. "I've actually stolen time from you. I can never do enough to fix that." His phone buzzes in his hand, pulling his attention away from me.

"Go, take your call," I murmur, sinking back into the bed, flipping the cover on my tablet.

Charles looks like he doesn't want to take it, like he wants to keep this conversation going, but his phone keeps vibrating.

I don't start to really regret my words until it's night and I'm alone. Like the many nights preceding, Charles pushes the boundaries of visiting hours until one of the nurses threatens to call security. It's during these dark hours, when I'm left alone with the gifts Charlies has given me that I let my mind drift to this man.

It's bizarre how I've come to rely on his visits, even when he's working. It's been a different experience getting to know someone through watching them. We chat, of course, Charles telling me a little about what he does at a private equity firm his dad is the CEO of, but it's how his shoulders relax when his friend Jack is on the phone. When it's his father on the phone, his entire body reacts. He sits up straighter, any trace of a smile or a laugh on his face vanishes, and he uses what I like to call his "business voice."

When he and I do talk, Charles probes into easier topics with me: college, where I grew up, what my parents were like. He tries to avoid things that may have occurred in the last five years. It's a small mercy, one that I still try to puzzle out when I'm alone at night.

When I try to divert my mind from Charlie, my mind instantly clicks to Vivian. I reach for my phone a thousand times to call Vivian, but I stall, not knowing her number. My number is the same, and I know in my heart, somehow, that she's not in my life anymore. People change and grow, but we always texted daily, even when we were living together.

My loneliness only grows in the darkness of my hospital room, and while I stare out the window at the city lights, I wonder if loneliness is what keeps Charles here with me during the day.

Two

"I WANT to go back to my apartment," I say to Charles as he grabs my bag from the bed. I'm sitting in a wheelchair because it is hospital policy when leaving. I want to argue that I should be given some leeway since I do have to work on strengthening my knee. The threat of a seventh floor walk-up looms large over me, so I don't push it.

Charles pushes out a huff of air through his nose. He doesn't have to tell me he disagrees. He doesn't have to do anything else for me to know he disagrees.

"If that's what you want, Elia." Charles cuts an attractive figure in slacks and a polo.

Since my clothes were cut off my body the night of the accident, I was going to have to wear scrubs out until Charles gave me a simple beige dress. I nearly wept with relief at the buttons that ran down the whole front of it, making it easy for me to dress myself for the first time. It didn't need to be something fashionable, just something I could do myself and not worry about the cast on my leg or push my shoulder uncomfortably. Ashley, whoever she is, is a godsend for getting me clothes.

Our PickMeUp! driver is annoyed at how long it takes

Charles to help position me comfortably in the back seat so my broken leg can stretch out beside me. I've been told for a week how lucky I was. It was a clean break so healing should be easy. The knee surgery went well. My wrist could have been so much worse. My helmet saved my life. I could have broken my hip and more.

It's hard to feel lucky when you feel alone in the world.

I scroll through my contacts. Chinese food, sushi joint, a temp agency, and the law firm I worked for ages ago. I tried calling them one day when Charles was in his office for a meeting he couldn't avoid. The new receptionist didn't know who I was, and I left a message for one of the partners to call me back but they never did.

I know a person is never the best judge of character for themselves, but I like to think that I was a good person, a good worker, not the type of woman whose friends would be totally and completely AWOL, not the kind of employee that wouldn't even deserve a callback. I know I could check social media and find my friends, but I'm not sure I'm ready emotionally for any fallout from the last five years. For now, I can live in this little amnesia bubble pretending like none of this is real.

Pulling up to the building already tells me this is a bad idea, but Charles is too much of a gentleman to say otherwise. He helps me out, leans my new fashion accessory, crutches, against the car, and slings my purse over his shoulder.

"Put your arms around my neck," he offers when I've finally made it to the door opening. I fight to hide how exhausting just that was. I don't protest, sliding my arms around his neck as his hands grip my waist, pulling me out. We've moved past him needing to ask if this is okay; past me fighting him.

Charles' face is so close to mine that I can feel his breath tickling the hairs on my neck as he lifts me from the seat. My dirty brain supplies how easy it would be for him to lift me onto a table and press his hard body against mine, and damn it if I don't let my mind wander. He is singularly focused on getting me to my feet while I'm thinking about the thrill of having him close to me and the arousal that sends through my body.

"I think blue is more your color," I say, my voice ragged, gesturing at my purple purse hanging from his shoulder.

Charles gives me a grin, adjusting it on his arm. "I think this looks nice with my eyes." He smiles and I think, it does, it really does.

He pulls my keys from his pocket and gives me my crutches so he can open the doors. Directly beside my building, I see the name of the Chinese food restaurant and across the street is the sushi place. Awesome, I apparently never went far from this place.

I wish something would jog my memory. The smell of the trash on the street is not unique to this part of the city, nor is the smell of fried rice wafting through the doors of the restaurant. We walk through the entry and Charles stays behind me as I navigate crutches on the stairs. More than once, I get them stuck on a stair, falling back into his chest. His hands steady me, gripping my hips until I get them right again. I hope he can't hear the pounding of my heart when I lean against him. Two weeks in the hospital has destroyed my stamina, leaving me sweating as we make the climb.

"Sorry," I grumble, focusing on the next step.

"That's why I'm here." I can hear an edge of pain in his voice, but I can't look at him and see the pity I know is there.

The pain throbbing in my arm and leg makes me want to cry. I shouldn't be using both crutches, but I didn't want to leave the other one at the entrance of the building to be mistaken for trash. Hitting the landing on the fourth floor, I see the error of my ways when I just can't do it anymore. I throw one crutch and then the other at the wall before sitting on the stairs and crying. It's stupid and vain, but I hate how weak I feel. I hate how my body feels like it's betraying me for being injured and I hate how unfamiliar this place is.

Charles looks unsure at first but then braces one hand on the wall and the other on the railing to look at me. He's more in my face than usual, an annoying wrinkle of concern between his brows. I don't expect him to comfort me—we hardly know each other—but it does force me to stop crying.

"I have your pain meds in your bag if you need," he offers, his voice low.

"I don't want medication. I want to be able to go to my own apartment without needing your help or needing pills. I hate that I can't even get up the stairs. I am an independent person."

"I don't doubt you," Charles says, moving out of the way for someone to pass.

"But I can't do it. I can't take the stairs. What am I going to do when I have to take the trash out or go to work or get food?" My voice breaks and fresh tears start. Through my blurry vision, I think I spot devastation on Charles' face but the look is quickly gone so I'm not sure if it was ever there in the first place. We're creating a traffic jam; people are trying to ascend or descend the stairs.

"Hey man, get out of the way," a guy trying to climb the stairs growls.

"Just a second," Charles says, not even looking over his shoulder. "What do you want right now?" He stares directly into my eyes.

"I just want to go home." I start to cry again and cover my face with my hands. I feel like I'm collapsing into myself. I don't see him move, too lost in my own grief. I feel an arm snake under my legs, hooking under my knees, and another arm around my back. He pulls me to his firm chest and I grip his shirt, hiding my face in it. He's careful maneuvering me around the turns, taking the stairs two at a time until we get to my apartment.

I expect Charles to put me down, but he slides the key into the lock. His hands are full with me, so he uses his foot to push the door open and if I wasn't getting snot all over his shirt, I might be turned on, but I'm in so much pain, so tired that I just hold tighter to him.

He kicks the door shut behind him, setting me onto the couch. He brushes a strand of hair from my face so he can look me in the eye. This is such an intimate gesture that I melt for a moment. He's squatting in front of me, this six-foot-something man who is pure muscle.

"I'm going to grab your crutches. I'll be right back. Don't run away on me," he says, trying to tease me and make light. I chuckle despite myself and this seems to be all he needs before he stands and leaves me alone in this unfamiliar place.

Charles isn't gone for long, but it gives me a chance to really look around the apartment that is apparently mine. It's small and feels impersonal. The couch, a dark blue loveseat from Ikea with light blue piping around the edges, is nothing special. My TV is resting on a small entertainment stand with DVDs and picture frames on it. The whole space is shockingly sparse. There are a few pictures of nothing special hanging on the walls. There is one of Paris depicting the Arc de Triomphe and another that features rows of flowers in Amsterdam, I think.

Charles opens the door and I notice that he's breathing a little heavily now. I think scaling those steps would wind anyone regardless of how fit. He leans against the door, a sweet smile on his face as he looks at me. I hate to think of what he must see looking at me, how my cast extends forward; I must look like this broken thing. This *broken thing* that needs saving. This *broken thing* to be pitied.

"What do you think about medication now?"

I scowl at him but hold out my hand, surprised that it's shaking. I don't want to need meds, but I need the pain to stop.

"Do you want me to beg?" I snap, my anger surfacing.

"No, Elia, I don't." He sounds sad, pushing off the wall to get a cup. I wonder if I'm pushing him too hard with my out of control emotions. Charles has been a safe place for me to take out my anger and I'm afraid that maybe I'm hitting his limit. He opens a few of the cabinets, looking inside. I turn to watch him, seeing the nearly empty shelves. From my spot on the couch, I can see just two glasses and a mug before Charles closes the cabinet, cup in hand.

I take the pill he hands me, down it with the water and wait for it to take effect.

"Sorry the place is a mess," I say, a frown tugging my lips downward.

"If this were a Spend The Night rental, which it looks like, I would probably give you zero stars. Terrible host, dirty, no dishes, and poor movie choices. What are these? Are they porn or slasher movies?" Charles squats in front of the TV to get a better look at the movies I have. The way he tugs his pants up before dropping into a squat makes my heart race, and I admire his ass all the way down. I can blame the racing heart on my medication, but not the way my eyes follow him. Charles holds up one of the DVD's, *Sorority Girls Nightmare: Wet T-Shirts with Blood*.

"That's not even clever." I snort, looking at the cover where coeds with big tits are fake screaming as they're sprayed with blood instead of water.

"I didn't take you for the type," Charles teases as he crosses the room to sit next to me on the couch. It's the closest we've been seated. I spent more time in the hospital bed, him across from me, than anywhere else.

The DVD collection is surprising. Can a person really change that much in five years that I wouldn't even recognize myself?

"I'm not. *Titanic* is too suspenseful for me to watch. And forget blood. It's probably for the best that I was unconscious after you hit me." I mean my words to be light, but from his visible flinch, they weren't. I can't take the words back now though.

"Come back with me. Stay at my place. Please."

I look into his brown eyes, not wanting to give up my independence. There is a different look in his eyes, not pity, not desire, but hope. Maybe he *is* just as lonely as I am. Or maybe he has a savior complex and he gets off on it. "But what if you're a serial killer?" I ask, leaning back against the couch.

He smiles, eyes marking every cut and bruise on my face. "Then it's already too late because we're alone in your apartment." His voice drops into an intentionally deep timbre when he speaks.

I laugh at his teasing. "Then I make a pretty easy mark, huh? You already know no one would miss me."

I'm quiet for a moment watching Charles analyze the room like he would a problem. "I always said if I was on my own I would at least get a cat to keep me company. I told my friend who I lived with that if she was moving in with her boyfriend that would mean I *had* to get a cat, but it would be a poor replacement for her. She wanted me to name it after her. I wonder why I didn't get one."

"Maybe because pets are hard?" Charles muses, handing me an ice pack wrapped in a musty towel before diving into cleaning out my fridge. When I try to get up to help him, he pins me back to the couch with a look.

"Play with your tablet or something," he says, turning his head away from the sink where he is pouring sour milk down the drain.

I get to my feet, grabbing a crutch, and hobble over to him.

"You realize you just issued a challenge, right *Charles*?" I emphasize his name so he understands whose home this is.

Charles hangs his head, a smirk tugging at his lips. I rest my crutch against the wall, reach onto a shelf, and feel around to see what's up there. I try to get on my toes, my fingers just skimming something, but I don't have the range of motion nor the leverage of two feet. Each touch keeps pushing the item further and further out of the way.

"I wish you would call me Charlie. Only my father calls me

Charles." He sidles up beside me before reaching above me with his stupid height that dwarfs my five-three frame. I have to try not to be affected by his proximity. He slides whatever it is closer to me so I can reach it myself. I pull it down, pointedly not looking at him or where his shirt has risen, showing off tanned skin just above his belt. I catch the sight of a happy trail leading from his belly button down to...

Above the belt!

I need to keep my eyes above the belt. I may not remember the last five years, but my body clearly remembers being very sexually frustrated. That at least explains why no boyfriend has come out of the woodwork looking for me.

When I see the green fuzzy thing in my hands, I yelp, dropping it. I forget that my leg is broken for a fraction of a second in an effort to get away from what was growing in the back of my cabinet. I stumble, my leg not bending the way I want it to, and pain lances through my body. I can feel it in the back of my throat. I expect to go down, wind up in the hospital again for my carelessness when Charles grabs my waist, hauling me against him.

"Thanks," I murmur, enjoying being in his arms far too much.

Charles is slow to let me go, the depths of his brown eyes searching my face for something.

"So eager to escape my company you would rather be back in the hospital?" He chuckles, grabbing the offending article. Even he makes a face, tossing what I think used to be English muffins into the garbage bag.

"Something like that, Charlie," I try out the nickname and decide I like how it makes him brighten up.

"Looks like you don't have any roommates or a boyfriend." His words are matter of fact as he pokes his head into the bedroom.

"I guess the slasher porn is from an ex?" I state, limping my way over to my inner sanctum. I expect to find more mementos or knick-knacks here. Maybe pictures that prove I had a personality, but there is even less. No pictures from college; hardly any personal touches. My family quilt isn't even out, but the photo of my parents from their wedding day is where I've had it for the last several years: a place of honor on my nightstand.

I want to cry. I want to cry because I miss them. They would know that I had been gone for two weeks. They would have reached out. Before they died, I would talk to them every day. Both were only children and so was I. It made us closer than most families because we only had each other.

Charlie watches me sit on the bed, which is unmade. Aside from the moldy food, it's some of the only evidence that someone actually lived here.

"Your parents?" he asks, probably already knowing the answer.

I see my family quilt across the room on a shelf in what only a shrewd real estate agent would dare to call a closet. I want to wrap it around myself and sob, falling back into that never ending pit of grief that had enveloped me after they died, but I can't find the words to ask for it. If I open my mouth, the tears will start to flow and I won't be able to stop.

"Yeah." I say softly, setting the frame back on the nightstand. Staying with Charlie is only going to be temporary. Leaving this photo here is proof that I will be back. I *have* to be back.

Charlie gives me my space and goes to my closet. "I want to find a bag to take some stuff for you." He holds up a small duffle bag, little more than a gym bag. "Is this okay?"

"Still convinced I'm coming home with you? You need to at least buy me dinner first."

He gives me a cheeky grin.

"If you really want to stay here alone, I'll leave you to it." His tone makes it obvious that he's not serious. It's the tone a parent would use on a stubborn child who is picking the exact wrong battle. I wonder what he thinks of the situation, and why that makes him so damn pushy to make amends.

"Fine, go ahead. But leave my underwear drawer alone," I say with a scowl.

"Do you even know which drawer that is?" he teases and I laugh as I throw a pillow at him. It should be too soon to make a joke like that, but it might be the only way we can get out of this with our pride intact.

Before we leave, I have Charlie set out my family quilt, laying it along the foot of my bed. He keeps swearing he can carry it, but the agony from the trip of the stairs is too fresh. Charlie might be in great shape, but running these stairs three times with my things and my crutches and me will be too much to ask. My heart aches, wanting that familiarity with me, but it will serve as my anchor. I will return to this apartment again. I will get my old life and my memories back.

Three

MY PAIN IS SO OVERWHELMING, I'm gritting my teeth by the time we pull up to Charlie's apartment building. He wasn't kidding about the proximity to the hospital. We don't pass it, but I do see signs for it as we approach. He carries the duffle bag full of the few belongings that we grabbed from the apartment. It's almost exclusively clothes. I've been wearing underwear purchased by someone else for the last week so I'm looking forward to wearing something that is mine, even if I don't recognize it.

"Benji!" Charlie calls out as we walk into the building. There is a liveried doorman standing behind a counter with a smile on his face. He looks young and like his uniform doesn't quite fit.

"Mr. Breckenridge," the young man greets Charlie with a smile. His green eyes skate over my face, pleasant, but committing it to memory. I wonder how many other women Benji has seen Charlie bring to his apartment.

"Charlie, *please.* This is Elia. She's going to be staying in my apartment for the time being while she rehabilitates from an injury. Please assist her in any way that you would assist me."

"Of course, Mr. Breckenridge. Welcome Miss Elia, please let

me know if there is anything I can do to make your time here more pleasant."

We ride the gilded elevator up and up and up, past the floor numbers that I expect him to live on. When we keep going, I wonder just how rich Charlie is. It occurs to me that I don't even know exactly what Charlie does.

"Did we, uh, miss your floor?" I ask as we rocket past the thirties and then the forties.

"Nope." Charlie rocks back on his heels, watching the numbers climb.

"What exactly is it that you do again?" I ask, swiveling to face him.

"Private Equity."

"AKA, you're filthy rich for no reason?" I ask, my tone barbed. It doesn't seem to bother him though.

"We take a majority share in companies with the help of investors and we make them better through restructuring and other corporate nonsense."

"Right."

He must see that my eyes glazed over at some point. "Are you tired or is what I do just that boring?"

The elevator finally stops and we step into a long hallway. I can barely keep myself upright from exhaustion that hits me. Maybe it's just the sudden stop of the elevator that seemed to fly, but I sway a little. Charlie reaches out to steady me again.

"Finance guys all think they're hot shit and what they do is *so* interesting." I try to stay light, but I can hear my words slurring.

Charlie takes the crutches out of my hands and leans them on the other side of the elevator door. I don't have time to formulate an objection before he's scooping me up again, watching my cast and making sure he doesn't smash my foot into the closing doors. I lean into his touch, tucking my head into the crook of his neck. He lowers his head just a little, pressing his cheek to the crown of my head. He's coming to my rescue again, and being in his arms, feeling his hands on me, and I don't mind too much.

"It's hard not to think that when women keep throwing themselves at me."

I cling to him, furious with myself for it. I breathe in deeply, not wanting my eyes to close, but it's a losing battle. With PT in the hospital, I would work my muscles hard and then go right to my bed and nap. The stairs, leaving the hospital, through all of it today I have fought to stay awake.

"You picked me up, bud," I remind him teasingly, forcing my eyes open. We're near the top of the apartment building and I want to see the spectacular space that he must live in.

"Only after you threw yourself in front of my car."

"Hardy-har-har," I respond, but I'm not sure he hears it because my eyes are closed before the elevator doors shut behind me.

I wake on the softest bed I think I've ever slept in. The bed is warm around me like a cocoon. I can pretend, just for a few minutes, that I'm back at my parents' house; before the fire that claimed their lives, before I went to college, before I lost my memory. The sun is setting and I can see a touch of the brilliant hues in the sky through the sheer curtains on the windows.

It occurs to me that I fell asleep in Charles, er, Charlie's arms. It occurs to me that he carried me to bed and tucked me in. It occurs to me that I should be embarrassed, but I'm not. He's had to leave the room so the nurses could help me use the bathroom so I didn't flash my bare ass at him. He's been there when I screamed and raged in pain, refusing an opiate. Somewhere in these moments, I caught feelings. It's not until I'm

33

lying in this bed realizing the weight of all these little things he's done for me, that maybe I'm not alone. It's not romantic, though the attraction is there, as much as I try to deny it. I think we're starting to become friends and maybe it's something we both need.

I sit up, my crutches leaning against the wall, waiting for me. On the nightstand sits a glass of water and the Ibuprofen prescription for my pain. I'm sore, muscle fatigue everywhere in my body, but none of the outright pain that was plaguing me earlier. Seems sleeping on something that's not a cardboard box will do the body good.

The room I'm in is simple and impersonal. This space looks more like a magazine style home instead of the short term rental style of mine. The room is all whites and beige; the only shock of color is the red and orange canvas feather above the headboard that I can see in the mirror directly across from the foot of the bed. I've seen hotel rooms with more personality, but I'm hardly going to complain. Charlie has given me somewhere warm and comfortable, with an elevator, to rest in while I recuperate.

I emerge from the room with a crutch tucked under my bad arm, to be further wowed by the apartment. He wasn't kidding when he told me that he had space for me to come stay with him. I didn't think that apartments in New York City actually existed with a staircase in them, but here we are. Unobtrusively set toward the far wall is one of those floating staircases that looks like certain death. The staircase doesn't take up as much space as you would expect, especially since the space is utilized with a bar cart under it. The couch that Charlie currently occupies faces the obscenely large TV that practically blocks the sweeping views of Central Park.

Floor to ceiling windows cover all the way up to the second floor of the apartment. Whoever designed the guest room must have done the same here. The couch looks new and fluffed, like he's barely sat on it. The kitchen that is right by the front door is large and gleaming with dark marble countertops. The space screams magazine representation of a bachelor pad.

"Hey, you're awake," Charlie says, closing his computer halfway and setting it on the coffee table in front of him.

"Yeah, I'm so sorry for—"

"Nothing, you have nothing to be sorry for. Can I get you anything?"

My eyes are drifting around the apartment now, registering the dining room table for six between another room on this floor and the living room space. Tucked under the stairs is a rowing machine with a massive screen that faces one of the dual exposure windows overlooking Central Park. Views like this are only supposed to exist in movies.

My stomach gives an undignified growl, drawing a laugh from Charlie. My eyes flit to his.

"I guess food is a priority for now. I can cook?" I offer, but it's just as much a question. I'm not great at cooking, and if I improved in the last five years, it's been lost. Muscle memory can only get you so far.

"No, you need to be resting. I did set up your physical therapy schedule three times a week. Assuming that's not a problem." Charlie comes behind me, placing his hands on my shoulder, slowly guiding me to the couch. He helps position me so my injured leg is extended on the couch, elevated by soft throw pillows.

"Thanks, Mom," I tease as I settle down. Charlie drops into a chair across from me, pulling his laptop back onto his thighs.

"What food are you craving? My FoodNow! account is seasoned with all the best in the area. Pick a takeout, any takeout."

"Where is my purse? Let me treat you to Thai. Do you like Thai food?"

"Love Thai food. Love Thai street food. Do you have a favorite?"

We go through ordering, though he blatantly refuses to

let me pay. One thing I thankfully didn't lose track of were my bank accounts, which have some funds, for now. Each time I try to do something: get up to help him or to pay, Charlie is right there, shushing me and taking care of everything. He gets up multiple times: grabs my laptop, then my charger, then my shiny new phone and tablet, and finally water.

"I'm thinking I'll take this week and work from home to help get you settled. The physical therapist is coming and I want to make sure they have everything they need."

"Don't you need to go back to work?" I ask, lowering my computer screen. I struggle to my feet, needing to move, needing to stretch my muscles. Charlie jumps to his feet, but I wave him off. Charlie eases himself back down, watching each of my movements, each wince. I think it's killing him a little bit to not help. The effort is over as quickly as the need to move overtook me, and I drop back onto the couch.

"No," he replies. "That's the glory of my job; I work for my father's company. I can tell him where to stick it without having to worry about job security. I'm just going to have a few calls. I'm supposed to be in Tokyo this month, but Jack is going in my place."

"You've mentioned him before."

"We went to college together. He's a friend and he works at the same firm as me. He'll do a good job." There's something in his voice when he says it.

"You sound jealous?" I ask, tilting my head.

"It's not jealousy, it's just pressure. My dad has these dreams of me taking over the firm by the time I turn forty-five. Naturally, when I said I was working from home for three weeks, I became a slacker. I've lost my drive. Clearly, Jack is the one who wants my job." He takes a sip from a dark liquor. "According to my father, anyway."

Charlie rises, offering me a hand. "I have more work to do.

You're welcome to stay out here and watch TV. I'll go into my room so if you need anything, I'll be close by."

"Where do you usually work?" I ask, taking his hand and rising. I have to learn to accept help from time to time. I have to learn that accepting help doesn't signal weakness, but an awareness of my limits. He's been a gracious host, but I want to get out of his hair, out of his face. I want time to dive into my emails. I was lucky that my computer didn't have a lock on it.

"I have an office upstairs, but I'll stay down here for you. I would rather be accessible to you."

I lock eyes with him and feel a flush creep up my face. "I appreciate that, but I'm not a child," I repeat. I wish Charlie would stop treating me like an invalid who needs to be catered to. I wish he would see past the injuries. There are times when I think he does, when his eyes peruse the length of my bare legs, but insecurity whispers that it's only a clinical look to see how I'm healing.

He nods, his eyes not dipping from my face. "I know," his voice is gruff. "Let me give you the formal tour of your room."

He leads me into my room. Being alone with him in here feels different from when we were alone in the hospital or even in the living room. He walks me to a door that I had discovered earlier leads to a private bathroom.

"According to my realtor this is considered the 'princess suite' since it has a full private bathroom. I didn't exactly have you in mind when I bought this place, but it works. I have some basic hotel shampoo and conditioner, but I can get you more. I imagine this dress isn't going to cut it. Let me know what you need. My assistant, Ashley, did some research on clothes that are comfortable with casts and braces and everything."

"Casts, and braces, and slings, oh my. I really don't need you to get me anything, I can order something online."

The bathroom is simple, a stall shower with plenty of space for the chair I know I'll need to order. The whole space is white, just like the guest room which makes sense.

"Please, let me. You can say I've done enough as much as you want, but honestly? If you sued me tomorrow, I would pay ten times what I am."

"I'm not going to sue you," I say, hobbling back to the bed.

"You would have every right to do so. I just want to do what I can to help you. Have you given any thought to my offer to hire a private investigator?"

I have. I have thought long and hard about his offer and I've waffled on it so much. I've thought about it late at night when I was awake in the hospital alone, eager to have someone, anyone, to reach out to. I wish that I had someone to text, someone to help to fill in the blanks, but my contacts being empty can't be a mistake. The lack of texts can't be a mistake. I would have thought that maybe there wasn't anything saved to the Cloud, but I did have text messages, ones from FoodNow! giving me updates on my orders, a few text messages about work and one mystery text that I sent.

Don't ever contact me again.

I don't know who it was to. The number was erased, and there were no other texts in the chain. Just the one message sent the night of the accident. Was this person the reason I was out in the rain? Did I go out because whoever this was upset me?

"Yes, and I still don't want you to hire a PI. It feels weirdly invasive, even if it is my own life. Two weeks. No one texted me in two weeks. No one sent me memes or stupid jokes. Someone who I thought was my best friend, who I used to text all day every day, isn't even in my contacts. I don't know what happened, but clearly we aren't in touch anymore. Maybe I need a clean slate. Maybe this is the universe telling me to take it."

Charlie's brow twitches in, just a second, before his face smooths. "As you wish. Just holler if you need anything," he says, turning toward his room.

"Of course, Dread Pirate Roberts. Good night," I call to his retreating form before flopping on the bed, wondering what I'm going to do with this clean slate I've been given.

It's awkward at first, the way living with a stranger in close quarters would be. We have morning routines to learn, like how he wakes up at four AM to get on his rower. Or that he can't even talk to me before my second cup of coffee.

I discover that he prefers his first coffee to be an espresso before switching to a latte and on particularly rough days, where he's barely gone to sleep before his alarm goes off again, he drinks an espresso mixed with *Mountain Dew*. I've learned to avoid him on days like this, his mood sour and mercurial, not because he's rude to me, but when he drinks that battery acid it's because his dad is putting pressure on him. It's pressure that he's getting because he's here with me, and I don't want to be an undue burden, not any more than I already am.

I send a thank you prayer to the god of technology that all my passwords are saved on my laptop. Getting into my emails helps to fill in some of the blanks, but not nearly enough. My emails are mostly shopping deals and other nonsense that was easy to filter out. I have emails about commissioned art pieces, and ones from a temp agency warning me that if I continue to be late, leave early or miss work completely, I won't be able to rely on them for a reference.

The rest of my computer is equally as empty. There are bank statements from the account I set up after my parents died. I have tax returns saved, but no photos on my computer, not even from college. All my social media accounts are shut down. I try to find ones for the illustrations I do, but it looks like I send them out to someone else to post.

I track my accounts like a forensic accountant, trying to go back and see if there are any hints to when things fell off with Vivian. The best clue I can find is from three years earlier, when I started to pay cash for most things, only finding cash withdrawals from my checking account. There are no names of places for me to reach out to that might give me some information about my life.

I'm glad to see that the nest egg my parents left me is still intact. I was lucky, after they died, that their lawyer who drew up their estate documents had the presence of mind to push to sue the contractors and suppliers that caused their house to burn down. The money I got from the lawsuit would never replace them in my heart or in my life, it won't give me back the moments they missed and are going to miss like this one, but it helped to ensure that I was able to find a real one bedroom and be able to do some of the artwork I had always wanted to.

Soon after I move in, Charlie gets a TV installed in my bedroom so I can retreat in there when he's working late. I'm in what I've come to call my room watching a TV show when he knocks on the door.

"Am I supposed to believe this show is still on? How have they not run out of plot?" I ask, waving the remote at the screen.

"Longest running medical drama on television. I think it's been renewed for another two seasons." Charlie leans against the door frame, arms crossed.

"Well, I have to rewatch the first ten seasons, and then catch up on the last five years, so this will keep me busy for the next several months."

"How was PT today?" he asks, noting the ice packs on my knee and shoulder.

"Good. Dan said that I was 'lucky' with the accident and it all could have been much worse. Says I'll probably be cleared for my shoulder before my knee."

"Makes sense. You can't really work your leg with the cast."

"Nope. He did say that was unlucky. He wants me on one of

those knee scooters, but I can't really put that much pressure on my knee."

"You're a mess," Charlie teases.

"Only the hottest. I did also find out that I had been doing some graphic design work, though I'm not sure what. I guess I had a tablet or something that we missed in my apartment. I have emails from people about my work. I figured out that I had to refund people money for work I promised and can no longer deliver on. I was also a temp with a terrible track record, so going missing for two weeks didn't seem like a surprise."

"You don't strike me as the type to be unreliable."

"I didn't think so, but maybe I was someone else's sugar baby, so I didn't need the money."

"I would think this sugar baby setup is preferable."

"For now," I tease, but for a second my heart sinks and I'm afraid he thinks I'm just here for the free food and rent. I dismiss the thought when he pushes on.

"Come watch a movie, unless you're heavily invested in Dr. Mcwhats-his-face and who he's screwing now."

"Do you have time?" I'm already turning off the TV though, eager to spend more time in Charlie's presence. I want us to watch a comedy so I can hear his laugh and catch him smiling. I want to have an excuse for him to touch me.

We settle on the couch, his phone and laptop accessible if need be. I'm stretched out again, leg elevated. Charlie made sure to set up the pillows, lifting my leg gently to set it on the pile he's made for me. I get a light shock when his fingers graze my knee when he places a fresh ice pack on it. When we touch, I wonder at what it would feel like to have his hands all over me. He sits down beside me, much closer than usual, but not quite touching. I can still feel the heat from his body, even at this slight distance.

"Is this okay?" he asks, setting the bowl of popcorn within reach for both of us.

"Yeah," I agree, trying not to be so affected by his presence. I can't go and fall for this man. I don't think my attraction to him is based purely on this savior complex, but he seems to genuinely be a nice guy.

Charlie braces his arm over be back of the couch, casting furtive glances in my direction. I try not to notice, but eventually I look up at him, realizing just how close he is to me.

"Can I help you?" I ask with a smirk.

"I'm just enjoying the movie and didn't want you to think that my arm was me trying to put the moves on you."

I try to pretend that it doesn't bother me that he's not. I'm not expecting this to become anything, as much as I would love to see his muscles in action up close and personal. But it would be nice to know that I'm still somewhat desirable in this state. "Because I'm so repulsive that you would never?" I try to inject a joking tone into my voice.

He pauses the movie. "Because I don't want you to feel like you're stuck with me and have no options. Because you're living in my house and I didn't want to make you uncomfortable." His voice is gruff. I can feel his gaze sweep down to my lips before he focuses intently on my eyes.

My eyebrows twitch down for a second in confusion. He's shown me such kindness, and I wonder if I were better, in a position to leave if he made me feel uncomfortable, if his stance on making a move would change. There is an odd sort of comfort in knowing I am completely safe with this man who, somewhere along the way, stopped being a stranger and started to be my friend. I wonder if he thinks about us being more than that. Is there anything more attractive in a partner than that?

"I'm not uncomfortable," I say. "So, let's go back to the movie."

Charlie nods and turns the movie back on.

The dance between us as we move closer to Halloween gets more awkward as I find myself looking for reasons to be around Charlie.

He takes me to my appointments and uses me as a way out of going into the office. I know he has friends outside of work, but it never comes up that he's skipping out on seeing them when he spends most nights either working or with me. I hate to see him working so hard with what seems like so little reward. He's making so much money, but what good is it if he's unable to take the time to enjoy it? Even though he's not in the office, he's still working just as hard if not harder, taking calls from the car, stepping into different rooms at the hospital during my check-ins to continue his calls.

The visit to get my arm and leg casts off is quick, but it delivers a hell of a surprise. Charlie admits that he has to go back into the office again. It was to be expected. I knew this day was coming, but it doesn't feel any less like a punch in the gut. I've grown used to having him around, finding any reason at all to be near him. It was inevitable that this was going to end, but his return to the office feels like it's hastening the timeline.

When we get into the apartment there is a long slender box sitting on top of the island. Charlie glances at it, then at me.

"Before you jump into the shower I know you're desperate to get to, this is for you." He slides the box closer to me. Glad as I am to be out of the cast, I still slip into a seat at the island to take the weight off my foot. It's going to take some getting used to the freedom and range of motion again.

I give Charlie a look, one that I know is useless. He's going to do what he wants, buy what he wants, regardless of my objections. I should have known what was in the box, but I can't stop the gasp that escapes my mouth when I manage to wrangle the box open.

Laying within it is a gorgeous long cane. The shaft of it is black, it has a mother of pearl handle, and intricate carvings along the side. Gently, I rub my fingers along it.

"Thank you," I manage to choke out. I've felt so clumsy using my crutches with my hand in a cast as well. My gait was thrown off by it, so having the cane, something that will make my life easier, even remotely, makes me want to cry. Even I hadn't considered what I was going to do. I figured when I did get out of the cast, I would limp along, probably causing more damage.

I don't hesitate to hop off the stool and throw my arms around his neck. My ear is pressed to his chest when his arms come around me, squeezing me. It might be my imagination, but I think that I can hear his heartbeat speed up just a little.

Releasing him, I give him a watery smile. To break the tension, I want to make a joke about how it looks like a cane my grandmother would have had.

"Wanted to make sure that you could still move and groove in style."

"Get me an old lady wig and my Halloween costume is complete."

Charlie snorts. I want to say something snarky to that snort, but we both hear his phone vibrate in his pocket.

"Let's take it out for a spin tonight. I might have lied on my schedule so we could go out to dinner to celebrate your cast coming off. I've got a reservation nearby that we could walk to if you're up to it." His phone vibrates again.

"That sounds good." I take the cane out of the box, testing the height, and how it works. I leave Charlie to take his call, using my new cane to cross back to my room, glad to not need a crutch jammed in my armpit anymore.

The water feels amazing on my leg as I gently wash it. And then wash it again. I like the idea of having a night out of the house. I swore I was going to start wearing leggings, but if we're going out for dinner, I want to dress up. That nagging insecure part of my brain tells me that I'm close to being fully healed and he's going to tire of playing hero to my damsel in distress. Charlie has only seen me as this damaged bird in need of saving, but I wonder what possibilities it would open between us if he started to see me as something more.

I go the whole nine. Clean hair, plucked eyebrows, shaved legs. Not that I expect Charlie to be touching my legs, but it still is nice to feel my smooth leg. I take the time to style my hair, surprised even after these few weeks that it's this shade of blonde.

I had once or twice toyed with the idea of dying my hair blonde after a college boyfriend said he liked blondes, but it was never more than that. It's definitely more platinum than I would have picked. I like to think I would have gone for more of a honey color, but it is what it is.

I wonder what made me dye my hair. They say after a serious break-up women are more likely to make a drastic change like this. Maybe I did have a boyfriend and we ended things. My hair is more grown out, obvious around the roots that I haven't touched it up given the darker shade there.

I take time curling it, letting it settle me. I'm surprisingly anxious about what a night out with Charlie will look like. I know that my clothes aren't the fanciest but I feel good, probably better than I have in weeks. It's amazing what some mascara, a blow dryer, and being able to move your ankle can do.

I practice using the cane with sneakers and my new boot. It doesn't make for the cutest outfit, athletic shoes and a forest green dress, but I make it work.

Charlie emerges five minutes after he said he would, but I'm not going to sweat the small stuff. He's dressed more formally than I expected. It's still casual, but office casual. His white button down is unbuttoned on the top and he has no tie, but he's added a suit jacket, and I can't stop the stuttering in my chest. The man is a walking sin.

I feel his eyes travel my body, admiring the length of my legs, up to my face.

"You seem to be tolerating the boot well."

"Wow, with romantic words like that, it's a wonder the ladies aren't breaking down the door," I taunt, pulling on the supple leather jacket that he surprised me with one afternoon after I shivered between the door and the cab going to the doctor's office. It's nice to have a real reason to wear it.

Charlie reaches forward, scooping my hair out so it isn't caught within my jacket. He's stepped in like that before when I was struggling with a jacket, bag and crutches, but now it's less necessary. Charlie's fingertips brush my neck when he does it and his eyes drift to the spot where he touched me. They flick to my lips then back to my eyes, a small blush on his cheeks when he sees that I've caught him.

"Oh, you know me, and all the time I have to woo the ladies." Charlie offers me an arm, pretending like none of that happened. Cautiously, I slide my arm into his, letting him lead the way.

The walk to the restaurant is slow. I'm still trying to get used to the different pressure on my foot. Charlie keeps an eye on me, looking for any stumble or weakness. The restaurant isn't far, thankfully, and we have a reservation so we're seated almost immediately.

Charlie pulls out my chair for me, and it starts to feel more like a date, which I'm not sure either of us is ready for. More than once, though, I feel like he's tried to have an excuse to be in my vicinity. It's been just about four weeks that we've been in each other's lives. I can't lie and say that I haven't thought about it more. Moments when he's caught me after I stumble, or when our eyes meet when reaching for the same takeout container and our fingers brush. I wonder if I'm the only one that imagines what it would be like to feel his bare skin under mine.

It's Mexican for dinner and that helps keep the mood light.

The server makes the guacamole beside us, letting me taste it as we go to make it to our specifications.

"How has the leg been feeling?" Charlie asks.

I take a long sip of the margarita I'm finally able to savor. Since I wasn't shopping for the alcohol myself, I wasn't going to add it to the list of things for Charlie to get. I skipped my pain medication today so I could have this one drink.

"That's a loaded question." I lick some of the sugar off the rim.

The sound of Charlie's booming laugh has the same effect as a sugar rush for me. "Alright, I know it's not going to be perfect, but how does it feel to be free?"

I grab a chip, plunking it into the guacamole and salsa.

"It feels weird. Sure, I can walk a little easier, but I still can't take the stairs on my own." I glance up in time to see Charlie's face falter before he throws up a wall, one meant for world and business calls and something to hide behind. I want to claw my words back, but instead my hand shoots forward and I grab his wrist.

His brown eyes study where we touch before he meets my eyes again.

"I didn't mean that I'm not grateful for you and for everything you have done for me. I am. I am tremendously thankful for you. I may not be free to run laps around Central Park for hours, but you set me free in other ways."

"How, Elia? You have no idea what your life was like before. What I took from you." He pulls his hand back, but I hold tight to it, the chips and salsa forgotten.

"Charlie, it's been a month. Other than the clients I owe graphics to, not a single person has come looking for me. I mean, sure, you can go a while without talking to friends. But a month without reaching out? No missing persons report? I'm a ghost, a nobody. I don't matter to anyone. The people I would matter to, the people I *did* matter to, are either dead, or they're not talking to

47

me. Don't ever think I'm not grateful for everything you're doing for me."

I pull my hand back when the waitress returns with our meals. The silence settles between us as we wait for her to leave, but she's attentive, too attentive when it comes to Charlie, and I am uncomfortable with my annoyance at that. He thanks her, nodding that he's good, even as her hand rests on his shoulder.

"Are you good, honey?" the waitress pushes.

"Looks delicious," he says when she still hasn't left or taken her hand off him, despite his visible discomfort.

"Smells amazing. Thanks again," I smile directly at her and reach for his hand, giving it a squeeze on the table.

He turns his hand over, sliding his fingers through mine, and the jolt I get from us holding hands like this is so foreign. His gaze heats as he looks at our hands then meets my eye. We've been in close quarters, in each other's space for the last month, both of us too afraid of crossing a line with the other, but this is openly, intentionally affectionate in a way that isn't strictly platonic. I hate how she made him uncomfortable. It was visible, obvious, but she didn't care. I have to wonder if I've just become this attuned to him after all the time we've spent together.

This is the hint that the waitress finally takes, with one last offer to get anything we may need. I draw my hand back and rest it on my lap, ignoring the amazing smell of the enchiladas sitting in front of me.

"Honestly, Charlie, I can't imagine I was very happy with my life before. Stop thinking about it as something you took from me, and think about it like it's something you gave me. A chance to do things differently. Don't minimize that because I'll be able to tell if it's going to rain because of my leg."

Charlie gives an undignified snort, but digs into his meal, accepting my words.

They weren't meant just to butter him up and make him feel better about the whole situation. It's the truth. It hurts that I don't have Vivian in my life, but something must have happened that I'm basically alone. I don't know what it means, and I'm not eager to look the gift horse in the mouth right now.

I refocus the conversation into what it was meant to be, a celebration of my achievements. A step toward the future.

Four

SURPRISE COLORS CHARLIE'S face when I remind him that it's Halloween. The way his eyebrows lift, mouth forming a perfect 'O' shape, makes me want to laugh and kiss those perfect lips. *Kiss*. I squash the thought almost immediately. I cannot think about how his mouth would feel on mine.

His surprise is followed by immediate panic at realizing that we have absolutely no candy to hand out to trick-or-treaters. I doubt that he has a costume either. I felt guilty for a minute, like I should have reminded him, but stop myself. Why should I? I'm not his wife or his significant other, no matter how much time we spend together.

"I can always go to the grocery store, or, you know, CVS or somewhere to get it," I offer, knowing that lugging the candy back to the apartment would probably be a lot for me. I'm still willing to try, willing to start again.

"No, no, no," Charlie declines. He reaches around me where I'm seated at the kitchen island to grab his wallet and keys. I try not to think about his proximity, how his body is almost pressed against me.

I should be thinking about getting back to my apartment, but my knee and ankle are both not healing the way they should. Each injury slows the other. If Charlie has noticed the bruise I'm sporting on my cheek from where I smashed my face when my knee gave out, he hasn't said anything.

It's a rare Saturday that Charlie has off and that he spends it running around the Upper East Side hunting for candy warms my heart. We haven't had heart-to-heart talks about our lives and how we grew up, but there is a different intimacy to seeing someone before they're ready to face the world with their armor on.

This is how he shows up almost two hours later, with his arms weighed down by bags and bags of candy. I laugh as I help him through the door.

"Do you really think we're gonna get this many trick-or-treaters?" I ask, starting to unload them into the cheap Halloween bowl that he also picked up.

"Maybe," he offers with a shrug. "I'm not usually home on Halloween. I don't know what kind of trick-or-treaters we get. If I'm not working, I have friends that will have a party or get bottle service at a club."

"Well, Benji said we just need to put this door hanger outside and trick-or-treaters should come." I falter as his words sink in about usually being with his friends. I look up at him, my head tilted toward him. It's a proximity thing again; I feel like he's been edging closer to me for weeks. "If you want to go out, you should. You don't have to stay home with me."

He hasn't said it, but there have been nights where I think he's had plans or had people he was going to see, only to stay in with me. Whenever the subject of friends comes up, he has a close group that he'll talk about, but when it comes to family, he gets vague, not wanting to go into detail. It's clear enough from photos around his apartment that he at least sees his mom, and he's mentioned that she's still alive, but there doesn't seem to be much of a relationship. His friends are his tether more than his family, and I understand that in a way I think few people do.

His brown eyes study me for a second. Study if there is anything hidden in my words, and of course there is. There is insecurity and fear and all those ugly emotions hiding. The truth is, I want him to stay with me. I want this to be more than just the hero-damsel dynamic it has been.

"They usually come throughout the whole building. I've seen them out and about. But no, I'm not passing on any exciting plans. Jack and his girlfriend are doing some haunted house and I don't do the gory fear thing." He touches my arm gently.

"Well, you got enough candy to last us through the next five years of Halloween. If you're feeling generous, we can just give each kid their own bag."

"I think that would make us the most popular apartment in the building," he teases.

Us. I said it first, but he echoed it. Does it mean anything more than just a slip of tongue? Is he thinking about me being in his life next year?

I let my mind wander to what the next year could look like with him. I envision staying with him in his apartment, because with the way he works it's the only way I would see him at all. My mind drifts of its own accord to how it would look with Charlie sweaty and above me, his body moving against mine, and I have to clench my thighs at the flood of desire. I hope to God that once I'm totally healed, he can maybe see me the same way.

"You can always bring some to the office," I suggest, clearing my throat. I set the bowl on the island next to the door so it's an easy grab and carry a smaller bowl to the couch, limping as I go.

"Ashley might kill me if I bring sweets in. She's got a sweet tooth the size of Russia and will eat the entire bag in a day."

"You need to do something nice for that girl," I scold, trying to stow the remaining bags of candy on a shelf.

"What makes you think that I don't take care of her?" Charlie helps me by taking the bags from my hand and sliding them onto the top shelf that I couldn't quite reach. Proximity, again. His body is near mine, but I can almost feel the strain in his muscles trying to keep from pressing against me, from touching me. I want him to give into the urge. I want him to see what it would be like. I banish the thought, focusing instead on talk of his assistant.

"Well, let's see. You work her super hard, you make her do shit for *me*, which is obviously above and beyond. And then you act like, I don't know, like she's just available to do anything you need, and she's your personal calendar. You need to do better by her."

Charlie throws his hands up before preheating the oven and pulling the frozen pizza from the freezer. It's stupid and arbitrary, but it makes me feel better if we cook in once and a while.

"I got her a Chanel bag for Christmas last year. She loved that! And I put cash in it. I swear, I thought she was going to kiss me."

Ugly, green jealousy stabs at me at the thought of him kissing Ashley. I don't know her, I don't know what she looks like, but how available Charlie is to her makes me envious.

Ugh. Who am I? Jealous of other women in Charlie's life? I don't have a claim to him. We're just roommates, forced together by a weird circumstance, not one that I would change.

"Try like three designer bags. She really saved your ass with me this year." Another reason that this spike of jealousy makes me feel weird. We haven't even met and Ashley has bent over backwards researching clothes, like dresses that were perfectly my size, that were easy with a leg cast and a brace. She even occasionally sent little helpful things like ultra moisturizer for my leg since it's been released from the cast.

"Did she?" he asks, tone light and teasing.

"Yeah, if you think about it, all of the clothes she's gotten for me. You know, I hate to imagine it, you having to go out and get me underwear."

"Okay, look, let's just stop it there." He blushes furiously as if he's never had to go out and buy a woman underwear before. Then it occurs to me. Maybe he hasn't. I don't really know what his past is like. I know that there was a woman at some point, but not anymore. I don't know what that means for us. I try not to read into it too closely; the way he blushes at the thought of getting me underwear.

The night is surprisingly slow, not many trick-or-treaters, but Charlie does agree to sit on the couch with me and watch Halloween themed movies, including and especially my favorite, *Hocus Pocus*, because that is the best Halloween movie that exists.

With each ring of the doorbell, we seem to be getting closer and closer to one another on the couch. I don't know if that's intentional or if it's just because we're trying to get to the bowl of candy that's between us. But I have to imagine it's intentional when his fingers find my hair, lightly toying with the end of my ponytail.

We stay up later than necessary waiting for those last minute trick-or-treaters, even though we haven't had one since 10pm. We watch movie after movie, never a scary one after I said I was scarred for life by the horror porno's at my apartment.

It's late when I feel my body get lifted off the couch, gently rousing me from sleep. I groan, and Charlie goes still, like if he doesn't move, I'll fall back asleep. I turn my body closer into him, my hand fisting in his shirt. Part of it is sleep, but a stronger, more awake part of me does it on purpose. It might be the only chance I have to feel this close to him, inhale that masculine scent. He sets me on my bed, surprising me with the brush of his lips on my brow before he slips out of the room, leaving me to drift back to sleep and wonder if this was all a dream.

It's the little things that Charlie does in the weeks between Halloween and Thanksgiving that start to make the difference between us. Like how he tries to be home earlier, or not work on weekends, saying he wants to make sure I'm getting out of the apartment. As much as we want it to be a daily thing, there is just no way that Charlie can get out of work early every day. We take the victories where we can. I start to crave this time with him. The way his eyes brighten when he comes home and finds me ready to go out. It makes me feel a little bit like a neglected puppy, but if I had a tail, it would definitely be wagging when he gets home.

"Are you doing anything for Thanksgiving?" I ask as we walk. We're two weeks out from the holiday. Charlie is holding my cane so I can try to push walking on my own. I was doing well until during one of these very walks, I was pushed into a hole in the ground by an errant cyclist.

Thankfully the sprain wasn't too bad, but it did slow me down for a week and this is my first walk since it happened. Still, I want to try without the cane.

"Probably not. I usually wind up working. Foreign markets and offices are open, and even if I am home, I'm just watching my emails. Sometimes Jack and I will spend it working together but since he started dating his girlfriend, he tries to get actual free time. I think he's proposing this year."

"When was the last time you took an actual holiday off? I mean, we've been together for like a month and a half now, and you work like a fucking maniac. You know, no reasonable person works every day of the year."

"I don't work every day of the year," he protests. His hand goes to the small of my back when he has to crowd close because another one of those bikers keeps skirting too close to the pedestrians. My heart races, and not because of the close calls we've had, but because I have to fight the urge to lean into him, into the lingering smell of clean laundry and coffee. I wonder for a half a second if he's as affected as I am, but he doesn't seem to be, so I bury the thought deep deep under my repressed desire for something, anything, to light me up the way he does.

"I find that hard to believe. You sat in my hospital room,

sending emails and taking meetings. You can't fool me, Mr. Breckenridge," I say with a teasing scowl.

He smiles at me. "So what do you propose?"

"Take the day off. Let me cook for you. Take the time to relax, watch some football, and drink some fancy imported beer. Put your feet up for once."

Charlie has put so much of his energy into helping me, that I feel helpless without doing something in return for him. At the moment, my options are limited. He's got more money than he knows what to do with, and I think it's the little things that mean more to him than anything else. It can't be that hard to manage a meal for two.

"You're an awful cook," he points out, and I realize he never removed his hand from the small of my back. His touch is barely there, ready to catch me if my ankle or knee decide they have had enough.

"It was *one* grilled cheese!" Who knew butter burned so fast? I looked at my phone for one minute, because he had texted in the middle of the day, checking in, and the next thing, my grilled cheese was blackened, the pan burned so thoroughly that I almost bought a new one to replace it.

"Case in point, Els, it was a grilled cheese. Even I was making those for myself when my mom or nanny wasn't around."

"Of course you had a nanny. Do you still happen to have the silver spoon that you emerged from the womb with?"

"I believe my mother has it in a nice frame beside my newborn hand and footprints. Before you ask, the frame is, of course, also silver."

I laugh again. "Please? Let me try? And at worst, you can save the day again and order takeout or we can eat leftovers, but let me try."

"How can I say no to that face? Of course you can try."

I clap my hands in delight, already starting to plan the menu.

That saying about biting off more than you can chew? Yeah, well, I'm a classic case of it. I have used possibly every pan in Charlie's kitchen trying to make mashed potatoes, green bean casserole, cheddar biscuits, stuffing, cranberry sauce, and pie for dessert. The main struggle, though, is not the many other things I'm making, but the tiny Cornish hens I'm terrified of burning.

My hair is swept up in a messy ponytail, half of it spilling out as I open the oven for the fifteenth time. Seeing that the hens are not burnt, I add a splash of milk and a glob of cream cheese to the mashed potatoes before stirring the stuffing.

"If you keep opening the oven door, it's not going to cook," Charlie tells me.

He's not patronizing me; he's genuinely trying to help, but I'm frazzled and in pain from hopping around the kitchen all morning. I can't help it, I snap.

"I know that!" I immediately want to claw back my words. I want to stuff them back into the place where my anger and frustration can live.

"Do you want help?" he asks softly, rising from where he's been sitting at the island, watching this catastrophe play out.

"No, I'm supposed to be doing something nice for you." I turn to face him, waving the potato masher in his face. A nice thick glob flies off the tool, hitting him smack in the face.

For a second, we're both too shocked to do anything, but he thumbs it off his face and pops it into his mouth.

"If you wanted my opinion, you just had to ask. It needs more salt." He gives me a rare goofy smile and it immediately puts me at ease.

I can do this.

I go back to focusing, finally calming when the food is all in the gorgeous double oven. Charlie keeps the rest of his commentary to himself, beckoning me to the couch to relax and watch some of the parade. The small collection of timers sitting on the counter are taunting me, even as I try to relax.

I nearly jump out of my skin when the first one goes off and the rest follow like falling dominoes. Charlie, who had been inching closer to me, snaps back to his side of the couch. He follows me, sitting again at the island, knowing that offering help again will only get his head bitten off.

I grab a towel off the counter, not sure where I've haphazardly left the oven mitts over the course of the day. I pull the stuffing from the oven, careful that I'm holding both sides of the pan. Once that is set on the side, I realize the green bean casserole and the cornish hens are burning. I try to grab them both, figuring that the pans should be light enough, but the problem is not in the pans, it's in that I haven't opened the oven door enough. Too late to do anything about it as the back of my hand grazes the door.

It's not a serious burn. Contact lasts only a second, but my immediate reaction sends the casserole pan and the hens out of my hands in a knee-jerk reaction. The moment seems to happen in slow motion, the pulling of my hand back toward me and the simultaneous release of the food. I can only watch in horror as the pan hits the oven door, food-side down, and the hens bounce on the floor followed by the clatter of metal on the tiles.

My tears are swift and immediate, and Charlie is right there beside me, hands on my back.

"Are you alright?" His voice sounds worried as I look up at him behind lashes laden with moisture. He reaches for my hand to inspect the small pink welt appearing on the back of it.

"I ruined dinner," I sob, unable to contain the tears, unsure of where they came from. I slide to the floor as the sobs wrack my body. I feel guilty over the ruined food, but it's more than that, more than just the pain from the burn. It's everything. It's two months of being injured. Two months of not remembering my own life. Two months of focusing on getting my knee and ankle working right. It's Thanksgiving: a holiday I would have spent with my parents, a holiday that I spent with my friend Vivian's family after the parents died, a holiday that's about family and yet I feel utterly alone except for Charlie. In him, I find a similar soul, cast adrift with no close family ties. When I asked him about spending the holiday with his family, he just shrugged and said that he hasn't done that in years.

Charlie is sitting near me on the floor and during my crying jag, he cradles me to his chest. He eventually lifts me into his lap, when he senses the shift in tears from physical pain to emotional pain. He doesn't say anything; he does try to shush my tears and soothe me. He rocks me against him, trying to find something without words that can offer me comfort.

We don't acknowledge the open oven door or the other food still burning inside.

"I'm so sorry," I finally manage once my crying has slowed. I'm reaching up and wiping my tears when Charlie pulls back and looks at my face. He's pensive, one brow ticking down.

"What for?" He brushes the hair from my face and gently cups my cheeks.

"Everything? I ruined dinner, to start. I've crashed into your life without a care. I've –"

"You've made my life so much more than it used to be," he says, his voice rough.

And then he is kissing me. His mouth is soft, so much softer than I would have guessed. I'm so startled that I don't even have a chance to react before he pulls away, a blush creeping up his neck.

"I'm sorry. I shouldn't have done that."

I open my mouth to object but the biscuits are now so badly burnt that smoke is wafting out of the oven. We both scramble off the floor, trying to get there first. Charlie turns both ovens off while I use an actual oven mitt instead of the towel I was using when I burned my hand. I drop the tray of blackened biscuits on the stove top and turn on the vent before looking back at Charlie, who has rescued the rest of the ruined dinner.

Laughter bubbles from my chest, such a change from the tears just moments earlier.

"So, Thai on me tonight?" I ask, finally earning a smile from Charlie, who still refuses to look anywhere near my lips.

Maybe I was wrong. Maybe I'm not alone in this growing attraction for the man who helped save me.

I wish I could say it isn't awkward after the kiss. Charlie is extra deliberate when he moves around me. Any attempts to try to get him to talk about the situation falter. He is always quick to change the subject, though I catch his eyes following the length of my legs or lingering on my lips.

After an insufferable, isolating week, I corner him the best I can in the kitchen. I brace one hand on the island and the other against the wall. He could easily move around me, but he doesn't.

"Can we talk?" I ask. It's late, it's really later than late. It's close to three in the morning, and I don't even care about the kiss at this point, I just want my friend back.

Charlie looks like he would rather eat glass, but his posture deflates just a touch and he nods. "I'm sorry things have been busy."

The excuse sounds weak to both of us, but I only cross my arms.

"You've been avoiding me," I correct.

He has the decency to look chastened. "You're not wrong, but you're also not right. I did have a tremendous amount of work to get done. With good reason."

"Are you going to tell me that reason, or am I going to have to hold my breath?"

He reaches toward me, his hand coming to my arm. I go still, surprised by the intentional touch.

"We're going to get out of town." His words suck the wind out of my sails.

"I'm sorry, what?"

"We're going to go on a trip. The neurologists have been saying that you need space; you need different stimulation."

My body flushes at the word stimulation. "What did you have in mind?" I am thankful that he's talking to me, so I let my annoyance rest.

"We have a flight tomorrow, which is really today, so probably too late for me to even have Ashley get you clothes, but really, it's not a big deal, if you just pack what you have it's fine. I have a bag you can use." He's rambling. This man, this perfectly polished, put together man with his smiles and his crisp hundred dollar bills, is incapable of stringing words together.

Is this the final hoorah? Is this how we part ways, a trip to soften the blow of 'get the fuck out of my house'? I can't believe how much the prospect of that makes me sick. The last thing I want is for us to say goodbye, for me to leave and go back to my solitary existence. I had that for a week while he bustled to and from work and I am not excited to do it again.

Still, the idea of going somewhere new, somewhere with Charlie outside of the monotony of our everyday lives, excites me. In the absence of Charlie I've started to wonder if I should consider what life after him would look like. I had resisted his offers to get a private investigator to find Vivian initially, but when I thought he was avoiding me, I started to change my mind. I needed time to find myself again before I could risk the hurt that reaching out to Vivian might bring. I might be blowing it out of proportion, but if I'm not, I wasn't ready for the potential fallout.

If this really is a goodbye trip, then maybe finding Vivian can keep me moving forward.

"Are you going to tell me where we're going?" I lean against the wall, letting him pass. This time, he doesn't crowd me, but the berth of space isn't as large as it was yesterday.

"It's a surprise," he says, his face closer to mine.

I think he might kiss me again, and I move, just a touch closer to him, but he pulls back, a smirk on his face.

"When do we fly out?" I refuse to look at his lips, no matter how badly I want to.

"Tomorrow night. I'm taking a half day, which is why I've been working like a dog. I wanted to make sure I can take the time while we're away." There is an undercurrent to his words, something he's saying without saying, but I refuse to read into it.

"They're really letting you do this? Right on the heels of taking time off after the accident?"

"They don't let anyone do anything. El, it's three in the morning and I still need to get work done tomorrow before our flight."

"I don't even know if I need my passport for this flight," I point out, and he grins.

"Remember when I had you fill out all that paperwork I said was for the hospital? I lied, sort of. Your passport expired, which I noticed when we got it from your apartment. I figured you would need it for something identification wise."

"Ashley?" I ask, already knowing the answer.

"Ashley," he confirms.

"You owe her the best gift you have ever given her. "

"I booked this all on my own, thank you very much."

"Shall I give you a medal for being able to wipe your own ass too?" I tease. I didn't realize how much I missed this banter until it was gone.

"I'll accept a pat on the back if you don't have one handy." He gives me a half smile. "But seriously, I need to crash. My alarm is set for three hours from now."

I pull away from the wall, heading to my room. The promise of tomorrow might prove to be too much for me. I don't know what to expect. I don't know what tomorrow is going to bring, but I know that Charlie is in it, and that is enough for me.

Five

⁓

I CAN'T SLEEP a wink on the flight to San Francisco, even with the cashmere blanket and eye mask that are gifted from the airline. Not even the comfort of first class can lull me to sleep. Every time I think I'm able to fall asleep, Charlie shifts ever so gently, pressing his thigh against mine. The one time I am able to let my mind drift off, all I can think about is how it would feel to have his thighs spreading mine as he hammers his body into me. I'm obviously more frustrated than I thought.

Charlie is plugging away on his laptop over some reports that are due while we're away. He tried to promise that this was the only time that he would need to work, but he and I both know that as much as he wants that to be true, it's not.

I'm too excited to keep my eyes closed for long, so I look out the window as we chase the setting sun. I open my mouth to make a snarky comment about time travel, but hold it in when I look at Charlie's face. His brow is furrowed as he concentrates on the spreadsheet in front of him. Every so often, he catches his lower lip between his teeth a second before sucking it into his mouth. I study his profile instead, the way he absently runs the back of his hand along his jaw, rubbing at the five o'clock shadow growing there. He catches me looking at him out of the corner of his eyes.

"Can I help you, Elia?" he asks, turning to face me. He lowers his screen, signaling his focus change.

"No, not at all. I was just watching you," I admit, delighted when he blushes. It's a quick stain on his cheeks, surprised by my attention.

"Oh really? See something you like?" he asks, leaning back. I love the way his eyes rove over my face. He's been tentative since the lines between our relationship started blurring. What was clear no longer is. Our kiss makes things uncertain. Was it a one time thing? Does he see me as more than the sad little injured amnesiac he's been hosting in his home? Does he think I see him as a very fit, good looking ATM with surprisingly soft lips?

"Plenty." I take my eyes off of him and take a bite of the salad we were served. The combination of spinach, walnuts, and goat cheese is a delicious distraction. There is so much I like about what I see when I look at him, but I won't say that. I enjoy his smile and the way his brown eyes twinkle when he's amused. I find myself blushing under his attention.

"Are you enjoying your first time in first class?" he asks, sipping his red wine. I would challenge him on what makes him think this is my first time, but my doe-eyed wonder as we settled in and were served gave me away, no doubt.

"It's not too shabby. I will say, I thought you were private jet rich, and you're just boring first class rich." I want to hide under the heady look in his eyes. He's felt guilty since the kiss, afraid of giving an impression of pressuring me. This is the first time I've seen something other than nervous trepidation while he tries to keep me at arms length.

"Someone has high standards," he teases.

"Only because you raised them," I say, taking a sip from the now warm champagne I've been nursing. "Do you think this is real crystal?" I ask, looking at the glass in my hand.

"Possibly. You know there is some asshole somewhere who whined that it wasn't." He signals to the flight attendant, who comes over.

"Felix, is this crystal?" he asks.

Felix smiles, delighted that it's an easy task. File that under things I appreciate about Charlie: he makes sure every person feels seen. Finding out Felix's name and treating him like a person was a small action that Felix seems to appreciate.

"Only if you ask for crystal specifically. Would you prefer that I change your glasses out?" Felix offers, already reaching for our glasses.

I pull mine back out of reach with a shake of my head. Charlie laughs.

"No, not at all, just a curiosity. Don't trouble yourself."

"Of course, Mr. Breckenridge," Felix says before disappearing back into the galley.

"Are you satisfied?" Charlie asks. The teasing tone is starting to wane, turning husky.

"Never," I say.

He looks like he wants more. Like he wants to reach out and take my hand or maybe even kiss me, but we're in flux. Neither of us knows where our relationship stands. Not that we have talked about it at all; his disappearing act only made me feel more unsettled.

Charlie checks his watch. "We have two more hours, might as well see if there is a movie you want to watch." He gestures at the screen in front of me. "The glory of losing your memory means you can rewatch all these things for the first time again. I almost wish I could re-watch *Infinity War* and *Endgame* again."

"*Infinity War* and *Endgame*?" I ask and he sighs.

He knows I don't remember, but it still surprises him when I forget about major events in the last five years, like how we wound up with a reality star for a president.

"Yeah, the *Avengers*?" he asks, concerned that maybe I don't know who they are.

My mind casts out looking for any memories I have of the superhero movies. "Yeah, I think the last one I saw had that robot in it."

Charlie shudders. "Well, I know what we're doing when we get back to New York. I'm locking you in my apartment and we're watching ALL of the *Avengers* movies. Pick something else to watch now. I still have to send a few more emails before the flight ends."

I pick a comedy based on a TV show from the 90s with a ton of lifeguards and can't help laughing out loud. A few of the pop culture references go over my head, but I still enjoy it deeply. Every so often, I catch Charlie peeking at me out of the corner of his eye, smiling as I laugh.

It's strange to think, but I am grateful that of all the people in New York City, Charlie was the one in the cab that hit me. He's given me a whole new life, one I never imagined myself living, and it's not just the nightly takeout or the swoon-worthy views of Central Park at dusk. It's having someone to share my life with. Even if he isn't my partner, he is my friend. This life we have come to share, I cherish so, *so* much.

The announcement that we are beginning our descent startles me. Charlie tries to send off a few more emails before Felix reminds him to put his laptop away.

"So, where are we staying?" I'm curious about what the plan is for San Francisco.

"Well, we still have another two flights." Charlie says, finally relaxing and closing his eyes for a moment.

"You're joking," I say, not liking the idea of being stuck in a tin can for much longer. I'm not uneasy about flying, but the thought of doing it for much longer is exhausting.

"Nope, we have a night in San Francisco and our next flight

leaves at noon. I booked us a hotel in the city before our next flight."

"And then what?" I ask.

The sound of the landing gear dropping grates my nerves. I reach out and grab Charlie's hand without thinking. My eyes slam closed, the unease working through my system. He threads his fingers between mine, letting me squeeze as hard as I need.

"I'm sorry, I'm just..." I trail off, trying not to think about the landing. It's irrational, but that's what fear is. It's the loss of control over what's happening as we descend that terrifies me.

"It's okay," Charlie reassures me, not letting go even once we have safely touched down. I keep waiting for him to let go, but he doesn't; he waits until I'm ready to let him go.

Six

"NO," I say emphatically, shaking my head.

Before us is a small propeller plane that Charlie wants me to get on. Our stay in San Francisco was short before we got on another flight to Tahiti. I'm about to get on a plane for the third time in thirty-six hours and my heels are dug so far into the ground that dragging me will rip up asphalt. We're standing on the tarmac, watching people board ahead of us for the first time on this trip from Tahiti to Bora Bora. There is no first class because the flight is under an hour and the plane has about ten seats. We're about to board a puddle jumper and I am terrified.

"No," I repeat, shaking my head again. "I have seen drones with better engines. I will not get on that plane."

Charlie is patient, watching me and listening to my concerns. "If you really feel that way, I can cancel the hotel and get us one here."

I look at his face and know he would do it in a heartbeat, even if there were some sort of penalty for canceling the same day. I can taste the acidity of fear in my mouth, or maybe that's just breakfast clawing its way back up my throat. My will to fight this is giving way to reluctance. I know that this is what Charlie wants to do.

69

He's asked so little of me that I can't deprive him of this. I pull my shoulders back, shaking off my fear as best I can.

"Fine, let's do this." I clench my teeth, marching up the stairs before I change my mind.

"It will be worth it," Charlie says. "I promise."

I keep my eyes squeezed shut the entire time, holding Charlie's hand. I don't care if it gives the impression of clinginess. He doesn't seem to mind, rubbing his thumb over my hand with the limited access he has under my crushing grip.

A car whisks us from the airport directly to our oceanfront villa. I'm unable to tear my eyes from the window, watching the car bypass the homes of the locals, shops, and so much more. The transition from homes to the resorts is abrupt when we get closer to the water.

Calling our hotel oceanfront is an injustice; it's so much more than that. From the lobby, I can see the branches of the villas extending over water. It's the sort of place that only exists on Pictogram influencer pages, available to the elite and wealthy.

The entrance is wide open with travelers coming and going from the resort to various excursions. Those that are milling around the lobby look relaxed, a mixture of sunburned and tanned with drinks in their hands.

The hostess is delighted to welcome us as she checks for Charlie's reservation. "Thank you so much for joining us. You are so young, is this your honeymoon?" she asks as she leads us to a golf cart.

Charlie wraps his arm around my shoulders and pulls me close against his body and giving me a cheeky wink. I inhale the scent of him deeply, but I'm still tense against him, not used to being so close to him or feeling the side of his hard body pressed to my breast. Even after days of travel, he smells like clean laundry and mint, like sunlight and a cooling breeze wrapped into one.

"You bet, but this was a surprise for my bride. Any chance you can have the local stores send up some simple attire for her? Swimsuits, cover-ups, and dresses." He glances down at me. "Anything else, dove?" he asks, smirking.

He is enjoying this immensely, watching me squirm under the discomfort of his generosity.

I smile and look at the woman driving the cart. "No, please don't have anything sent. It's really unnecessary," I plead, but if I'm being honest, I need it. I may have overpacked, but it's mostly leggings, sweaters, and long-sleeved t-shirts. I'm ill prepared for a beach vacation. Never in my wildest dreams would I have thought this was where we were headed.

He glances down to my feet, which are shoved into a ragged pair of Uggs. "Add some sandals too. You can have this all charged to my card after she decides what to keep."

I grit my teeth, vowing to challenge him when we don't have someone right there. If he wants to be flashy in front of others, then I'll let him do it.

She stops the golf cart at the entrance to the row of villas. The hostess leads us down a dock, which has villas on all sides, about twenty in total. Our villa is the farthest one from the shore. She's talking about the island and all the activities available to us, but I don't internalize a word she says. The water here is crystal clear and I can see fish swimming below. Every six feet, there is a pane of plexiglass, which leads us to look down at the fish beneath our feet. I pause at the first one to watch a school of fish swim by.

He was right; that last flight was worth it.

"As requested, the two villas on either side of you are vacant, and this is where you will be staying. I have noted that you would like breakfast served in the villa."

She unlocks the door, letting Charlie and I walk in. Inside there is a rowing machine in the living room, and honestly I think we have an entire house, not a hotel room. The main living space is open concept with a dining area, couch, and small kitchenette. On either side of the living space are doors that lead to the bedrooms and bathrooms. The doors to a patio are open so that the wind is blowing the sheer curtains inside.

"Your rowing machine per your request, Mr. Breckenridge," she says as she waves her hand towards the exercise equipment. "We also have the fridge stocked with water. Through this doorway is the first bedroom with a queen bed, but this is the master."

She leads us into the larger of the rooms, completely ignoring the first room. I have to remind myself to breathe when I look at the space. It's large, nearly larger than my entire apartment. A four poster king bed sits against the far wall with a mosquito net around it that's pulled back for the time being. Through a doorway I glimpse which I imagine is the bathroom. I can't be positive of that because on the water side of the room, there is a large soaker tub, certainly big enough for two, that looks out a set of French doors that lead to an outdoor patio. The tub in the bedroom says it all. This room is for fucking. Out on the patio, there are chairs and umbrellas spread out, wrapping around back to the living room. There is also a hammock that sits over the water and a plunge pool.

Charlie is just as in awe, taking in the sights of the villa. Neither of us can believe this place is real.

"Thanks. That will be all," he says, slipping the hostess money. "Can you have some breakfast sent to us now?"

"Of course, sir. Right away," she says before slipping out.

"Charles." I turn to him, his body so close to mine. I have to use his proper name because of how lavish the space is.

He cuts me off, waving a dismissive hand. "Don't. The doctor suggested a change of scenery might help your brain relax a little. So I figured this would be relaxing," he says earnestly.

"Yeah, a change of scenery. Like, maybe a cabin in the Catskills away from the city. Not fifteen hours away on an island in Bora fucking Bora!" I say looking around. I throw myself on the couch, dramatically. I don't let him answer before barreling on.

"And the clothes? Really?" I ask, not even sure where to start. I let my arm drape over my face.

"Look, I've been a Scrooge with money. My biggest extravagance was buying my apartment. I am otherwise a workaholic. You see how bad I can get. I needed this break just as much as you and I needed a good reason to spend my money. This makes me happy. Seeing your face when you watched the fish made me happy. If you told me that you wanted to stay another two weeks, I would say to hell with my father and we would stay another two weeks."

I glower at him for using how hard he works against me. He sits beside me on the couch, lifting my feet so they settle on this lap. His finger digs into the sore muscles around the scar on my knee, massaging it. He doesn't let me object.

"Let me have this. Let me enjoy making you happy with breakfast in our villa, snorkeling, sleeping in, and whatever the hell else you want to do. They have yoga classes here that you can take. We can snorkel and scuba dive and ride horses on the beach at sunset for fuck's sake. We can do everything or nothing. Just let me enjoy spoiling you."

He's relentless in his kindness and how hard he works. I throw my hand dramatically over my face again as I lean back into the plush pillows.

"If you must buy me new shoes, then you must."

He laughs and starts to rub my feet. I take a peek at him from under my arm, swallowing hard. Vacation Charlie is a different person: the set of his shoulders, the relaxed facial expression, his phone not glued to his hand.

"So, what do you want to do?" he asks, eagerly. It's late afternoon in New York, still so many hours of work to be done, but he doesn't even look toward his laptop.

"I have no idea! I don't think I even have a swimsuit. It was winter in NYC when we left. Can't you just do your workout while I shower and think about it?"

He pats my foot, rising to his feet. "If that will make you

happy, sure. I'll call the front desk and ask them to at least make it snappy for the bathing suits."

"You are so fucking bossy," I say, shaking my head. I grab my bag, carrying it to the smaller of the rooms. Regardless of his kindness, I wouldn't even consider taking the master.

"I think you like it," he says with a smile, disappearing into the master with his suitcase.

I blush, thinking that I would indeed love to have him boss me around, particularly between the sheets. A flush spreads on my skin at the thought.

The room is small, space for the bed with a dresser and mirror. This room is not meant to be stayed in the long term. It's a way station, a place to rest your head between sundown and sun up.

I step into the shower and let the water wash away the past two days of travel. I wonder if when I was in that accident, I actually landed in a coma and this is all just part of some weird dream my brain invented to cover for the crash. The smell of the coconut soap is soothing as I take my time under the rainwater shower.

I close my eyes, letting the water hammer against my skin and letting my mind drift to the accident. I haven't told Charlie that I've started to remember that night. Mostly what has come back are fragments of the actual accident, but nothing more. I remember the rain on my skin, unable to see where I was going. I try to capture feelings, why I was out there, but nothing holds. An overwhelming panic as headlights blind me. I can't tell Charlie how I remember him hovering over me, trying to shield my broken body with his as water loosens his perfectly styled hair so it hangs in his face.

I don't want to think about what it could mean, remembering. I almost prefer not knowing what happened, not remembering the trauma. I'm afraid to find someone that didn't think I was worth looking for. I'm afraid to find out that I didn't like my life very much before and be stuck right back in it. Worse, I'm afraid to find that I was happy and it means losing Charlie.

When I emerge, Charlie is on the rowing machine. I can see his earbuds in, so I don't bother him, choosing to watch him instead. The small dining table has been loaded with various fruits, pastries, eggs, and crepes. I know I don't have allergies, so I'm comfortable picking at unknown foods and drinks. I grab a fruit smoothie and take a long sip from the straw, the mango refreshing on my tongue.

I watch Charlie, the explosive movement as his strong legs push the seat back. He leans back, flexing his abs before pulling the bar back with his powerful arms. He makes it look effortless, but I can hear how his breathing is controlled so he gets the maximum out of the exercise. More than once he has tried to show me how to do it, but the way I was hurt - my knee, my ankle, and my shoulder - means that it's still too painful to try.

It's calming listening to him sucking in air as he drives with his legs before a sharp exhalation as the seat slides forward again. I'm mesmerized watching his body move so in sync. Legs, core, arms, legs, core, arms. It's motions that he's comfortable with, familiar with. He did them through college on the crew team, and after graduating, he stuck with the machine.

When he finishes, he turns to face me, his t-shirt soaked in sweat. It doesn't stop him from using one of the dry spots to wipe his forehead, giving me an eyeful of the abs he has worked so hard on. It would be rude to not appreciate them, and I do, taking peeks at them before meeting his eye. The smirk he's suppressing tells me that I've been made.

"Oh good, you're out." He gestures at some bags sitting beside the door. "That's what they could round up on short notice in terms of bathing suits. Pick one out and we can finally relax." He checks his phone quickly, his brow furrowing.

I grab the bags and slip into my room, to see what the options are, leaving him to scroll through whatever email or text he just got. Somehow with all the flying we're only five hours behind New York, which means Charlie is seeing what his team hasn't done.

The bags contain endless treasures. There are a few decent

bikinis and one pieces tucked against coverups and lounge shorts. I slide on a simple purple bikini that straps on like a bra and high rise bottoms. When I emerge after trying them on, I'm disappointed to see that Charlie is still in his workout gear on his phone.

In taking care of me after the accident, he was accused of being too lax with his work. Initially, they were understanding, his guilt over the accident won him sympathy. Like all bosses, they wanted to ensure that he was still focused on work and when he landed a huge deal, they backed off. This trip comes with strings, and while he isn't working his usual eighteen-to-twenty-hour days, he still has to be plugged in.

Charlie glances up, registering my movement. I watch as his eyes rove over me in a way they haven't before. This is the most I've been exposed to him ever, and he's capitalizing on his chance to drink me in. He studies the swell of my breasts and the curve of my hips, cataloging the various scars I have from the accident. There aren't many, but he studies the few, namely along my knee where they had to do surgery to repair the ligament. I wouldn't say our dealings were platonic before this, but they certainly didn't have the heat behind them the way his gaze does now.

"I'll shower off and meet you by the pool." His voice is husky as he drops his phone on the table. His hand reaches out, groping for a piece of fruit, not taking his eyes off me. I can feel a blush stain my cheeks, the heat in his gaze transferring to me.

"Sure, I've got my book." I walk past him, grabbing my book from my carry-on bag. Clear skies and the sound of the ocean below me are instantly calming.

I think about wanting to text my best friend about what just happened. My thoughts stray to Vivian. She would love this place, and would balk at the idea that I'm here with the hot millionaire. The thought throws me. How much money does Charlie have that he's renting out the cabanas around us too? I can't go down that rabbit hole. The last I remembered was that Vivian was graduating law school. Then again, last I remembered, I was working as a receptionist for a law firm.

So much is different from five years ago. I want to change that, but I don't know where to begin. I have no contacts to start to reach out. I have no old friends I can text or email to ask for Vivian's contact info.

I throw myself onto a lounge chair, trying to invest myself in the book. I've read the same few pages over and over again with nothing really sticking. My mind keeps moving back to Vivian. Maybe she would help ground me, tell me that this is, in fact, not all a dream where a gorgeous millionaire whisks me off to an island. The only thing missing from making my life a romance novel is mind-blowing sex.

When I get back to New York, I'm determined to find Vivian and figure out what exactly went wrong between us. She was there when my parents died, she was my first friend in college, my room-mate, my sister. Whatever happened between us had to be rough. That thought gives me pause. Maybe reaching out would be a bad idea.

Charlie finally emerges, but he has his laptop in his hand, his swim trunks hanging low on his hips. He's done me the dishonor of wearing a shirt, which blocks the view of his perfectly sculpted muscles. If he's going to ignore me so he can work, then he could at least do it shirtless.

"I'm sorry, I have to answer emails and do some work. I promise the entire trip isn't going to be like this," he reassures me, but it's an empty promise because he's a slave to work, even if he doesn't want to be.

"Charlie, even if it was, that's fine. You have taken so much time away from work to try to help me. You're in the dog house with your bosses. I get it."

He settles at a table in the shade. His brown eyes lift to mine as his computer starts up. "I'm glad you're so understanding, but it's really unfair to you and to me. I have a thousand days of unused time off, I should be able to take a vacation once every five years," he says, sighing.

I set my book aside to slip into the infinity pool. The water is surprisingly warm from the harsh rays of the sun, so it doesn't bring the cool relief I expected. The displaced water slips over the side with a soft splash.

I stand in the water and lean over the edge, looking out toward land. Palm trees are dotted along the shore, offering shade to those along the waterfront. I can just make out people playing along the water's edge.

It's watching a pod of stingrays swim by that I decide I must have died and now I'm in heaven. There is no way that I have found myself in paradise like this.

The water around me ripples as Charlie gets in the water. "How are you feeling about all this?" he asks, sitting on the stairs, keeping his distance.

"What specifically? This coma dream my brain has cooked up wherein I've been rescued by a handsome man, or are you talking about being in Bora Bora with you?" I stand in the water, watching him.

He smirks at my words, but turns serious again. "I meant mentally being here. I wanted to see how you were doing," he prods.

"If you're asking if I remember anything, the answer is no. But I wish I had someone I could tell or brag about being here on Pictogram or something. I was missing my friend earlier."

Charlie raises his eyebrows. His elbows are braced on his knees as he studies my face. "That's the first you've mentioned wanting anything from your past life," he says softly, watching my reaction. He's gotten good at knowing when I'm frustrated or angry, but lonesome is new for him.

I look away, wanting to squirm under his scrutiny. I tread water, lifting my feet up from the shallow water. The pool is small and not deep; when I stand, the water barely skims the bottom of my breasts.

"I had this girlfriend, Vivian. She was my best friend. We went to college together, pledged the same sorority, and we were room-mates right out of school. Last I remember, we were still living together, but were discussing what to do when our lease was up because she wanted to move in with her boyfriend. Did that happen? Did we stop talking because of that? I just don't know. It's like pausing a movie in the middle of a big scene and then picking it up years later, in a totally different scene. Maybe you're right, maybe I should see a therapist when we get back to New York." I had fought Charlie on this tooth and nail, not wanting to admit that there was anything wrong with me, but maybe I did need help.

I needed someone to help me sort through the issues so I didn't spiral. There were little things I could remember: trying a restaurant, a different temp job, fighting with a guy I had been seeing. They were snippets, the random pieces of a puzzle whose colors were too muted for me to know where they fit within a larger picture I couldn't see.

"Anything you need. If you want, I can get someone to track down your friend." He stops when he sees my face. "I'm not saying investigate her. I'm saying get a phone number for you so that when you're ready, you can reach out to her." He lets this offer sink in. I remain silent, considering it. Charlie wades into the water, staying on the opposite side from me, maintaining his distance. "You don't have to decide this minute. Sit on it until we get back to New York. We're not in any rush."

I nod, knowing that the answer is going to be yes. These last few months have been scary without anyone I know around. I have come to trust Charlie, but only because he was in my hospital room every day I was stuck in there. He kept me company while letting me get to know him. It would be good to have someone who knew me in my corner.

"How is work going to handle you in a different time zone?" I ask, shifting the conversation off me.

"Jack said that he will double down. He gets it." Charlie hesitates, scratching the back of his neck. "Well, not really."

"When will I get to meet this Jack character?" I ask. I've heard stories, and I've also heard Charlie yelling at Jack on the phone, but he is otherwise a mystery to me. Charlie has minimized his social life, focusing instead on making up for the work he missed since we met. Now he's here with me, instead of spending time with them.

"You can meet him when we get back. He's jealous that you have been monopolizing all of my time lately."

I lay back in the water, letting my blonde hair fan out around me with my eyes closed. Charlie approaches me, causing the water to ripple against my skin. I open my eyes briefly when I feel his hands gently touching my back, supporting me. I glance at him out of the corner of my eye.

"I'm sorry," I say, closing my eyes, letting him hold me up.

"What could you have to be sorry for, Ellie?" he asks.

My whole self softens at the nickname. Elia is already a short name, so it's rare that it gets shortened. Hearing it on his lips makes me gooey. He's trying it out, Ellie. I've been El to him before, but Ellie has a different vibe to it.

"Everything. I feel like I've caused so much trouble for you. I'm probably healed enough to go back to my own apartment." I feel like this trip is the perfect time for us to reset our boundaries at home. Going back to my apartment might be the best way for Charlie to not feel obligated to take care of me.

"Is that what you want?" His voice is gruff.

I open my eyes to find his brown ones boring into mine.

"I hate being a burden to you. You're spending your money on me: getting all these fancy doctors and specialists, hiring private investigators, and calling in your connections. I don't understand why."

He lets me go, forcing me to right myself so I'm standing in front of him. He's so tall that he towers over me. I squint looking up at him, finding his eyes burning.

"I don't know how many times I can tell you that you being in my life has changed it for the better. I was going through the motions of living before. I had a job and an apartment and I would bounce between the office and the penthouse, but it wasn't anything more than a place to sleep until you got there. I'm just going to be direct: I want more with you." He pauses, wetting his lips, his eyes flicking down to mine. He's thought about this; his statement isn't flippant. He brings his hands up to my face, cupping it gently. Charlie's brown eyes search mine, setting my soul on fire. I want to feel his lips on mine again, our first kiss was surprising and too quick.

This time, he's slow about lowering his mouth to mine, letting me object if I want. I have no objection, only an objection to him not kissing me yet. The world stands still when his lips finally meet mine. My arms wrap around his middle tentatively, my fingertips grazing his side. I'm surprised by his thumbs grazing my cheeks. I open my mouth to him, deepening the kiss. His tongue sweeps into my mouth, brushing against my tongue. I moan, leaning in, pressing my body against his.

He breaks the kiss off, rubbing his thumb over my lips. "I thought I made it clear to you that you're so much more than some charity case to me. That collision changed both of our lives."

I want to believe him. My heart nearly jumps through my chest to hear him say the words out loud. Isn't this what I want? A confirmation that he's feeling even remotely the same? So why do my thoughts go to war with heart? Is it to temper these budding feelings?

I'm saved from having to address his statement or my feelings when I hear his phone beep with an incoming email. I take the easy escape. "Don't you need to get that?" I ask, my voice low.

"No, I don't. I have much more important things to do." He

kisses me again, this time a little harder. His hands drop to my hips, pulling me against him where I can feel his erection. I moan again, opening my mouth. He seizes the opening, his tongue dancing against mine. He lifts me, pressing me against the wall of the pool.

His kiss is desperate as he holds me against his rock-hard body. I spread my legs, hooking them around his hips in an effort to get closer to him. I can feel his hard-on straining against his bottoms, urging against my core. Charlie's hand comes up behind my neck, tangling in my wet hair. His other arm snakes up my back, crushing me against him. I lean up, at a severe disadvantage, overcome with the need for more. There will be no coming back from this moment.

I don't want to come back from this moment.

His phone starts to ring.

"Ignore it," he says breathlessly, not moving his mouth from mine. He starts to kiss down my neck, one hand sliding down my bathing suit strap. His fingers dance along the edge of my top, over my breast, teasing as he goes. I groan as my body comes to life under his touch. I can feel a fire kindling between my legs, so I dig my heels into his bottom, pulling him closer to me, closer to that heat. I know I've had boyfriends before, but never in my life have I been this turned on. The phone stops ringing as Charlie slides my other strap down. My hands are more tentative with him. I run my hands along his shoulders and then up to his hair. I've imagined what it would be like to run my hands through his golden locks, and I'm so glad to finally do it, finding them silky in my fingers.

Charlie's phone starts to ring again. He groans, hesitating for a minute, moving his mouth down to my jaw.

"If it's important they'll leave a message," he says.

I hope they don't call again.

He cups my breast through the bathing suit top, his lips leaving a fire-hot trail down my neck that he sucks and nips at, his tongue soothing as he goes. I release his hair and reach behind me to unclasp my top, which I struggle to get a grip on. He has me pinned firmly against the side of the pool. I whimper when he finds a sensitive spot along the column of my neck. Charlie grins at the noise.

I'm thankful that the villas around us are vacant. At this moment, as his hand starts to tentatively tease into my top, I wouldn't even care to find out that there was someone watching. The phone stops ringing while I fumble with the strap. I'm just about to get it undone when it rings a third time.

Charlie lets out a frustrated groan, dropping his head onto my shoulder. His lips are swollen as he steps away from me, staring into my dazed eyes. I can read his mind, the apology written on his face without him even needing to say a word. Charlie doesn't cross back to the stairs; instead he braces his hands on the deck and hauls himself out of the water. He strides over to where his phone rings. He checks the caller ID before answering. With his free hand he adjusts his bottoms, trying to hide the evidence of his arousal.

"What, Jack?" he snaps, opening his laptop, prepared for whatever might have come up. "What is so fucking important that you couldn't handle it?"

I take this moment to fix the straps on my top, making sure I'm still covered in all the right places.

Charlie goes quiet, listening to the other end of the phone. His eyes flick to me, then back to the computer, apology written within. They talk business a little more, Charlie dropping into the seat with an aggravated sigh. Jack's a good friend, an old friend, so he doesn't hold back letting him know just how frustrating he is being.

"Yes, Jack, Bora Bora is fucking amazing. I literally went to an island in the middle of the ocean to get away from you. Now leave me alone unless you want me to kick your ass when I get back." He ends the call and looks at me.

I am still flushed, sitting in the water under the golden sun. I climb out of the water, wrapping a towel around my chest, feeling too exposed.

"I'm sorry," he says, looking at me over the top of his laptop screen. The set of his shoulders tells me that he's settling in.

"Nothing to be sorry about. I'm going to cool off inside for a little while." I need to cool off both from the temperature and my emotions. I may not remember the last five years, but the ache between my legs tells me it's been too long since I've been truly satisfied.

"I want to pick up where we left off. Maybe get a closer look at that tattoo on your back." He gives me a sheepish and then devilish grin. This time, I know the blush I'm feeling is from him.

I step into the cool AC, goosebumps breaking out over my still wet skin. My phone sits alone on the table where I left it, no messages or emails waiting for me. Technology hasn't changed much in the five years that I lost, but I'm still getting used to the nuances. There wasn't much to be transferred over from the Cloud outside a few innocuous photos of food and flowers. I won't forget the anguish on Charlie's face when he handed me the phone and saw that I had no photos in there as a reminder of who I was.

I give in to the urge to download Pictogram. I may not have anyone to follow me, but it doesn't mean I can't start to rebuild my life. At some point I had one, posting silly photos and videos from college, but I can't remember the handle or log in info. I try searching for my name but with no result. I then search Vivian's name and am delighted to find her but that is quickly overshadowed by disappointment that her page is private. My thumb hovers over the request button, uncertain if I should.

Charlie walks in to find me lost in my phone. He's quick when crossing to me and then takes my phone and sets it aside. I raise my eyebrows at him, at the audacity of him censoring my phone time.

He sits down, apologetic. "I am really so sorry. I told Jack to fuck off."

"I heard," I say, interrupting him, tucking my feet under me. This is uncharted territory for me, for us. I always had clearly defined relationships, not chaotic make-outs with my what, roommate?

"Let's head into town, walk around, and get a feel for the place. Go shopping, find somewhere to eat lunch, and then when we get back it will be late enough in New York that Jack will be too tired to bother me again."

"I'm not sure it's ever going to be too late for Jack to bother you. I've seen the hours you work. But sure, just as long as we pick up where we left off at some point," I say, glancing at him out of the corner of my eye.

He reaches out and tilts my chin toward him. I can feel the heat building again between my legs as I meet his eye.

"Any time you want," he says, pressing his lips against mine. I refuse to be swept up this time, so I pull away and earn a wry grin from him. I float into my bedroom and sift through my bag to see if I have anything reasonable to wear. Spoiler alert: I don't. So I dig through the bags sent over by the front desk to see if there is a cover-up I can reasonably pass off as a dress. I manage to find a wrap one, keeping my bathing suit on underneath in case an errant wind blows the skirt up.

I want to stay in this villa and explore my relationship more with Charlie, shamelessly explore his body more. But we have the next two weeks to do that and everything in between. We could afford to take it slow with each other.

After weeks of walks in the city, Charlie has become conditioned to stick to my left side, ready to catch me if my leg gives out. We visit a nearby shop with some bitchy saleswoman where Charlie flashes his black card and buys the cheapest thing he can, a simple emerald-cut aquamarine, my birthstone. He spends just enough to show what type of sale this woman lost out on: a *Pretty Woman* moment for sure.

I can't stop toying with the jewel as we walk, and I let Charlie take a drastic lead. "I am still injured, you know," I call after him.

He's so excited to explore that, for the first time, he's not cognizant of how far behind I've fallen. He's not on New York time, relentlessly speed-walking from point A to point B. He's on vacation and needs to slow down and remember that I have little legs. Charlie knows where he's going now and is on a mission to get us there quickly. At my protest, though, he slows, offering his arm to me. I let him lead the way as we go, eventually stopping at a Mexican restaurant.

"I made reservations," he says, holding the door open for me, letting me enter first.

"When?" I ask incredulously as Charles approaches the hostess desk.

"Okay, so maybe the front desk made the reservations for me," he admits, grabbing a mint and popping it into his mouth. His eyebrows rise dramatically in a waggle and he gives me a self-satisfied grin. The hostess leads us to our table, winding us around empty chairs to a secluded corner. The building has an open-air courtyard with tables all around it.

There is a live mariachi band playing next to a fountain in the courtyard. It's a late lunch so the restaurant is mostly empty. We order drinks, a mojito for Charlie and a margarita for me, and an app, chips and guacamole, to start. He looks so relaxed, sipping his drink, with the top two buttons of his shirt undone. I wish everyday Charlie was like this.

"I studied abroad in college in Scotland. I've been to Europe, but this is something entirely different," I say, looking around. "This is just so surreal."

"I know what you mean. I've been to Europe a few times and went to Thailand for a friend's bachelor party, but nothing quite like this. It feels like paradise."

"You're stupid rich, let's just move here forever," I say jokingly, taking a sip from my drink.

"I would love to, but my father, well, he wouldn't love that idea."

"You're the heir apparent, right?" I ask.

He seldom talks about his father and for good reason. I can hear the edge to his voice whenever they're on the phone together.

"Ah, yes. He's fast-tracked my advancement through the company. It helps that I haven't really had a personal life recently, present company excluded." We never venture into the conversations of past flames. He has a bunch of extra toothpaste and travel-sized women's deodorant packed away in the bathroom, which makes me think that he wasn't exactly celibate, but it's weird to think about.

"Were you serious with anyone before the accident?" I try to muster up as much nonchalance as I can before shoving a giant chip in my mouth. The hard edges poke around my mouth and I know I look more foolish for doing it. Maybe that will shut me up and keep me out of his business. Then again, what happened in the pool makes it my business. The waitress drops off our orders, whisking away our empty glasses. Charlie waits until she steps away before answering me.

"I did, once. But I wouldn't have been kissing you if there was someone else. That said, you've seen how I work; I didn't have enough hours in the day to keep her happy." He sounds regretful about how things ended.

I don't know what he thinks this says about me. He wants to explore a relationship with me, he has said as much, but what does that look like for us? What kind of relationship? Does he think that I'll be more okay with how hard he works because I'm going into it with both eyes open? It's hard to put myself in the headspace to know if that would be the case. Until I'm on my feet, able to have an identity outside of being Charlie's broken pet project, I'm positive I would go crazy relying only on him for company. But the angel on my shoulder, the one that sees everything Charlie has done for a stranger, insists that he's worth that and so much more.

"Can you tell me more about her?" I ask, unable to filter the question.

He laughs, but it's hard and joyless. "Is that really what you want to talk about right now, while we're in paradise talking about quitting jobs and living here forever?"

I take a bite of a taco.

"Yes," I say, covering my mouth with my hand.

His brown eyes harden as he sighs. "Fine. We were engaged. When I wasn't around to listen to bands or visit venues, she decided this wasn't the life she wanted. We went our separate ways. That was a year ago." The finality in his voice shut off any further questions about his ex.

"If I had relationships to remember, I would tell you about them," I say honestly.

The last guy I remember dating steadily was during college and we broke up just before graduation because he was headed across the country. I wasn't interested enough in him to try long distance, and I tell Charlie as much.

"I'm aware that I'm at an advantage since I can actually remember the past five years," he says with a sigh. "Can we go back to talking about happy things and not dwelling on the past? I'm really not in the mood for this sad walk down memory lane." He takes a sip of his new drink and gestures to the waitress for more.

"Fine, we can talk about how rude it is that you want me to go clothes shopping after stuffing me with tacos and margs?" I complain, eating another taco.

"You know you're perfect. The doctor even congratulated you for putting on weight and finally being more than skin and bones."

"This has *nothing* to do with my weight and *everything* to do with how bloated I'm going to be from all this food! Already, I have a food baby. His name is Rex and I am taking you to court for child support," I say patting my bloated belly.

"Is a shopping spree not enough?" he offers with a chuckle.

"I accept your terms, but for the love of all that is holy, keep your long-legged running around town to a minimum. Not only am I damaged from the accident, but now you're going to have to roll me out of here," I joke.

He doubles down by ordering flan for dessert.

The rest of the afternoon is uneventful as we do some light shopping, finding more reasonable shops that I can get some clothes and accessories in. I try to object to him paying again after I get an entire vacation wardrobe from one shop.

"Please, let me pay for something," I say, reaching for my small wristlet.

"I doubt that your credit card covers international fees. Also, no," he says, handing over his black card, pushing my hand away.

The hotel sends a taxi to collect us and as soon as we get back to our villa, I let out a huge yawn. As much as I want to pick up where we left off, I can barely manage standing on my own two feet. I rationalize that I'll just go into my room and lie down for a minute. I rest my head on the pillow and fall into a deep, dreamless sleep.

Seven

I WAKE up dazed the next morning and emerge from my room to find Charlie hunched over his computer with his glasses on, a steaming mug of coffee beside him. The table has a fresh breakfast spread. I pad over, grab a strawberry, and then wait until he is at a pausing point in his work.

He finally looks up at me and leans back in his chair. He's wearing a green t-shirt with his alma mater emblazoned on it. If he's already working, it means I missed out on the morning workout show.

"Welcome to the land of the living, sleepy head." He smirks, taking a sip from his coffee.

"I guess the jet lag hit me harder than I thought," I say, pouring myself a cup from the carafe. "Not all of us can be used to jet setting around the world." I smile when he laughs.

"Well, it's good since you obviously needed the rest. I think we both forget that your body is still healing," he points out as I rub my shoulder, trying to loosen it after a night of sleeping awkwardly. Of all my injuries, my shoulder healed the fastest. Still, it likes to remind me that it wasn't just my leg and head that were damaged.

"PT Dan is going to be really mad at me. We are three days into this trip and I still haven't done any physical therapy." I try doing a few easy stretches just to get my body looser.

"Dan will be fine. Besides, aqua therapy is a thing. We'll just have to make sure we go swimming a lot. There is an awesome hike that I was thinking we could do, but only if you're up to it. I know your leg isn't always the most cooperative. I think it would be a good challenge nonetheless." He folds his hands behind his head, watching me as I pick out breakfast foods.

I want to squirm under his keen eye. He seldom wears glasses, but has broken them out a time or two when his eyes are fatigued from all the screens. If our relationship were more familiar, I might brush a lock of blond hair from his eyes and remark on how it makes him look like Clark Kent.

"Do you order breakfast like this all the time?" I ask, looking at the fresh fruits, pastries, and yogurt.

"It's part of renting a villa; we get breakfast every morning. I just tell them the night before what time I want it and if there are any special requests." He motions at his usual omelet: egg white with vegetables.

"You are so spoiled," I say, sitting down and taking a bite of a chocolate croissant.

"I'm less picky than others. Some people want all the mirrors removed or they want specific soap in the bathroom. You name it, someone requests it. They just need a more streamlined way instead of me having to call and ask for what I want for breakfast." He is on a roll, ready to keep talking about this issue. "Example: I asked for my usual omelet."

I cut him off. "Egg whites, spinach, tomatoes, and green bell peppers with a dash of garlic."

He smirks. "Right, so today, they brought me all those things separately because when I ordered, I said 'salt and pepper on the side.' Whoever wrote the order wasn't clear or whoever made it was confused, whatever the case may be. I ate the omelet and moved on with my day. Other assholes may not."

"You sound like you know 'other assholes,'" I say.

"I was raised by other assholes. My dad once threw a 14-ounce porterhouse at a wall because it wasn't rare enough. That's the mildest I've ever seen him overreact. There is a reason why he is working on divorce number four." Charlie's mouth purses as if he's tasted something sour.

"How much work do you have?" I ask, changing the subject.

He shakes the cobwebs free from his mind, dropping the train that was steamrolling right into negative territory. "Always a never-ending amount, but I already had a call with Jack this morning and he said that we should be in good shape. The hotel dropped off snorkeling gear and a waterproof camera. If you want, we can go snorkeling and you can take photos. You mentioned you liked photography." There are two cameras sitting out: an underwater camera and a digital SLR.

"All of this is making me uncomfortable," I say honestly. My reaction is not what he expected and he is clearly dismayed. "I don't want you to think I'm ungrateful because I'm not. I just...you're so generous, and I have nothing to offer you in return. I'm not loving this power imbalance," I say, holding the box for the digital SLR in my hands.

He gets up and walks over to me. "Can we start with the facts again? Fact one: my car hit you, a person on a bike. You suffered serious injuries, including a traumatic brain injury that resulted in you losing five years of your life. You tore ligaments in your knee, had bones protruding from your ankle, and broke your wrist, among other injuries."

He takes the box from my hands, setting it back down. "Fact two: this accident resulted in a loss of income, a loss of your bike, and actual memory loss."

He brushes a strand of hair away from my face. "Fact three: having you in my life has made a difference. For the last two months, I find I'm happier waking up in the morning, I'm working a little less, which is better for me emotionally, and even my mom said that I seemed different."

His golden brown eyes bore into me. "You have changed my life for the better. I don't care if it costs me every cent I have. Do you know when was the last time I actually watched the Macy's Thanksgiving Day parade? Or even had something better than a turkey sandwich for Thanksgiving? My mom would try to get me to meet her and my stepdad in Vail but I've still never been because I'm always working the holiday. Stop acting like you're this terrible financial burden on me. At this point, I have still spent less on you than on my car."

I overdramatize my shock by dropping open my mouth and clapping my hands to my cheeks. All to cover my actual shock because I know my hospital bills were not cheap.

"If anything, the power balance here is in your favor."

My eyebrows shoot into my hairline at this statement. He looks away from me finally.

"Why do you feel so responsible? You weren't driving," I point out.

His hands slide into mine. "Because if I had left work at a decent time considering there were hurricane force winds bearing down on the city, that car never would have been there at that time. There would have been no collision in Central Park. Seeing you lying on the pavement was a wake-up call. It was heart-breaking to know that I had caused this and yes, I am still making amends with myself for the harm I have caused. But I'm thirty years old and my closest relationship is with my rower. Even Jack has a girl. I could barely sleep the days you were unconscious in the hospital because I was afraid they would wake me up and tell me you had died. I couldn't do it." He swallows. "I know I've said it a thousand times, but I'm sorry for hitting you. I'm sorry for all the physical and emotional pain and distress I have caused you.

"I'm not sorry we met. I'll never be sorry for having you in my life."

I lean forward this time and kiss him, placing my hand gently on his cheek. Usually he will initiate any sort of touching but I'm feeling brazen after yesterday. The confirmation of how strong his desire is makes me comfortable to take this step first. I kiss him softly, then with more insistence, pushing him back against the couch. He lets me do this, his body soft and willing.

I shift my body so I can rest my hands on his chest and then straddle him. It belatedly occurs to me as my core makes contact with his shorts that the only piece of clothing I managed to take off last night were my swimsuit bottoms.

I grind against him a little, feeling him harden in response. Then I deepen the kiss. At first, he does nothing with his hands, almost holding them back and away from me. He then shifts them to my hips. I feel his fingers dig into my skin, urging my hips forward once, twice. I let him guide them as I feel a pulse of desire ripple through my body. One of his hands moves up into my hair, holding me close against him. The only thing separating us is my cover-up and his clothes.

I open myself up to him in a way I never have. I separate my lips, and my tongue drives into his warm mouth. With one hand in my hair and the other wrapped around my hips, he urges me forward again and I willingly comply, taking over the tempo he sets.

He places both hands on my ass as he stands, prompting me to squeak in surprise. I wrap my legs around his hips and let him carry me into his bedroom. I had forgotten just how enormous his room is, with the tub inside it. He deftly carries me and gently lowers me on the bed. He doesn't follow me down. Instead, he pulls my hips back to the edge of the bed, grinding his hips against mine, teasing me.

"Tell me to stop," he whispers, giving me an out.

Instead, I shake my head, reach forward, and pull off his shirt. I want to be skin-to-skin with him. "No," I whisper.

His eyes flash with lust as he lowers his hand to my knee, his fingers dragging lightly along my scar. He leans down to kiss the edge of the scar gently before his hand moves to the inside of my thigh. I bite my lip, anticipation driving me wild, wondering when he's going to find what he is looking for.

When his fingers graze up my hips, his eyebrows shoot up in surprise to find that I have nothing under my coverup. Surprise gives way to delight as he smirks and rubs his thumb against my clit, testing different motions and pressures to see how I respond. I moan, arching my head back, unable to get enough of him touching me.

He watches my body writhe, seeing which motions get the best reactions from me. His tawny brown eyes are intent on me as he first rubs his fingers up and down, then side to side, and then in circles. He slips one finger and then another inside me, steadily moving inside me. My whole body is hot under his scrutiny as he watches me.

I close my eyes, bite my lip, but I'm unable to stop the moaning and whimpering in response to him. I'm surprised when he kisses the inside of my knee, tracing kisses inside my thigh. He rubs his nose against me gently as he works his way to my center, working me over with his fingers.

"Did you know you have a birthmark, right here?" he asks, pressing a kiss to the spot along the crease of my hip, usually well-hidden by underwear. His teeth nip gently at the skin on my thigh before he takes his fingers away. He has worked my body into such a frenzy that I cry out as soon as his tongue touches my core.

My hands reach out, diving into his hair, and I pull his head closer without even thinking about it. I never thought oral could be as good as it is right now, and Charlie is more than capable at helping bring me to the edge. My other hand is fisted in the sheets, my body wanting to squirm, but he holds my hips in place with his free hand.

I can't stop the moan that rises deep inside me and claws its way out. There are no coherent words, just sounds I never knew I was capable of making. My body is a jumbled spent mess as he coaxes the last waves of pleasure from me. Charlie pulls away, wipes his mouth, and stands up.

I open my eyes, looking at him as he grins with smug satisfaction. I rise onto my elbows, fighting a contented smile. When Charlie drops on the bed beside me, stroking along the outside of my leg, I can see domesticity reaching for us from the future. It's a future that I want to see come to fruition.

I reach for him, kissing first his chest, then working my way along the ridges of his abs. God bless the rowing machine and whoever invented it. Charlie stills my hands and then leans me back until I'm flat on the bed. His lips meet mine and I can faintly taste myself on his mouth.

"This is about you and you alone. Don't worry about me," he says, but I still want to get him over the edge. I want to mark what his face looks like when he falls into the well of ecstasy that an orgasm brings.

"Are you sure this is real life? Are you actually Mr. Perfect?" I kiss him back and he grins, his tongue flicking against mine.

"I can honestly tell you that I am not Mr. Perfect. I'll show you all the ways that I'm not," he growls, capturing my mouth with his. I run my hand over his hard-on and when he doesn't object, I rub him again. He pulls back to watch me as I slide my hands into his shorts. I hold eye contact as I rub my hand down his shaft loosely to get a feel for him before speeding up my movements. My thumb plays with the head of his cock, a small bead of sticky moisture there as I tease him with the very tips of my nails, gently grazing his sensitive skin. He shudders under my touch, and I exact the same sweet torture he used on me just minutes before. He closes his eyes tightly, his head falling back with a groan.

"Oh, don't stop," is all he manages to get out between gritted teeth. I work my hand over him, eliciting a moan as his own climax makes his body tense under mine. His breathing gets ragged as he cries out while I draw the last waves of pleasure from him. I extract my hand when he's a limbless mess. We both sit there for a minute, a little out of breath, before he stands.

"I am going to get cleaned up," he says awkwardly, pressing a kiss to my forehead.

We're still trying to figure out each other's quirks and habits. I don't begrudge him this as he struts into the bathroom, grabbing a bathing suit as he goes. I slip out of his room and go into my own bathroom to wash my hands. My cheeks are flushed and I look lighter, somehow I feel it too.

I wonder when the last time my body felt that release was. How long was that pent up inside me? I change into a bathing suit, knowing that Charlie wants to go snorkeling today. As I do, I realize that I'm not ready for any more activities. I haven't waxed in ages and I consider for a second that I'm not on birth control. I used to have an IUD and the hospital confirmed that I don't still have one. Protection was the last thing I thought I needed, but now I'm angry with myself for not having it. Good thing there are plenty of other activities we can get up to, though the thought of having him inside me isn't far from my mind anymore.

He emerges from his bedroom clad in his bathing suit.

The waterproof camera is charging as Charlie approaches the breakfast spread and pops a blueberry in his mouth. The tension is thick in the air and all I can think about is how his tongue felt on me and how I want to feel him inside me. I'm startled by how strong these thoughts are, how badly I want them.

"You wanted to swim," I manage to squeak out from the couch. His head lifts from picking over the food and he looks at me, really taking in the sight of my bare skin. I watch his eyes follow the edges of my top to my bare stomach and along my legs. I cross my arms over my stomach, trying to hide myself from him, as if it would make a difference.

Charles strides over to me, crossing the room in two steps before kissing me on the lips. His mouth is minty fresh, surprising me. He cups my face in his large hands and I melt inside, kissing him back. I rest my hands on his hips, digging my fingertips into his skin.

"Yes, let's go swimming," he says, pulling away and offering his hand to me. I take it, ready to go wherever it might lead.

Eight

I FEEL like I blink and our first week of vacation is gone. We both agree to take it slower after that first day, trying to let cooler heads prevail. This hasn't stopped me from waking in his bed naked a few times after late nights spent exploring each other's bodies.

He learned that I'm ticklish around my sides and I learned that kissing below his ear makes him weak in the knees. I would wake most mornings to find him gone, already plugging away at work, six hours behind what everyone else was doing. Charlie tries to keep his work time limited once I wake up, even if it means he has to wake early to accomplish this.

He and Jack were able to find a nice rhythm that involved Charlie both setting Jack up for the next day and taking care of loose ends at the end of Jack's day.

On this particular morning, I wake to find Charlie propped on an elbow, watching me. I groan and pull the sheet up over my bare torso to cover my face.

"Don't do that, I look like a mess," I whine, not ready to expose my morning breath and mussed hair, though he's already seen it all. I enjoy the sound of his laughter as he pulls the sheet down and away from my face. He rolls over so he is on top of me, one knee gently spreading my legs apart so he can settle between them.

"Why not? I love looking at your face." He presses a kiss to my jaw. "And kissing you and making sure you know that I will worship your body as long as you let me." His mouth drops over my nipple and he sucks on it.

Over the week, he has discovered many ways to awaken my body from its deep slumber. Right away, I feel a rush of desire as he gently rocks his hips into mine, and I let out a noise that can only be described as a whimper. I am embarrassed by how easily he undoes me.

"I have morning breath," I object. "Don't we have to go on a massively long hike tomorrow? You can't tire me out today." My objections fall on deaf ears as Charlie leans up to kiss me on the mouth, a hand tangling in my hair.

"Yes, we do have the hike tomorrow, but only if the weather cooperates and it looks like we're due for a rainy day," he confirms, sitting back on his haunches. I wait, knowing that there is more to come.

"Today, I scheduled a boat tour and guided snorkeling, so you need to wake up. I waited as long as I could but we're going to be late."

I grab his pillow and pull it over my face. "But we're on vacation and that means sleeping however long I want," I whine.

Charlie promptly pulls the pillow away, pushing the stray strands of hair out of my face. "That is not the point of *this* vacation. We have already had five days of barely leaving this villa or even getting dressed. We have things to do, like massages and snorkeling. We cannot lie around in bed all day."

"Challenge accepted. Besides, I couldn't get up if I wanted to." I sit up on my elbows, leaning forward to brush a kiss against his neck. He's been talking about wanting to get out and see more of the island so I won't begrudge him these adventures, but I'll put off getting out of bed as long as I can.

"And why is that?" he asks dubiously, his finger tracing a line down my neck, following the curve of my breast.

"Someone is in my way," I say, looking at him, raising my eyebrows. He rolls over to his side of the bed and I smile, thinking about how easily we fell into his and hers sides of the bed.

"Now you have no excuse. I've already worked on three different deals today and you are still in bed!" He gets up and walks over to my side. My eyes track him as he moves around the king size bed. He leans over as if to kiss me, before just scooping me up in his arms. One hand slips under my knees and the other rests comfortably on my back, holding me tightly against him.

"What are you doing?" I ask, my body tense with alarm. He walks into the bathroom, stepping into the large walk-in shower. I start squirming, murmuring my protests before he sets me down. I think for a moment I'm spared, but then he twists the knob, starting the spray.

"Oh my God," I exclaim as I am pelted with ice cold water.

"CHARLES!" I shout, trying to get out of the water, but he presses me against the wall, pinning me there with a kiss. His arms and legs bracket me to where I am, and after more kissing, I barely notice the water temperature.

We manage to shower, purely shower, together before getting ready for a day out on the boat. I wrap the towel around my hair, walk back to my room, completely naked, to get clothes.

"You are a sin, woman," Charlie says, watching me walk away. I glance at him as I turn the corner and catch his eyes on the bare skin of my back. "Move your clothes in here," he calls after me. It gives me a thrill, the thought of him not being able to take his eyes off me.

I air dry as I pick out what I want to wear, not bothering with drying my hair since we're going swimming. I tease Charlie a little longer by gathering my clothes in my hands and returning to his room, still bare-ass naked.

He grabs me and pulls me against him. "I swear," he growls in my ear, kissing me as he runs his hands from my back to my ass, which he uses as leverage to pull me tighter against him.

"Charlie," I admonish gently as he gives me a raspberry, ticking my neck.

The stirrings of a relationship were there before we came here. It's only blossomed without the confines of the city and the apartment.

He lets me go so I can get dressed and he can take one last look at his emails.

"How long have you been up?" I ask, finally putting on clothes.

"Since about four. I wanted to get work done before I was completely incommunicado for the rest of today. Jack cried like a baby when I showed him the pictures of the dolphins yesterday morning," Charlie calls as he walks into my bathroom and grabs my scar cream. It's become a ritual every morning and night. He squirts a little onto his hand before coming up behind me and rubbing it on the exposed scar on my knee. His fingers work in circles around the raised tissue, digging deep.

I realize then, as he focuses on rubbing his fingers into my tender skin, that I've been falling in love with Charlie this entire time. Each time he caught me before I fell during PT, ignored a work call to take a call from a doctor, every offer of support made me feel cherished in a way I hadn't since before my parents died.

I was falling in love but was afraid to say it. Would he think I was only in love with him because he was rich? Would he think I was using him for this lavish lifestyle?

I turn to him, and kiss him, gently resting my hands on his chest. I pull back, tracing my fingers along the giant white D on his green shirt for his alma mater. My hand slides into his as I give him a broad smile.

"Let's go have an adventure."

Nine

⤬

I AM HOLDING on tight to my hat as the speed boat whisks us out to sea. Charlie and I tried to start a conversation, but the motor drowned out our voices. We both stopped screaming, content to be nestled side by side. His arm is wrapped around my shoulder, the other resting on my knee as we both pretend we can hear the captain when he points out various things on the coast. I can't wait for us to stop so I can take pictures of the white sand beach against the dramatic green mountains behind it.

I'm already taking mental snapshots, imagining blowing them up and hanging them in my apartment whenever I return there. The boat finally stops and the captain points at the small little dock at the back of the boat with a ladder leading right into the water.

Once the camera is in my hand, I can't stop taking photos. I take pictures of the island and of Charlie as he gets himself ready to go. I sneak a snap of him checking his phone and again when he glances to take in the view himself. His blond hair isn't slicked back like usual; it flies free in the wind. His sunglasses block what I expect is a pensive look on his face. I managed to get one shot of him pulling his shirt off from behind, and that photo is all for me.

I set the waterproof camera on the deck before tossing aside my cover-up. Charlie's head snaps to me, his eyes raking over my skin as if he hadn't seen me naked just an hour ago. I'm in a red swimsuit with one shoulder bare. It feels dangerous to wear, as if my boob is going to sense the freedom and spring from my top without warning. But I liked how it looked and how it made me feel. There is a cutout over my cleavage, but I otherwise feel supported, despite the gaping hole, which surprised me .

The snorkels and masks are set on the lower deck atop towels for our inevitable return. Charlie goes down first and helps me onto the landing before pulling his snorkel on. I snap a goofy photo of him wearing it, giving a thumbs up before he enters the water first, ready to help me down.

The water is warm as I slide into it. Charlie has his hands and feet braced on either side of the ladder so I sit on his lap before he pushes us away, his arms folded around me. The captain follows us into the water, ready to point out the different animals we see as we swim around the area.

I take photos of the brilliant fish and stingrays as they swim by. I keep trying to sneak a few of Charlie, but I'm stunned when I watch a sea turtle swim by. I'm so transfixed by it, barely remembering to snap a picture as it glides away. The captain leads us over to a place where we can stand and he can tell us more about the ecosystems and the wildlife in the area.

I giggle as the captain guides my hand over a stingray, my fingers slipping over the slimy skin. Charlie's hands rest on my hips as the captain takes a few photos of us so when we look back, I'm not behind the camera the entire time. He walks us onto the beach, where there is a cabana set up with a table and chairs. I glance at Charlie, who gives a shrug of his shoulders as if trying to say this was not him. The smirk tugging at his lips tells a different story.

Every moment of the day was carefully orchestrated by him to get us to this moment. I settle into the surprisingly plush chairs,

Charlie taking the time to push my seat in, with a gentle kiss on my cheek. Out of the forest come two musicians, one playing a small guitar-like instrument and the other a woodwind of some sort.

"You're something else, sir," I say as he sits across from me. I drop my elbows onto the table and rest my chin on the back of my hands.

"I thought this would be nice. It's less about you and more about me wanting to have these experiences for myself. Like going to Thailand was really cool, but we didn't do any of the cultural stuff. I would have loved to visit some of the temples and learn more than the best bars they have," he says.

"Or the best strippers?" I joke.

"Or the best strippers," he confirms, a blush tinging his cheeks. "I thought Bora Bora was nice because it's more of just a resort destination. I want to learn the important details of the area."

I nod, dragging my finger along the condensation on my glass.

"Like, when we were little, it felt like my dad would bring us on these business trips just to shut up my mom, who would complain that she never got to go anywhere. We went to Sydney for two weeks during the Olympics. I left the hotel once for a swimming match, but as soon as we got there, my little brother threw up all over my dad's business associate. I was in Sydney, at the Olympics! But no, I didn't even get to Bondi Beach or the Opera House. Thinking back on that has made me want to make sure I'm getting the full experience when I travel. Ergo," he gestures at the table in front of us. A server comes over with plates of chicken and rice and we dig in.

"I don't remember you mentioning a brother," I say, watching him closely. That snippet of information makes me realize just how little I know about Charlie.

"No, I wouldn't have. We're not close. I was about 10 when that incident happened and he was five, probably my parents' last ditch effort to save their marriage. It was already on thin ice at that point. My mom was wife number two, and my father never let her forget that he had an iron clad prenup. If she left him, she got nothing, and that included her sons. Not that he wanted us. When we got back to the hotel from the swim meet, my dad was rough with Brad. He yelled and shook him, scolding him for embarrassing the family in front of a client. That was the last straw for my mom and she left, taking my brother with her." He takes a sip from his drink, the ever-classy piña colada, his eyes sad. "My dad fought for me in court because I was old enough to take care of myself. From there, I went off to boarding school, then college and then working at his company. I don't think he's seen a picture of my brother since he was five."

I reach out and take his hand, sad that he has this fractured relationship and that his father has done so much damage. There aren't any right words for this moment, for the way he is baring his soul to me.

A part of me regrets that I don't have more recent memories to share with him of travel or of more. I want to get those memories back. I want to be able to talk to him about more than just childhood trauma or the death of my parents as a defining moment in my adult life. I want to be able to commiserate over bad breakups and have something to add to a list of great places to hang out that aren't closed or the Chinese food place across from my old apartment.

"Sorry, I didn't mean to drag the mood down," he apologizes, letting the last wisps of the bad memory slip away. "I would get some holidays with my mom and brother, but we were raised so differently, and I wonder if he thinks that I picked dad."

"You were a kid. You shouldn't feel guilty for anything that happened then," I say.

"Yeah, you say that, but I was a huge dick to him. I was so mad that we were only out of the hotel for maybe two hours and I hadn't gotten to do or see anything, all because this kid binged on whatever sugar he could get his hands on." He sounds disappointed with himself; his child's reaction to the situation.

"You were a child. I'm sure I did some pretty shitty things when I was ten, too. I know I was an asshole to my parents when I was a teenager. You can't be too hard on yourself. Besides, there is still time to fix it. What are you doing for Christmas?"

We had danced around the upcoming holidays after Thanksgiving. I hoped I would be back in my apartment before then, but stairs were still a struggle, no matter how much work I put in. Part of me hoped that I could find another apartment on a lower floor, but my landlord wasn't sympathetic to my plight.

"Well, I haven't thought about it, honestly. I wasn't sure what your holiday traditions were. I'm embarrassed to say I don't know what faith you follow." His words highlight just how much more we have to learn about each other.

"I am a non-practicing Catholic. I used to be a C&E Catholic, but after my parents died, I had a falling out with God," I admit easily. Even calling myself a Christmas and Easter Catholic was a stretch. I would only go if my parents were going and too often we were busy with something else. Once I made my confirmation, it was all over.

"You never talk about them," he says, pushing his empty plate away. "Now that I've spilled my family history, the floor is open, if you want it."

My fingers trace the condensation on my water glass as I think about my parents. "There was a fire in their house after I graduated college. It turns out the home improvements they had just done were not up to code and the electrician cut some corners. Because of the origin of the fire, they never had a chance. The settlement money is what pays for my apartment; at least that's what my bank account tells me." I try to be glib about it, but I still miss them. It was actually eight years ago, but in my mind, it's more recent and the wound is still fresh.

"Thank God you were a good record keeper," Charlie says.

"My dad was really good at keeping files and it sort of rubbed off on me, I guess. Good thing, too." Around us, the attendants start to clean up, putting away the cookware and folding the canopy. One of the attendants comes over and asks if we want a picture together before we have to put an end to the dream. I say yes with enthusiasm, jumping out of my seat.

The man fancies himself an amateur photographer, taking candid photos as well as staged ones. I hear the shutter close a few times as we align ourselves on the beach. I turn to look up at Charlie, finding his eyes on me. There is no awkwardness, no question of what is okay or hesitation for how to proceed. We each wrap our arms around the other. I grasp my wrist around his middle, grinning at him. Charlie leans down and kisses me, slowly, not caring that there is a camera on us, going off wildly. The way he looks at me. makes me forget that I don't entirely know who I am. It makes me think that I might be okay with that. I won't let Charlie become my whole world once I know what I'm doing, but I want to stay in his orbit as long as he'll let me.

When I realize we have to swim back to the boat, I groan.

"Don't make me. I'm going to get a cramp and sink and die," I whine, stepping into the warm water.

"You will not. I won't let anything happen to you," Charlie reassures me, taking my hands and kissing them.

I let myself float, his large hands tugging me toward him. "Easy for you to say, you can stand and be fine. I'm going to be carried off to my watery doom."

Charlie laughs, never letting go of my hand as we swim out, carefully tracking when the sand bar ends.

Slowly, we make our way back to the boat, the small dot slowly growing closer. I wasn't wrong about my side cramping up as I tried to keep up with Charlie. He lazily floated along as I was struggling. He lets me hold on to him and rest as he swims towards the boat. When we get back, I cling to the ladder and rest against it so I can catch my breath. Charlie comes up behind me, bracing his feet on the bottom step so I can lean against him. His hands grip the metal, letting me just enjoy the feel of him.

"Take your time," he teases as I slowly climb onto the small deck. I grab the digital SLR to take more photos as the sun makes its final descent. Charlie moves past me, up to the deck. When I finally put the camera down, Charlie has glasses of champagne for us. We sit in a comfortable silence, letting the boat gently rock us.

I make Charlie take a few selfies with his phone. We take some goofy pics, some smiling, and a few of us kissing like we're teenagers. On a whim, I upload one of them to Pictogram, even though I have no followers and I follow no one. I want to document this adventure so when I'm old and think this was all a dream, I will have something tangible to hold on to.

Ten

THE LIGHTS ARE on in our villa when we get back. There are petals all over the place, leading from the doorway into the bedroom. The silky rose petals cover the king bed, and on each nightstand, there is a bucket with a bottle of champagne in it. The tub water is flowing over the infinity edge, casting petals down the drain. The door is open so we can look out on the night sky full of stars, twinkling just for us. There are candles burning at various heights around the rim of the tub and the entire room.

I'm pleasantly surprised by this. I turn to look back at Charlie, expecting him to look pleased with himself, but he looks as surprised as I do. Drifting farther into the room, I walk over to the tub and dip a toe in, finding the water piping hot, as if it was just filled.

"This wasn't you."

"No, not me." Charlie walks over to a little card, set between two kissing towel swans, in the middle of the bed.

"'Happy marriage, Mr. and Mrs. Breckenridge,'" he reads, fighting a smile.

"We should have corrected someone along the way," I scold, taking it from him and reading it for myself.

"Nah, it's better this way," he says, leaning down and kissing me. He is not slow or soft this time. There is heat behind it as he walks me backward onto the bed, demanding that I yield to him, and I do. My heart melts along with my body, nervousness giving way to burning desire.

I sit down, my hands fisted in his shirt, tugging him with me. His hand cups the back of my head as he lowers me all the way down onto the bed, and then he slowly climbs on top of me. I let go of his shirt to shimmy back further onto the bed. I would laugh as I scramble backward, watching him toss the swans off the bed, but the way he looks at me, like he's seeing my whole self, makes me feel exposed. It's not a bad thing that he's seeing all of me. I find it makes me freer, knowing that he's seen me at one of the darkest moments in my life and he's still here.

He follows me, crawling across the bed, eyes not leaving mine before he kisses me again. Charlie's progression starts down my neck, nuzzling me gently as his hands find the hem of my dress and lifts it overhead. He nips my ear before tossing my dress on the floor.

Charlie trails his fingers along the edge of my bathing suit top, the featherlight touch almost tickling me as he pulls down on my one shoulder strap. A gentle kiss is placed on each of my shoulders as he pulls the strap completely off my arm, freeing my breasts. My hands go to his sides to take his shirt off, but he is already reaching behind him, pulling it over his head and absently throwing it across the room. I tell myself to play it cool when he does that because my mind goes blank watching his muscles flex. He has the body of an action figure and for some reason this wonderful, caring man has chosen to share a bed with me.

I lean forward and press a kiss to his sternum, running my hands up his back to pull him toward me. Charlie resists me, guiding one knee and then another between my legs. He tugs at the one-piece, pulling it down, lifting my hips so the suit can be removed entirely. He smirks the whole way as I gladly spread my legs for him.

"You've got me indecent," I say, my voice coming out breathily. There is an ache between my legs, caused by him, and I want to rub my thighs together to relieve the pressure. More importantly, there is an ache growing in my heart, and it's full to the brim with wanting him, not just between my legs or in my bed, but in my life. I can't go back to a life without him in it, and that realization is startling and scary.

Charlie pushes me down gently while his eyes rove over my exposed breasts. He reaches a hand out to palm one. His other hand is light on my skin as it makes its way between my legs.

"You're right. Hardly seems fair."

I suck in a breath as his fingers start to lazily circle me. I reach for him, but Charlie lets go of my breast to pin my wrist, leaving me powerless to do anything about it. Not that I try very hard since I am enjoying this, as my body arches into his.

Charles focuses on how my body reacts before lowering his mouth to my bare nipple, his tongue swirling around it. I never had particularly sensitive nipples, but right now my entire body feels like a band ready to snap. I want him in a way I've never wanted anyone or anything. This goes past desire and excitement, this is a need. He is a necessity, like the air I need to breathe. I let out a moan and Charles grins before he releases my breast from his mouth. With better access, I fight with his bathing suit tie, finally managing to undo it.

I struggle with pulling it down, finally seeing his cock in full for the first time. I run my hand along the length of him, letting it be his turn for attention. For all the fooling around we have done, he's focused the exploration on me, but now it's my turn to return the favor. I tug on his cock with one swift stroke, watching how his body responds. Charlie lets out a sharp breath, watching as I stroke him again, teasing him as I go. He kisses me hard on the mouth, tugging me close to him so our bodies are almost flush against each other. Charlie pauses before going any further, pulling away from me. The fire in his eyes still smolders, but his brow is creased in concentration.

"I don't know what my birth control situation is." I prop onto my elbows as he reaches for the nightstand. Of all the things to not know, this might be the most inconvenient.

"I am nothing if not prepared," he says, pulling free a roll of condoms like a 17 year-old boy hitting it big. I laugh as he rips one off, sliding it on without complaint.

"Someone had high hopes for this trip," I tease, fighting the smirk that threatens to break on my lips. I'm willing to admit to myself that I did too, and with each kiss, each touch, each tender moment, my hope grows past the idea of a casual hook-up. He flashes me his devilish grin and I feel my heart slam in my chest at the look.

"After our first encounter, I wanted to be prepared if it went any further. I grabbed these at the gift shop. Value size was all they had," he says, sheepishly. Even his level of preparedness is turning me on and I can feel heat flood my core.

"Less talking, more kissing," I order, grabbing his face with both hands and pulling him close to me. I'm afraid that if I don't feel him inside me right now I will cease to exist, the desire burning me up from the inside out. I feel the pressure of him at my center begging for entrance, but he stops.

The concern drifts across his face again, stopping his movements. His hands are braced on either side of my head.

"I just," he stumbles, lifting a hand to run his knuckles along my jaw. "This is okay? I want to make sure you're alright. I don't want you to feel like you have to do this because of everything that's happened. Say stop and this stops." His voice is rough, chock full of everything that he's holding back. It makes my heart burst that he is so ready to do this, but is willing to forgo his pleasure if I'm not ready.

But I am ready. I am so fucking wet and ready and just want to feel him inside of me.

"Yes, I want this. I want you, Charlie," I say, tilting my hips up to meet him. I feel the pressure of his tip as it enters me. We both hold our breath for just a moment before we moan in unison. Charlie watches me closely as he eases inside of me, tracking the way my head tilts back, exposing my neck to him as the smallest noise of desperation claws from the back of my throat.

My hands clutch his sides as he moves slowly to start, waiting for me to change my mind and tell him to stop. When I don't, he grows more insistent with each thrust, lowering his mouth to my exposed neck. My back is arched into him, but I need him closer, deeper, and at my speed.

I roll onto my side, facing Charlie, and push him gently away with a hand. He's so eager to be mindful of my needs that he doesn't hesitate to back off, worry flashing on his face. But I roll with him, and when he realizes exactly what I'm doing, he grins. I hover, making sure that we're centered before I lower myself down on him. The sound of pleasure he makes sends a thrill through me. I want to bottle that noise and hear it whenever I can because that noise is like a drug. It makes me feel powerful as his fingers dig into my hips, pulling and pushing gently.

Our bodies are moving in rhythm, like this is the hundredth or thousandth time we've done this together, not the first. I expected the awkwardness of new lovers, but it's not here. This isn't the routine of old lovers, either. There is grace and frenzy and seduction in how our bodies fit together. He reaches out to grab my breast, teasing my nipple with his fingertips. Needing to feel that same power, I grab both of his wrists, forcing them back on the bed. I hold them there, the roll of my hips getting more insistent. I can see the control he has slipping and I let my body relax as he flips me onto my back.

His hand is hooked under me and his fingers dig into my shoulder. He pulls me as close as he can, plunging himself deep inside of me. I can feel the rising tide as my climax overpowers me. My eyes flutter closed and I want to bite down on my lip, but instead I cry out, not bothering to contain it. His hands clench on my shoulders as he reaches his own climax. His hip movement grows more frenzied and I hear my name on his lips as he roars his release. His iron-tight grip on my shoulders loosens as he thrusts a few more times before pulling out.

I lie there a moment, dragging in each ragged breath that I can. Charlie looks at me, quiet, as he hovers over me before pressing a gentle kiss to my lips. His movements are graceful as he climbs off the bed. My hand drops onto my stomach and I will my heart rate to slow. I twist on my side, toward the bathroom, as he ambles away to clean up.

I admire the shape of his body, especially his ass, as he walks away, and a feeling of contentment settles into my bones. Charlie remains silent as he runs the water to wash his hands. Left to my own thoughts, I rise and cross over to the tub, pensive.

I've never had sex like that in my life, and from the delicious ache that gathers in my muscles, I can guarantee I haven't had sex like that in the last five years. It would be so easy to dismiss what is growing between us as lust, and I worry for a second that maybe this is that moment in a show where the two leads get together, thinking they have real chemistry, but they don't. One look at Charlie where he faces the mirror earns me a wink and a sly smile and I know that my life isn't a TV show. What I have is so much better, and the warmth in my limbs has nothing to do with my need to have him inside me again, but everything to do with the half smile and rumpled hair of that gorgeous man.

I settle into the warm water of the tub; steam is no longer rising off the surface. I sink into the water and pull my hair up into a bun. With nothing to clip it, I release it and slip further in so my breasts are covered. Behind me, I hear the champagne bottle pop before Charlie places a glass into my hand. The water overflows when he climbs into the spacious tub beside me.

"You should pinch me," I demand. I let the champagne bubbles fizz in my mouth before I swallow.

"Why would I do that?" His tawny eyes watch me closely.

"Because it's the only way you can convince me that this isn't just my coma brain dreaming this all up." I love the sound of his laughter when he barks it out.

"This is very, very real."

"There is no way that I'm sitting in paradise having been hit by a car that had a millionaire playboy riding in it. That shit just doesn't happen in real life. I figure I was hit by a car and this is all the in-between world while my mind heals itself. I mean, what kind of name is Charles Breckenridge? You sound like some prep school douche."

I don't expect the quiet that follows my words, but a smirk does lift his lips. "I am very, very real. This is very real."

Charlie places his hands on my hips under the water, pulling me toward him. I suck my lower lip between my teeth before looking at him through my lashes. If I'm right, if the perfect man has fallen into my lap, I don't want to waste another minute of my time with him.

"I think I'm falling in love with you, Charlie," I whisper. The thought is out of my head before I even have a chance to process it, and I curse my lips for going faster.

My words hang in the air between us. I swear my heart stills for the space of two beats while I wonder if I've made a tremendous mistake letting the post-orgasm haze loosen my lips.

He leans forward kissing me so softly, I'm not even sure it happened. His wet hand rises to my face, tracing my jaw with a finger.

"That's just the endorphins talking." Charlie's voice is quiet when he responds, like he's trying to convince himself.

It's hard not to be crestfallen that he would dismiss my words so easily, but I want to make him understand. "Charlie, no I--"

He silences my objection with another kiss. There is a sadness in his eyes when he does, trying to bury the comment and the feelings with it.

I want to talk about this, open more than just my legs to him, but the story about his father nudges my mind, and I know that as much as I'm thinking this is a coma dream, he could be thinking something similar, trying to hide from these emotions that have grown much bigger than this villa. I wrap my legs around him, my softness pressed against him, giving him an out of this conversation.

"Don't worry, I won't hold you to it when we get back to New York," he whispers, wrapping an arm around my back. The strength of his arm pulls my body flush against him as he tangles a hand in my hair. This vulnerability from him holds me in place. An ex broke his heart once, leaving behind a man who is afraid to let love back in.

I don't expect to be the woman that makes him love again. But if this is real, if there is any chance that he is not a figment of my imagination, then I want him to know that he is worthy of love. Even if it means I can only love him for a little while.

Charlie tries to appease me by waving a coffee under my nose, but I only growl at him. Our two weeks in paradise have ended and now I have to get back on the death trap they call a plane. We never talked again about how I told him I was falling in love with him, letting the rhythmic movement of our bodies communicate our feelings toward each other.

I grew up lucky, with two parents who not only loved me, but loved each other. By showing me what that looked like, they set me up for life with high standards. It also made me yearn for that own love in my life to the point of bad relationship decisions in the past. My parents showed me that love is more than hugs and kisses. It's in how my mom cut my dad's hair because he swore no one could do it better even when it was a little lopsided, or how he would make her banana pancakes on her parents' birthdays to ease her hurt. It made me able to recognize love when Charlie massages my scar with the cream nightly or wakes me with coffee, the precise amount of creamer stirred in.

"Are you sure we have to go back?" I ask, taking one last sad look around the villa, coffee in hand. The last week of the trip was spent with both of us naked almost the entire time. Our villa's location meant that even when we went swimming for midnight dips in the ocean, there were no prying eyes to see what we were getting up to, even if we weren't the best at keeping quiet.

I have always laughed at the term 'lovemaking', thinking of it as something reserved for cheesy love stories, but that's the only appropriate word I could come up with. We took our time together, always touching each other. We would spend hours not necessarily chasing release, but trying to learn the dips and valleys of each other's bodies. It wasn't about getting there fastest or the frenetic need that would sometimes overtake us. It was about finding out that Charlie is ticklish around his hips or that he enjoys tracing the wing tattoos on my low back first with his fingers, then his tongue. Even when we weren't being intimate, Charlie always found a reason to find his hands on me: smoothing back my hair, pulling my feet onto his lap, holding my hand while we went for a walk.

I had joked that the value pack of condoms was ambitious. However, when we left, there were only two left and they got tucked into Charlie's laptop case.

Charlie's thumb grazes my lower lip, pushed out into a pout. I nip at him, teasingly, earning a gentle spank on my ass.

When we arrived two weeks ago, we had two carry-on bags.

Now, we're departing with two checked bags stuffed to the gills with clothes and silly souvenirs purchased on our rare trips out. I pull the worn green baseball cap I stole from Charlie down over my sunglasses, gesturing for him to lead the way. He steps in my way, tilting my chin up with his hand and using the other to remove the hat so he can see my face better.

"Hey, hey, I promise we can come back," he swears, and it sends a thrill up my spine that he's seeing a future for us together.

He leans down and kisses me, short and sweet. Charlie keeps his hand on the small of my back or on me somewhere else the whole way back to the airport.

I may have misjudged Charlie. His love language is touch. The way he brushes hair from my face, or how he kept a hand at my elbow when we went for walks in the park early in my recovery. But giving gifts is also his love language. He's nonstop showered me with technology, and clothes, that beautiful cane and this trip.

While at the airport, I post a silly photo of us pouting on the tarmac before boarding the plane. His stubble is rough on my cheek as he kisses me for a second photo. Charlie grips my hand, knowing that taking off makes me want to puke. Our first flight is the same short trip to Tahiti on a propeller plane that takes off only after people switch seats to rebalance the plane.

When we land in Tahiti, I'm surprised to see that I have two followers. Sitting in the airport lounge, I show off to Charlie, who has already cracked open his laptop.

"I have followers on Pictogram! Now, you have to take me somewhere on the private jet so I can show I am one with the influencers," I joke, settling into the corner booth we've staked out for ourselves. There is an icon on the app, showing that in addition to the followers, I also have a message.

"Oh, ew," I mutter as I read the text on the screen. I am somewhat surprised and yet not at all. Charlie's hand is rubbing his chin as he reads an email when I distract him with my reaction. I pass him my phone so he can see what caused my response.

"'Be my sugar baby as you ride my big fat cock.' Oh! And there's a picture of that big fat cock. Classy. Will your new sugar daddy be picking you up from the airport?" Charlie says, amused.

A mother sitting nearby with her children glares at us, pulling them closer to her. I quickly block the sender and delete the message, while I deal with the strong urge to scrub my eyeballs and brain to remove the image.

"Did you miss the part where I said 'eww'?" I ask, bumping him with my shoulder.

"Well, I assumed you just didn't want the dick pic. Maybe you were looking for another sugar daddy now that you have me wrapped around your finger, " he teases, pressing a small kiss to the palm of my hand. I let out an unattractive snort, trying to hide my smile.

His attention turns back to his laptop, while I look at the other follower. My entire body goes still when I see it's Vivian and that she's accepted me as a follower. I didn't think I had requested her when I found her that day at the start of the trip, but I must have.

I struggle with going through her photos to see what her life has been like for the last few years. I wonder if there will be some kernel of what happened between us. I let my curiosity win, scrolling through her pictures.

I'm surprised when a recent photo is of her hand with a gorgeous canary diamond on her finger. If it's the guy she was with when I knew her, he really took his time. I scroll through and see a photo of her and who I assume is her fiancé ice skating in Bryant Park. Definitely not the same guy, but he looks familiar, and I'm annoyed that I can't place him. I wonder if I do know him, if I've met him in the last five years and that's why he feels familiar.

I scroll and scroll and scroll, looking for the last time I was in her pictures. I know we both had Pictogram at one point so I have to hope that I will be there. There were countless brunches where we thought we were so bougie, having just graduated from college and living in the big city. I have to scroll all the way to the start of her account to find a photo my parents took of Vivian and I at our college graduation with our honors cords and diplomas in our hands.

I'm shocked by how young we look compared to the woman she is now and the woman I am now. It makes me feel ancient, looking at the hope and excitement on our faces unlined by years of worry. I scroll back to more recent photos, looking to see when I dropped off, but it's unclear, as if I've been scrubbed from whatever posts she could delete me from. Charlie glances at me out of the corner of his eye, finally looking away from his emails.

"Seeing if your suitor has more pictures for you to admire?" he teases, but his face melts from joking to concerned as he really looks at me.

"What's wrong?" he asks gently, reaching out to touch my shoulder.

Part of me wants to kiss him and ignore this subject the way we have ignored so many. I consider brushing it off, but my heart hurts, and if I'm being honest with myself, I do want to talk about it.

We've danced and sidestepped the issue, but I want to talk about being confused as to why my best friend in the world didn't know I was hurt, why no one was looking for me after the accident.

"This is Vivian," I say, holding the phone out to him. Something crosses his face quickly, but it's gone before I can even interpret it. He hasn't pressed me so I won't press him. "I apparently requested her on Pictogram and she accepted. She's engaged. I don't know what to do next."

He hands me back my phone, silent for a minute. "Do you want to talk to her again?"

"Yes. I mean, it's awkward, right? We had to have this whole falling out because the only photo of us together is from our college graduation. But whatever happened was so bad that she deleted all of our photos? I can't imagine anything being that bad that I basically stopped existing in her world. I would check my old Pictogram, but it's gone, deleted. There are so many questions that I don't know the answers to."

Charlie closes his computer, turning to face me entirely. "If you want to talk to her, then do it. If she wasn't interested in reopening your connection, then she wouldn't have accepted. You're worried about all these bad what-ifs, but what if she can enlighten you about what you're missing? What if she can help you understand what happened not only between you two, but what you were doing the night of the accident?"

The accident. The other big mystery in my life. What was I doing on my bike in the pouring rain in the middle of the night? My life has become a huge question mark. Maybe talking to Vivian again would help straighten that out. Maybe I could start to find more of myself again.

"Well, I have an eight hour flight to obsess about it. She looks so happy." The wistful tone in my voice emerges when I hold up the photo of her ice skating. Charlie leans over, pressing his lips to my forehead. I lean into it, even if his two week old stubble scratches my face.

"For what it's worth, I think you should talk to her. I think you've been stuck with me and doctors for the last few months, and you could use a girlfriend to gush about what a great guy I am."

My eyes nearly roll into the back of my head as he wanders off to get more snacks. When I search for him, after he's been gone for a while, I see a woman running her finger down his arm. She is clearly asking him something but whatever he says in response causes her to pull her hand back like she's been burned, and then she stalks back to her friends.

I refuse to ask him about it when he comes back and Charlie refuses to offer an explanation. We sit in silence until I finally break, turning toward him as he's putting a spoonful of parfait in his mouth.

"Make a new friend?"

"As a matter of fact, yes. She wondered if I was going to be on the flight to LA, which I confirmed. She invited me to join a special club while on the plane, but I had to decline." Amusement is threaded through his tone.

"You had to decline?" We never set up the boundaries of our relationship. We didn't say we were exclusive or if I was going to move back to my apartment or if he wanted me to keep living with him.

"I did. I said that my pregnant girlfriend didn't do too well flying."

I scowl at him, making him laugh deeply.

"You know, if you wanted to, you could join her special club during the flight." I try to keep my voice casual, but from the way his spoon pauses halfway to his mouth, I know I failed.

"Do you want to have that conversation now or wait until we're back in New York and not jet lagged?"

I grab the glass of champagne that he brought with him as well as a handful of snack mix. "I didn't want to assume anything."

"What do you want, Elia?" His hand lands on my bare knee, forcing me to be more angled toward him. Rubbing the stubble on his jaw, he continues, "Since I'm sensing your hesitation, I'll tell you what I want. I want you to be happy and comfortable. I'll be honest, you know how much I work. But I want this, us, to work. It might be cheesy of me to say, but I think fate intervened so I could meet you."

I open my mouth to respond, but he silences me with a kiss.

"I don't want an answer right now. I want you to take your time to think about it. Take a week to decide what you want from this. Just one more thing to think about while you're stressing over Vivian. For what it's worth, I want you to stay with me until physical therapy clears you. If you want to go back to your own apartment, I get it, but I don't want you to run away on my account and just hurt yourself."

I reach out, pressing my hand to his cheek, without saying anything. His last relationship failed because of his outrageous work schedule. There is no denying that not everyone could deal with such strenuous hours. But like all things in life, relationships require work, and for a man like Charlie, for someone with a golden heart, it's worth it. It will be a challenge, but I'm willing to put in the effort. I'm willing to show Charlie that his parents' marriage wasn't what love should look like. I might be incomplete, unsure of who I was, but I know what I have wanted in a partner, and I know that Charlie has those things.

I never really get a chance to finish the conversation with Charlie before an email catches his attention and we board our next flight. A wink from him is the acknowledgement that we both know I have a lot to think about.

My book doesn't offer a good distraction. I'm too overwhelmed with thoughts of the accident, Vivian, and Charlie. I give myself a headache trying to call up any memory from the last five years. There is nothing there, not even a flash of a movie or a brunch or birthday party.

I hardly sleep on our next flight because I can't stop thinking about these decisions. My mind keeps turning over and playing out each eventuality. I play out staying with Charlie. I play out meeting up with and reconnecting with Vivian. Being invited to her wedding and her being invited to mine with Charlie. I see myself making the decision to go back to my small apartment and having no contact with either of them, no friends and no one to tell me what my life was like. My brain has made it a zero sum game: either I do both or I do none.

Charlie is using the last two flights to catch up on work that he's been neglecting in favor of afternoon delights and midnight dips. I have on an eye mask to block out the light but nothing can block my mind as I think about Vivian and seeing her when I get back to New York. I sit up and message her before I can change my mind. I ask if she would be willing to chat with me. I don't know what time it is for her, so I turn off my phone and finally settle down to rest.

Eleven

WHEN WE GET BACK to the penthouse that night, I am exhausted. Charlie ordered food ahead for us while in the cab, knowing that the fridge would be empty. We're both surprised by flowers and balloons. Charlie sets our bags aside in the foyer, going immediately to the note on the flowers.

"'Happy Honeymoon!' Oh, what an asshole." Charlie's laughter fills the empty quiet of the two-floor penthouse. "It's from Jack. I told him that everyone thought it was our honeymoon so they kept giving us shit. I encouraged him to play it up for his honeymoon, so he sent this."

He laughs again, sounding delirious, going on more than thirty hours straight of traveling. Charlie doesn't give it a second thought, kicking off his shoes at the door to wheel both of our bags into his room. I'm not sure where I fit in here, where I'm supposed to sleep. We're no longer in our sex bubble that was Bora Bora. We're back in our real lives with real people. Christmas is next week and we haven't really discussed what we're doing about that.

"Charlie," I call, still standing in the doorway. He walks back out of his room, looking at me, waiting. Before I can open my mouth, his phone rings. It's the front desk letting him know that the food is here. Not once does he drop his eyes from me, silently pleading with me to have this conversation. He turns his full attention to me, waiting for me to go on, unbuttoning his shirt.

"Charlie," I begin again. "What are we? I hate to try to put a label on us, but should I be looking to get back to my own place? Should I sleep in the guest room? What are we doing?" I see hurt flicker in his eyes at the suggestion that I go back to my old place, but he still walks over to me, taking my bag off my shoulder and slinging it over his.

"I meant what I said at the airport. I am going to follow your lead in this. If you feel like you need to move out and get space, then you can do that at any time." Now it's my turn to feel like I've been punched in the gut even if I'm the one who started this. "That said, I would love it if you stayed. If you want to know how I would introduce you at parties, sex kitten is the obvious choice, followed by girlfriend." There is a knock at the door, giving me a moment to think, even if it is only just a second while Charlie thanks the delivery guy.

"I'm in this as long as you are," he continues. "If you want to slow this down, we slow it down. But from where I'm sitting, I'm holding the winning hand and I'm all in." He's being cheesy, and he knows it, but the smile that spreads on my lips is real.

I close the distance between us, rising to the tips of my toes to kiss him, pulling him to me. His hands go to my hips, pulling me against him, when my stomach lets out an undignified growl. Charlie's laughter rumbles through my body.

"Let's get you fed. Unpack the food, while I put your bag in our room. Unless you have any objections?" He pauses letting me have my chance and I choose not to take it. I've already spent the last week in his bed; all this does is add me to his full morning routine.

I'm sorting the Thai food when he emerges. "What is the plan with Christmas later this week?" I ask, not wanting to push him too hard on it. The apartment is just as spotless as we left it, the whirlwind mess that I am contained in the guest room, now my old room.

"Probably working from home most of the time. Mom usually tries to get me to meet her halfway on a ski-slope somewhere, but since this is a divorce year, my dad is probably spending it alone. You're a wild card now too. I honestly hadn't thought about it." Charlie isn't looking at me as he says this, carefully unpacking each of our dishes and sides. As usual, he's gone overboard with options to make sure I have something leftover for lunch tomorrow, or as a late night snack when he comes home from work.

"Is your mom going to Vail again?" I ask, taking a bite of a spring roll, remembering a previous conversation about a family house out there. Charlie slides my favorite, chicken pad see ew, to me after taking a helping for himself.

"No, she might be in New York this year. My brother is in a graduate program at Columbia, getting his JD/MBA, so I think she's here visiting him."

I pause, lifting the chopsticks stuffed with food to my mouth. "Do you want to see them?" I have to tread carefully. "I'm not angling to meet your mom or anything, but, like, I don't want you to worry about me, you know, meeting your mom and that's why you're not seeing her."

Charlie is quiet as he thinks about this, stuffing pad see ew into his mouth to delay responding. I let him think before I take another bite.

"I..." he starts before stopping again. Charlie places his chopsticks on the table to give me his full attention. "I...I do want you to meet my mom. I would rather you meet her before my dad. If you could never meet my dad, that would be preferable. I probably feel the same way about my mom and brother that you do about Vivian. There is history there, a lot of hurt, that I don't think we can get past."

I brush his dirty blond hair out of his face where the long

strands have fallen, covering his reaction. "Maybe this is the year of new beginnings. You've brought me mine. Let me help you with yours. Is there somewhere neutral where you can meet them? If you want to, that is." I watch as he drags his knuckles along his chin, deep in thought.

"I have to think about it. Did you ever hear back from Vivian?" His change of subject tells me that he doesn't want to talk about it.

My phone is a cold paperweight at the bottom of my bag. When we took off from Tahiti, I turned it off. I turn on my phone now, leaving it on the table. For the first time, I'm anxious to turn it on, unsure of what it will hold. Will Vivian have ignored my message? Would that mean she never wants to see me again and only wants to rub my face in how great her life has been? Maybe she regrets accepting my request. Or she was drunk when she decided to follow me.

I'm incapable of playing it cool while I wait, drumming my fingers on the table. I grab my phone as soon as the screen lights up, even though I still have to wait for it to fully power up. The phone makes a sound and my anxiety leads me to nearly chew through my lower lip as I pull up her message. I quickly scan what it says and then pass the phone to Charlie. His eyes rove over the screen, a smile tugging at the corners of his lips.

"I think brunch tomorrow sounds perfect. Suggest Claudia Jean's on the West Side. I know the hostess so I can get you a reservation."

"But you're going to come too, right?" My voice is strangled by my desperation.

Charlie's eyes soften, and he cups my face, his thumb caressing my cheek. I've come to rely on his friendship in the time I've known him. I may have known Vivian well, but she's outside my comfort zone now. He must see it written on my face.

"Absolutely. If you want me at the table, I'll sit with you, otherwise there is a countertop area I can wait at."

My heart fills suddenly, and I rise to kiss Charlie, tongue sliding between his lips, which he opens willingly to me.

"What did I do to deserve you?" I ask, closing up my left overs, cleaning up his as well. We've done this before, gotten takeout and talked, hanging out like friends, but it feels different now.

"You got hit by a car," he deadpans.

I was afraid going to bed that night was going to be awkward, but we are both too exhausted to overthink it. We naturally gravitate toward the same sides of the bed that we used in Bora Bora. Charlie then moves closer to the middle of the bed as I turn my body and curl around him in the same nightly routine we had for the last week, drawn to the other for safety and comfort.

Twelve

CHARLIE WAKES me the next morning with a kiss on my neck. I don't move yet, waiting to see what will happen next. The bed shifts below him as he stretches closer to me, kissing my lips gently. I roll over, placing my hand on his chest, feeling his rock-hard muscles under my fingers. I could get used to waking up next to him for the rest of my life.

I press my body against his, my fingers dancing their way to the elastic of his boxers. I tease along the strap and his Adonis belt before slipping my hand into his boxers to find that he is already at attention. My eyes flutter open to find his Cheshire Cat grin hovering over me. I stroke him a few times with a firm grip before he rolls over on top of me, pressing his hardness against the softest part of me.

Charlie leaves a trail of kisses from my neck down the vee of my shirt. I wish I hadn't worn a shirt to bed now, with Charlie's intended direction clear. One hand finds its way under my shirt to my breast, and his fingers graze over my peaked nipple, exciting the raw nerve endings.

"Good morning, beautiful." Charlie's voice is a low whisper, rough with sleep. Yep, I could definitely get used to waking up to the way he looks at me. Eyes bleary with sleep, he reaches over to the nightstand and grabs his wallet, which has the last two condoms from Bora Bora.

My hand starts working him more urgently as I think about how good it's going to feel with him inside of me. I can hear my breath coming faster and more labored. This morning isn't about gentle exploring or trying to draw out the last throes of pleasure.

He pulls his boxers aside, rolling on the condom before easily slipping inside me, wet and ready for him. I roll over so I am on top again, this time controlling our rhythm. His eyes are alight with passion as he watches me on top of him. I think he likes it when I take charge. Charlie's hands grab at my hips. My shirt is chafing my skin and I hate the barrier between us. I free myself from the shirt, pulling it over my head and tossing it to the side.

"Oh God, Elia." Charlie's voice breaks while he reaches for my bare breast. I'm quick, though, grabbing his hands and stopping him. I want to feel his hands on those sensitive nerve endings, but I also want to be in charge. I pin his hands above him, ready to make him beg for it, but too quickly I'm climaxing. I release his hands and dig my nails into his pecs. My head drops back and I'm unable to hold back the moan that scrapes the back of my throat.

With the last shudder of pleasure wracking my body, he swiftly flips me over so we can continue together. He pulls me back from oblivion and I let him. For the first time I can remember, I feel a second smaller loss of control as our moans harmonize. Each of his thrusts become faster and more frenzied and we climax together. As his orgasm floods my body, I drag my nails along his back, needing something to hold on to. We lie there like that for a moment, foreheads pressed together, our hearts beating in tandem. I tilt up and capture his mouth with mine. Charlie leans into the kiss, his tongue slipping into my mouth, before pulling out. He's quick to clean up the condom after, shuffling into the master bathroom.

"Good morning to you too," I murmur as I follow him into the bathroom.

"Sorry, you just looked so tempting."

"You are literally insatiable," I chastise.

Charlie turns on the shower and the hot water quickly steams up the large mirror. The bathroom is dreamy. It is certainly one that I have dreamed of. The shower has no door, just a solid glass pane. There are six water pressure nozzles to ensure no stone is unturned. I realize that this is my first time really seeing the space.

There is a gorgeous soaker tub opposite the shower and I'm certain that it's closer to a hot tub fit for three. My mind immediately goes to soaking my weary bones in it after physical therapy.

Charlie kisses the top of my head before getting into the shower. His boxers are tossed haphazardly at his hamper. While he showers, I admire yet again how beautiful his penthouse is. The bathroom is white and grey marble all over. Even though it's his bachelor pad, the vanity has double sinks with vanity lighting around the mirror.

I join him in the shower, wrapping my arms around his midsection as he wipes soap from his eyes.

"Can I help you?" he asks, hands sliding into my hair before it gets wet.

"Didn't want you to use all the hot water." I step under the spray of the hot water. Charlie finishes showering first, giving me some alone time while he gets ready.

I thought the shower in Bora Bora was luxurious but it had nothing on this shower. Above me is a pressurized rainwater shower head that massages my scalp as another nozzle sprays directly at my chest, middle, and legs. There are additional nozzles that spray from the side and the only way I could be covered in more water is if I took a bath.

I scrub the thirty hours of travel off me. There is something that feels just dirty after sitting in recycled air that long. I should have showered as soon as we got home, but between the food and the excitement about brunch, I just pushed it off. Brunch. I think about what I'm going to wear today and what I'm even going to say to Vivian when I see her. We finalized details, including swapping cell numbers, the night before, and the plan is to meet at one. I suddenly realize that my clothing options are limited. Either I have the same threadbare black shirt I've been wearing off and on for months with shorts or a coverup from the beach, neither appropriate for December in New York City.

When I get out of the shower, Charlie is arranging a rack of clothes in the bedroom.

"What fresh hell is this?" I ask, gesturing to it as he starts to remove some of the garment bags.

"I may have had my assistant pick up some clothes for you?" He holds his hands out in a 'what are you going to do' fashion before returning to what he was doing.

"When?" I ask, puzzling over the clothes he's still organizing.

"I may have asked Ashley to drop clothes off while we were away. Now just seemed like the perfect opportunity to share them with you." Charlie doesn't seem to be bothered by the extravagance, but I am. At every turn he's whipped out his credit card to pay for things, and I'm left feeling like Julia Roberts in *Pretty Woman* without the prostitution, but now that we're sleeping together, maybe even that line is blurred?

"Why is it you couldn't keep a woman before?" I ask, walking over in my towel to see what Ashley picked. Each price tag is higher than the last and I must look like a cartoon with my eyes bulging out of my head. I start again from the beginning of the rack, looking for the cheapest items, which included a pair of $200 boots and a wool dress.

"Something about being married to the job meant I couldn't be married to her." Charlie's voice is dark as he says this, a subject barely broached. I smash my lips together, watching him turn his back on me to pull on a shirt. The damage his father did to him as a child is still far-reaching.

When he thinks I'm not looking, Charlie pulls the tags off a few of the other pieces, and I'm reminded that his love language is more than touch, it's giving gifts. It's making sure I have everything I need even when I don't know it. I haven't met his father, but something tells me he wasn't the touchy feely type. I may not have been able to remember the last five years of my life, but all the psychology classes I took in college seem to have stuck.

"Please have her return the others. I don't need this much. It's not like I leave the house, anyway," I point out, scrounging in my bag for my lotion and scar cream. Charlie plucks my scar cream from my hands, applying it to my leg while I put lotion on my arms.

"You really enjoy that, don't you?" I ask, watching as he works deep into the tissue with it. I have to bite back a moan that is part pain and part pleasure at how he works the underlying muscle and tissue.

"Think of it as my penance." The gruffness in his voice is hard to miss, as his fingers reach the very edge of my scar. The tone of his voice breaks my heart, filling in the cracks with the need to assuage his guilt. The ache from the residual pain slowly fades from that spot with each tender affection he shows it. It's become routine how he starts at the top slowly winding his way down along the side of my knee until he reaches the thinnest part of the scar.

Charlie drops onto the edge of the bed, eyes watching me finish getting ready. He's wearing jeans and a cranberry red sweater that has two neat buttons on the top near his neck. With his hair combed back, he looks like he just walked off a Ralph Lauren catalog page. I can't help but think about how amazing he looks and how lucky I am to be with him. The circumstances that it took to find each other may not have been ideal, but I don't think I would change it. If someone offered me the chance to undo the accident, I don't think I would take it. The thought of losing what we have isn't something I even want to think about.

I change into the wool dress and a pair of leggings, hoping that it looks good enough for an Upper East Side brunch. I hope that the outfit is cool and sophisticated and doesn't say desperate to reconnect. I am desperate to connect. I'm desperate to talk to Vivian. Someone who knew me before. Someone who knows my secrets and dreams. But also, I want to have someone else to talk to, someone I can laugh with. As much of a joke as it was about needing someone to swoon with about how great Charlie is, I do need that. I feel isolated and alone otherwise. I need a friend.

I stand between his legs as he sits on the bed, reading an email. He's always reading an email. I take his phone and drop it to the side. He immediately looks at me, his phone and email forgotten.

"This hostess with the mostess that got you this reservation, is she a former fling?" I ask, knowing I had a jealous streak in college. Knowing what an incredible man Charlie is only makes that jealous streak stronger. He's a catch, and I, well, I'm a mess. It's a dark, insecure thought that needles at me, but the reminder that it's my body he's touching helps shut that voice down.

I know that information like this will just hurt me, but I have to ask. I thread my fingers through his hair, pressing my nails into his scalp. If he were a cat, I think he would purr, the way his eyes start to drift closed. Realizing I've asked a serious question, his hands are on my hips to steady me, and he looks me straight in the eyes.

"Yes, but a very distant one. She's more a friend than anything else. She's in business school now at Columbia and does the hostess gig to pay her way. We went to Dartmouth together," he admits, ready to put every card on the table.

"Quite the pedigree," I say casually, thinking of my state school education. Most of the kids I went to school with came from working class families with not many aspirations past earning a basic degree because our guidance counselor in high school said we had to. Even I had to admit that my chosen field had led nowhere for me. Before the void of memory, I was working as a secretary. It seems like my missing time was filled with doing commission work: drawing book covers and fan art, taking temp jobs, trying to find a way to cover my bills.

I feel lost not knowing what direction my life was taking before the accident. Was I drawing because I liked it or because I felt the need to monetize my hobby and earn money? For months I've been able to hide from it, under the purview of focusing on my healing, but what would come next for me?

"I like your pedigree better." He moves lightning quick and flips me over so I'm on my back. I let out a surprised yelp. "Believe me when I say you have nothing to worry about."

His words jar me from the unexpected downward spiral in my thoughts. The one thing I miss most is the self confidence that I had before. How can I be confident if I don't really know who I am?

"I do. I trust you," I say, because it's the truth. In the short time I have known him, he has been up front and honest about everything.

The kiss we share is long and deep, his fingers running through my hair before drawing away from me. As much as I would love to let him distract me from this brunch, I know I have to get ready. I still have to fuss over my hair and make-up. Charlie pulls back, rolling to the side of the bed so I can get up.

I used to be skilled at blow drying my hair, easily turning the brush in my hand, the heat encouraging me to quickly move through the motions. My hands are clumsy now in a way I don't remember them being before. I hate that I have no idea if it's because of my nerves now or a change in my habits in the last five years. Did I not do it as frequently?

I pull my hair back into a ponytail, away from my face before letting it down. I toy with the blonde strands. Even after all these months have passed, looking at the light color surprises me. I twist the edges, running a hand through the top, flipping it this way and that before putting it back up again. I let my thoughts stray to getting it colored back to my natural shade, or as close to it as I can get. Charlie lets me panic and sort out my anxiety on my own, knowing I need the headspace for myself. He lets me carry on until I have no choice but to leave it and hope that things with Vivian aren't beyond repair.

Thirteen

⨖

WHEN WE PULL up to Claudia Jean's, I stare at the building and the people on the street finishing their last minute shopping. I hesitate before opening the door.

"I'll be inside the whole time," Charlie reassures me. Ever the gentleman, Charlie opens the door to the vestibule erected by the restaurant for the cold winter months. I steel my nerves, pushing ahead to the second door, and walk in before I change my mind. A pretty redheaded hostess is ready to greet whoever enters or to be the fierce gatekeeper to the inner sanctum. Her hair is mostly pulled back with a few strands framing her face as she studies the seating chart in front of her.

"Name?" she asks, barely looking at me.

"If this is the sort of service you offer, I'm sorry I got you this job." Charlie's voice is booming as he teases her, soliciting a response. Her head snaps up, finally looking at Charlie and then me. I'm quickly forgotten as she flashes her perfect white teeth, coming around from behind the podium to squeeze him in a tight hug. I feel a jealous twist to my heart and I hate it.

"Chuckie!" she exclaims, kissing both of his cheeks, beaming at him. Her attention shifts to me and she drinks in the sight of me.

The plain ponytail, the edge of the wool dress peeking out from beneath the parka, something that is thankfully my own. "You must be Elia. It's so nice to finally meet you. Charlie was giving me a rundown via text last night. I'm Taryn." She's trying to put me at ease but her gregarious nature is overwhelming. I want to retreat back to the safety of Charlie's penthouse, away from prying eyes. Taryn stretches out a hand so we can shake. She seems to sense that I'm a frightened bird, ready to flee. The look she shares with Charlie makes it all the worse.

"Vivian is already at the table so I'll take you to her."

I'm confused that she knows Vivian's name but assume it's because she checked in ahead of us.

Charlie swoops down to kiss me. It's soft and gentle, a barely-there brush of the lips. Another element to our relationship seems to have been added to the mix. Gone are Bora Bora Elia and Charlie; in their place Elia and Charlie in New York emerged, and now, a third facet of our relationship: Elia and Charlie in public.

"I'll be here the whole time," he promises again, squeezing my hand before walking further into the restaurant, leaving me to follow Taryn. My heart slams against my chest and I wonder if it's possible to break a rib this way. I inch my way through the cramped walkways of the bustling restaurant, worried that I made a mistake.

Vivian is sitting alone in a booth, scrolling through her phone. I can see the massive canary diamond on her finger, accompanied by her perfect manicure. She glances up when she sees Taryn approaching and when her eyes land on me, my heart stops in my chest. She looks so happy to see me and it hurts how surprised I am by that. Why did I feel like this was going to be awkward? Vivian looks happy and healthy, her auburn hair loose around her shoulders, falling in picture perfect waves.

This crushing weight of heartache and loneliness hits me from nowhere. I suspect it's feelings I can't pinpoint because they're from the last five years. She pops out of her seat, initially reaching to hug me, but she hesitates, the past five years hanging over her in a way that they don't for me. Whatever happened that we lost touch is still there for her, putting me at a loss. One of us is going to have to make the first move; she's already opened herself up to reconciliation by accepting my request and responding to me, so I take the next step forward.

I open my arms to her awkwardly, without thinking about what I'll do if she rejects this advance. Vivian doesn't hesitate when she steps forward, arms folding around me. It settles me in a way that I didn't know I needed, giving me the reassurance and security I was missing. Charlie has done everything right since we met, but nothing can beat the arms of someone who has known you and loved you through some of your darkest moments. Vivian was there for me when my parents died and after a brutal breakup in college. She was there for me when I got my nipple pierced on a drunken dare and was there to help inspect it when it got infected and I had to take it out. It's not always about the men in your life, but about the women too. The ones who are there to hold you up when you don't think you can do anymore and to help build you up when you have nothing left to give.

"I've missed you so much," she whispers, squeezing me tighter. I feel her face shift into my shoulder against the hood of my jacket.

"I've missed you, too," I say, feeling my eyes well up.

"Thanks, Taryn," Vivian says, as we break apart and sit down. "Enough about that. I've ordered mimosas so tell me what has been going on. You were in Bora Bora, what the actual fuck? That's awesome," Vivian blurts, trying to keep the flow of conversation. It's easy to start with the superficial and rebuild just some of the rapport we had, but I came here for answers, for some sort of insight into what happened.

"I mean it was amazing, but I was hoping you could tell me what's been going on. I was in a car accident in September. I don't remember a whole lot about the last five years." The words rush out of my mouth before I have a chance to really think about what

I want to say. I take a nervous sip of my water, hoping I haven't scared her off. The appearance of a waiter cuts off any other embarrassing babble. Quickly, I look at the menu and pick the first agreeable thing I see.

"Shut the front door! Tell me more," she says, resting her elbows on the table with her chin perched on her hands as she listens with rapt attention. I realize just how badly I missed this, how badly I missed the way that Vivian could make you feel like the center of the world with her words. She was always a tremendous listener.

"Yeah, literally. So, I was hit by a car that had this guy who works in the financial district in it. He's been nursing me back to health this whole time. I mean, he's stupid rich and flew us to Bora Bora for two weeks. I feel like I have to be in a coma and that none of this is real," I say. Vivian reaches out and pinches my arm on the small spot of skin where I rolled up my sleeve, careful of her manicured tips.

"Ow," I say, rubbing my arm, pouting at her.

"Seems pretty real to me. Where are you living these days?" she asks, taking a sip of her drink as if this were the most normal thing in the world.

"Actually, with the guy. His name is Charlie and he's been really fantastic." I swing around to peek at him, but he's on his phone again. When I turn back to Vivian, her eyes are still on me. "I was living in a seventh floor walk-up in Washington Heights and I couldn't handle the stairs."

"Charlie is a pretty great guy, isn't he?" The way she says this makes me pause. I cock my head to the side, waiting for her to go on. When she catches my confusion, she continues. "My fiancé, Jack, and Charlie are friends. Jack's been bitching that Charlie isn't around for him to hang out because of some new broad. Imagine my surprise seeing a photo of you two on Pictogram."

I know the smile on my face is fake as fuck, and she can tell, but I keep it there frozen while I process this information. Puzzle pieces that seemed to have no home suddenly fit in ways I didn't expect. I realize the reason that her fiancé looked familiar is because there are photos of Jack and Charlie in his apartment from college and beyond. Which means that Charlie knew who Vivian was when I showed him the picture. I don't realize that Vivian is still talking until I look back at her.

"I'm sorry, I missed that. Can you repeat it?" I ask, focusing on her. I have to try now in a way that I didn't before. Why didn't Charlie mention that he knew Vivian? Is that why Taryn knew her name when we got here? For every answer I thought I was going to get, I find that I just have more questions.

"I was just saying that I'm glad we could reconnect after so many years." Her sculpted eyebrows quirk down in concern, but then her face shifts back to excitement. I don't have the time to worry about that right now since she's given me the opening I need.

"What happened? I mean, as far as I can remember, which for me feels like a few months ago instead of five years, you were moving in with Connor. And then I have nothing after that." Her moving in with Connor had been natural. They started dating in college and were still together for years after. So, as our lease was ending, it was the obvious next step for them.

"Nothing?" Vivian asks, uncertainly. There are cracks in her façade showing as she sips her mimosa.

"Nothing. I only knew my address because of my ID. Otherwise when Charlie asked, I would have said our old place."

She seems to consider this, her lower lip sucked into her mouth. Vivian was never very good at hiding her thoughts. I could always read them on her face. But something changed and I realized I don't know what she's thinking right now.

"Do you trust me?" she asks, seriously. Whatever it was, I wasn't expecting this question.

"Is there a reason for me not to in the last five years?"

"No, but believe me when I say, let's leave it in the past. The reason isn't a problem anymore, so it would be pointless to bring up that ugliness."

"I get that, Viv, but I really want some answers. I need answers. I don't know who I am anymore. I'm blonde, something I never thought I would do, and not like honey blonde. I'm platinum blonde." I pull my hair out of the ponytail to show her. We're silent again as the waiter delivers our food, both murmuring our thanks to him, as she decides what to reveal. Vivian looks pained when she finally opens up.

"You started to see someone new. His name was Ben or Brad or something. I honestly don't remember because I never met him. If you hung out with him, it was always at his place, and any time he was supposed to come out with us, he flaked. He seemed like kind of a dick, but I had just moved in with Connor and I was busy with my last year of law school and my internship. We started talking less and less until we just stopped. You asked me to remove all photos of us from Pictogram and then, nothing. The night I got engaged, Connor threw a big party and you just didn't show.

"I tried texting and calling. Any time I did, it said the number was out of service. This was maybe like three, four years ago? We've been out of touch the whole time. I assume that you're not with that guy anymore if you're living with Charlie. Since this version of you values my opinion, I, ten out of ten, highly approve of this match."

"I just cut you out?" I'm so confused, so lost. The words come out sad and desperate. Her hand reaches out to my wrist, grasping it gently. I think about the memories, or I think they're memories, of me arguing with a faceless man. Is this the same guy? Did things with this Ben or Brad guy end and I felt like it was too late to fix things with Viv? No way I was in a relationship at the time of the accident; otherwise, he would have been looking for me.

"You have me now. That's all that matters. Let the past be the past. I don't care. Really, I don't. I'm getting married and my fiancé's best man actually hit you with a car. If that isn't fate, I don't know what is."

I laugh and swipe at the tears that threaten to fall. "Well, I don't have much to tell you about the last five years, so what have I missed?"

Any trepidation that may have been simmering under the surface fades. Vivian launches into what the last five years have looked like for her, starting with breaking up with Connor after catching him in bed with someone else. I finish my avocado toast in the time it takes her to explain all of this.

"How did you meet Jack?" I fight the urge to look back at Charlie. This is the first glimpse I'm getting into his world that he hasn't provided himself and I'm excited to learn more about the people in his life.

"So, I'm at this bar after breaking up with Connor, trying to, like, get out there and feel like myself. There is this guy who literally won't take no for an answer no matter how many times I tell him to stop touching my ass and that I don't want him to buy me a drink." Vivian barely pauses to get air, clearly used to having to tell this tale in the cutest and most charming way she can. "Well, someone taps me gently on the shoulder, and I think it's the guy so I throw my glass of red wine in his face, saying, 'No means no, asshole.'" She's struggling not to laugh. "And there is Jack, sweet Jack, standing there with my coat in his hand, his white shirt covered in red wine. He licks his lips, tasting the wine I just threw in his face. And he goes, 'Well, I hope that wasn't expensive because I'm not going to buy you another one.'" She laughs to herself at the thought of it.

"My coat had fallen off my chair, so he was just trying to be nice. I felt so awful and ordered a club soda to try to fix his shirt. While we waited for the club soda and while I tried to help him clean his shirt, we talked. It was the best careless move I ever made." Her voice takes on this faraway, dreamy quality. In the years I've known her, I don't think I ever heard her speak that way.

"That was maybe two years ago? You and I were already out of touch by then, so you never met him."

I reach out and take her hand the way she did mine earlier. "I'm sorry I wasn't there." I wish I could go back and be with her through all this; through breaking up with Connor and meeting Jack. I worry that I don't deserve this second chance I've been given with my friend, but I know I'm not going to squander it.

"You're here now and that's really all that matters. Jack and I are getting married next fall, a little less than a year. Now, it's all about wedding planning and figuring out what our future looks like together."

Vivian fills in the blanks on what our friends have been up to. I missed weddings and babies and bachelorette parties. Peppered in are stories about her attending some of these events, but she never mentions seeing me there. I'm content listening to her, wondering if we can find the old groove we had of weekend brunches and drinking till we were tipsy.

"So, what's your plan now?" she asks while I'm trying to catch the waiter's eye to get the check.

"What do you mean?" I ask, unsure of what she's getting at. I turn back to her.

"Well, you said that you were doing freelance work before. Are you going to go back to that? Are you moving back into your apartment? What are you doing?"

I look at her, unable to come up with an answer. "I don't really know. I've been so focused on my recovery. I broke my ankle, which has been a bitch to heal. If it was just one injury, it would be easier to figure out moving back to my apartment, but I messed up my knee and shoulder and wrist. The icing on the cake was, of course, amnesia. There have been so many doctors and evaluations to see about doing something about that, so I haven't thought much about what I'm going to do next. I was working on commission, and the temp agency has filled my role, so I don't really have anything to go back to. It's both freeing and terrifying all at once."

"What's the deal with you and Charlie, anyway? Jack's been agonizing over it since Charlie whisked you off to Bora Bora."

I'm sure she saw the photo of us kissing that I posted on Pictogram. Just thinking about us being together makes my insides melt and my cheeks flush. Did I dare imagine a real life with him? I glance over at where Charlie sits, chatting with someone at his table. It's like he knows I'm looking because he turns his head and catches me watching him. He gives me a wink, letting me know that I've been seen, and that he's still here, waiting for me. I feel my whole body grow tight, the thought of getting to go to bed with him every night.

Vivian snaps her fingers in my face. "Earth to Ellie," she says, bringing me back to our conversation.

"We're together," I say tentatively and she doesn't even fight the grin. "It kind of happened on our trip. The week before we left was Thanksgiving and I made us these ridiculous cornish hens since a turkey would have been too much food. I burned my hand and ruined dinner and proceeded to sob on the floor of his penthouse. He kissed me while consoling me and trying to figure out why I was crying. Neither one of us knew what to do about it, so we just pretended it never happened until we were in Bora Bora. I was living with him but sleeping in the guest room and now I sleep in his bed."

She looks like she's fighting laughter at the ridiculous story, and it really is just that, ridiculous. It was like an extreme 'meet cute' that nearly ended with me dying, but instead, I found this incredible man.

"God, he's a fox, let me tell you," Vivian says. A quiet lull falls between us and I get the feeling she's working herself up to something. "Why didn't you call when you woke up?"

I hate how small her voice sounds and that I'm the one that made her feel that way.

"I don't have a good reason, really." I look away from her, tugging at the napkin on my lap. If there is anyone in the world I can open up to, it's Vivian. "I was too afraid of the reason why we weren't talking anymore. That it was this terrible thing and you hated me and you wouldn't take my call. But if I never tried to call you then I couldn't get hurt, so I hid behind my accident, and little by little my heart healed. It also didn't help that I didn't have your number."

Vivian's hand flies out to grab mine where it was reaching for my water. She opens her mouth to say something, but her eyes dart behind me and she jumps out of her seat with the same enthusiasm she had when I showed up. I twist as she flings her arms around the newcomer before kissing him.

"I've missed you," a deep male voice rumbles.

"It's been like four hours, Jack," she admonishes, but a sly grin is on her face. Vivian is elated to have this love and attention on her. I stand up and am dwarfed by him.

"This is my fiancé, Jack. Jack, this is Elia, Charlie's mystery girl."

I smile, offering my hand to him. The smile I receive never quite reaches his eyes, but he takes my hand, squeezing it with an unexpected strength. It seems with Jack I'm already starting behind the curve and am going to have to work hard to earn his approval. I try to squeeze his hand back, but it's already too late. Jack pulls his hand back as Charlie approaches.

"Chuck, this is the girl you've been hiding from us?" The look between the two men is significant. I may have only known him for mere minutes, but it's clear that Jack is not a fan of me. Vivian is putting on the performance of a lifetime trying to cover that up, trying to keep me from fleeing and Charlie looks downright pissed with the frosty reception I'm getting.

Charlie wraps an easy arm around my shoulder, pulling me into his side. "Siren Hotel's happy hour starts in ten, and I got us a table for four. You two ready to head over?" Charlie asks, his voice forceful. Jack slides his green eyes to me, then looks back at Charlie, a similarly fake smile plastered on his face.

"Absolutely," Vivian says without hesitation. Jack, to his credit, smiles indulgently at my friend.

"What the lady says goes." Jack doesn't sound too happy about it.

Charlie helps me into my jacket, taking my hand in his as he leads the way out of the restaurant. When I whisper to Charlie about the check, he confesses to having taken care of it. Taryn waves goodbye to us all as we depart and begin our walk to another restaurant. Vivian links her arm with me as we walk behind the guys.

Jack is a little shorter than Charlie, but they have a similar slender frame. Something about how Jack holds himself made me feel so small beside him, when I've never felt anything like that from Charlie. I want to hear what the two of them are whispering about as we begin our trek over the nine blocks. Charlie's hands are shoved deep into his pockets, their conversation only ceasing when Vivian and I catch up to them at a corner.

Vivian has always been great at filling silence. I let her chatter about wedding planning and her new job while I turn over the last two hours in my mind. Charlie's deception weighs heavily on me, but confronting him about it now isn't possible. I'll have to ask him about it when we get home.

The Siren Hotel is a cute little seafood place with great happy hour deals on drinks and oysters.

The booth we are seated in is in the back. Already the place is packed with a line out the door. I'm glad Charlie got us a reservation, given the crowd. I slide into one side of the booth, Vivian across from me and Charlie right beside me, his hand resting on my knee as soon as we're seated. It's clear that this place is a regular spot for them because none of them look at the menu, ordering a round of appetizers, oysters, and drinks.

"So, my boy here hit you with his car?" Jack asks as if he hasn't heard the story from Charlie.

I debate if I have the emotional wherewithal to give Jack the performance that is required to appease him. Whatever actually happened with Vivian and I taints what Jack thinks of me. I'm not sure I will ever be good enough for his best friend or his fiancée. I could choose to fight this battle, but it might mean fighting him tooth and nail every step of the way.

"I'm sure you know more than I do. I don't actually have any memory of the accident." I haven't told Charlie yet, that I have a snippet of that night. A flash of a memory of his rain-soaked face hovering over me. I don't know if it's real or something my mind conjured for me, a mechanism meant to fill in the gaps that have appeared in my memory.

"That is true," Jack concedes, leaning back in his chair, his hand on Vivian's. Each movement they make is in sync with the other. They anticipate each other's needs without so much as an acknowledgement that they're doing it. The bread bowl is dropped at our table with a variety of breads and immediately, Jack grabs one with tomatoes baked into it, dropping it on Vivian's plate. A hum of contentment escapes her while she reaches for the olive oil and salt to pass to Jack. It's truly mesmerizing to watch. I hope that someday I can find that level of comfort with someone.

"Your dad is pretty pissed, dude," Jack's tone is dismissive of me, turning to Charlie.

"My dad is always pissed," Charlie says, sipping his bright pink drink. Somehow his arm has found its way from my knee to around my shoulders, an idle hand twirling my ponytail around his fingers.

"Yeah, but he found out that you were slacking for two weeks and that I was covering for you, so he told me that I could have your bonus."

Charlie seems unbothered by this, dropping a piece of bread on my plate. I had hesitated to dive into the platter, wanting to save space for the oysters we ordered, but the fresh scent wafts up, making my mouth water in response.

"He tells you that every year. He can tell me all about it

tomorrow when I'm back in the office." Charlie's voice has taken on an edge to it heard only when he's angry. He wants to let the subject go so I open my mouth to try to change the subject, but Jack barrels on, needing to needle his friend.

"He said you need to stop thinking with your dick and do your job." Jack's deep green eyes slide to me and I see Charlie's jaw tick.

He squeezes my shoulder reassuringly, but I can't help but worry about all of the strife I have caused. "I can talk to my dad about it tomorrow." Charlie's voice is hard, making it the final word on the subject. Even Vivian looks uncomfortable, shooting Jack a questioning look.

I seize on the moment of silence prompted by the waiter dropping off the oyster platter. "So, Charlie told me you two got engaged over Thanksgiving? He, of course, was sparse with the details. How did you propose?" I ask Jack, hoping, praying, that he takes the redirect.

Vivian doesn't give him a chance to blow it, plowing right on in. We hadn't gotten a chance to discuss the magical proposal earlier and I'm delighted to hear her side of it.

"He actually rented out the whole of the Bryant Park ice skating rink. You know me, I hate ice skating. I was pretty hesitant but when he promised to rent it for an hour, just for us, I begrudgingly agreed."

"I know someone who operates the ice skating rink, so it was easy to manage," Jack interjects with his part, clearly a practiced maneuver with the way they tell it.

Vivian beams. "So, he gets me on the ice, leading me around slowly before taking me to the center of the ice. I, of course, hate this and hold on to him for dear life because there is no railing for me to clutch, just him. He's careful about letting me go as he gets on one knee. Suddenly, there are these soft booms, and I almost fall because I'm startled, but it turns out it was rose petals shot out of confetti cannons all around us, and I'm just stunned. I was so stunned that I actually left him hanging before saying yes. We went to Nobu for dinner before going home. It was honestly such a dream," she says looking at Jack.

My heart fills for them. Jack may not like me, but his love for Vivian runs deep, and I cannot begrudge him that.

With our food being served, conversation starts to circle around what their mutual friends are doing for the holidays, and I am quickly the odd man out. Both Charlie and Vivian do their best to include me, Charlie explaining who people are and Vivian mentioning old friends we shared, but Jack is determined to make sure I feel like an outsider.

I'm not sure if he doubts that I'm interested in Charlie or that I'm in it for the long haul with Vivian. In either case, I'm not sure it will be possible for me to win him over. I excuse myself to use the restroom, leaving them behind. As I turn a corner, I see Charlie watching me before reaching forward and punching Jack in the arm. Jack, to his benefit, doesn't bother to ask what he's done wrong, he just scowls at Charlie, his mouth twisted as he makes his case.

I sit in the bathroom longer than necessary, contemplating if I really, genuinely, want to return to the table. I don't want to go back out there and talk to Jack if he's going to be all subtle barbs and attempts to exclude me. Convincing him that I'm in this, both with Charlie and Vivian, is not going to happen over one happy hour. Frankly, it's not his business to determine if I'm worthy of Charlie or not. It's going to be a long challenge and I'm not sure he will trust that I'm not with Charlie for his money. I can only imagine the stories that Vivian told him about our days of eating ramen during the week, so we could scrape by with rent and hit bottomless brunches on weekends. Vivian catches me gently dabbing at my eyes to not smudge the few swipes of mascara I managed before leaving the apartment.

"Ellie?" she asks, touching my shoulder. Her face is apologetic, eyes turned down, with a mixture of shame and apology. "I'm sorry Jack is being a dick. He's just," she takes a deep breath in, "protective."

"I get that, Vivian, I do, but I'm fighting an uphill battle with him. I'm not going to win it with you and Charlie fighting it for me." My words are sharper than I intend, my frustration with Jack being taken out on her. An annoyed growl escapes my throat as I toss out the towel.

"I know, it's just, I feel responsible. I poisoned the well and I never should have."

I grab her hand. "Is there more that you're not telling me? That Jack knows? Because he's being a douche canoe to me and it feels disproportionate if we just grew apart. I had no contacts in my phone. None of our other friends in the city or sorority sisters. No one." I lean against the counter, hugging myself.

Her silence all but confirms that more must have happened, and I'm thankful that she's willing to move past it.

"I mean, honestly, Viv, no one from my past cares about me. Charlie asked a friend if a missing persons report had been filed and to tell him if one is filed. Nothing. I've been living this weird fantasy life for months and no one wants to know where I am. No one is worried about not hearing from me for three months. Three months! Like, I'm an adult and, obviously, people have lives and don't talk to everyone all the time, but you're telling me there isn't one person I talked to with enough regularity to miss me? It was a huge red flag that there was nothing from you on my phone. I had more old texts from my Chinese food delivery guy and verification texts than I did messages with any real people. No texts from Jordan or Sarah or Sam. I didn't even have social media on my phone."

Vivian wraps her arms around me, hugging me close as I cry for the first time since Charlie kissed me on Thanksgiving.

I used October and November to focus on healing and to turn my anger and loss into something more. Sadness was never an emotion that I warred with. There were mostly tears of frustration during physical therapy, but now as I think about all I've lost that I don't even know I'm missing, I cry.

"Did you come here for dinner or a show?" I hear Vivian snap after the door opens into the small bathroom.

She shushes me and rubs my back, holding me close against her as I get it out of my system. How many times did she hold me like this through college, through my parents' deaths? How many times did I do the same as she cried about heartbreak, about the Sarah McLachlan animal commercials, and the death of McDreamy?

"I'm sorry you feel like you've had to go through this alone, but you don't have to now. Charlie is smitten with you. I can see it on his face when he looks at you. And you have me. For as long as you will let me be here. We made a blood oath during pledging to be sisters no matter what and I'm not letting that change now. I promise you, the only thing I didn't tell you was that we had a fight about us growing apart. It wasn't the thing that broke us up but it was rough. It's not anything that's going to keep us from being friends now."

I nod, remembering the drunken oath we took the night we accepted our bids, cutting our hands on the jagged edges of a beer can. I'm grateful for her capacity for forgiveness. She's tender with each movement, blotting at the streaks of black down my face from the obviously not waterproof mascara. I do as I'm told, holding wet washcloths to my eyes, to try to bring down the swelling while she tends to the rest of my face. Together we take a deep breath before I have to face her caveman fiancé.

I try to admire Jack's protectiveness of them both, clearly the most important people in his life, but I'm annoyed at how he has decided this means he can treat me whatever way he wants. Charlie stands so I can slide into the booth. He keeps his face carefully impassive as he studies my swollen eyes and tight jaw. His brown eyes cast a death glare at Jack, who acts oblivious, resting a hand on his fiancé's knee.

"Since this week is Christmas, Jack and I are having a small engagement party for friends on Christmas Eve. You should come, Ellie."

I glance at Charlie since he hadn't mentioned the party at all, which he cops to immediately, hands raised defensively.

"I didn't mention it because I assumed I was in the work doghouse and it was only a fifty/fifty shot I would get out. I will make it work though. Dress code?" Charlie threads his fingers through mine and I worry about needing more new clothes. I'm driven further and further into debt with Charlie, though he never makes me feel it.

Vivian seems to have the same thought. "Ellie, why don't you come help me set up that day and you can borrow something of mine," Vivian offers and I am so thankful for it. "We've always been a similar size and that doesn't seem to have changed."

"Yes, I would love to help out," I agree, relaxing into my seat.

Having been shamed while I was away from the table, Jack remains quiet until we pay the check and leave. I'm loath to leave Vivian behind after just getting her back, but Jack looks eager to get home. I hug her tightly before we part ways, each in our own PickMeUp!. Vivian promises to send me details for the party, and for a brief moment, it feels like nothing has changed.

I waste no time interrogating Charlie once we're alone.

"You knew?" I ask, trying to hold back the accusation in my tone.

"I knew," he says simply, sliding his phone in his jacket pocket. "It was such a weird coincidence and I didn't want to add more pressure to you seeing her again. The last thing I wanted was for you to go into that brunch feeling like you needed to make nice with Vivian if it turned out that what happened between you was catastrophic. I didn't know until you showed me her picture in the airport. Jack didn't fess up about knowing until I texted him once you had your brunch set up. I hated keeping you in the dark, but I wanted you to know you were still making your own choices without my interference." He takes my hand in his. "My finger-prints are all over your life now. I didn't want you to feel like Vivian was more a part of me than she was a part of you."

I lean over and kiss him, my hand firm on his jaw. "I appreciate that, but I do wish you had told me so I didn't look like a dumbass for not knowing there was this connection."

"I'm sure you didn't look like a dumbass." He's sweet and I let him go on thinking that.

"You also didn't need to hit Jack," I admonish, and he smirks.

"He was being a dick and he knew it. He deserved it. I've hit him over much less."

I squeeze his hand. "While I appreciate you defending my honor, I'm going to have to fight this battle with him on my own. It's going to be a slow burn with him. Whatever happened, he doesn't trust me. Did he tell you why he doesn't like me?" I'm curious if he has a different story from the one that Vivian told me.

"Just that you dropped your friends like hot cakes because of some guy. Vivian didn't get into too much detail about it. She told Jack she didn't remember him well. She said she didn't even meet him."

"Well, that's not going to happen again," I swear.

The chime on Charlie's phone is like a Pavlovian ring, alerting him to emails he's been graciously ignoring in favor of happy hour.

Giving him the break he needs to address it, I pull out my phone, deciding to get in some quick online shopping using my own credit cards. Not that we need it, but I order some sex toys and a few teddies online for Christmas. Things are so new with Charlie that I wouldn't even know what to get him for the holi-days. It's a cheap way out, but I think he will enjoy it all the same. I press order as we pull up to the apartment, and I spend the rest of the day holding on to this quiet excitement for things to come.

Fourteen

MONDAY MORNING IS the first time since getting back from Bora Bora that we have to return to our regularly scheduled lives. I hear Charlie's alarm go off; he's quick to silence it and get out of bed to change into his workout clothes. When we got ready for bed the night before, Charlie warned me that he was going to be super busy with work, playing catch-up and giving Jack a break before his engagement party. I check the time and see that it's only four AM. I groan, pulling a pillow over my head to try to go back to bed.

I manage to get sleep in small bursts after that, but what keeps me awake more than anything is the dream that I'm having.

I'm riding my bike, furiously pedaling, trying to keep my emotions together. The rain is falling harder as I remember that we're getting the edge of a hurricane before it heads back out to sea. I have a small regret as I push myself, but only that I didn't opt for the subway instead.

The weather and the late hour means that there aren't going to be as many people on the road, so I take a chance turning the bike down the 97th Street Transverse. It's tight and can be risky for a bike, but it's faster if I go this way. I can feel my heart breaking, leaving a

158

breadcrumb trail of itself behind as I pedal harder. My adrenaline rush from what just happened is wearing off. I feel lost, uncertain about what I mean to do with my life now. My head is bent low, and under the brim of my helmet, I can see a large puddle ahead. Living in New York for the last seven years has taught me one important thing: never trust a puddle. You never know how deep it might be. I'm coming at it from a slight downhill, picking up speed. I'm desperate to get home, so I don't bother with the brakes, swerving to avoid the puddle. Only, I've avoided the puddle, but moved right into the path of a car. My only thought as I tumble onto the pavement is that this might be easier than facing the question of tomorrow.

My eyes fly open and I sit up, unable to get the image of the blinding headlights out of my eyes. I'm still seeing spots when Charlie walks into the room, drenched in sweat. A glance at the clock tells me it's only 4:45 AM. His earbuds are still in as he lifts the bottom of his shirt, wiping at his forehead, and then pulling his shirt up and over his head before casting the shirt to the side. Spotting me, he silences his music, a frown tugging his lips down.

"I'm sorry, I didn't wake you, did I?" he asks, his voice a quiet whisper, as if I might be lulled back to sleep. I'm afraid that if I open my mouth to answer I might throw up. So, instead of speaking, I just give a little shake of my head. I'm not sure I can go back to sleep at all, no matter how much I want to. I'm ready to sit and cry, the waves of fear, distress, and pain washing over me, but with Charlie looking at me like that, I can't let those feelings overtake me. His guilt over what happened is already too much; it has too much of a grip on him. I can't add to it. I won't add to it. It is a burden to be shared, but there are moments I catch him watching me limp if I'm tired, a pained look on his face washed away before he thinks I see.

"Is something wrong?" He's so attuned to my emotions that it makes hiding anything difficult. He lowers himself onto the bed beside me, concern on his face as he pushes hair from my forehead.

Feeling the cool air on my skin, I realize that I had been sweating in my sleep. I draw my knees up to my chest, keeping my mouth shut, still not wanting to burden him. He puts his hand on my knee and shakes it a little, a silent plea for me to open up to him. The heartbreak on his face is too much to bear, and I know keeping it from him will only be worse, so I take the leap.

"It was raining super hard because of a hurricane that had worked its way up the coast." My words are quiet, hanging in the air between us. I don't have to say any more for him because there hasn't been a moment where he hasn't thought about that day. He knows the conditions from that day; he recalls seeing my body lying broken in the street.

"You're remembering." It's a statement, one that has so many implications.

"Pieces. For now, just the accident. I'm remembering some feelings and the accident itself. Nothing before or after."

"I don't want you to take offense to this, but I think it would be really good for you if you get a therapist. The doctors mentioned it a few times and you seemed to brush it off, but there are a lot of complicated feelings around what happened. I want you to feel like you're supported and have a safe space to parcel out what you remember and deal with what you don't." He glances at the clock and curses under his breath. "I have to finish getting ready. I've got a meeting with my dad first thing and I want to get there before him. Dan is coming over at eight for your PT and I can have my assistant get you a list of trauma therapists if you want." He twirls a strand of hair around a finger.

"Can I decide in January?" I ask. I look around the apartment and realize it's not even decorated for Christmas but I still say, "I want to enjoy the holidays as best I can without feeling broken."

"You're not broken." He presses a kiss to my forehead, his hand cupping the back of my neck and drawing me closer to him. "You don't have to do anything you don't want to."

I don't distract him further but I do watch him strip off his boxers before he strides into the bathroom.

"I was thinking about trying a hypnotist," I confess when he emerges, bare and clean. He's rubbing the towel in his hair, leaving the rest of his magnificent body on display. He glances at me with interest. I had honestly only thought of it in the time that he was in the shower, but it was still a consideration.

"What brought this on?"

"I feel like I should want to get my memories back." Ever since seeing Vivian, I keep thinking that maybe I should let the past stay in the past, but shouldn't I want to remember? Shouldn't I want to reclaim that history?

"We can talk about it later, but only if you really want to." Charlie disappears into his walk-in closet to get dressed. When he emerges, I admire how good he looks in a suit. He looks classy and elegant, like he belongs on a GQ magazine cover, not heading to the financial district for work. His hands are quick and practiced as he puts on a fresh tie.

He catches me watching him in the mirror. "Stop undressing me with your eyes," he says, fixing his belt. "I might just let you actually undress me."

I smirk at him. "Maybe later," I promise, thinking of all the things I want to do to him. I'm not interested in furthering what must already be his father's frustration, so I keep my come-hither looks to myself. He gives me a quick kiss before running out the door.

After physical therapy, I drift back to the guest room I had inhabited for two months. The queen bed is freshly made, a pair of pajamas neatly folded on the corner, waiting for my return. I had been prepared to move my clothes into Charlie's room and then realized that it would have been too presumptuous. I'm stuck in limbo with him, unsure what to do about my clothes. I settle for grabbing my toiletries and moving those into his shower because at the very least, I'll be showering there.

After showering, I email the temp agency again, trying to get back in their good graces. The response I get, a mere hour later, is full of explanations as to why they would have to consider it. In the last two years I'd worked for them, I had a poor track record when it came to being on time and missing work. News of the accident didn't sway them at all: they politely promised to be in touch after the holidays and that was all. I have about as much hope in that as I do in Jack having a change of heart tomorrow.

It had been one thing to let myself feel aimless and adrift before our trip since I was still focusing on getting better and stronger, testing my limits. The swimming we did in Bora Bora, or water therapy as I tried to call it with Dan, helped some, but I still have aches when standing too long. Overall, though, I've been feeling stronger, so I want something for myself. If that's a job, a hobby, or a volunteer position, I don't know. What I do know is that I don't want to feel so reliant on Charlie for everything, especially now that my relationship with him has changed so drastically. I can't just float around the apartment with nothing to do while Charlie is at work. My convalescence was a mixture of watching TV and reading books to pass the time. He was working long hours before he spirited me off to the other side of the world and I know it's only going to get worse now that we've returned. With PT taking up less of my time, I need a new focus.

Tired from physical therapy, I take the stairs to Charlie's office one at a time, carefully testing the strength of my knee as I go. I love the space he designed here. There are wall to wall bookcases ringing the room but they're bare. His desk is positioned at the window, providing him with a sweeping view overlooking Central Park. There is a half-scribbled-on notepad sitting just to the left of the desk, his handwriting smudged by the way his left hand drags across the page.

Setting my laptop on the desk, I contemplate what it is I'm doing up here. Very briefly, while I was in the hospital, I saw a therapist. It was short-lived because my anger was still too fresh for me to be open about what I was feeling. One of the tips she gave me before departing was to try journaling about my feelings. I had dismissed the suggestion, not wanting to admit there was anything wrong with me.

So today, I write. Similar to how I was one day ready to reach back out to Vivian, I'm finally in a headspace that will let me look on the events of the last few months without a dark heart closing me off. Bora Bora was exactly what the doctor ordered. It cleared my head for me to finally really process what happened in the accident outside of this closed off apartment.

I open a document and I pour all of my thoughts and feelings out onto the page, not wanting to stop. I write about the changes in myself and how it feels to have lost so much time. The document grows in length as I talk about the things that I had taken for granted, things so simple, like knowing my own favorite restaurants, like having friends.

The whole exercise is unexpectedly cathartic and I curse my stubbornness for not trying it sooner. It's a perfect way for me to work out how I've been feeling about the accident. When my words approach Thanksgiving and the trip, I hesitate. This is only for me, but writing about it makes it so real. Charlie has grounded me, stopped my emotions from casting me adrift.

I feel more alive with him, like I've touched something deep inside me that was dormant a long while before the accident. The feeling, I think, is hope, and I don't know what to make of it. I let my feelings settle and I sit back, looking at the length of what I've written. I catch the sob that tears through my chest before it reduces me to nothing. Eyes squeezed shut, I force the tears back down.

I begin to dig through my old emails to find my landlord's contact information and send him a message to find out what requirements there are for subletting the place. Then I spend what feels like hours deleting all the old marketing emails I've accumulated. Once my inbox is empty, it feels like a weight has been lifted from my chest. I feel like I'm on a roll, so I text Vivian, thanking her for brunch, for forgiving me, for being my friend. I knew I missed having someone to talk to, but until I had Vivian back, I hadn't realized how badly I needed it.

It's lunchtime when Charlie texts that he's going to be home for dinner and will finish work from here instead. Dinner for Charlie could be anywhere from six till ten, so I still have almost an entire day to come up with something to do. I reason with myself: I'm trying to return to work, so what does it matter if I charge a few more things on my already bloated credit cards? The apartment is in desperate need of sprucing up. I've learned about the rise of same day deliveries over the last five years, so I order a few things with a guaranteed delivery for today. Four hours later, I'm catching up on another procedural show when I get the call from the front desk that my packages have arrived.

One of the doormen, Benji, knocks on the door with the boxes. My eyes want to bulge out of my head when I set my sights on them.

"Hello, Miss Elia," he says, setting the boxes inside. I feel guilty that I have no cash to tip him and make a mental note to get him something nice for the holidays. I know Charlie had mentioned needing to tip the doormen after all the packages and guests they have had to accommodate since my arrival. I'm hardly the worst of the residents here, but I know how important our front desk is to keeping things running.

"Hi Benji, thanks for your help."

We chat for a bit about what I'm doing, and he loves the idea so much that he offers to come up and help after work, which I politely decline. I want to do this for me and Charlie, for our first Christmas, even if our relationship is just a fledgling one.

I work up a sweat hanging tinsel and lights around the stairs to the loft. I'm winded by walking up and down the stairs over and over again, struggling to wrap the delicate garland through the banister. My knee aches from using it like this, but I try to focus on how excited Charlie is going to be to see it all. The fake frosted window spray goes on easily. I can barely keep myself from dancing with delight as I spray it on, trying to make snowflake patterns as I go. The floor-to-ceiling windows make it difficult to get to the top, and it's going to be a bitch to clean up in a few weeks, but it's so bright and beautiful. Maybe I can convince him to let it stay until February. Little vinyl decals stick neatly to mirrors in the house, presents and snowmen in little crevices where he wouldn't expect to find them. I can only hope that Charlie is as delighted with the space as I am. All we need now is a Christmas tree.

Our relationship has done everything out of order, like living together before even kissing. However, I think of the magic and whimsy behind my grandparents' courtship: it was a no-nonsense arrangement, quick and full of love. They wasted no time after finding each other. I thought love stories like that had been lost as we started to expect more and want more from our partners. These days, knowing someone for only three months wasn't long enough to get engaged or married, but my grandparents' courtship had lasted only eight months from meeting to marriage. I knew the story well: of how my grandparents, both immigrants, met at a club and for two weeks straight, they talked. Tired of waiting, my grandmother demanded to know when he planned to ask her out. He proposed three months later, on Christmas Eve, and they were married the following May. Perhaps this was my chance at a whimsical love story. Maybe everyone had one, but they just didn't see it when it came around.

I'm reading on the couch when Charlie gets home at nine. I lean my head backward so I'm looking at him upside down when he enters. He drops his bag off to the side, shrugging his coat off and then hanging it up with care. Routine finished, he zeroes in on where I'm sitting, crossing to me in three easy strides before dropping to his knees to kiss me upside down. I see the allure of the Spiderman kiss as his tongue grazes mine.

"I'm sorry I'm late," he apologizes, standing. He pauses, finally noticing the change in the space around him. Christmas lights are flashing from the stairs, a different strand hung around each doorway, painstakingly coordinated to match his pre-existing décor.

"Did you do this?" he asks in wonder, picking up a nutcracker. Carefully, he fiddles with the lever behind it, his eyebrows lifting in surprise to find that it functions.

"No, I took a shower and came out and it was like this." I shrug, like it's the only thing that makes sense. I dig around for my bookmark, the one I always seem to misplace, and cram it into the spine.

Charlie sees the bowl of walnuts on the table, tests out the nutcracker, and a delighted laugh echoes in the room following the crunch. A smile tugs at my cheeks as I pad into the kitchen to start dinner. The burner clicks three times before the flames appear and I set the pot that's full of water atop it.

"You didn't eat yet?" he asks, eyes flitting all over the apartment, skipping from one decoration to the next. His voice is far away as he asks, a finger touching gently to the frosted windows, coming away with the artificial snow. Dumping the jarred sauce into a pan, I nearly drop it when Charlie strides over to me, pressing an urgent kiss to my lips. His lips nudge my mouth open, tongue darting against mine. I wrap my arms around his neck, and I stretch up on my toes so Charlie doesn't have to hunch as much. But he wants more, he wants me closer so he lifts me up by the waist and settles me on the counter beside the stove as the water is starting to boil.

"Thank you for doing this." The sincerity in his voice makes me weak.

"I was happy to." I loosen his tie and unbutton the top few buttons of his shirt. I stop before I go any further, knowing that if I keep going, I'm going to burn the water on the stove. "Go, get out of your work clothes while I finish up."

He kisses the tip of my nose, stepping away so I can finish making dinner.

"I need a job," I shout to him, stirring the pasta sauce. I'm balancing on my bad leg, trying to strengthen it. Little tasks like these, like slowly lifting onto the tips of my toes, make me feel better about myself.

"You do not need a job," Charlie says, returning to the kitchen. He's distracting, wearing just his boxers, and I have to focus, really focus on what I'm doing as he sets up his laptop, never far from work.

"Says the guy who leaves the house every day for his *job*," I emphasize, turning to face him. I refuse to let my eyes dip from his face when he walks over to me to taste the sauce that I've been haphazardly dropping seasonings into. "I do PT and then I just read or watch TV or stare out the window. I'm a drain on resources. I need to do something fulfilling." I drop the spoon onto the bright red spoon rest, something I rescued from my old apartment. Something that made Charlie's space just a touch less "aggressive bachelor pad that could be used for photoshoots."

I don't face Charlie, dumping the pasta into the water, trying to keep my mind on the task at hand. He wraps his arms around me from behind, grinding against my bottom. I go perfectly still, like an animal caught in the sights of a predator. His fingers slip into the band of my shorts before grazing lower, lower, lower, hitting home when he finds the apex of my thighs. I bite back a harsh breath as his fingers start to make lazy circles against my clit. He kisses my neck, nipping at my ear.

"I'll give you something fulfilling," he growls, rubbing my most sensitive spot. I let out a noise, somewhere caught between a moan and a squeal, squirming away from him.

"That is *not* what I meant, and you know it," I admonish.

He laughs, stirring the pot for me. "Your focus for the last few months has been healing. You still technically have a traumatic brain injury. You need to give yourself some grace." He starts to pull out plates and the parmesan cheese. "If you want, I can fire my assistant and then we can have hot sex while I'm on mute during a conference call."

I grab the grater, and turn to him, pointing it at him threateningly. "A, don't fire Ashley. B, you say this like you have experience." I tickle his sides, making him squirm.

"No, but someone else did once and forgot to mute it. Never did find out exactly who it was," he says as he plates the food. "But I get it. You're bored, and I've somehow managed to become the center of your world with all things, unintentionally. What do you want to do? You were working on art before. I don't think you ever told me what your major was in college. You enjoyed taking photos on our trip, maybe look into that. But please don't feel like you *need* a job right now. I just want you healthy and whole." He kisses my forehead. "Bon appétit, baby."

It's a lot to think about and I appreciate the latitude that he's giving me. I decide to walk around Central Park tomorrow and take photos for a few hours while I try to answer the age-old question: what do I want to be when I grow up?

I'm unsure of how to broach this next subject. Once we're seated, I mull over how to dive in and decide to attack it head first.

"Have you reached out to your mom?" I ask, taking a bite of pasta.

He looks up at me and then over at his phone. "I did. She invited us over for Christmas dinner. Well, she invited me and I told her that I would have a plus-one." He sounds nervous about all of this and I wonder if I've made a mistake pushing him on this.

"If you want to spend time with your mother and brother without me, I'll understand."

We'd gone from zero to sixty in an unbelievable amount of time. We never have to worry about introducing him to my parents, but how do we explain how we went from strangers to living together in three months, even if it was out of order? I wonder if his family will think I'm just a gold digger, taking advantage of Charlie's generosity.

"No, I don't want that. I want you there. I'm just not looking forward to the questions and the judgment that's going to come with it. There is no getting around how we met and why we are living together. As much as I think it will make a great story someday, the wounds are still very fresh," he says, reaching over to the raised scar on my leg.

"Did you know my grandparents had a whirlwind romance?" I turn in my seat to look at him, pushing away my plate. My hand goes to his on my knee, turning it over so I can hold it. He has so much strength in him, but I think he prefers to hide behind it instead of letting himself be seen. "They met in October, got engaged on Christmas Eve, and got married in May. My dad was born in January of the next year." I hop off my chair at the island and swivel him so I can settle between his legs. Gingerly, I brush a blond lock out of his face. I never get tired of the chiseled features of his face, as if Michelangelo himself had carved him from marble.

"I don't think there is a right or wrong amount of time to know someone or to be with them. I really believe that when you meet the right person, you know." I kiss him softly on the lips, then below each ear, taking his face in my hands.

"Besides, the hard part is living together. Seeing if you can tolerate their quirks, and we have been doing that pretty well for the last three months. That could make or break a couple."

He cups my face in his large hands and I lean into them, into the unexpected warmth. "I'll text her and tell her we're coming."

All talk of his mother stops as he hops off the stool, the rest of his meal forgotten. He kisses me gently, pulling my body against his, first by my waist and then his hands travel lower, to my ass. He squeezes my cheeks, walking me backward to the bedroom. We move like we've done this before, going from the kitchen to the bedroom, a tangle of limbs and kisses, trying to claim more of the other. He pushes me back on the bed, following me as I go. I scoot back so he has more space but then I stop.

I wish he had something on so I could use it to pull him toward me, but I settle for his face, palms grazing a fresh layer of scruff on his cheeks. I don't know what I did to deserve such a guy, but I'm not going to let him go.

Charlie must see the hungry look in my eyes, "We have all the time in the world for us."

He lowers his body down to mine, kissing my mouth and my neck. I fight a giggle as he tickles my neck, his hands working their way up my sides to take off my shirt. In my rush to sit up to aid him, I bang my head against his, and we both rub the spot I hit while laughing.

"I said *patience*," he orders, taking my shirt off and casting it aside.

With one hand he teases my nipple using his finger tip to draw circles around it before taking the raised center between his forefinger and thumb pinching gently, waking up every nerve in my body. His other hand continues to travel down my side to my pajama bottoms. He doesn't move to my core; instead, he grips my hip and rocks against me, his mouth finding mine. I feel his hardness against me, almost whimpering at the solidness of his cock.

I reach for his boxers again, and he grabs my wrists, setting both hands above me, gentle and forceful at the same time. I'm glad then that I'd ordered handcuffs and restraints for Christmas, for some light fun later on. He lets me go so he can take off his boxers. There is a silent command in his brown eyes to stay where I am and to not move a muscle. I obey willingly.

Charlie whips his boxers off, leaving them in a puddle at his feet. He stands beside the bed, erect and ready for me. I look at him from head to toe, admiring, always admiring the Greek god of a man who decided that he wanted to be with me. He grabs a condom from the nightstand, sliding it on before he settles between my legs. I reach for him, but he's lightning quick, capturing my wrists and holding them above my head as he teases me with the tip of his cock. I try to lift my hips to meet him, and he pulls back, watching me squirm.

"This is fifty shades of fucking unfair." My voice is strangled, and his laughter rumbles until he thrusts deep inside me. I cry out, calling his name for the first time, and I love how it sounds. He takes his time, slowly drawing sounds of pleasure from me with each move of his hips. My back arches and I press hard into him as the pressure inside me builds, growing with every movement he takes. Charlie's face is in the crook of my neck, his mouth nipping and sucking as he helps me reach release. My whole body feels limp under him, but I keep my hips moving in rhythm with him.

He's not done with me yet, as he flips me over, giving me a different angle and pleasure point. Charlie grips my hips, starting slow again, seeing what speed and depth drive a bigger reaction. His fingers trace the angel wings on the small of my back.

"I don't know how I could forget about this," he purrs, gripping me tightly.

"Oh God," I pant as he picks up speed, slamming into me to the hilt. My face digs into the pillow in front of me and my hands clench the headboard. A moan, deep and feral, escapes my throat as I have a second orgasm. I can't see Charlie's face, but I can imagine how smug he is. His movements slow, and he withdraws. I collapse facedown in a heap, boneless and spent.

"You didn't finish," I point out as I flip over and he starts to get off the bed. He doesn't say anything, only offering a small shrug. I scooch to the edge of the bed, grab his shoulder, and stop him. I tug him back to me, pulling his face to mine. The kiss is slow and deep, my mouth opening to him, our tongues dancing against each other. The kiss moves from sweet to hot.

"I want you to come," I insist as I eyeball his cock, which still appears to be ready for me. His Adam's apple bobs as he looks at me.

"I won't argue with that." He places his knees on either side of me, lifts my legs so that my ankles are on his shoulders, and he kisses the insides of my legs. He presses a kiss to the scar on my leg. Gripping my hips, he tugs me against him, and he thrusts to the hilt. I cry out, biting my lip at the suddenness and he stills.

"Don't stop," I plead.

Charlie doesn't and I can see the pleasure on his face as he moves slowly. His thumb moves between my legs, rubbing small concentric circles around my clit. There is power in watching the impact you have on your partner as they move to the absolute bliss that an orgasm brings. A smaller wave of my own pleasure follows.

"That feels like a record," Charlie teases, an eyebrow quirking upwards. He climbs off me and heads to the bathroom. I follow him and watch him in the mirror as we both clean up.

"Someone seems proud of himself."

He kisses the top of my head. "Seems like something I should be proud of: getting a woman to orgasm three times in a row."

Even I can't help the smirk on my face. "Two and a half," I say, trying to keep his ego in check.

"Sure." He nods, his face burying a smirk of his own while also telling me that he doesn't believe me at all. "I still have work to do. You should get some sleep and we can talk more in the morning."

I gnaw on my lip, trying not to feel like a child being put to bed. I know he probably should have stayed at work later and made a huge sacrifice by coming home when he did. That car had hit me at two in the morning, which had been a normal time for him to leave.

I bury that feeling, though, because I know that he's trying to manage both work and a new relationship. I don't know much about his ex, but I know that the relationship collapsed around his work schedule. I'm determined not to give up on him. I'm exactly where I'm meant to be.

Fifteen

IN THE MORNING I broach the subject of needing a key to the apartment for myself. I'm hardly held captive here, free to come and go as I please, but usually one of the doormen has to let me back in when I return. Charlie admits that I have a point and that night when he comes home, he hands me a small box. I shouldn't be surprised when I see a key sitting inside, but I still am.

"What will I give you for our first Christmas now?" he moans, feigning dismay.

"You're sure you're okay with this? Giving me a key? You don't feel like we're moving too fast?" I ask, holding it in my hand. The key is on a bicycle keychain. For a moment, I can't decide if it's too much dark humor, but then I smile. It's just the right amount.

"Do *you* feel like we're moving too fast?" He ducks to look me in the eye, his fingers grazing my chin, lifting my head to look at him.

My lips twist into a scowl. "Answering a question with a question is so annoying," I retort, stalling. "I'm okay with it, but I'm not the one whose friends and family are worried about me being manipulated by some gold digger."

Charlie takes my hands, with the keyring wrapped around a

finger, and plops next to me on the couch. There is no hesitation to what he has to say. "Fuck them."

I laugh.

"No, seriously, fuck them. I think we can both agree that you hardly sought me out. You didn't dive in front of my car knowing I was in it, planning to get my money. I think we can also agree that this has been something more for a while, even before the trip. I know I was afraid to say anything to you." He pauses.

"We both spent so much time worrying that the other might feel they were being taken advantage of, that we never said what we meant or what we wanted to say. At least, I did for those first few months. So I'm going to say it." He pauses again and looks meaningfully into my eyes. "Move in. Keep your apartment if you want, so you know you have somewhere to fall back to, but I told you before and I'll tell you again: I'm all in."

I kiss him, squeezing the key between our hands, the ridges imprinting on my skin. A brief thought dances through my head: maybe it's finally time to visit my old apartment, now that I'm in a different headspace.

I wait for Charlie to leave for work the next day before heading for my old apartment. My first obstacle is the stairs down to the subway and my second is the stairs back up again. I've lived in New York long enough to know that you don't get into an empty subway car when the other cars are packed and you avoid the elevators unless absolutely necessary: two lessons I learned the hard way.

I regret my bravado when I emerge from my old subway stop and realize that I still have to climb seven stories up to the apartment. I walk slowly despite the frigid temperatures, stopping for a coffee on my way. I rest my leg and savor the gingerbread latte, letting it warm me from the inside out. The scar on my leg is throbbing, the muscles overused and tired from physical therapy the day before.

Standing at the bottom of the stairs and looking up at them, I have regrets. Regrets about coming here, regrets about not taking a cab, regrets about ever having thought that a seventh floor walk-up would be fine. I can't imagine ever thinking it was a good idea. I try to get up the stairs through sheer force of will, but by the third floor landing, I have to sit. For an angry moment, I don't even care that I'm blocking the stairs. I almost want an old lady to trip over me so I don't have to walk all the way up.

A hand rests on my shoulder and gives me a shake. "Shit or get off the pot, girlie," a grizzled voice says from behind me.

I twist quickly and spy a spry older woman, almost like I had willed her into existence. Her long coat is open and she has a colorful, homemade scarf that matches her striking ice-blue eyes. She narrows her eyes at me before recognition brightens them.

"Elia?" There is a touch of kindness in her voice that I didn't anticipate. She had seemed like the quintessential New Yorker, in a rush to get where she's going, intolerant of obstacles.

"Yes. Do we know each other?"

Her eyes harden, so extremely expressive. "We've only been neighbors for two years." When I don't confirm I know her, she continues. "What, you hit your head or something?"

"Actually, I was hit by a car, if you must know. I don't remember much from the last few years."

She seems to consider this as she walks around me, making an unintelligible noise in response to this revelation. "Good. Means a nice clean slate. Maybe you'll make the right call and move out of this miserable building. Where have you been?" She stops on the landing in front of me, waiting for an answer. She doesn't seem callous or mean, just matter-of-fact.

"I don't know if you would believe me if I told you." Sometimes I don't even believe it.

"Well, good for you. Are you home for good?"

"I think I'm just going to live on this stair for the rest of my life."

"It's hardly the best that the building has to offer. What's wrong with you?"

"I broke my ankle and hurt my knee. This building has a lot of stairs."

"That's why I like it. Keeps people from visiting me." Her brow is scrunched, still puzzling over me. She reaches into her bag to pull out a bottle of acetaminophen with a bright red arthritis-friendly cap. With ease, she opens it and deposits two into her hand, handing them off to me.

"Thank you." I dry-swallow the pills, grateful for them. "I'm sorry, but I don't remember your name."

She waves me off. "Letty. I live across the hall from you."

I realize then that she might be my best link to my missing life...or at least the last two years. "Letty. Did I have a lot of visitors?"

She regards me shrewdly, her thin lips twisting. "It's best to leave the past in the past. You seem healthy despite the bum leg. If you found a place with an elevator, stay there. Nothing good will come of poking about for skeletons in your own closet." She checks her watch and I notice that it's an old-fashioned analog one.

"That's not an answer," I point out.

She doesn't care, continuing down the stairs. "If you're smart, girl, you'll listen to me," she grumbles, adding under her breath, "Not that you ever did before."

She doesn't give me another chance to question her, disappearing down the stairs. I let the mystery of Letty hover over me for a few more minutes before dredging up the strength to continue on my way upstairs.

My faded welcome mat still greets me, informing anyone who

knocks to not bother unless they have tacos. I twist the key and am met with a dusty smell, a reminder that the apartment has been vacant for months. My first visit had been so disorienting, warped by a haze of pain and confusion.

The heavy door slams shut behind me, enclosing me in the apartment. It's more space than I remember, a rare find in New York City, a genuine one-bedroom that didn't cost a small fortune. I walk into the bedroom, my fingers grazing the blanket my mother knit for me when I went to college. It's on top of the family quilt that luckily survived the fire.

The first apartment Vivian and I had shared in New York had heat that would cut out unpredictably during the winter, so my mother had overnighted me the quilt with a handwritten note: *May the love of family help keep you warm during these cold winter nights!* On the back she'd hastily added: *No boys!* I know I saved the note and I hope I can find it somewhere.

Looking through my closet now, I find that weeding out clothes is quick and easy: I soon find that most of the clothes are the wrong sizes, and I can't imagine ever wearing some of what hangs in there anyway. Most of it is flowy and loose, and maybe I could have gotten away with wearing some of it, but I know that it would be better to just donate the lot.

There is a nearly-empty box of trash bags under the sink and I use the last of them to bag everything up, telling myself that even if I can't find somewhere to donate the clothes today, I can always leave the bags in the apartment to take care of later. I snap a picture, sending it to Vivian with an emoji with crossed eyes. Her response is immediate: she's nearby and offers to meet for lunch. The idea of leaving and coming back is unbearable, so I invite her over instead.

She steps into the space with a similar reaction to mine. The apartment could be a short-term rental, for all the personal touches that are around -- a handful of photos tacked to one wall are the only giveaway that someone lived here, that it wasn't just tired travelers coming and going. The Ikea furniture is bland and beaten and there isn't any art to lend some personality to the white walls, whose paint is peeling in corners and around the door jamb. I've seen vacant apartments look more inviting than mine.

"So this is it? Well, I don't blame you for staying with Charlie considering that those stairs are a bitch." Vivian is breathing heavily, bracing a hand on the back of the couch.

"This is it, yeah. My humble abode. I was just cleaning out the clothes I have here." I wait a beat before continuing, "Charlie asked me to move in with him for real."

She looks like the cat that ate the canary, eyes bulging just a little, biting her lip to prevent the smirk from spreading. "So, are you?" she asks mildly, but I'm not fooled. The excitement brims in her voice. Vivian snoops nonchalantly around the bookshelf, skimming the titles of the books and movies. When she reaches the DVDs, she grabs *Sorority House Horror Three: Topless and Terrified,* holding it up and looking at me with surprise. "You *hate* horror movies."

"I know!" I exclaim, dropping onto the couch. "Yeah, I think I will. I mean, on the one hand, we've known each other for such a short amount of time. But on the other hand, we've already been living together for almost all of it anyway. As soon as I was discharged, he moved me into his place, after coming over to see what the situation would be here."

She picks up a picture frame that had been face down on the bookshelf. I'm the only person in the picture, the Eiffel Tower behind me. It's an older photo, my eyes shielded by cheap sunglasses and a wide-brimmed sun hat.

"I took this picture." She's smiling wistfully, as she returns it to its spot. "We went right after I moved in with Connor. It was part of my post-bar trip. We spent two weeks eating baguettes and getting drunk under the Eiffel Tower."

My heart breaks that I don't remember this at all. "We'll make new memories." My voice cracks awkwardly, but Vivian offers a smile, squeezing my shoulder.

"For what it's worth, I think you and Charlie are good together. Also, like, special circumstances. I know it's reality TV, but there *is* a reason that relationships start on Big Brother. You're in close proximity, you're limited in what you can do, all your time is spent with the other person. Ainsley couldn't handle not being the center of his world, but you're more independent than that."

I'm looking through my desk drawers when she says this and I spin around. "Ainsley?" I ask, hoping that my voice isn't too colored by curiosity and jealousy.

"Yeah, his ex-fiancée. They broke up about a year ago, maybe? She hated the long hours that he worked and bounced. They were supposed to get married this fall." Vivian isn't looking at me because she's poking around in the bags of clothes. I'm glad she's not really paying attention to me, because I feel like I've been sucker punched. Did we go on his honeymoon? Is that why we got the champagne and the flower petals? My heart sinks. Vivian finally looks up and sees the look on my face and even after years apart, she's able to read my mind.

"Oh, honey. I doubt that's what your trip was about. And even if it was, *you* were with him, not her."

I try to take her words to heart, but I know I'm going to have to talk to him about this later; this feels like another pretty large omission on his part. Now I feel even more concerned that maybe we are going too fast.

"I don't know how independent I can really claim to be, since I'm living with him, not working, and spending all my time with him."

"Okay, well, again, extenuating circumstances. Besides, you made it here all on your own. These setbacks are temporary. What's with these clothes?" Vivian attempts to redirect the conversation.

"I'm just going to donate them all."

She nods absently and sits on my bed, running her fingers over the quilt. "I think about your mom a lot. Whenever I'm about to make a big life change, I wonder what she would think. She always had the best life advice."

"Like 'If the sex isn't good don't waste your time,' you mean?" A wave of grief hits me.

"I think the exact saying was, 'If it's not giving you an opportunity, an orgasm, or joy, then fuck it, but not literally.'"

We laugh, both fighting back tears now.

"She would have loved Charlie. She would have seen how much he cares about you and how much he has taken care of you." Vivian squeezes my hand and I know she's right. We reminisce some more about college and our first apartment, while I move to the bathroom to clean out my medicine cabinet. I pause, fishing out a bottle of allergy medicine. I look at it, confused for a minute, before setting it back where it was, tossing an expired prescription bottle into the trash.

"You have allergies? Since when?" Vivian asks, sitting on my suitcase to cram my blankets into it.

"I don't know." I look at it, wondering whether I should hold on to it, but decide to leave it on my shelf. Passing back through to the bedroom, I collect some picture frames, the photo from Paris and one of my parents from my graduation, and make sure they are in the bag I'm taking back to Charlie's.

Our trek down the stairs is slow and full of slap-happy giggles as we both struggle. Maybe it's going down instead of up, maybe it's the Tylenol from earlier, or maybe it's just having Vivian by my side, but my knee doesn't bother me as much. We split a cab back downtown, since, she says, she's played hooky from work long enough.

Vivian has gotten me thinking again about who I want to be and where I want this relationship to take me. I know that in time, Charlie and I will figure out the 'getting to know each other' part. I tell myself that the important thing is that I don't hate how he chews or whether he leaves his cup of water beside his bed all night and day.

Benji offers to help me with my bags when I get back to the apartment, but I decline, determined to complete my task myself. I started out on my own and I made it back to the apartment on my own too.

Once the task is complete, I'm filled with pride. The first thing I take out of my bag is the photo from Paris, but the buzz of my phone on the table startles me and I drop it, frowning when it hits the ground. The text is innocuous, just Vivian saying that she hopes that we can hang out soon, even if it means earning the ire of her boss, but the back of the picture frame has popped open.

Scooping the picture off the ground, I see that there is a second photo tucked behind the one of just me. In it, my arms are looped around Vivian's middle, her arms around my shoulders, both of us grinning like we'd won the lottery. Behind us is Notre Dame, so I assume it's another picture from our mysterious trip to Paris. I swap the pictures, placing this one in the front of the thankfully uninjured frame, and find it a home on top of the dresser.

After unpacking the rest of my meager possessions, I dive into the next herculean task I've assigned myself for the day: sorting through the hundreds of photos I took during our two weeks away. I have two cameras and a phone full of pictures to inspect and I'm eager to order pictures to hang on the walls.

I start with Photoshop, another charge to my credit card to worry about later. Muscle memory seems to kick in as I remember which tools I need and where to find them and I work hard, sharpening some parts and lightening others. I fall so deep into editing the photos that I'm startled by a knock at the door. I holler that I'm coming, taking care to save my progress before hurrying to the door. Benji smiles behind the peephole and I pull the door open, confused.

"Deliveries, Miss Elia."

I smile as I open the door, not sure what it could be now. He hands me the boxes, and once they're in my hands, a muted clink of metal on metal tells me exactly what's inside. I fight the tug of a different sort of smile on my lips while Benji is still standing there. Once the door is closed, my body shivers in anticipation, thinking of what is contained in the light box.

Charlie texts as the sun sets, telling me that his debt has come due and I shouldn't wait for him for dinner, that he's not going to be home until late. I give it the old college try to wait for him anyway, finding some movies from the last five years to try to watch while snacking on leftover pasta. It's an abject failure when I fall asleep on the couch.

My dream involves dancing baguettes and the Eiffel Tower exploding like a giant bottle of champagne, the bubbly beverage frothing over until the Seine flows golden with endless amounts of the liquid. Distantly, I hear the front door close and am startled awake. My nerves still seem to be frayed, given how easily I've been startled lately.

"What are you still doing up?" he whispers, as if he can lull me back to sleep. My back arches as I stretch, a huge yawn giving away how tired I really am. The clock on the cable box tells me that it's after one in the morning, practically an early night for him. I toss the blanket aside, rising from the couch onto my toes as I deepen my stretch, my tank rising up, showing my midriff. Setting his laptop on the island, Charlie's eyes drink in the length of my legs and the bare skin of my torso.

"I was watching a movie and must have fallen asleep. How was work?" I ask, leaning up to kiss him. This taste of domesticity reminds me that my feelings for him are real. I want this life with him, even if that comes with late nights. It's worth it with him.

"Ah, you know, same old shit. My dad is riding me about having been out for two weeks, but that's nothing new. For a CEO he's really too invested in a lowly Managing Director like me."

"Something about that job title doesn't scream lowly to me." I take his mention of the trip as my opening. "Can I ask you something?"

He nods, getting himself a glass of water, and I think affectionately of the collection of empty glasses I had cleaned up earlier in the day.

"Was our trip supposed to be your honeymoon?"

Charlie chokes on his water and sets down the glass, looking alarmed. "I'm sorry, what gave you that idea?" he asks, not answering the question.

I stay silent, fighting the urge to cross my arms, not wanting to seem defensive or confrontational. When I say nothing, he leans against the counter, crossing *his* arms -- definitely defensive.

"No, that's not what that trip was. I'm going to guess Vivian told you?" He doesn't wait for my response before continuing. "Ainsley and I were supposed to get married the weekend before the accident. She called it off during Christmas last year after I spent Thanksgiving, Christmas Eve, and Christmas Day working. She threw the ring in my face and left. We were supposed to go to Seychelles for our honeymoon. I can't tell you how often it crosses my mind that if I had gotten married, I wouldn't have been in that car that hit you. And you would be whole now." He scratches behind his head, looking away from me. His tone shifts from defensive to angry. "She is in my past. If it makes you feel better to know that you're not a rebound, I went on a few dates in the spring. Do you want to know my number? Fifteen. I will tell you anything and everything you want to know. I have no secrets. You don't need to go behind my back to find anything out," he bites out that last, pushing past me to go to the bedroom.

I follow him. "I didn't go behind your back. Vivian mentioned it, so I asked. I do feel like I'm entitled to know." I hate that I feel defensive now, but his tone set me on edge.

"Entitled is one word for it." His laugh is harsh as he starts to undress. He's rough about tugging out his tie, haphazardly dropping it off to the side. Charlie doesn't look at me as he unbuttons his shirt, peels it off, balls it up, and throws it at the hamper with force. I'm standing next to the hamper when he does this, and I flinch, turning my head away from where it landed just short of its target. Charlie goes utterly still at that, his eyes searching, looking for something, anything, to explain my reaction. I'm just as aware of it as he is and for a moment neither of us knows what to say.

"Do you think I would hit you?" he whispers, horrified, not moving. There is something like betrayal laced into his voice, that I could think he was capable of raising a hand to me.

Eager to change the subject, I sit on the corner of the bed, closer to where he stands. "No, I don't think that. I don't know why I did that." I take a breath. "Entitled was the wrong word, but you asked me to live with you, past just my recovery. I didn't go behind your back, it came up. I knew there was an ex-fiancée, you did mention her, but I guess I had envisioned her in the far-away past, not that this was the week that ended your engagement only last year. Can you blame me for being a little insecure? I'm afraid that this is just some hero complex where you feel like you need to save me and take care of me after the accident and that after I'm healed you won't want me anymore."

Charlie still doesn't move from where he is, and for a moment, it hurts that he doesn't come to me since I have just laid bare my biggest fear. I would be less vulnerable if I was naked.

"Baby," his voice is soft as he finally crosses to me. His large hands are gentle as he places them on my shoulders, as if trying not to startle an injured bird. They trail slowly down my arms to my hands, which he wraps around his waist, hugging me to his stomach. "It's like Jack; only time is going to prove it to you. I'm not going anywhere and you have nothing to be insecure about. I haven't heard from Ainsley since she moved out. I bought this apartment to start over, away from any memories that we had in our old place. There are no ghosts of fiancées past lingering here. This place is all us and *our* memories."

I pull away gently, pressing my forehead to his chest, then my lips to his stomach as I hold onto him.

I rise to kiss him softly on the mouth, both of us focused on giving more of ourselves to one another in any way we can. He lifts me, my legs wrapping around his middle, as he leans me back to the center of the bed. My lips won't leave his, not even to take off my shirt, so he just pushes it up, his hand palming my breast. I fumble with his belt, pulling him back against me when he tries to pull away to handle it himself. I don't care that it's needy of me but I just don't want him to let go of me at all. Charlie doesn't bother with taking his pants off, pulling himself free, pausing at my entrance. He's fast with the condom, pulling it from thin air and sliding it on. He thrusts inside me, slow and insistent, and I don't stop him.

Our lovemaking is slow that night, each of us giving to the other in turn. We don't care about the late hour. We take our time, wait until our partner is satisfied and their needs are met. We fall asleep cuddled close, each providing safe harbor for the other in the storm.

Sixteen

A TEXT from Charlie warns that he will be home by seven for dinner. A surprise, to be sure, but a welcome one. I assumed that leading up to Christmas Eve all his work nights would be late, like the previous evening. The goodies I had ordered online were burning a figurative hole in my head. All I want to do is break them out, unable to wait until Christmas. I had a terrible habit of keeping surprises, often giving my parents gifts before their birthdays or holidays, too eager to see their responses.

Charlie keeping me updated on his trip home means that I can whip out some of what I bought without waiting too long in an uncomfortable g-string. I spend the hour before he gets home lighting candles and struggling into a lace bustier and a black thong. I pull my blonde hair up away from my face in a hasty clip, imagining myself pulling it out and letting my hair tumble around my shoulders while I ride him. After several curses I forgot I knew, each more imaginative than the last, I manage to attach the garter hooks to the stockings.

The full length mirror offers a perfect glimpse of how it will look when Charlie gets home. I alternate between barefoot and black stilettos, admiring the length they seem to add to my legs.

The stilettos might be overdoing it, but I feel sexy and powerful wearing them. I slip the silk robe on and try out a few poses for how he will come home to find me. Should I be lying in bed, waiting and ready? Should I greet him at the door? I check myself out in the mirror again, admiring how full my breasts are and how my ass looks thanks to all the squats I do in physical therapy.

While in my apartment the day before, I came across a vibrator in my nightstand and was surprised. I had never really taken things into my own hands, having had a steady stream of monogamous relationships from high school through college. Masturbation for women was so taboo, that I never thought much about it. But now with the weight of it in my hand, I wonder what it would be like to do it. I wash it off, careful of the battery. I know enough to grab the lube from Charlie's nightstand. Even if I don't do it before he arrives, maybe we could play with it some, or I could use it tomorrow to pass the day away.

I sit on the edge of the bed and turn it on, feeling it shake in my hand. I smirk, checking my phone and seeing that Charles' ETA is in five minutes, so maybe I can get myself primed.

I move the fabric of my thong to the side and press the vibrator to my clit gently at first, testing. I let out a hard breath and wonder why I haven't tried this sooner. I increase the pressure, my breath becoming a little more insistent as I squirm against it, trying to figure out how to move when a cock isn't involved.

I'm so alert, and on edge, that I hear the jangle of keys as the first of the three locks is undone. I quickly turn off the vibrator and stash it in my nightstand for later. The heels slow me down as I try to be silent, moving on the balls of my feet so Charlie doesn't hear me get into position. I let the silk robe drop off my shoulders and gather at my elbows, and I try a few poses quickly to see what feels more natural as the second lock clicks. I put one hand on my hip, then the other, and then both, before settling on just one. I cock my hip to the side and brace my hand against the door jam. I hear the last lock click and the door swings open.

"Hello, Mr. Breckenridge," I purr, only to scream when I see that it's not Charlie at the door. I quickly pull the robe around me and stand up straight, desperate to cover as much of my skin as possible. The man before me is Charlie, but aged thirty years, a permanent frown line creasing around his mouth. I know that face because I've seen it in pictures in the apartment, somehow looking disapproving even in photos where he should be happy. I quickly tie the robe shut. All euphoria that has been building in me is gone. My hands clasp on my chest to further keep it closed, as if he could see through the dark fabric.

"You must be the strumpet that has kept my son from doing his job for the last few months." He takes off his coat, seemingly unbothered by my state of undress. He hangs the coat up in the closet and makes himself at home as he shuts the door behind him.

"You must be Charlie's dad," I respond, my voice sounding strangled even to my own ears. His name eludes me and I wonder if I've ever actually heard it. I guess it makes sense that his father would have keys to the apartment, in case of emergencies, but this is so far from an emergency, no matter how on fire my face is.

"I have to guess by the way you answered the door that Charles is not home yet?" he asks, already knowing the answer. I'm practically dismissed as he unpacks his laptop, setting it on the island. I'm still frozen in place, distinctly aware of how see-through the bustier is and that I am wearing a thong. The robe is barely long enough to cover my ass entirely, and I think his father has already had enough of a show. The key to survival in this moment is making no sudden movements.

"He should be here any minute. He was picking up dinner because he had to work on a proposal tonight."

Charlie's dad walks past me and sits on the couch, crossing his legs and grabbing a magazine off the table as if this was a waiting room. I tug the robe down as far as I can, my face still burning with embarrassment. The shock is wearing off and other emotions, namely horror, are sinking in.

"So you, what, thought you would distract him further with sex?" He glances over at me, taking in the sight of the kitten heels and garter that peeks out under the robe. "You remind me of my ex-wife." The way he says it tells me that's not a good thing.

"Can I get you anything while you wait?" I ask, slipping back into receptionist mode, the only way I will survive the ticking clock until Charlie gets home. I try to push past the feelings of objectification.

"I'll have an espresso."

I slip back into our room while his attention isn't on me, grab a pair of sweats, and pull them on over my stockings. I abandon the heels and pad barefoot back to the kitchen. I look at the time and say nothing as I flick on the machine, letting the water warm up. I never have the drink myself, but I took it upon myself to learn how to make espresso when it became obvious that Charlie preferred to drink them while working for hours on the weekends.

My breathing is focused as I try to work through the next few steps that I'm going to take in getting through tonight. Give Charlie's dad his drink and then get changed into the largest clothes in the apartment. I focus on willing the drip to go faster so that I can get the espresso to Charlie's dad and then put on more clothes.

Charlie walks in as I hand his father the drink.

"So, I know how you said you love soup dumplings so I got an order to go from that place in Chinatown that you mentioned you like. It took a little longer than I expected to get here from downtown. I tried to mislead you a little with my ETA," Charlie announces as he walks in the door, proud of himself for the surprise. He sets the bag of food on the island and then his eyes land on his father. He subtly stands taller, and his voice gets a little deeper.

"Dad." Charlie doesn't know where to go next. "What brings you by?" Clearly, Charlie wasn't the only one with a surprise on his mind.

"I wanted to go over your proposal. I went by your office and you were gone so I came here, assuming you would be home. Imagine my surprise." His father sips his drink, clearly unbothered by the discomfort in the room. His cold brown eyes flit to me for a half a second, before dismissing me.

"Right, I'm going to get changed and then we can talk over dinner. We have plenty of extra food." Charlie grabs my arm gently, leading me into our bedroom and cutting off any response his father may have. Charlie leans against the door, closing his eyes.

"Not exactly how I imagined meeting your father," I quip, trying to lighten the mood. Charlie opens his eyes, reaches forward, and unties my robe to get a good look at what I'm wearing. He groans.

"Shit," he bites out, not angrily. "You answered the door in that?" He reaches a hand forward, rubbing his thumb over my breast before withdrawing his hand quickly. He walks around me to his dresser and starts pulling out clothes to change into. I take off the robe, toss it to the side, and bend over to grab my own clothes to change into. Charlie catches a glimpse of me bent over and through gritted teeth, he curses again. I don't even hear him cross the room, before I feel his hands on my hips, pulling my ass against his rock hard cock. He gives me a playful spank.

"My God, what I wouldn't give to have gotten home before him," he says into my neck as I stand. I do the man no favors by grinding against him before pulling away.

"Unfortunately, you were not and now your father has seen me half naked." I gesture to my body and the lack of clothes. Charlie fights to hide a smirk. "I swear to God if you laugh I'm sleeping in the guest room tonight."

He quickly smothers the smirk and bites his lips, but his amusement still shines in his eyes. I would tease Charlie, peeling the clothes off slowly, but I'm too frantic and worried about his father sitting outside.

"Can we also talk about the fact that your father has a key to this apartment?" I ask as we both strip.

"How about we save this argument for later, dear?" Charlie agrees tersely. We emerge from our room, both in t-shirts and sweats, eager to be done with his father's visit.

In the living room, we find his father has moved from the couch to the table, his laptop open before him. His father won't even look up at us.

"That was fast. With a body like hers, I would have taken my time," his father says, a plate of soup dumplings in front of him.

Charlie places his hand on the small of my back. "Dad, that was seriously uncalled for." Charlie grits his teeth as he says this. My cheeks are burning for the second time tonight.

His father doesn't apologize but he stands up and joins us at the island. "I'm Charles Senior, and you are?" He offers his hand to me, a bare minimum of respect. I hold my head high, determined not to be cowed by this man. I have nothing to be ashamed of. He's the one who should feel dirty talking about his son's girlfriend like she's a commodity and right in front of her, no less. I'll never have to wonder why he's on his fourth divorce.

"Elia," I say, taking his hand and shaking it. Just as quickly as he introduces himself, he dismisses me. He starts in on Charlie about investment figures and quantitative analysis for the proposal. I feel largely forgotten as I suck down my soup dumplings and rice, standing inside the kitchen. They go back and forth trading numbers and jabs about how best to handle the deal.

I shouldn't have let the insecure voice in my head win out, because I know Charlie. He presses a kiss to the side of my head before placing his hands on either side of me on the island, pinning me in place. Of course I wasn't forgotten. I feel his breath on my neck, surprising me.

"I know my dad, so this is going to take a really long time. Why don't you turn in? No need to wait up for me." He kisses me again before moving their operation to the dining room table.

I settle into my spot on the couch, legs curled under me. I set my laptop on my knees and go back to editing my photos. I post a few of my favorites to Pictogram and order a couple of canvases to hang up. I look at some of the commission work I was given, trying to get a feel for what I had been doing before. Most of the commission pieces have been passed on to other artists due to my extended absence. My tablet sits on the coffee table and I'm not sure yet if I'm going to pick up the work again. Much of what I had done was fan work based on books. There was little income from that but it was enough to fuel my sushi addiction.

I consider picking up the pen again to draw, color in the sketches I've done, but my heart just isn't in it. My ears perk up when I hear Charlie and his father mention Christmas.

"I think I'm going to spend it with mom," Charlie says, not looking up from his laptop.

His dad's head snaps up and he stares intently at Charlie. I catch the look on his face and how he's trying not to look disappointed by the news. This uncaring man seems to have a heart after all.

"She's coming to town? I know you have Jack's party tomorrow night."

"Yes. She's visiting Brad for the holidays."

I start to feel bad that he will have no one to spend Christmas with, but then I remember that he called me a strumpet and objectified me in front of his son, and the feeling passes.

"Wish your mother and brother well for me then. Are you taking the girl?" his dad asks.

"Stop pretending like you don't know her name. I've mentioned Elia plenty of times in the last few months. You have known her name and exactly who she is," Charlie objects, his tone low.

"Look, she's sexy and I understand why you want a woman who answers the door dressed like that, but she's not wife material. She's definitely not your wife material," Charles Senior continues, popping another soup dumpling in his mouth.

"Stop. Right now," Charlie warns, his voice flirting with anger.

He's trying to keep a level head for his father, his boss, but I'm not sure how much more he can hold back.

I try to let his father's words roll off my shoulder like I'm Teflon, but I can't pretend the dig about not being wife material doesn't hurt. I'm trying my hardest to do what I can to help Charlie when he comes home: keeping the apartment clean, taking care of the laundry, and even trying to have meals ready. I told Charlie that having a housekeeper was redundant before we left for Bora Bora. The need to feel like I was contributing meant that I kept things clean before our relationship became more. After we got back, I insisted that I could manage doing something like cleaning up after the two of us. Still, his housekeeper comes once a month to do a deeper clean.

"You know it's true. Jack's told me some things about her and I don't know if this whole amnesia thing is for real. It's a little too convenient that she's some freelance artist and now she gets to restart her life? Maybe it was true after the accident, but I doubt she still doesn't remember," his dad says, barely below his normal speaking voice. He wants me to hear what he has to say about me. "I heard Ainsley has been asking about you."

"Enough," Charlie's voice is lethal. "If you want to work on the deal, then stay and work on the deal. Otherwise, you can get out of my house."

His father leans back, looking at his son, trying to see him in a new light.

Quietly, I close my laptop, calling out that I'm headed to bed as if I hadn't heard a word of what was said.

Charlie calls out a brief goodnight, his father seeming to have taken the offer to keep the focus on work. One glance at his father confirms that he wants to make sure I know where I stand, that he sees me as a distraction. I offer him my best fake smile.

Closing my eyes, fighting the tears back, I tell myself that it doesn't bother me, when it completely does. I'm left wondering what Jack knows about me that I don't.

Seventeen

I GET to Vivian's apartment fifteen minutes early and I debate if I should go in early or just wait. The doorman, annoyed with my loitering, asks what I'm doing there and when I state my intended destination, he waves me up. I can't wait to see her apartment and as the numbers go higher, my excitement rises as well. When I get there, she's standing in the door, waiting for me while directing people where to put things in the grand space. Someone, the caterer I assume, is setting up in the kitchen area and grumbling about preferring to be behind closed doors. The apartment is an open concept with the entry flowing easily into the living room, which is hugged by the kitchen.

She's across the park from me on the West Side and I'm glad that I have her this close. Vivian welcomes me with a hug while I check out the rest of the apartment. The living room has a set of double doors leading to a balcony where space heaters are being set up if anyone wants to brave the cold. From what I can see, it offers a sweeping view of Central Park, nearly directly across from Charlie.

"So, I know I told you I needed you here early for prep stuff, but I really just wanted some time with you for myself."

I hope my relief isn't visible. I'm glad she doesn't want more from me; my muscles are quaking from physical therapy that morning. After telling Dan that I had gone to my old apartment, we discussed what I felt like during that endeavor and how best to strengthen those muscles. As a result, he worked me a little harder than usual.

Vivian and Jack's apartment is spacious, but only one level, unlike Charlie's place with the loft area. She tells me there are three bedrooms and two bathrooms so they have plenty of space to grow into it. This is the kind of apartment people dream of when they come to New York before being faced with the reality that they're only able to afford a 450-square-foot shipping container unless they want weird roommates they found online.

She's had their living room furniture put in storage for the night and there are tall tables set up for mingling, with chairs interspersed for people who become too tired of standing in their heels. This is a classy affair and I doubt that I've ever owned anything fancy enough for tonight. About thirty of their closest friends are coming to this party, a combination of work friends or, in the case of Jack, his fraternity brothers.

I hadn't realized that dating Jack had thrust Vivian into the upper echelons of society where there was this expectation to be perfect at all times. By extension, through Charlie, I was now in that league too. Grateful doesn't cover it when Vivian tells me she's having a hair and make-up trial for the wedding before tonight's affair and she asked if they could work on me too.

"Not that you need it," she says, settling into a chair for her hair and make-up with a glass of champagne in her hand.

I laugh, taking a sip of my own drink. "Sure, I'll believe that someday," I agree with a laugh, but I'm not overly worried. The jet lag has passed and my tears last night weren't enough for me to look swollen this morning. "Who is coming tonight?"

"I do want to warn you, and I cannot be clear enough that Charlie didn't know, but Ainsley is going to be here."

I pause, the champagne flute lifted to my lips but not quite touching them. Charlie's fathers words still ring in my mind: I'm not wife material, Charlie should move on from me and settle down with someone else. I don't blame Charlie for not kicking his dad out immediately; I would have had a hard time balancing the urge to respect my parents and stopping the disrespectful things coming out of their mouths. He shut it down as quickly and respectfully as he could, considering the man speaking the words is also the man who signs his checks at the end of the day.

I have no reason to think that Charlie would stray, regardless of his shared history with Ainsley. We still haven't spoken in depth about it because it is something I feel like I shouldn't push. If he wanted to be with Ainsley, he would be with her and not playing house with me.

Vivian reaches her hand out to tug at my blonde tresses. "You should go back to your dark hair; this blonde does not suit you," she says, wrinkling her nose. The hair stylist grips her face sternly to try to get her to stop moving but Vivian was never any good at sitting still.

"For now, I'm just going to grow it out. It feels brittle, like too many bleach jobs have stripped my hair. I think it needs a break. I was thinking about getting it cut soon anyway." I pull at my long hair. Naturally, it's a dark chestnut, which is something that's showing around my roots. If I cut away all the blonde, there should be enough left to gather it into a ponytail, but not much. I planned to give it another month or two before hacking it off. It was startling to see when I caught sight of myself in the mirror for the first time. The blonde has started to grow on me, but not enough to want to keep it long term.

"It's gotten so long." Her fingers wind their way around the ends before she's tugged back into place again. She narrows her eyes at the stylist, but thinks better of it.

Vivian points at the door, where a garment bag is hanging, and winks. She did promise to loan me something for tonight's formal affair. The dress glitters as I reach out to touch it. It's a sleeveless gown that is a blue ombre, from light blue at the top down to a midnight blue at the bottom. It's a slim cut that leaves nothing to the imagination, with a plunging illusion neckline. I turn to look at Vivian and she shrugs.

"I got it for something or other and never wore it. I think you will look amazing in it though." She smiles behind her glass of champagne, only setting it down when she's scolded by the make-up artist working on the wedding "trial" look. Vivian offers next to no commentary, seeming to care little about how she looks. Her wedding is about her marriage to Jack and I think she would be happy to walk down the aisle to him in a paper bag.

It feels like we're back at our sorority formal, helping each other get ready. Except instead of changing into cheap dresses we found in a thrift store, we're putting on dresses found on the racks of Nordstrom or a posh designer. She's more excited to get me ready, zipping me up and directing the stylists on how she wants my hair and make-up done.

Vivian is wearing what can only be described as a wedding dress. It's an a-line gown with a chiffon skirt, a lace bodice with no back, and finger loops hooking the long sleeves over her hands. The gown is elegant and understated. I am so glad that we reconnected so that I get to see her on her wedding day. Looking at Vivian now, I can see what a beautiful bride she's going to be.

Charlie and Jack arrive straight from work together. We can hear their voices in the hallway talking business before they even walk through the door.

"I'm telling you, this is a good company and we need to act while we can." Jack's voice is urgent as he gives a server his coat.

Charlie hands off his coat, with thanks, while holding onto his laptop bag. "And all I'm saying is let's wait until the new year," he insists.

Jack's eyes find his fiancé first and he lets out a big whoosh of air as he takes in the sight of her. "God, I am the luckiest man alive.

I feel like it's bad luck seeing you in this," he says, walking over to her. There is no hesitation as he kisses her passionately. Jack's arm snakes around her waist, the other holding the base of her neck as he dips her backward, following her body with his.

I can't help but smile. As much as Jack hates me, he loves my friend more. At the end of the day, that's what really matters: how they feel about each other. Connor was an alright guy, but this is clearly where her heart is meant to be.

I look and find Charlie's eyes devouring the sight of me. There is a slit in the skirt, which comes up my thigh, showing the very bottom of the pink puckered skin that is my scar. He walks over to me, his fingers grazing that spot gently. It sends a thrill up my spine, feeling the brush of his skin against mine.

"I have to disagree, Jack," he whispers, the words meant only for me. The fire in his eyes makes me wish we were anywhere but here, especially after the letdown the night before. Charlie's movements are controlled as his hand slides up the nape of my neck, gently urging me toward him. I lean up to kiss him on the mouth and his tongue slips into my mouth, flicking against my tongue. My hands go to his hips and I pull him against me, feeling him stiffen.

"Seriously, you two, this is my engagement party," Jack whines.

Charlie and I break apart, breathless and grinning, eyes only for the other.

Vivian hits Jack, an equally wide smile on her face. "Jack, let them be happy," she scolds. Jack's blue eyes linger on Vivian before he casts them to me, still distrusting.

Charlie pulls me close to his side. "What can we do to help finish setting up?"

"Just the favors are left." Vivian doesn't seem concerned as she says it. Charlie dumps his laptop in their bedroom, so we can help finish setting up the favors and gift table.

"I didn't bring a gift," I whisper to him, embarrassed. I hadn't thought about needing one. Hindsight being what it is, it was dumb of me not to think about it. Charlie reaches into his suit jacket, flashing a crisp white envelope. My body nearly sags in relief.

"All over it." His sultry voice earns him a quick kiss on the cheek. I'm full of nervous energy waiting for people to arrive. My glass of champagne is my body armor as people slowly start to trickle in. Here, a law school friend of Vivian's whom I vaguely remember; there, some friends from college who I thankfully remember; and then, Charlie takes great pride in introducing me to his college friends. His arm is wrapped around me, steadying me, holding me close to reassure me that I'm not alone in this sea of unfamiliar faces.

"We missed you at Homecoming," one of them says pointedly, after politely acknowledging me. Eyes flit over me, not giving me much more attention than that. The accident is another thing I hadn't considered coming up while we were at the party and I wish I had a chance to talk to Charlie about how we were going to address it.

"I was playing nurse all fall. I hit Elia with my car after work one day and she's been staying with me while she recovers." His arm tightens as he presses a kiss to the top of my head.

"So you brought your community service project to the engagement party?" some girl asks, confusion and disgust registering on her face.

I fight the urge to pull out of Charlie's grasp, to separate myself from him. He's stuck trying to justify me to his friends, who don't seem to understand what hitting me has to do with my presence here.

"Actually, we're dating." His tone is annoyed. "And she's Vivian's friend." If Charlie pulls me any closer to his side, our hips might actually fuse together.

I plaster on a fake smile and excuse myself the first chance I get.

I seek out Vivian, who is chatting with some of our sorority sisters.

I need friendly faces, and not only are these women familiar, but they hug me and tell me they've missed me. Vivian did the hard part, telling them I was in an accident and didn't remember the last few years. I was grateful for the cover, tired of having to tell the story for the fifth, sixth, or seventh time tonight.

It's easy enough to cover my missing time with them since it's unlikely I've seen them since shortly after graduating college. We make the usual small talk, catching up before Vivian slides off to her other guests. They're all in varying stages of life; many married, some with kids, and they all seem happy, and genuinely glad to see me. When the conversation shifts to child rearing and pregnancy, I slip away to grab another drink.

Charlie is mingling with a group of men I haven't met, but his raucous laughter reaches me across the room. My lips twist in a smile and I drop into a chair that looks out on their patio and farther, the park itself. My leg burns from standing on it in heels for so long.

I reason with myself that no one is setting me apart from everyone else, I am doing that to myself. Charlie and Vivian both want me here. Hell, even Jack "wants" me here because Viv does. Charlie finds me across the room, offering me a wink, and I know that I need to get off my sorry ass and join him. I can't let my own insecurities get to me. I may not have gone to a college covered in ivy, but it doesn't mean I'm less or don't deserve to rub elbows with this crowd. Charlie doesn't stop his conversation when I approach; he just wraps his arm around me, easily folding me against him.

An elbow nudges me and I turn. It's Taryn, who is standing next to Charlie.

"So glad to see you," she says, ignoring the conversation in front of us. A burly man with a ferocious beard is recounting a story from their freshman year of college that involved getting picked up by campus security after passing out in front of them.

"Me too. I could use a friendly face." I am genuinely glad to see her. We didn't talk much when we met, but she seems warmer now than the hostess who greeted me the first time I met her.

"Eh, they're all just drunk idiots. Don't pay them any mind. You look absolutely smashing."

I offer her a tight smile. "I'm just lucky Vivian had this in her closet to spare. I swear I have never owned anything this nice."

"You wear it well. I'm sorry if I was kind of a bitch when we met, but the restaurant industry will eat you alive and then some."

I shake my head emphatically. "No, I get it. You have to play gatekeeper. And Charlie mentioned you're still going to school?"

"Yes." She nods, her dark brown eyes staring into space, before looking back at me. "I'm getting my MBA from Columbia, which has its own challenges."

"I bet."

Our conversation fizzles when someone taps her on the shoulder to greet her. Charlie seizes on the opportunity to take my hand and separate us from the crowd.

We step out into the bitter cold air and I shiver until I move close enough to one of the heat lamps. The idea behind setting them up outside was nice in theory. String lights help create a romantic ambiance, but in reality, it's just too cold, even with the lamps.

Charlie pulls me close to one that's at the edge of the patio, where we can see the lights of the city below us. This isn't the penthouse apartment, but we're still up there on the thirty-seventh floor. I can't make out any figures down below but the sounds of the horns and Christmas music filter up, muted by the distance.

"I'm sorry about before. Some people can be such assholes."

I want to wave him off, tell him that it didn't bother me, that I have thicker skin than that. But I can't tell him that it didn't hurt, so I do the next best thing. "Don't worry about it. It's nice to be around people other than you and PT Dan, even if those people are dicks."

He laughs. "Glad I rank up there with PT Dan."

"So, I wanted to tell you, I had an OB/GYN appointment this morning."

Charlie looks up sharply at me. I wonder if his father has been warning him about me trying to get pregnant to trap him. An annual visit with the lady doc was never the top of my to do list, but I realized I didn't know enough about my body to keep going on in ignorance. Since I couldn't provide a medical history, the hospital ran a litany of tests, including an STD panel, so I knew I was clean in that sense.

"I went to find out about getting an IUD," I rush on. "I had one before and they confirmed I don't have one now. I figure this way, we know for sure I won't get pregnant."

He lets out a woosh of air and puts his hand to his chest.

"I thought..." he trails off.

I try not to take his relief personally. I am in no way ready for a baby either, but the insecure part of me adds this to the tally of reasons we don't fit, like this is evidence that he doesn't think I could be a mother to his child.

"You thought I was going to tell you I've been poking holes in the condoms and baby trap you?" I force a smile. "Hardly. I feel like we jumped into this so fast we never even had the conversation about what we saw for our futures." I leave an opening for him, an opening for a conversation that maybe this isn't the best place to have. I need to jump at the chance to talk to him about it now though. Each night, he comes home late or he comes home and keeps working. We have enough time for a good fuck and then we pass out.

"I don't know. I mean, I was ready to settle down with Ainsley and get married, so I know I'm a marrying man." He rubs the back of his neck, not looking at me, focusing on the city beyond. "But I don't know about kids. You know how my lifestyle is. I don't know if I could do that. Put all that pressure on my wife to raise our child. My wife would effectively be a single parent. I'm basically just good for child support and sperm."

I rest my hands on his cheeks. "You're worth more than just child support and sperm. Your penis is pretty fantastic too," I tease and he nips at my hands. My heart opens to him; there is so much struggle and pain behind this question. His father is on his fourth divorce. He saw what it is like to be a child when the father has a demanding job like the one he does. I wonder if kids were a deeper problem with him and Ainsley, but I don't press that. This conversation is about us and what potential we have for a future.

"What about you?" he asks tentatively. Kids are a big conversation. He's basically laid out that he's not sure he could see himself having children.

"When I was a kid, I was never interested in playing mom. I had more fun playing with the dog or something. My baby dolls were never my favorite. It didn't matter how many I got, I preferred other games. Kids always felt like they were the logical next step. First comes love, then comes marriage, then comes Ellie with the baby carriage. Now?" I lean against the railing, looking up at Charlie. "I just look at them and think that I don't want the hassle. I'm not a baby hater, I just don't know if I'm mom material."

"For what it's worth, I think you would make a great mom, if you wanted to have kids. But it sounds to me like we are on the same page." Charlie twists a stray strand of my hair around his finger.

"I think so. For what it's worth, having kids or not having kids isn't a deal breaker for me. For the right penis, I mean, guy, I would put it back on the table."

He snorts into the champagne glass he rescued from a tray sitting outside. "Ah, so it's about my dick, not my money." Hot breath brushes the hair on the nape of my neck when Charlie lowers his head to my shoulder. The cold of his nose makes me shiver as he traces it along the curve of my neck, pressing a kiss below my ear.

"Every day of the week, baby." I press my body against his.

His fingertips dig into my hips, pulling me firmly against him. "Any chance that outfit from last night makes another appearance?"

I cast a surreptitious look back at the party, confirm that we're alone, and then drop my hand between his legs. Feeling the hardness there, I push the heel of my hand down the length of him, stroking him over his pants.

"There might be something even better under this dress."

His eyes are hungry and his kiss even more so as he devours me, pulling me against him. He claims every part of my heart and soul with that kiss.

"Charlie, someone said you were -- oh, I'm so sorry!"

We break apart like teenagers caught by our parents. Charlie turns around, very obviously pretending to look over the balcony to fix his pants as if the newcomer hadn't said his name.

The new arrival is a petite woman with natural blonde hair, pulled up and away from her face in a low ponytail. Her short light pink dress has straps that cross several times on her ample cleavage. I'm not sure if it's the coloring of her dress and hair or the flush of the cold that gives a rosy sheen to her pale cheeks. I don't know how she can stand to be outside for even one minute in the cold. Charlie turns around finally to face this woman.

"Yeah?" I feel his body go completely still behind me and I wish I could see his face. "Ains," he breathes her name almost like a prayer that escapes his lips.

That one syllable tells me everything I need to know, and it simultaneously pulls all of my insecurities to the front. She's gorgeous with her full lips, parted gently in confusion, and green eyes that are trained on Charlie. I feel inadequate just being in the same vicinity as her.

"I'm sorry. Jack just mentioned that you were out here. I

thought you were alone." She sounds disappointed, her conviction to find Charlie wavering. "I wanted to talk to you."

The symbolism of how I stand between them now, an obstacle to them being together, burns away the feeling of that kiss.

"I'm Elia," I say, reaching out my hand. I hope the wavering in my voice can be explained away by the cold, while wishing that speaking up changes something. Charlie is frozen with the spell of Ainsley cast over him.

"Ainsley," she confirms, shaking my hand. There is a question in her eyes, wondering who I am and exactly what she interrupted. I take another step away from Charlie, aching when he doesn't seem to notice.

"I'll let you two talk." I force a steel rod behind my words, trying to lend them a strength I don't feel. Charlie's eyes find mine, having woken from the daze of Ainsley's presence. I give him a nod, letting him know it's okay as I leave my boyfriend with his ex-fiancée. My head is held high, totally cool, totally unbothered.

Vivian and Jack's bedroom is off limits, but I discreetly ask her if I can use her master bathroom, citing a line at the other. She squeezes my arm with a nod.

The bathroom is smaller than Charlie's but held enough space for us to get our hair and make-up done earlier. The mirror is long, the same tiling covers the floor and the walls in the Japanese style for the ease of cleaning. I drift to her side of the double sink, marked by her various lotions and creams around it. The silver nob twists in my hand, cold water gushing from the spout. I focus on that, the feel of the water in my hands and the feel of it on my face as I splash it up, not caring about my make-up. I force a shaky breath out, trying not to think about what they're talking about outside or how he reacted to seeing her. I stare into my own green eyes, focusing on how far I have come and how far I have yet to go.

"You are smart and beautiful and college-educated. You were probably fine before Charlie showed up in your life and you will be fine if things end. You have endured storms worse than a breakup and you have weathered them with grace. You have come out better for every challenge. He has not broken up with you yet. You're blowing this way out of proportion."

I let my insecurity burrow deep inside me, letting it take root for too long. Seeing how they look at each other, that history of love, that history between them is difficult to deny. I try to use these words of affirmation, to assure myself, to try to bolster my own self-confidence.

I hear a throat clearing and jump as I see Jack leaning against the door frame. Anger rises in me, seeing him so nonchalant and relaxed.

"You did this on purpose." I turn to face him, drying my face off with a towel.

"I did," he confirms.

"Why? What did I do to you?" I ask. I throw the towel down on the counter, bracing a hand on it.

"It's what you did to Vivian. I won't let a manipulative back-stabber back into her life and I want you out of Charlie's."

I have to admire his devotion to them, but he's so wrong about me. He's not interested in letting me prove myself to him.

"Do you actually hear yourself? The blatant hypocrisy? *You're* manipulating the situation."

Jack's face doesn't show any reaction to my words. He stays where he is, unmovable. I push past him to get back to the party.

"I'll do whatever I have to to protect them," he warns as I walk back into the party. I'm flustered when I enter the main room, angry and embarrassed by this whole night. Vivian, still radiant, spies me, walks over, and grabs my hand. Seeing Jack behind me, she smiles, completely unaware of the tension between the two of us.

"Oh good, he found you."

I turn to look at Jack, then back at Vivian, swallowing my anger.

"I told her that Charlie left. She was just coming to find you and say bye." Jack's blatant lie shocks me, but I'm not going to call him out for it and ruin Vivian's night.

I fight with warring emotions inside me. A slap in the face might have had less of a sting. There is static in my ears as Vivian talks -- thanking me for coming, I think. Jack is ready with my purse, coat, and Charlie's laptop case, eager to see me off. He is practically shoving me out the door, but Vivian doesn't seem to notice as someone else comes up to congratulate them. I offer a quick farewell, eager to be out of the room that suddenly is too hot and has too many people in it. I wrap my arms around Vivian, congratulating her and wishing them both a Merry Christmas before I depart, alone.

I'm so confused. Why did Charlie leave? Where did he go?

I can't focus my emotions as I ride the elevator, which was empty but then picks up more people as we make our way to the ground floor. I'm angry and hurt. I feel betrayed and alone. It's not just Jack and his meddling, but Charlie and his reaction to Ainsley. I try to reason that I should be patient, that I should give him time to open up about her, but I'm shaken by his reaction to her. Was that desire? Longing? Lust in his eyes?

I brace myself, stepping out into the cold street air. An errant taxi lays on its horn as a pedestrian takes their life in their hands by jaywalking against the light, taking their sweet ass time as they do it. The pedestrian doesn't look up but, instead, flips the bird at the taxi as they continue to walk their way. I aspire to this level of unbothered; I need that level of unbothered right now. Pacing under the awning of the building is Charlie, running his hand through his hair. His eyes light up when he sees me and he hurries to my side.

"Oh, good, there you are!" he says as if I'm the one who has been missing this entire time. I chalk this up to Jack delivering the wrong message intentionally and let out a ragged breath. The devil works hard but Jack works harder. I resolve to not push it with

Jack. If he wants to be a dick, fine, but I'm done trying if these are his tactics.

"Yeah, sorry, it's hard to pee in this thing. You left." There is a hint of accusation in my tone that I can't keep out. Charlie glances up from ordering the PickMeUp!. I remain silent, hoping this will encourage him to talk. It's almost midnight on Christmas Eve and I don't know where we stand.

"I'm sorry," he starts. "I'm sorry. I was so thrown off by Ainsley that I wasn't thinking straight. I shouldn't have left, but Jack said you were in the bathroom and it was too hot in there all of a sudden. So many people in that space, I mean. It had to break fire codes or something." He brings his fingers up to his mouth, as if to take a drag from a cigarette, but nothing is there. I wonder if he used to smoke, adding it to the list of things I don't know about him.

I open my mouth to say something when the car pulls up and we climb in. We're silent in the car. This is not the place to have this conversation, to talk about seeing his ex-fiancée after his father said I'm not wife material.

I pick a mantra and repeat it in my head: *You are smart and you are powerful and you have weathered worse storms. You are smart and you are powerful and you have weathered worse storms.*

I repeat this over and over in my head as we slowly creep along, the traffic unbearable just to go through Central Park. We drive the transverse that our accident happened on and Charlie reaches for me, squeezing my hand. It's obvious that his own memories of that night are surging up. We keep up the silence, even once we reach our building and ride the elevator to our floor. This silence is torture. I'm sure my face looks grim, no secrets hiding there. Catching sight of me in the mirrored wall of the elevator, Charlie runs his hands through his hair, leaving it in disarray. Once the apartment door is closed, I pause.

"What did you two talk about?"

His eyes fall on me. There is a level of exhaustion I haven't seen on his face as he casts aside his laptop case and jacket. I wait anxiously for an answer. He toes his shoes off, leaving them on the rack. I do the same, taking off my jacket, leaving my purse on the island haphazardly.

"I honestly didn't hear a word she said. I was too surprised to even really register her presence and then I left. I told Jack and Vivian that I had to leave and I did. It was just jarring to see her there."

"Jack didn't warn you?" I gather my dress in my hands, walking into the bedroom.

"Warn me?" he asks, pulling his tie loose.

Vivian's warning echoes in my head; she was specific in saying that he *didn't* know. But I feel like her tone, her wording, made it seem like he should have known before that party.

"That Ainsley was coming." I set about getting ready for bed, a headache starting to form at the base of my neck. I shift my hair aside, stretching my shoulder to its limits while reaching for the zipper.

Charlie comes up behind me, his fingers brushing mine aside to take over. His lips brush the top of my spine as he slowly pulls the zipper down. Goosebumps break out on my arms as his hands follow my shoulder blades, pushing the dress off my shoulders so it slides off my body, pooling on the floor.

Under the dress, I had on a black lace teddy with an equally plunging neckline. He kisses the back of my neck, his hand tracing the inside edges of the teddy from my shoulder down to my breast. He pauses there, rubbing his thumb over my hard nipple, breathing heavily against my hair. I arch my back into him, desperate for him to continue. This is easier, connecting on a physical level rather than actually talking about anything.

"We're not done talking about this," I gasp out.

His hand finishes the trail to just below my navel, where he slides his finger in between the material and my skin. I should stop him, tell him we need to talk, but a gasp escapes my lips when he finds my clit, alternating circling and applying pressure. I lean my head back, resting against his collarbone as my breath starts coming out in quick, short bursts, matching the tempo of his fingers.

I spin around, kissing him passionately, my body primed for him. My nipples chafe against the rough lace and his body. He lifts me easily and I wrap my legs around him, still wearing my heels from the party. He carries me to bed, his hands gripping my thighs as he lowers me onto the pillows.

"I am not interested in Ainsley. I am not interested in talking to her. All I want, all I need, is right in front of me. If you think there is more to talk about, then we can talk about it, but right now, I want to focus on doing all the things I've thought about doing to you since I saw you tonight." He unbuttons his shirt as he says this.

Stopping is not an option. Do we have things we still need to talk about, like his meddling best friend? Yes. Am I going to let that interfere in our relationship any more than it already has? Absolutely not.

I undo his belt, pulling it out, keeping my eyes locked on his. My fingers fumble as if these are the first pants I've ever undone and it makes me want to laugh and scream all at the same time. I roll over as he starts to pull his pants off.

"Going somewhere?" he asks, reaching for me. There is a hesitation in his voice, worried that he's reading the conversation wrong, that maybe I do want to stop and talk about this. It's been hot and heavy between us, physical and full of need. I keep my hips raised, my ass in the air for him to ogle. Thongs are probably the worst invention ever, as I have never found a pair of more uncomfortable underwear, but knowing that I have Charlie's full attention on my ass makes it at least somewhat worth it.

I reach for the bottom drawer of my nightstand, grabbing some of the toys I bought. I pop back up with a riding crop and a strap that matches one I have already attached to the bed. When I turn, Charlie is in his boxers with an eyebrow raised.

"I didn't realize you wanted to 'Fifty Shades' it."

I smack him gently on the chest for that comment. "I don't want to go all red room, unless that's the other shoe that's still got to drop. I thought it could be fun. That's the best part of a new partner, right? Exploring what turns them on and what doesn't. Merry Christmas," I say as I grab the other strap from the opposite side of the bed.

"Merry Christmas, indeed." He smirks, letting me push him down on the bed.

I grab his already hard cock and stroke him, teasing, watching what earns a reaction and what doesn't. It's in the subtle movements: the bite of his lips, the burn in his eyes that tells me what pressure to apply, where to touch, how to get him going.

His hands are reaching for me, but I'm mostly out of his grasp, sitting further back on his thighs. I wrap the straps around his wrists. They are light and fun, easy to stop using if we decide we don't like it. The whole time I'm velcroing him in, Charlie looks delighted. He tugs at the bindings, feeling their strength, and I wonder if it will hold. I pull a condom from the nightstand, his eyes on me, and I slowly slide it down over him.

He can only watch as I slowly lower myself onto him, a throaty "Oh" the only noise I get from him. My own whimper escapes, my eyes locked on his, as I pause and take in the fullness of him. He tries to fight against the restraints to reach me, but I shake my head, letting my hair down from the clip it's been in.

I set the pace, moving my hips, gyrating, tempting, teasing, and pulling at the threads that hold us. His breathing is labored as he tries to shift his hips up, but I won't let him, pulling myself up and away. The sound of his growl sends a thrill up my spine. His hands wrap around the straps, holding tight to them as I move him closer to climax.

He doesn't need to warn me, though he opens his mouth to do so, because I'm hitting the same stride. My body clenches around him and my head falls back as I moan loudly. My body seems to take over, knowing what it needs to do to ride this wave. I dig my nails into his chest, needing something to hold onto, something to ground me as my whole body tightens and releases like a coiled spring. I roll my torso forward, pressing my forehead against his, both of us panting for breath even as I rock my hips a few more times, his body still shuddering. I reach over and undo the velcro on one hand before moving to the other side. I kiss him with my body folded against his. His arms come up around me, hugging me to his chest.

"Next time, it's your turn to endure that sweet torture," he murmurs, kissing my lips.

I want to lock us in this moment, in this room, away from outside voices like Jack and Ainsley. I want to hold on to this bliss but I know it has to end. I climb off him, gingerly, before sweeping my hair up as we both wash off.

"You forgot the riding crop," he jokes when we're back in bed, tugging my body close to his under the covers.

Eighteen

WE WAKE UP NATURALLY, with no intentions for Christmas morning. Charlie folds his arms around me, holding me close to him as he presses a kiss to my head. I groan, pulling the blankets over my head.

"What if we never left this bed?" I ask, knowing the answer. Charlie tucks me closer to his body, my back against his chest, and he kisses my neck, nipping at my ear.

"We could. I have no strong feelings about seeing my mother and brother."

I let him kiss me. I let him distract me and soothe me. There are probably a thousand reasons why I shouldn't even be in bed with this glorious man, but that's why I refuse to see a psychologist. I don't want to hear it.

"When was the last time you saw them?" I ask. I roll over to face him, my finger tracing along his face and jaw. I catch the muscle tightening there as he holds my gaze.

"After Ainsley and I got engaged, we had a get-together with the families to celebrate."

I kiss him on the lips. "We need to have a longer conversation about her eventually, but you should see them sooner rather than later."

He kisses my nose. "Ask your questions. I don't want you to feel like you're being compared to her at every turn. I know I'm not the most open book, but in my mind, she's behind me. That's why I never bring her up or talk about it."

I don't tell him that he's on the money, that I feel like I'm being compared to her. "Okay, I get that, but I feel like I've had the hood pulled over my eyes with you knowing Vivian and then with Ainsley, it's just... it's been confusing." He's open to answering my questions, so I push forward. "How long were you together, how did you meet, and how much did everyone in your life love her?" The words come out fast and furious. I feel better having let them out but I hold my breath a little because I'm worried about the answers.

He doesn't belittle me or make a joke of it. He answers me, honestly and quickly. "We met in college. We started dating our senior year. She went to Harvard for law school. We broke up because I was working miserable hours and couldn't handle long distance. When she moved back to New York for work, we reconnected, as friends. We didn't start dating again right away because she was a new associate and working long hours too. After her first year, we ran into each other at a party and then started dating again. I proposed about two years ago and then we broke up a year later. My family has known her since I was a freshman in college, so they're comfortable with her." He runs his knuckle along my cheek. I hook my leg over his hip pulling him close to me. I feel his hardness against my leg.

I kiss him gently.

"Have you talked to her since the break-up?" I feel like it's a game of twenty questions.

"No, we haven't talked. She didn't even have to coordinate getting her stuff out of our apartment. We were engaged for so long because I couldn't commit to a wedding date, but the way she cut me out was," he pauses, "efficient." His fingers twine around my hair, tickling the nape of my neck.

"What changed?" I whisper, unsure why I should expect this to be any different.

"Everything. I hit you with my car, Elia. That was a big fucking wake up call. I wasn't driving but if I hadn't been working late? If I hadn't been so focused on work, so focused on squeezing every minute out of every day, then..."

"Then we wouldn't have met."

"Let's stop talking about her," he orders as he rolls over on top of me. He slowly slides into me and my hands grasp his shoulders. We slowly make love. I hold him close to me as I climax, savoring him. He kisses my forehead and pulls out without finishing himself. I start to object and he waves me off.

"I shouldn't have done it without a condom to begin with."

I get out of bed, kissing his shoulder. "I would have objected if I had a bigger problem with it."

I jump in the shower, humming Christmas carols. We never did pick up a tree but I resolve to find one for next year, if there is a next year. Charlie is no longer in the bedroom when I emerge, but I can hear the sounds of his rowing machine. The man never misses a day.

I have a few more surprises up my sleeves for the day, starting with matching flannel pajamas that I got for us with dancing reindeer all over. I set Charlie's pair on the bed for him. Even if he doesn't want to wear them all day, I want to get at least one photo of the two of us in them.

I head into the kitchen, pulling out the brand new *pizzelle* maker I ordered. Charlie's even strokes and breath provide a steady background noise while I get to work making the treat.

When Charlie hops in the shower I start to press the wafers, making a few test ones to ensure that I'm making them right. I wasn't expecting a fresh wave of tears and longing to hit me when I broke off a piece of the first batch. The taste, the smell of the dough baking, makes me miss my parents in ways that are intangible. I miss their guidance and love. I wish they could meet Charlie and tell me if I'm doing something stupid. I want to know they would approve of him. I think he would pass muster and they would love him like a son. I blast Christmas music from the speakers in hopes of drowning out the insistent sorrow.

Charlie emerges, in the matching pajamas, and I double over in laughter. "I look ridiculous," he declares as he smiles indulgently. He lets me dress him like this and follows along without question, which makes my heart swell.

"You look adorable. Sit and eat your breakfast." I set out a plate with Italian treats while I fry up eggs for us both. I flit around the kitchen, trying to keep an eye on the eggs while starting the next batch of *pizzelle*. Charlie is silent as I work and try to keep from burning anything. *Pizzelle* cook so fast, it's hard to manage more than just the wafers.

"So in sixth grade, we started to take language for the first time ever. I took Italian because my mom's family is Italian. Then at Christmas time, we learned about *pizzelle* and I got totally obsessed with them. For Christmas, my parents got me a maker so we could make them at home. It sort of just became a tradition after that. The first few years, it was a disaster but then we figured out the best way. We always had matching pajamas and stockings stuffed with our favorite candies and little bullshit knick-knacks that my mom would pick up throughout the year."

I stare off, thinking about the last Christmas with my parents. My mom would use hot chocolate with whipped cream to rouse me from my bed and tease me that she let me sleep long enough. Now, I sip my coffee, though I don't need the added caffeine because I'm already bursting at the seams with energy. Charlie watches me the whole time in quiet contemplation.

"Did you have any traditions?" I ask, finally sitting down beside him. Platters piled with *pizzelle* as well as bacon and eggs are set between us so we can make our own plates.

"Coffee," he says, taking a sip from his cup.

I giggle. "Coffee is your tradition?"

He smiles and lifts his cup for a refill, "No. I just need more. We didn't really have traditions since Dad was always working. Mom tried to make things special when I was small but part of our family was missing, so it was kind of empty. But, as I grew older and Dad continued to work, my mom would take us skiing. Sometimes it was just to get away from my father."

"Well, we can make new traditions." I kiss his temple before I eagerly run into the guest room to grab the presents stowed there.

"So, don't think anything too crazy from the number of things here, but, Merry Christmas."

He is frozen, staring at the presents in front of him, obviously not sure where to start. He starts smaller, carefully tearing at the wrapping paper so as to not destroy it. Within the packaging is a leather wallet engraved with his initials, something simple and useful. The next few gifts are all various photos from our trip together.

He holds the picture frame with a photo of the two of us on the beach after snorkeling. Charlie smiles as he rubs his thumb over our faces.

"I love them. Thank you." He leans over and kisses my forehead. He gets up and goes to the bedroom, bringing out two items.

"I cannot take credit for the wrapping job. Ashley was kind enough to put me out of my misery and wrapped them for me."

I open the slightly larger one and find a beautiful silver picture frame inside. I flip it around and there is a picture of two kittens in the frame. I look up at Charlie, confused by the cute but odd stock photo. I'm glad I ordered extra prints from the trip to put inside it.

"It's a beautiful frame. Thank you."

He laughs, taking my hand and threading his fingers with mine.

"Pets are not presents, but if you want, these two kittens are reserved for us to adopt."

I look up at him in surprise. "Really?" I look at their little faces and am more in love with them already than I am with Charlie.

"Really. Back when we were talking about you going to your apartment, you mentioned how lonely it would be once you were there alone and said you wished you had a cat to go home to. I'm not saying you should move back home, obviously, but if you want them, they're ours."

I love the sound of that, our cats.

"We may never want human children," he continues, "but we can always have cats."

"Yes, yes! I love their faces." I trace a finger over the curious little faces. Then I hug Charlie, gripping the frame in my hands, imagining having them home with us.

"They still need to be spayed. Once that happens, they're ready to come home with us."

I grab his face and kiss him. Charlie looks so pleased with himself that he's practically preening.

He places the next box in my hands and moves back, eagerly watching my response. I open it and see that signature blue box with a white bow wrapped around it. I'm surprised to see it, Tiffany's is such a grand gift, but I can't stop my smile. It's a long box, so I know it's not a ring, and that is fine by me. It's a simple pendant on a platinum chain with four marquis diamonds in a floral design. I let out a breath.

"It's beautiful, Charlie. It's, I mean, it's gorgeous. Thank you." I lean forward to kiss him, setting the box on the counter. I'm not sure I've ever owned anything so grand. I hop off the stool and get between his legs. He brushes powdered sugar off my face. If I was going to say it, now would be the time to tell him I love him, that being with him might be the best thing that ever happened to me. But I already tried to tell him I was falling in Bora Bora and he dismissed me. I'm not sure after what happened last night, my heart could take it again.

"Your last gift is one that we will also have to pick out together in the spring. I figured it's time I replaced your bike."

I snort-laugh at this. With everything going on in our lives with my recovery, I forgot I was even on a bike when the accident happened. It was never part of my daily routine five years ago, so I forgot it even existed.

"As long as you get one too, then that's perfect."

Charlie kisses the tip of my nose, "Deal."

"I think we knocked our first Christmas as a couple out of the park," I say.

Charlie opens his mouth to agree but there is a knock at the door. I can tell by the look on his face that he doesn't know who it is.

"Mom," he says, surprised, as he opens the door after checking the peephole. A tall, slender woman, her blonde hair pulled into a ponytail, pushes past him with five tote bags slung over her shoulders. Behind her is a short balding man with grays where he does still have hair. He's dragging two wheeled suitcases behind him. The last to enter is a young man who looks like he could be Charlie's twin with the same strong jaw and Italian nose. Charlie has deep milk chocolate brown eyes, but this man's eyes are blue. Charlie has blond hair that has a way of breaking free of being tamed; this man has chestnut brown hair that is slickly combed back.

"My son." She hugs Charlie closely, squeezing him around the middle. Charlie hugs her back, but his back is rigid, arms stiff as they wrap around her.

"Vince, Brad." Charlie shakes their hands, stepping back and taking in the sight of all their bags. He crosses his arms across his chest defensively. "What's going on?" he asks, not introducing me just yet.

I stay where I am, standing beside the island, even as his mother drops her bags from her shoulders.

"That apartment above Bradley had a terrible leak and the heat wasn't working. I just knew that my Charlie would have space for us, so here we are." Charlie looks like he would rather stick his arm in the garbage disposal. "Who is this?" his mother asks, finally catching sight of me.

She looks me up and down from my still damp hair down to the pajamas and slippers on my feet. It's obvious to her that I am not a new arrival, but rather spent the night in her son's home.

"Elia, this is my mother, Barbara, my step father, Vince, and my brother, Brad. Family, this is my girlfriend, Elia."

I swoon being introduced as his girlfriend. I'm saved only by his arm wrapping around my shoulders, keeping me tight to his body. His mother looks like she tasted something sour and doesn't reach a hand out to me. Vince takes pity on me, offering me his hand, shaking it firmly. Brad looks at me curiously, hesitating before finally shaking my hand.

"I made some *pizzelle* for breakfast and can make more if you want. We also have some eggs and I think cinnamon rolls." I step back toward the kitchen, ready to spring into action.

"You can take our bags to the guest room to start. I'll poke around the kitchen and see if there is anything to make. Oh, I just miss making breakfast for my boys on Christmas morning." His mother finally takes in what Charlie is wearing and she laughs.

"She's not the maid," Charlie challenges, reaching back to me so I don't walk away.

She blatantly ignores him and says, "Go change out of that ridiculous outfit and put on some nice clothes."

I regret encouraging him to mend fences with her already.

"I can put your stuff in the guest room, but you're not staying. I'll book you a hotel before you spend the night here," Charlie says, grabbing the bags and moving them out of the way. Vince is quick to help, eager to be useful and do something. Brad doesn't bother to help, sullenly going to sit on the couch. I can't believe he hasn't said anything yet. There is so much going on that I almost miss his mother trying to throw out our Christmas gifts to each other.

"I've got those." I move quickly to get them out of her grip, taking them into the bedroom. Charlie comes in a minute later and closes the door. He leans against it, his eyes closed.

"I have regrets," I confess immediately, prompting a rueful smile from him.

"She can be intense," he admits.

I'm so frustrated, I start to unbutton my top, angry that she made me feel stupid in this outfit. Charlie's hands still mine, finishing the task and holding my eyes.

"I'm not kidding, Charlie. I have to fight to prove myself to everyone in your life. Not a single person is willing to give me a chance. Jack actually sicced Ainsley on you last night, your father called me a strumpet, and your mother almost threw away our gifts." I have to actively try to not stomp my feet like a petulant child. I'm pacing around the room, topless and angry. I'm so mad that I forgot that I was going to get changed.

"I don't..."

"I cannot fight them all, Charlie," I cut him off. I know I must look crazy, my eyes wild, tits flopping around.

He reaches out, takes my hands, and pulls me to a stop. "I can go nuclear today. It is guaranteed to ruin the morning, but if we drink enough, it has potential for entertainment."

I consider it, but not really. Driving a wedge further between him and his mother might win me brownie points with his father, but will do me no favors anywhere else.

"No, I don't want to ruin your relationship with your mother. The whole point of this was to try to mend fences, not attach rockets to them and light them on fire."

Charlie takes off his shirt. He sidles close to me, in my space, his fingers gently tugging my pants down by the waistband.

"If you think..." I start and he cuts me off with a snort.

"Relax. I'm just keeping this moving. My father may have endorsed a quickie while he was outside, but my mother will not."

I pull out a gray sweater and plain black leggings, the festive spirit having left once his mother started to take over my Christmas morning. There is a brief sad look in Charlie's eyes as he watches me get dressed and I'm sorry all over again for the trouble I've brought him. I hope that this guilt will relent soon. The pounding in my head starts, and I rub at my temples, willing the headache away. I shouldn't be surprised, but I am by the sight of Charlie's phone in his hand, no doubt shooting off an email or two for work, never taking a day of rest. When he opens the door, his mother is standing right outside and I want to die.

"I was just listening to see if you were coming out soon. I was going to make you some breakfast. How many eggs do you want?" She is outright ignoring me at this point.

"Elia already made us breakfast. I was just texting dad to let him know that you were going to be here when he came for lunch."

His mother's journey to the kitchen stops abruptly and she turns to him, her whole body rigid.

"Your father is coming," his mother states. Her wrinkle-free face seems almost impassive, but there is a flash of annoyance in her eyes. Her eyes flit to me before going back to her son. Charlie has the same golden hair she does, but all his other looks come from his father. I can't imagine how it must have been raising two boys that are the mirror image of a man she hates.

"Yep, it's a divorce year." Charlie shoves his hands in his jeans pockets. He gives me a wink and if he wasn't thirty-two I would be suspicious that he was trying to Parent Trap his own mother and father, but I get the feeling he just wants them to fight each other instead of picking on him.

"Good, the more the merrier, I say. Ainsley said she would be here at noon, too."

Now Charlie is the one to still.

"No," Charlie's voice is hard and angry.

His mother spins around to look at him. "No?" She is incredulous.

Vince and Brad are watching the exchange from the island. I notice *pizzelle* on the plates in front of them.

"No," he confirms forcefully. I reach up and start to play with my necklace, watching this moment unfold. I want to disappear, become a piece of furniture, so I don't have to witness this battle of wills.

"Who do you think I am, that you can say no?" She puffs out what I think is meant to be a laugh through her nose.

"I think you're my mother. I love you, but Ainsley and I broke up. And I won't let you disrespect Elia like that in my house." He glances at me and amends, "Our house."

"I see." Her tone is cold as she walks away into the kitchen.

"So, text her and tell her not to come," he pushes.

"Only if you text your father not to come," she counters.

"Only if you don't spend the night."

She sighs dramatically. "You would really kick your poor mother out on the street on Christmas?" She pouts, actually sticks out her lower lip, while her hands are braced on the counter.

"Yes. Your husband was an early investor in Amazon. I've seen his portfolio; you can afford to buy an apartment for the night, let alone get a hotel."

She opens her mouth to push further when Brad interjects.

"Ma, drop it," Brad says, taking a bite of a *pizzelle* and still scrolling through his phone. I think I might have found an ally, for once. He glances up at me and sneaks a wink my way, before indulging his mother in some eggs.

A huff is her only indication that she's giving in. The rest of the day, she eyes me suspiciously, while glancing at Charlie to see whether or not he is willing to relent. I try to fade into the background as much as I can, while trying to encourage Charlie to talk to his family.

After the early morning theatrics, we manage to get along well enough. Brad fancies himself an amateur photographer, so he helps show me how to rate photos and adjust the balance and exposure. Charlie and Vince talk shop about investments they see going big and ones they don't understand are exploding with popularity.

Barbara tries to insert herself while I start to cook lunch, but Charlie kicks her out with a look. Vince, however, manages to sneak in. He offers me a few tips to help keep the process going and sweeten up the meals. I share a secret smile with Charlie as he talks with his brother about school and the city.

We manage to survive without any nuclear fallout, though Barbara and I keep away from each other. When we have down time, I pop into the bedroom, wanting to give them space. I want to finish unpacking the stuff from my old apartment. Charlie's mom strolls by the room and sees me pulling out the blankets to set them on the bed. I wanted to take them out the day I brought them over, but my conversation with Vivian weighed on me and it never felt like a good time. Today, now, feels right.

"These don't really match the décor," she says, her fingers running over a frayed edge of the quilt. I sigh as I look at the bright colors and mismatched fabric. As sections got more worn, they would be covered by new fabric, sometimes in hodgepodge ways and other times just by covering the old fabric entirely. My fingers graze the lace from my mother's wedding dress, glad that I have that after the fire.

She had been saving it for me to wear, not all of it, but to have pieces of it for my something old. On her own wedding day, my father stepped on a part of her train, ripping a huge piece that was impossible to fix at the time, while they were taking photos. My father was more distraught than my mother, who reached down and tore off the ripped piece, handing it off to be saved with the rest of their things.

"They don't, but they're terribly warm and comfortable. They're also extraordinarily sentimental."

She raises her eyebrows at me. So I tell her about their origins.

"My mom sent me the family quilt for my first winter in New York. I think it was her way of telling me that I was never alone. Their house burned down in a fire a few years after that, and it's one of the few surviving things I have to connect me with them." Anything else that survived the fire was put in a storage unit, for me to look at when I was ready. I hand her the photo of me and my parents at my college graduation. I swallow the golf ball-sized lump that's lodged in my throat. I will not cry in front of her; she will only think they're pity tears.

"They haven't been able to help after your accident?" She's fishing. Clearly, Charlie has filled her in on my origin with him.

"They died in that fire." My voice is matter-of-fact. I set the frame to the side until I can figure out what I'm going to do with it.

She gasps at this news. "Oh, honey, I am so sorry." This admission flicked a maternal switch inside her. Before I know it, she's pulling me to her chest with her spindly arms.

"You must miss them so much at Christmas."

I hate that she's put into words what has been hurting my heart all day. I've felt so alone in my experiences, but this is one that I can share with someone, something that people can understand. Explaining grief is easier than explaining amnesia. People can relate to grief in ways that no one else can relate with me.

I stay silent, afraid to break this tentative truce that has settled between us. I suppose if having her give me a chance is too much to ask, I will settle for pity.

After I have gathered myself, we both exit my bedroom. Charlie picks up on the shift between the two of us but doesn't comment. When they all leave for their hotel that night, Barbara actually gives me a hug.

"Hopefully, we can plan a longer visit soon. The five of us can have a nice dinner at Nobu or Le Cirque." She pats my cheek in a motherly way, winking at Charlie.

I wonder if maybe we might have someone on our team yet.

Nineteen

SINCE CHARLIE and I are both decided we're not interested in becoming parents, I get an IUD between Christmas and New Years. It leaves me laid up in pain, but one little text asking Charlie when he's coming home, and he leaves work to take care of me in my pain and discomfort.

If I wasn't so miserable, I would be impressed by how Charlie manages to multitask, working while intermittently stroking my hair while I lay there with my head in his lap. Anything I need, he jumps up to get, from painkillers to a heating pad.

Still trying to be accommodating a few days later, Charlie mentions that Jack is coming by to work on a presentation. I'm less thrilled to have Jack in our space, but I also don't want to come between them. I know they have to do this just because Charlie has been here trying to take care of me instead of focusing on his job.

For Charlie, I will do this. I will smile and scrape and bend to make Jack happy, because at the end of the day, he is Charlie's best friend. There is no universe where I make Charlie pick between us.

I try to be ready for when they get home: carefully watching the pasta and checking and rechecking the recipe I had open on my tablet. Charlie smiles at me when he walks through the door, dumping his things on the table before kissing me. I don't want to rub it in Jack's face, the affection that Charlie shows. I gently push Charlie off, even as he nuzzles my neck.

"Dinner is just about ready. Nice to see you, Jack!" I greet, trying to offer him a smile. Jack, to his credit, offers me a wan smile and keeps his thoughts to himself. Maybe there is a chance for us yet.

"Well, it smells delicious," Charlie says, getting set up at the dinner table as the meal finishes. I beam at him, delighted by the compliment.

"So, were you guys friends before college or is that what solidified your friendship?" I ask, taking a bite of pasta. Charlie and I quickly learned that my cooking skills extended as far as boiling water, but I do try during the day to refine some skills. The *pizzelle* is an exception, honed by years of practice and knowing to double the batch because inevitably, the first few are either undercooked or burned beyond repair.

"Dartmouth has this tradition called Trips: freshman year you get to pick a different activity and they set you out in the wilderness for a week with two upperclassmen. We both went kayaking and went the wrong direction the first day. It was pretty great," Jack reminisces, shoulder bumping his friend. "We met Ainsley there and are actually still friends with most of the people from that trip. We stayed friends, pledged the same frat. Charlie got me the internship at his dad's company and that led to my current job."

"Sounds like it was an incredible experience. It's hard not to see how a bond like that could be forged in those circumstances."

Jack gives me a polite nod of agreement. I have to pretend like I'm not watching him eat my food, checking that he's enjoying it.

"So what's this I hear about Charlie finally getting a pet? Not you, of course, but an actual animal whose survival he will have to ensure?"

"Hardy har." Charlie grimaces at the feeble attempt at a joke.

"Yeah, we will be picking them up soon. I'm looking forward to it." I've already ordered a ton of things for the kittens, including a huge cat tree and several kinds of treats.

"Well, I'm just going to warn you, you're the first thing that Charlie has managed to keep alive in his care. Even then he did almost kill you at first. The dude kills cactuses."

I'm unsure what to make of Jack's constant reminders that I'm only here because Charlie almost killed me.

"Well, I'll gladly be here to save the day." I excuse myself, cleaning up dinner and the plates to let them work. If Vivian's experience is anything like mine, I'm sure she will appreciate having Jack home sooner rather than later. Charlie calls after me before I close our bedroom door so that I can read.

"Jack has just reminded me that I have events on the social calendar that I need to run by you. On New Year's Eve, we usually do a thing at a bar with table service. I'm happy to cancel if you don't want to go." He sounds hopeful, like I will say I would rather be anywhere else. I'm tempted to say that I want to stay in and have a quiet New Year's kiss. But, I need to make a good impression on his friends, and canceling their annual get-together would not endear me to them.

"The second is a charity gala at The Met. Our company got a table, so attendance is expected."

I lean against the door frame to the bedroom, imagining Charlie in a tuxedo, and I feel a rush of desire.

"Gala sounds fancy," I comment, fighting the urge to bite my lips. Since getting the IUD, I haven't wanted to be touched, let alone have sex, but now I'm desperate to be alone with him. Just sitting at the table feels like he's too far away from me.

"It is fancy, very fancy, black tie fancy. Vivian offered to go shopping with you to get a dress."

I groan, thinking about the credit card bill with a dress from Nordstrom on it. Any funds I had tucked away are quickly dwindling from all the knick-knacks and other treats I've purchased. I needed to get another source of income, and quickly.

"Take my credit card when you go shopping. There are certain expectations for events like this." He glances back at his computer and focuses on it.

"I really hate doing that." I say under my breath in an unnecessarily annoyed tone.

Charlie lifts his head from his computer to look at me. Jack studies me from the corner of his eye, but doesn't involve himself.

"We can talk about it later." His voice tells me this discussion is over.

Never in my adult life has the urge to stomp into my room and slam the door been stronger. I do step inside the room and close the door, however, so that I can be alone with my thoughts as Jack and Charlie work in the living room.

I go back to editing photos on my laptop and toy around with the idea of selling some as prints. I make a note to look into it tomorrow. One of the photos I'm editing is of Vivian and Jack from their engagement party. They absolutely shine together. His arm is around her waist and his forehead is pressed to hers. Their smiles are radiant as they stare into each other's eyes, love emanating from their entire existence. For all the faults I can find with him, there is no doubt in my mind that he loves Vivian. I soften the picture, adjust the lighting, and then order a print of it for them as a late engagement gift.

I must doze off because I stir as arms wrap around my knees and my back as I'm gently lifted and shifted to my side of the bed. I feel my blue light glasses pulled off my face and a soft kiss to my forehead.

"Jack?" I mumble with a grin.

"Hey now," Charlie objects, pulling the blankets back to climb into bed beside me. "If you don't remember who I am, I'm happy to show you." His words are half-hearted, exhaustion lurking behind them.

I roll over to face him and rest my head on his arm. I open my eyes, meeting his tired brown ones.

"I could never forget you, Charles. Even if I got amnesia again," I reassure him, pressing my lips to his arm. He folds the arm I'm resting on around my shoulders, tugging me closer to him.

"That's good," he whispers. His fingers are drawing circles on my skin as he studies me. I could live the rest of my life beside him in this way. I rest my hands on his chest and tilt my head up to him, locking eyes.

"I love you, Charles Breckenridge." I've wanted to say the words for so long, afraid that he would rebuff them the way that he did in Bora Bora, believing himself incapable of being loved.

He leans forward, presses his lips against mine, and rolls us over so he is on top of me. I look up at him, my eyes searching his face for any glimpse of what he might be feeling. I expect to find his emotions shut behind the wall he uses when working on deals, but instead, I find he's relaxed and open. Open to me, open to what I'm saying.

"I love you too, Elia Daniels. I'm not going to stop loving you, not today, not tomorrow, and not ever. Fate binds us together."

I don't fight the grin on my face, the feeling of safety and love that he provides. He pushes my hair out of my face, kisses me again, and crushes his body against mine.

I feel his arousal in my core and I gently lift my hips against him, letting him know I feel it. I snag his lower lip between my teeth, tugging at it. I could have waited my whole life to find the right time to say those words, but my confidence in our relationship only grows.

"Say it again," I beg.

He laughs, propping himself up on his elbows. "I love you, I love you, I love you."

I reach my hands between us, pulling him free from his boxers.

Charlie huffs, thrusting into my hand. I slowly pull on him, watching his reactions to my touch.

I pull aside my sleep shorts and guide him to me. We take it slow, until we both grow impatient, wanting that release. I hold him close to me as I climax and quiver, his own orgasm coming at the same time.

I nestle close to him when we're done, back in the original positions we were in, and I whisper that I love him until I fall asleep.

Twenty

ALTHOUGH I AGREED TO IT, by the time New Year's Eve rolls around, I hate the idea of having to go out. Maybe it's the constant conflict with Jack, but the idea of having to dress up to go out isn't appealing. Maybe I turned into a homebody during the missing time. The thought of prolonging the year by staying up until midnight is not appealing.

"Wouldn't a better way to ring in the New Year be by starting it six inches inside of me?"

Charlie laughs, walking over to me as I decide between earrings to wear. He grabs my hips and pulls me against his bare chest.

"I would love to start this year like that but I made a promise. I will make one to you now: next year, we can start it in our pajamas, snuggled with our kittens, watching the ball drop on TV."

My body hums at the idea of being with this man for another year. I will be with him for a lifetime if he will have me.

His fingers go to the edge of the dress, which ends just above my mid thigh. It gives new meaning to the term micro mini and I love how sexy I feel in it. When I picked it up the first time, I joked that someone would confuse me for the New Year's ball itself.

The dress is black and covered in sequins and rhinestones, long sleeves to short skirt. The neckline in this dress isn't as dramatic as the one I wore to the engagement party: it is wider than that and it does wonderful things for my cleavage. Charlie's eyes have barely left my body since I put it on. Twice, I've caught him buttoning his shirt wrong. If anything, this is making the case for why we should stay home.

"You're positive I won't be underdressed, as in, having the least amount of clothing on?" I ask, tugging the hem down as if it's going to suddenly grow another six inches by doing that.

"Baby," he starts, and I grin like a teenager, "you are going to be the hottest woman there. I'm going to be fighting assholes off you all night."

"I only have eyes for you," I reassure him, kissing him deeply. His hands start to wander and I pull away.

"Jack and Vivian will be here for dinner any minute," I warn, and the look in his eyes floods my veins with desire. The knock at the door stops us from taking it anywhere, though my hands were reaching for him.

Charlie groans in frustration, pressing a quick kiss to my temple. "Coming," he calls at the door.

"You wish," I mutter with a smirk as he slaps my ass before going to get the door. Now that they're here, I know that I need to hurry. I slide into the bathroom to finish my makeup, sorting through it to see what will match best with the black dress. Vivian comes and finds me and is in an equally short, long-sleeved royal blue dress.

"I am going to freeze my ass off," I say, looking at her in the mirror as I apply my mascara.

"At least you will look hot doing it?" she offers, leaning against the counter.

I glance at her out of the corner of my eye. "We said 'I love you' a few nights ago," I confess to her, smug as I say this. Things with Charlie have been so physical, the words felt like affirmation that what we have is deeper than just great sex.

Somehow, the sex has gotten steamier, as he works to elicit each noise I am capable of. He's pleased, preening like a peacock when he discovers a new one, doing what he can to draw it out again and again. When he comes home from work, I make sure he knows that he may be the boss at work, but he isn't once he crosses the threshold. But I want more: I want a life together that is more than sex, more than orgasms and noises, more than accidents and making amends.

"You two are something else. Jack says that you've bewitched Charlie with your pussy."

I burst out laughing, nearly drawing my eyeliner across my face. "And here I thought it was my sparkling wit." I plant my hands on the counter looking at Vivian. "Honestly, Viv, how long is it going to take me to win him over?"

She sighs and stands up straight. "I don't know. I'm trying to work on him but he's stubborn and hard-headed. I think he feels betrayed by the break-up with Ainsley and he's upset."

"Okay. Well, A., Jack didn't break up with Ainsley, Charlie did. B., I didn't break them up. And, C., He doesn't trust me because of what happened between you and me."

"I hate to keep rehashing this because it's like cutting open a scar to see if you're healed underneath. The root problem was a guy who you're not even with anymore." She takes my hand. "We're good, I promise." She holds out her pinky and I link mine, a long ago forgotten tradition of drunken pinky promises.

"Are you ladies ready? We're going to miss our dinner reservations if you don't shake a leg," Jack calls just before we emerge.

"Beauty takes time, my dear," Vivian says, walking over to her fiancé as he holds out her jacket. For a moment, he only has eyes for her, and then he shifts his gaze to me in greeting. His eyes catch on the necklace that Charlie gave me for Christmas, which rests on my collarbone. Something flashes in his eyes and I reach out and touch it to confirm that it's on right. The moment is forgotten as Charlie shakes my coat for me to step into. The coat is so long that it covers the edge of my dress. The idea of greeting Charlie in just the coat flits through my mind before I dismiss it. I'll have to think more about that another time.

The restaurant is a beautiful Michelin-starred place that I'm excited to try. Charlie made us reservations, which ensured we had a table. I've never eaten somewhere that was fancy enough to take our coats before seating us. Jack keeps it civil during the meal, but I swear he grimaces every time Charlie touches or kisses me. I think Jack actually gags when Charlie tells me I need to try something from his plate and he feeds it to me. I don't stifle the groan of delight as I savor the different flavors. When I do that, Charlie leans over and whispers in my ear.

"I haven't heard you make that noise before." His breath is hot on my neck, raising goosebumps on my skin. I blush at his teasing, but I glance at him, my eyebrow raised suggestively.

"Oh, get a room, you two," Vivian says playfully, sneaking a bite from Jack's plate.

"Seriously. Get a room," Jack's deadpans, killing the mood.

Later, when we're waiting for the car to the club, I'm alone with Jack. Charlie undertook the task of getting our coats and Vivian ran to the bathroom, leaving me with just a small window.

"Seriously, Jack, I thought we moved past this overt disdain."

"You say you're not a gold digger, but you're walking around preening, wearing a ten thousand dollar necklace," he hisses at me.

I reach up and touch my necklace, embarrassed by the cost and the fact that I had no idea. "I'm sorry, it cost how much?" I whisper, but my words are drowned out by a group arriving for dinner. Charlie choses that moment to return with the coats. I wish I had just a few more minutes to puzzle out this necklace business.

"They got them confused. Here you go, love," he says to me, opening the jacket so I can slide my arms through. I want to run back to the apartment, take the necklace off, and lock it in a safe. I'm not sure I've ever owned anything this expensive. My gift for Charlie barely covered the taxes on mine. How am I supposed to fit in this world? Vivian is able to rise to their ranks with her education and job, but what do I have that gets me through the door besides a bewitching pussy?

I'm quiet the entire time we ride to the club. I'm worried I'm putting too much pressure on Charlie by being in this relationship. He wants to be with me, I know he does, but I'm scared that my love for him isn't enough to overcome these hurdles between us. My insecurity about us is starting to be a problem for me, and I know I have to seriously consider therapy.

There is a line around the corner for the club, but we walk straight up to the front of the line. There are people standing at the front, glaring at us as we approach and I can't help but wonder how long they have been waiting.

I hug my coat closer to me as a harsh wind blows through, feeling its bite even through my layers. There is a bouncer with a clipboard checking names and I wonder if we're on it. I'm sure Charlie and Jack look suave enough to pass, their hair slicked back and in their fine clothes. If I can remember anything from before, it's that women get a pass into most clubs, so Vivian and I should be covered. Although, I see plenty of women freezing in the line for who knows how long. If it gets me into the club and out of the cold, I can be okay with blatant sexism.

"Mr. Breckenridge," the bouncer says as Charlie shakes his hand. Folded between Charlie's fingers is cash that he passes on, a move I've seen him perform numerous times with the air of someone who knows that cash is how you get things done.

"Reggie, I hope the wife and family are well."

The man smiles easily. "My wife is due in two months."

Charlie slaps him on the shoulder before reaching into his pocket for more cash. I can never get used to Charlie pulling out his wallet, a hefty load of bills clipped away. He's not even embarrassed or worried about it when he does things like this.

"Put this toward the college fund." There are groans from the line, angry that we've just strolled up, in our warm coats and flushed cheeks, to get in ahead of them. There is, of course, one guy who has to say something about the injustice.

"You're going to let these pricks in ahead of us because of a bribe? If that was all it took, I've got twenty bucks right here!"

Charlie spares a glance at the guy before looking at Reggie with a smirk.

Reggie frowns. "He just slipped me five hundred bucks and dropped twenty Gs on bottle service and you want to give me twenty bucks? Get the fuck outta here." Reggie waves us in, wishing us a 'Happy New Year' as we go.

"Do you ever get tired of throwing your money around like you're Mr. Monopoly?"

Charlie's mouth quirks up at my question. "Not if it still impresses you." He swoops down, kissing my cheek.

The entire club is throbbing from the loud music and movement of the people dancing inside. It's nearly pitch black inside; the only lights in the cavernous room are strobe lights. A hostess leads us to our table, which is tucked in a corner. Our group has already started to gather around the table with bottles of liquor sticking out of ice buckets. College turned me off vodka, after being served the cheap shit in high-end bottles too many times, and gin always tasted like dirt to me. I can't help the downward tilt of my lips, knowing I'll just suck it up and drink the vodka. No doubt this is good stuff, and hopefully it doesn't send my stomach turning at the first taste.

Charlie catches my frown, waiving the waitress back. "What do you want, love?"

My head snaps to the term of endearment. "I'm fine with this," I say, starting to mix a drink for myself.

"You're not. What do you want?"

Vivian must see the war on my face. She knows bottles at events like this are several hundred dollars. Seems kinda ridiculous considering I could go to the store and pick up this shit for pennies compared to what this club charges.

"TEQUILA FOR THIS BITCH!" Vivian shouts at Charlie over the music.

The waitress, who is anxiously looking around at her other tables, just raises her eyebrows to Charlie for confirmation. He hands her his credit card, ordering her to keep the tab open. Behind Vivian, Jack frowns, and I know it's just another nail in my coffin with him. I reach up to my necklace, worried now that someone will steal it right off my neck.

I see Taryn sitting down, with a space open beside her and I move in to greet her. She welcomes me with a hug and I'm grateful for this new friend.

"I'm glad you decided to come. I wasn't sure if this was your sort of scene," she shouts to be heard over the music.

"I'm not sure it is either, but I'm here."

She pours me a vodka cranberry and shoves it into my hand. "The drunker you are, the easier it is to ignore the come-ons. Not that Chuck will let anyone lay a hand on you." She glances over my shoulder. "I was just telling your girlfriend what a catch you are."

Charlie smiles, locking eyes with me and I feel his eyes burn for me. Right now, I think we're both wishing we were anywhere but here. His button-down has the top few buttons undone and he's already rolled up his sleeves. Taryn clinks her plastic cup with mine before tossing it back and I follow suit. My reaction isn't as strong as I expected, but I'm glad that I won't have to drink much of it.

"Thanks, Taryn, I really needed the upsell." The tequila is delivered with some lime slices and a small salt shaker and I have flashbacks to when Vivian and I first moved to the city and we were eager to get drunk as cheaply as possible so we took to doing shots whenever possible. At this time, Vivian and I each salt our hands and hold the glass and a lime. Charlie and Jack join us, along with a few others I recognize from the engagement party a week ago.

"To old friends, new friends, and the love that bonds us all," Vivian toasts.

The salt is coarse on my tongue as I lick it, dulling the taste of the liquor until the lime helps to soothe the burn. I haven't had a serious drink like this in, I don't know how long, so I have no clue what to expect from my tolerance. Although I have to bet it's poor, just from not drinking the last several months. I can feel the liquid warming its way through my veins, spreading to my fingers and toes. Charlie grabs the back of my neck and pulls me to him, kissing me hard.

"And here I thought I was going to be the lush," I tease as we break for air.

We take a second and then a third shot in rapid succession. Charlie told me that he tended to be in the work hard, party harder camp, but that implied that there was eventually a party.

"Let's dance!" he shouts over the music and I follow him onto the dance floor. This is a completely different side to Charlie that I haven't gotten to see, and I love every part of him.

He keeps my body close to his as we move with the music. One leg is between mine as his hand is palmed against my bare back, holding me close. Periodically, his mouth finds mine, his tongue slipping between my lips. The friction of him between my legs makes my head swim, but I hold on to him. At first, Charlie can't keep his eyes off me, his brown eyes locked with my own as we do what can only be described as eye fucking. Eventually, his eyes slip closed, giving in entirely to the beat of the music and the sway of the bodies around us.

Occasionally, other guys will try to dance around us, often quickly getting the hint that our party is invite only, and for now, there are no invitations. Another man comes up and starts grinding against me, sandwiching me against Charlie. I'm out of space to get closer to Charlie in an effort to get away from him, but this guy won't take the hint. The motions he's going through aren't so much dancing as he's blatantly dry humping me, his erection pressing against my ass with each thrust.

Charlie's eyes open, finding mine after sensing my unease, the change in the way I'm dancing. His eyes flash to the guy over my shoulder.

"She's taken," Charlie shouts. He's short of lifting me off the floor when he starts to pivot me away, neither one of us looking to get thrown out for a confrontation with this guy. Charlie might be a high roller, but at a club like this, he's hardly the only one. The guy runs a free hand along my side, and my insides crawl from the unwelcome touch.

"No reason you can't share," he says, and I feel several shades of disgust.

"How about I'm not interested," I shout, pivoting again.

"Sounds like a good enough reason for me. Get lost," Charlie shouts, no longer dancing.

The guy stops dancing. "Stuck up, bitch," he shouts at me before turning to dance with someone else.

Charlie looks like he wants to go after the guy but I grab his arm and shake my head.

"He's not worth it. Let's get another drink. I'm thirsty, anyway." My mood is killed. I'm eager to get some water and then work on getting my buzz back. I pour Charlie another drink and instead of a lime, I cover his mouth with mine. He greedily takes the kiss, leaning back, pulling me with him, so the length of my body is pressed against his. We sit back down beside Taryn, drinks in our hands. Charlie's arm is around me, resting on my hip, his fingertips teasing the hem of my dress.

More of their friends have shown up and I start chatting with them, learning more about Charlie in college. I'm more relaxed now, liquid courage burning through my veins. I feel more on equal footing with his friends now, drinking at a club, than I did when we were dressed in our finest at the engagement party. They talk about his role in getting an army of goats unleashed on campus as a senior prank, the vacations that they took together, the drunken frat parties. We're all laughing for a moment, totally at ease.

"Remember that time you and Ains got caught doing the Dartmouth Seven?"

Charlie's face instantly sours and Taryn goes still beside me. I don't know who the person is that's talking, just that he's one of the fraternity brothers. I may not know what that is, but from the reactions, I have my own assumptions.

"I was there, in the stacks, when you made her scream like that. I mean, you promised you would share your tricks." The guy stands and grinds his hips against the air like he's smacking an ass.

"That was hardly the position he had me in," a female voice says, and I shouldn't be surprised to see Ainsley in a gold glitter dress, radiant like the sun. Her blonde hair is braided in a crown around her head. Her steps are uneven, like she pre-gamed before coming here, but her intention is clear. She moves straight to Charlie, straddling him before leaning back, grabbing the collar of his shirt, and swinging her legs up so her ankles are on his shoulders. I watch as she grinds her hips against my boyfriend and my skin flushes with anger and embarrassment.

I'm shocked dumb that she would do that. I like to think that I would be clever and witty should a situation like this ever happen to me, but I'm not some heroine, ready with a comeback at all times. I can only watch, horrified, that this is happening.

"It was more like this," Ainsley says, her voice husky as she swivels her hips again.

Charlie is beet red, his hands not touching her intentionally. The rest of the group is stunned silent. The guy who started this story sits, unsure of what to do next.

When Charlie doesn't say anything, one of my friends jumps in. "Ainsley, this is Elia, Charlie's *girlfriend*," Taryn says frostily.

It was nearly worth Charlie not saying anything to watch as Ainsley nearly falls over backward getting off him. I love Taryn for not saying I'm his new girlfriend or limiting our time together. I am his girlfriend and that's what matters. When Ainsley scrambles off Charlie, standing before him, I notice the bulge in his pants and look away, embarrassed by the whole situation. Ainsley looks at me, recognition flaring. I must not have been clear with her the night of the engagement party last week.

Who did she think I was when we met? Did she think Charlie picked up some random girl to bring to the party to make her jealous? A sick thought hits me: is that what Jack told her?

"Girlfriend?" she sputters, her eyes flashing to Jack, then back to me and Charlie. She notices how his arm is around my shoulder and she takes one stumbling step back.

"I am," she starts, closing her eyes, and taking a breath, "*so* sorry." She turns to leave. Jack jumps up and grabs her arm. She yanks it out of his hand, and for a second I think she might punch him. I wish she would.

"Fuck off, Jack," she spits, before heading for the door.

Even with the noise of the club, our group is subdued, still trying to figure out what to do next. I hate the curious glances at Charlie and me, waiting to see how we both react to this heinous situation. The guy who started all this rightfully looks embarrassed and takes a sip of his drink.

"So, uh, tonight's on me," he says, forcing a laugh. The waitress is taking a peek at our bottles to see if we need anything more, so he seizes on the opportunity to switch cards.

I want to ask her if there is somewhere I could disappear to, away from the prying eyes. I put my hand on Charlie's leg. "Are you okay?" I ask, trying not to think about how many times Charlie and I have been in that exact position.

He seems to come to life at my touch and he reaches out, running a thumb over my cheek. "I'm so sorry that I didn't say anything." He kisses me on the lips then stands. "I have to make sure she's okay."

My mouth drops open, unable to comprehend that he would pick her in this moment. My eyes drift closed, as I realize that no matter how long I could be with Charlie, he will always have a space for her in his heart. The whole room is hot, too hot, and I want to get outside and away from these people. But I can't escape Charlie's friends and go outside since that's where he went to follow her. I grab the tequila and pour myself a double and knock it back, shuddering at the taste. I didn't even want to come tonight and I wish that I had pushed harder on staying home. But if I had stayed home, I wouldn't have learned that I will always play second fiddle to Ainsley.

Vivian, who had been in the bathroom during the whole sordid scene, returns and asks, "What did I miss?"

Taryn grabs our hands and drags us to the dance floor. "We're going to dance," Taryn says with urgency to Vivian. Jack moves to follow but Taryn turns on him, ferocious. "I think you've done enough for tonight," she scolds, pulling us away from the group. Vivian opens her mouth to ask what happened, but the look Taryn gives her could shrivel balls.

The three of us dance and I try not to think about my boyfriend chasing after another woman. I try not to think about the lengths Jack will go to break Charlie and me up. I take a drink from the waitress, not caring about the cost, not caring about anything as we dance. I ignore the random guys that come up and dance with us, even giving in a little when I feel someone's hands on my hips. I try to let my mind drift to the past when Vivian and I would go out and see who could get the most free drinks.

My eyes are screwed shut, until fingers thread through mine. They're larger and rougher than Vivian and Taryn's. I know these hands; I've felt them on every inch of my skin and inside me. I open my eyes, finding Charlie standing before me.

"Can we talk?" he asks. The DJ lowers the music, alerting us to the impending countdown. I don't know how long I've been on the dance floor, but it was too long, any amount of time was too long for Charlie to have been away with someone else on New Year's Eve.

Taryn rolls her eyes when Jack comes over to grab Vivian for a midnight kiss. She lets out a strangled, disgruntled noise as she looks to the guy next to her, opting to not make him her first kiss of the new year. "I guess I'll just go fuck myself then," she hollers over the music to no one in particular before disappearing into the crowd.

I let Charlie lead me down a hallway where the music isn't as loud and wait for him to say something.

"I'm sorry." He sounds sincere, but I only cross my arms, not as willing to let it slide like I did last week. Or before that with his father's comments.

"I followed her because I had to find out what Jack did," he tries to explain, desperation in his voice. I want to make it go away, how he feels, but I hold tighter to my anger, willing it to stay with me.

"No, you really didn't."

"Yes, she embarrassed herself in front of all our friends. Because of lies he told her. All of these people invest with our company. Our reputations matter. And Jack sacrificed some of that with his lies. And no one, not even Ainsley, deserves that kind of embarrassment."

"So you're saying that she would have done that if you were still engaged?" I counter, my focus is wavering, my anger slipping. I focus on trying to count how many shots of tequila I have done, how many of them I did to punish myself for Charlie's actions.

"Well, no," he objects.

"Then she was trying to stake her claim to you. Even if we weren't together, she wants to get back with you, Charlie. That is so fucking obvious that even Stevie Wonder could see it."

Charlie runs a hand through his hair, ruining the gel styling. I look closely at him but I can't tell if he's as bombed as I am. I give him a light shove to get him to look at me.

"*I* am your girlfriend, not Ainsley. I am the one you're supposed to turn to first. She embarrassed herself by pissing on you like a dog on a hydrant, but she also embarrassed me. You want me to fit in your world? You want your friends to respect me and our relationship? Don't go chasing after your ex. What the fuck were you thinking, Charlie?" I challenge, blinking furiously. He looks heartbroken at how hurt I am.

"I don't know!" he shouts, shifting his weight.

I gently touch the inside corners of my eyes, hoping to catch the tears before they fall and ruin my makeup. "I love you, Charles Breckenridge III. I love you in ways that I didn't know I was capable of, but I do not deserve to play second fiddle to anyone. I won't do it," I say sniffling.

He grabs me and kisses me then but I push him back and he huffs through his nose. He runs his hands through his hair again.

"You will never play second fiddle to anyone. I told you I loved you and that's not going to change. I had no heart before, but you are my heart. You make getting up in the morning worth it and coming home worth it. Did you know I have a couch in my office? I used to sleep on it four nights a week.

"Never in my life have I been home before ten. *Never*, that includes when I was engaged to Ainsley. I come home to you, to us, because I love you. I've loved you for a long time, since before Bora Bora and Thanksgiving. You have given my life meaning in a way that I never had before. I'm sorry, I fucked up."

I waver, looking at him, knowing these things are true. I kiss him then, pulling him against me.

"You are mine," I say, pulling away, looking him in the eyes, "You come home to me."

I kiss him again, reaching down between his legs to rub against him, so that I'm the reason he's hard. Charlie spins us, so I'm pressed against the wall, as he opens his mouth and heart to me, kissing me hard. His hands slide down, cupping my ass, picking me up. I wrap my arms around his neck and he pins me against the wall, crushing me there. He unzips his pants, pulling himself free, not caring that we're in the back of some club.

"I am yours," he confirms, sliding his arm under my leg so it's hooked over it. With that hand, he pulls my underwear to the side and thrusts himself into me.

"I am yours," I echo to him, my voice ragged and breathy. I lean my head back, hitting it against the wall, moaning as he slips back out of me then slams himself home.

Charlie moves his hips in rhythm to the pulsating music around us. I bite my lip and tangle my fingers in his hair as he presses against me.

"Oh God," I moan. I can feel the tide rising in me, the crush of my orgasm ready to render me spent. He must feel it because he uses his other hand to cover my mouth as my moans get louder. He kisses and sucks my neck, a hickey no doubt forming, while shushing me. The tawdriness of it only riles me up further, a throaty moan escaping, despite my best attempts. He bites on my shoulder as he comes, his movements frenzied. Our movements slow as we come down from the release.

There is a banging on the wall next to us around the corner.

"You two better wrap it up. I would hate to kick you out, Mr. Breckenridge," Reggie calls out.

I fix my dress as we both catch our breath. Charlie fixes himself before pulling money from his pocket. He reaches his hand around the corner, without taking his eyes off me.

"This better be from your clean hand, you hear me?" Reggie laughs, before his footfalls fade.

I look up at Charlie who kisses me on the mouth.

"I'm the only one who can make you make those noises." His voice is rough when he says it.

"I'm the only one you're allowed to make those noises with," I counter, unsure if we ever really resolved this.

"I fucked up," he admits, holding his hand out to me. "But I love you and I'll make it up to you. I promise. And I can promise that you are my priority. I can't excuse going after Ainsley. I can, but it just doesn't matter as much as you do."

"I hope you don't plan to make it up by buying me another ten thousand dollar necklace," I scold gently.

He grins, tilting my chin up to look at him. "Nah, that one will probably be twenty thousand. I fucked up big."

I swat at him gently. "Buying gifts is not the way to my heart. Loving and respecting me is the way to win me over. Listening to me is. Sex is great but it's also not the answer to our problems."

He blows out a long breath of air. "I'm sorry. I get it. I'm in the dog house, but can we salvage tonight? Maybe do more tequila shots until I get to take you home and make love to you properly." Charlie walks behind me before scooping down to kiss my cheek, then my neck.

I want to push him about Jack, but now isn't the time. We're both a little drunk and already on edge.

Vivian and Taryn greet us with trepidation. I give them both a nod, leaning into Charlie. For now, we're okay, until I have to lay into him about his friend's attempts to sabotage us. Charlie offers me a drink and I take it. The group of us make our way onto the dance floor and I find myself not caring what his friends think or what they have to say about me or what I do. It can't get lower than watching him follow his ex-fiancée after she gave him a lap dance.

I don't let Jack bother me or Ainsley hang over our heads. I give myself to Charlie entirely, dancing until the club shuts down and I send my wishes for the new year out into the universe.

Twenty-One

WE DON'T WAKE up until the afternoon. Staying up and eating pizza helped to curb the hangover somewhat. Charlie rises before I do, making coffee and getting his laptop, which is how I find him when I wake. I have no intentions of getting out of this bed.

I glance at Charlie out of the corner of my eye. I shouldn't be surprised that he's working, but there it is. What I haven't been able to suss out is if Charlie does this to himself or if it's all pressure from his father. I have to imagine a mixture of both. He catches me, before turning in my direction.

"Can I help you?" he asks, lowering the screen so his full attention is on me.

"Coffee would be wonderful." I mean it as a joke, but Charlie goes and gets my coffee and then returns to his laptop. As I sip my coffee, I continue to watch him. Once again, he lowers his screen and turns to me.

I bite my lip before plunging ahead with my thoughts. "It's going to sound insecure, but are you willing to tell me what you and Ainsley talked about?"

He lets out a sigh, figuring this was coming. I want to feel confident, not only in myself but also in our relationship. But so much has happened that I just can't feel secure. I'm going to have to give both time, but I hope having answers will help build up my confidence. Charlie closes his computer entirely and places it on his nightstand.

"We didn't talk about much. She apologized profusely. She actually wanted me to apologize to you on her behalf. She said she's too embarrassed to show her face around you. She said she was under the impression that I was still single, and I let it drop from there. I was only outside for so long because I wanted to make sure she got in the right PickMeUp! since she was a little unsteady on her feet." He turns to face me better. "You don't sound insecure and you have every right to ask. I am an open book and will tell you anything you want to know."

Content, I open my book, knowing that even if he did chase Ainsley outside, I'm the one in his bed now. It might make me a coward, but I put off confronting him about Jack, knowing that conversation isn't going to lead anywhere good. I'm in no position to issue an ultimatum about his best friend. While I know that Ainsley won't break us up, I believe that Jack just might be the thing that does.

With the gala coming up, I oblige Charlie and go dress shopping with Vivian and Taryn. Unfortunately, Taryn looks the worse for wear, holding a thermos in her hands.

"You okay?" I ask as I meet her outside the store.

"This is full of Dayquil," she says with a sniff. "I can't afford to take time off work, so I'm pushing through. I think I have a head cold."

"Probably because you work too much," Vivian, the last to

arrive, scolds. "I'm sorry, I had a deposition run late. Let's find you a dress."

We spend a few hours going through so many dresses that my head spins. Taryn and Vivian play dress up with me, making me try on some ridiculous options, including one that has an all feather cape.

As I emerge in that dress, I frown. "I feel like a bird," I pout, prompting the two of them to burst into giggles after snapping a photo.

They give me a romper meant to look like a suit. "What are you two wearing that you're putting me in these ridiculous dresses?"

"Well, I'm not going, for starters. Each table is like, a hundred thousand dollars, and my fuck buddy isn't invited, so I don't get to go. I'm here for moral support." Taryn sniffles, sipping from her thermos.

I open my mouth to object, but then back up. "Saying your fuck buddy isn't going to be in attendance implies that there is a fuck buddy in the picture," I point out, slipping back behind the door to try on the next outrageous dress. At this point I know it's for fun, but, my God, do people actually buy these things? I step out in a riff off of an Elizabethan style dress complete with a tall collar that extends over my head, except that the sleeves are clear and the skirt is tiered.

"Seriously?" I ask, stepping out to more giggles, and then I look pointedly at Taryn.

"Sooo, there might be someone I am having a lot of inappropriate sex with."

"As long as it's legal and whoever it is isn't married, I don't see a problem." Vivian shrugs and I nod in agreement, posing for their silly photos, stepping back to put my clothes on.

"Well, if we were going based on when Ellie's dress was from, it's totally illegal."

"How's that?" Vivian asks.

I emerge with the dress we picked an hour ago, its hanger slung over my fingers.

"Well, it was frowned upon during Queen Elizabeth's time to fuck brothers."

"I'm going to need you to elaborate on that," I say. I'm still fretting over the price of the dress when Taryn elaborates, albeit unwillingly.

"Well, and please don't hate me, but I slept with Charlie and now I'm sleeping with Brad."

Vivian spits out the sip of water she was drinking.

"Shut the fuck up. I did not hear this. La la la la la." I try to plug my ears as I hand over Charlie's credit card to pay.

"I can't tell what bothers you more: that I slept with your boyfriend or that I'm sleeping with his brother."

I glare at her, taking back the card, carefully stowing it and the receipt away. "Definitely that you're sleeping with his brother. That is something Charlie should know and I can't tell him. So, now I have to keep something from him. But if you insist on talking about having sex with my boyfriend, I'm going to get mad about that too."

The shopkeeper almost looks disappointed when we walk away.

"I'm going to do both of you a favor and shut this shit down right now," Vivian says with a shake of her head.

"We're in a class together. We were studying and... " Taryn doesn't finish as she spreads her hands and shrugs.

"I didn't realize the anatomy of a penis was relevant to a business degree," I hiss. I'm more stressed over knowing this than I am about Taryn and Charlie sleeping together. I knew they dated and a part of me must have known that they slept together. It's nauseating to have it confirmed.

"They are if I ever want to get a job. I'm going to have to get on my knees to get an interview. So yes, pensises matter for a business degree." Taryn sneezes. "I wish it were easy for me the way it was for Charlie; he got his job because of Daddy. And Jack...well, being Charlie's best friend certainly helped him. Hell, the elder Breckenridge will probably even move people out of the way for Brad." The bitterness in Taryn's voice is almost tangible.

"Listen, I have to get back to work. You two promise that you won't kill each other?" Vivian says as she tries to break away.

I look at Taryn, feeling guilty for snapping at her. Why do I even care if she's fucking Brad? What business is it of mine? And really, this is what this poor girl has to go through in order to have a career?

"I'm good as long as Elia is," Taryn says and looks towards me.

"All fine. I'm sorry it's so rough for you, Taryn." I lean forward and hug her, but she shrugs her shoulder with nonchalance.

Taryn offers to drop off the dress at my apartment because I have one last errand to run. I have to get my kittens. Charlie tried to promise he wouldn't be too late but I know he can't really make those promises with his job. His dad gave Charlie an informal review and told him that he's been slacking off since the fall and it would not be tolerated any longer. I assured him he didn't have to worry about me with the kittens. I am determined to find something to do with my time. The temp agency agreed to give me another chance and is working on finding me some opportunities. Until then, I'm happy to be a stay at home cat mom and try my hand at illustrating again.

The little balls of fur cry the entire way to the apartment. Bonsai and Mochi are contained to our bathroom at first. Watching them explore on the slippery floor both breaks my heart, because they are struggling with getting any grip, and makes me squeal with delight. I don't stop taking photos, finding everything they do adorable. I don't send the pictures to Charlie, knowing that it's cruel to tease him with them when he can't be here. I should leave them in the bathroom until they get used to the space, but when mischievous gray Bonsai sneaks out, I have no choice but to let them into the bedroom.

When Charlie gets home, he finds me spooning them in bed. I hear the bedroom door click shut as he enters. My book is still in my hand where I fell asleep, lights on for Charlie's return.

"I'm sorry, I didn't mean to wake you," he whispers, keeping the light dim. "Any room for me in the bed?" he asks, stripping and climbing in. I'm well-ensconced on my side of the bed, no threat to Charlie's side. He moves to my side, spooning me. We fit together so easily, like we have been made for each other. One arm slips under my neck, folding over my shoulders. One leg slips between mine while his other hand extends over my middle, finding a small pile of fur purring in their sleep.

"Always," I whisper, turning my cheek to him for a kiss. His lips press against me before we both fall into a deep sleep.

Bonsai and Mochi are photo gold as I follow them around, taking photos of them in the beams of sunlight streaming through the windows. I edit their pictures as they nap on my side, exhausted from playing.

It's midday when there is a knock on the door and I jump up, expecting it to be Benji with another package, but it's Charlie's dad.

"Mr. Breckenridge." I'm sure the surprise is all over my face as well as in my tone. I tug on the bottom of my shirt, wishing I was wearing a bra. My shorts are indecent, comfortable in the heat of the apartment, but the arrival of Charlie's father has brought a chill with him.

"Elia," he greets me as he pushes past me into the apartment.

I close the door and follow him inside.

"Charlie isn't here."

"I came here to see you."

I cross my arms waiting.

"I need to close a business deal and I need Ainsley's father to do it." Charlie's father sits on the couch and disturbs the sleeping kittens, who move to the other side, away from him.

"He's an old friend, and when the kids called off the engagement, well... Let's just say the relationship soured. I'll have an espresso," he orders, in the middle of his villain's monolog.

I want to tell him exactly where he can put that coffee, but the sooner he leaves, the better.

"As I was saying. You seem to be of humble stock, state school, no further aspirations past college, no additional degrees. Your work history indicates you dabbled in office work. Your parents were blue-collar folks. Respectable. Your mother was a real estate agent who sold your father the family home before they fell in love. Your father owned a local hardware store which, you sold for a pretty penny after their deaths. The wrongful death lawsuit certainly helped bolster your savings, but student loans and a vacant apartment are quickly eating away at it. By all accounts, you were raised by honest God-fearing folks." He leans back, sipping his coffee.

I stay perfectly still, watching him. Charlie may not have done a background check to find out who I was but his father certainly did.

"You seem like a nice girl and I have nothing against you. But you have to see that you're just standing in the way of the inevitable. Ainsley and Charlie have been like two magnets circling each other, never the right side facing the other. But now, we have a chance to give them a real shot that they can only take if you step aside." Charlie's father sets the cup back on the table.

"Your upbringing did not prepare you for the type of life you will have with Charlie. Sure, you're fine with him working night and day now, but what happens in two years when you're lonely and you start to wonder if he really is working late, or if he's meeting with Ainsley or some other woman? Those doubts will never stop nagging you as you wonder if your country bumpkin upbringing is enough to dazzle him when he's surrounded by women raised like him. Women who went to boarding schools and had private tutors. Women with families that have jets and yachts, while all you have to offer him is a piece of ass. Something he can get anywhere and not have that piece nag him about how lonely she is in his penthouse apartment taking pictures of cats."

I clench my teeth, refusing to look away.

"I'll write you a check for however much you want. I know your funds are dwindling from the settlement and the sale of the business. Even if you wanted to keep up, you could never." He unfolds his hands, slides off the couch, and heads to the door.

"And listen, if you want a job after, I can get you a position as an assistant at any company. You make a mean espresso and that counts for something." Charlie's father doesn't wait for any sort of response before walking away, leaving me with his words.

My body is quaking as he leaves. He was right about everything: my parents, my upbringing, even my thoughts and concerns. It's as if he plucked my worst fears from my head and gave them a voice. Alone in this apartment, I try not to consider how right he might be.

Twenty-Two

THE GALA IS two days away and I'm sitting in bed with Charlie as he plugs away on his computer. I lean over and kiss him gently on the neck.

"I love you, but I really need to get this done," he says looking at me, his eyes strained from staring at the screen. It's been days since we were home together and I was awake enough to hold a conversation. Try as I might to wait up for him, I can never manage it. His father's words feel like a burden I've been carrying alone, despite my desire to talk to my partner about it.

Without talking to Charlie to curb the nasty voice in my head, it grows louder. This voice screams and shouts at me that I am the other woman in this love story. I can only assume that the one-sided conversation was intentionally timed. Charlie has a deal he is desperate to close and has been working nonstop on it.

I spend my days replaying the conversation, visualizing the ways I would have told him to fuck off. In most of them, I dump the coffee on his lap, doing irreparable damage to what I imagine is his favorite bit. I imagine telling him that he can't kick out the mother of his grandchild, his only shot at it since Charlie decided to get sniped, both lies, but I enjoy picturing his face when he realizes that I'm forever tied to him. I want to be forever tied to him because I love his son, and if loving Charlie means listening to his father primp and preen, then I will do it. Maybe I should get a job to prove that I'm not a gold digger.

"Do you think I should get a job as an assistant?" I ask, broaching the subject. Charlie sighs and pauses for a moment. There is so much communicated in that one sound.

"You don't have to if you don't want to. If you want, I can make some calls, but really, Elia, I do not have the time or energy to fight with you about money."

I lean back away from him. "I'm not trying to start a fight." But my words have an edge to them. Maybe I am looking for somewhere I can work out my frustration, someone I can shout at, someone to just listen to me. I go quiet, watching as he closes his computer and gets out of bed.

"I'm going to go work in my office. Don't wait for me," he says, kissing the top of my head before he walks out, his footfalls heavy.

I can't sleep, leaving things like this, but I have to try. I have to hope we find time to talk before the gala. As I toss and turn, I realize that everything right now with Charlie is a waiting game. I'm waiting for the right opportunity to talk about us and about what his father said to me. But Charlie is worth it. Worth every minute and every worry because when we are focusing on each other, everything is perfect. There is no nagging voice telling me I don't deserve him. I need that voice quieted for good.

When the gala rolls around, I have run out of time to talk to Charlie about his father's offer to pay me off. He gets home an hour before the gala with barely enough time to get changed. At his insistence, I have a professional come to do my hair and make-up. It was a simple and direct order: ask Vivian who she is working with and schedule an appointment with them.

When he walks into the bedroom, I'm seated in the bathroom, getting my hair done. The woman has been talking ad nauseum about a famous client she had who she can't name because of nondisclosures, but who definitely shaved her head once. I try to look interested in what she's talking about, but she never gives me a chance to get a word in edgewise so it doesn't matter. She blatantly ignores the book in my hands that I'm so close to finishing but can't focus on because of her talking.

"You dyed your hair," he says, taking off his tie and tossing it aside. I meet his eyes in the mirror.

"Yeah, a few days ago. It's my natural color."

His lips twitch into a smile as I wince, the hair stylist pulling my hair back. The chestnut color makes me feel more like myself. I had gotten used to the blonde but this feels right. Both hair stylists told me to avoid bleaching my hair again because my hair will just get more brittle and break. It's taken extreme conditioning to get it back to a manageable state.

"I'll get dressed in the guest room. You look beautiful," he says before disappearing.

"He's quite the catch," the hair stylist says, wrapping another curl around the wand. She leaves me with enough time to slip into my red dress and put on my jewelry before leaving.

We both emerge, ready to go, with only fifteen minutes until the start of the event.

"We're going to be late," I point out, stepping into the living room while putting on my earrings.

"No, no one is on time for these things anyway. Who are you wearing, by the way? The photographers are going to ask." He isn't looking at me as he focuses on his cufflinks. When he does, I feel like my entire body is on fire, his eyes licking up my body. My whole being burns and I want to forget the party and jump him in his trim cut tuxedo. The suit jacket is open, revealing the tight white shirt underneath.

I'm in a floor length, a-line red dress. It conforms to my every curve, including the draping along my cleavage. My movements have to be slow and controlled because one wrong move and I'm afraid a seam will split. It feels like one already split since there is a slit on one leg that ends at the crease on my hip. This is, of course, the leg with my scar. My friends insisted that they didn't notice and no one would be looking at the scar anyway. I yearn for the days when Charlie would massage the wound for no reason other than to have an excuse to touch me.

"I think we're going to be a little later than planned." Charlie walks over to me and kisses me on the mouth. He doesn't know where to put his hands, skimming along the outside of my body, from my shoulders down. His hands settle on my hips, moving up my back where he finds that the dress is backless.

"You undo me," his voice is breathless. He steps forward, forcing me back one step at a time until I'm pressed against the wall, my head knocking into a picture. He plants his hands on either side of me, grinning like a fool. I can see the things he wants to do to me playing in his eyes like a movie. I bite my lower lip, wishing we could play them out.

"I refuse to go to this event looking like a trollop because you couldn't keep it in your pants for a few hours." I gently push him off me.

He groans, dropping his head to my shoulder, pressing a kiss to my neck. If he pushed, even just a little, I would let him take me. I would let him take me on every surface of the apartment. My laugh comes out a little breathless.

"I did want to ask. Do you think I should let the makeup artist cover this up?" I don't have to point to my scar because we both know what I'm referring to. It's not as bad as it once was but it is still pink and noticeable. He shakes his head, stepping away from me so he can pay the hair and make-up people, who have cleaned up and are waiting near the front door.

"No, you don't need it." He waits until they're out the door before he drops to his knees before me. I wonder for a second what he has in mind. His lips graze my scar with a sweet kiss before he moves his head between my legs. I gasp as he lifts one of my legs and rests it on his shoulder. My breaths are coming rapidly, his face moving my skirt to the side. His hot breath against my middle makes my knees weak and I'm glad he's there to support me.

"When we get back here, I am going to taste you. To remind you of every reason that I think you're beautiful and that this stupid scar doesn't matter."

I know that I'm already wet. "Why don't you just show me now?"

"Greedy girl. I thought you didn't want to show up looking like a trollop." His hands slide up my legs to my hips before pulling down my underwear. He hooks my other leg over his shoulder, balancing me there. It's precarious but the moment his mouth touches my wet folds, thoughts evacuate my head.

I moan, fingers threading through his hair, my hips swinging up to meet his lips as he sucks my clit. One finger, then a second, pump into me greedily, guiding my body to the edge.

"Oh God, Charlie, oh."

He quickens his pace until I come to the precipice of oblivion, and I don't just fall into it, I dive. My body clenches around his fingers and my ears ring from the power of my orgasm. If this was supposed to convince me to go to the party, it has the opposite effect.

Gently, he sets me down, one foot and then the other, making sure I can stand on my own. His eyes search mine greedily, watching my face as I come down from the high. He drags the back of his hand over his lips.

"It's been too long since I've tasted you. Too long since I heard those noises." He kisses my lips. The taste of me on his mouth is surprisingly heady.

"You have been," I let out a steadying breath, "busy." I follow Charlie to the bathroom, quickly scooping up Bonsai because she was clawing at the edge of my skirt. Charlie vigorously brushes his teeth and I press a kiss to Bonsai's head before setting her down.

"I promise, this project is ending soon. I think I'm going to need a few days after to put some things in order. After that, maybe we can find a cabin with no internet that we can escape to and then I can screw you on every possible surface."

"I like the sound of that." I thread my fingers in with his, leaning into his side. "Besides, we have a lot to talk about once you're around for more than just fifteen minutes at the start of every day."

"Well, that sounds ominous."

It's a testament to his faith in us that he's not worried about our relationship when I say that.

I'm blinded by flashing lights when we get to the Met. Charlie's hand on the small of my back helps to keep me in the moment and from getting too overwhelmed. He holds me close to him as we pose for pictures, even though I don't understand why we're being photographed. I hope I don't seem too oblivious to what I'm supposed to be doing. I place my hand on my hip, Charlie's chest, turning this way and that.

Charlie leans down and kisses me, grinning as the cameras snap furiously. As promised, they ask about the designer of my dress and Charlie answers easily, having checked the tag in the limo. His father arrives, requesting they take some photos of the father and son power duo. Charlie's eyes question me, looking for permission.

The look from his father is enough for me to give him a reassuring nod. Charlie lets me go for the first time with a quick kiss. They look powerful and fierce in their matching tuxedos. I can see one of Charlie's possible futures standing beside him if he follows in his father's footsteps. The future beside him is long hours, divorces, and alienation from his child. I can only hope that me being in his life doesn't lead him down that path.

I'm politely standing off to the side when his father waves a few other people over. Among them is an older gentleman and Ainsley. The similarities between them tell me they're related. He's small like her, only a hair taller than her, but even during an event like this, he has a grim set to his mouth. The four of them stand together, the fathers bracketing their children between them.

Ainsley looks classic beside Charlie in a strapless white gown and natural make-up. Even with the fathers in the photo, it looks like it could be a snapshot from their wedding. The mermaid-style gown she's wearing has beading all up and down the bodice in intricate designs. When asked about it, I think I hear her comment that they're Swarovski crystals. The lower half of the dress flares out with small chiffon layers that give it a feathered look.

Beside Charlie, Ainsley looks like the wife, resplendent in white. And with me dressed in red, I look like the other woman, the mistress, the one that is on the outside. Ainsley is angelic in white, her blonde hair gathered in a simple updo, tendrils framing her face. I have a glittering dress that's low cut with a high slit, and my dark hair is free in finger waves. I feel like the whore his father said I was. One glance from his father tells me he knows exactly what it looks like. There are cameras on me, and I hold my head high, biting the inside of my cheek to stop myself from crying.

Ainsley looks at Charlie with deep love there. It's the same look my parents would share and it only serves to deepen the feeling that I'm the third person in this relationship, not Ainsley. I see her mouth move, a furtive glance at Charlie, as she smiles for a photo. He answers her, his hand carefully set on her shoulder in a platonic touch. She surprises me, when her eyes find me, and she waves me over.

I step forward into the pictures and Ainsley stays there for a moment, turning her head this way and that before stepping away. Charlie's hand rubs my bare back, moving to settle on my hips in a very un-platonic way. We head inside, out of the freezing cold, leaving the photographers to their work with the next crowd of guests.

We're barely through the door and away from the overwhelming attention of the crowds looking to spy a celebrity when Ainsley approaches us.

"Charlie, can I speak with you alone, please?" Her voice is pleading as her green eyes flit from Charlie to me and then back again, trying to prove that she's not ignoring my existence. I start to pull away from him, to let them talk, but Charlie's muscles tense, holding me closer to him.

"Ainsley," he starts, but stops, blowing out a hard breath. "No." His voice is firm and final as he leads me to our table.

There is a small reception area as we enter, where there are people welcoming the guests and directing them to the party. Even the staff is dressed in gorgeous gowns, hair perfectly coiled up in intricate updos and make-up expertly applied. The stage is set up in a stunning room with glittering lights and priceless jewels on display. I realize I don't even know what this event is raising money for, but at a hundred thousand dollars a table, they surely have raised plenty of funds. I'm pretty sure the wealth in this room would be enough to end world hunger if they wanted. My dress alone cost five figures, and I'm positive mine is bargain-priced compared to these other ones. Across the room, I think I glimpse an A-list celebrity and his attorney wife chatting with the mayor. Magazines and media don't do these events justice. There is a series of ornate chandeliers hanging over the space and a stage is set up in the center of the room with what appears to be a small moat around it.

Before we go to our table, I snag Charlie's arm, stopping him. I take his hands in mine, giving him a reassuring squeeze.

"I think you need to talk to Ainsley," I urge, and he looks confused. "I think you both need closure. I don't know if she's still hoping that you can get back together or if that's just what everyone keeps telling her. As the other woman who is being told that you two are inevitable, you need to close that door if that's how you feel."

His brow wrinkles. The crestfallen look on Ainsley's face when Charlie walked away from her was heartbreaking. I want both of them to be put out of their misery.

"Who is telling you..."

I cut him off with a kiss. It's quick, sweet, and meant to silence him. He doesn't even have a chance to react before I pull away. "We can talk about it later, but think about it."

Our table is perfectly situated with a view of the stage and not overly close to any speakers. Since events like this are sold by the table, I know that we're going to be with Charlie's co-workers and, likely, his father. Vivian explained that these tables rake in two hundred thousand dollars each. Getting a table is like paying for the option to buy season tickets. A filthy amount of wealth is sitting at them.

"You look expensive," Jack says, shaking Charlie's hand as I hug Vivian. "What's the nightly rate?"

"I said enough," Charlie's voice is furious as he glares at Jack. I wonder how much Jack's been in Charlie's ear at work. For the first time, I consider that as bad as I've been hearing I'm not good enough, he's had it worse surrounded by it all day at work. My heart swells with love for this man who would defy those in his life to love me.

Even Vivian looks furious with Jack, but she's never been the public outburst sort of person; she is unwilling to make a scene anywhere, let alone at an event like this in front of Jack's bosses. Her pursed lips and raised eyebrow tell me that he's going to get it when they get home. I almost wish she would lay into him; maybe it would finally shut him up. I squeeze her hand, reassuring her that I'm fine. Jack holds his hands up defensively.

"I can take a hint when my jokes aren't funny. I apologize, Elia. You look lovely." He doesn't sound overly apologetic, but I dip my head to him, accepting it anyway. Charlie pulls out my seat for me and I try not to let this dampen my mood.

Charlie's father is seated at the table and so is Ainsley's dad. The empty seat beside him tells me that she's supposed to be seated here as well, but it remains empty for most of the night. It's only filled by those hoping to talk to her dad. Charlie's father keeps looking at the empty chair and then at his son, disappointment in his eyes.

We spend the next few hours chatting as we eat. Charlie is between his father and I, letting me talk to Vivian as she talks about this ass of an attorney she has to deal with. During the speeches, I learn that the fundraiser is for the Relocation of the North American Deer from the Northeast. It's so oddly specific, and to me, utterly useless, but I guess they were just looking for a reason to have a party.

"Do you donate to actual legitimate charities as well?" I ask Charlie as the last course is served.

"This is all dad, though I did have to chip in for your seat. I'm all for saving the West Coast otters, but I don't think they need the funds."

"North American Deer," I correct.

Charlie snorts into his whiskey. "That must have been last year. But yes, besides your medical bills, I do make some regular donations. The trust fund is set to make automatic quarterly donations to the charities of my choosing. If there are any causes you feel strongly about, I'm happy to add them to the mix."

"Trust fund? Are you real? Maybe this is still a coma dream."

He laughs, his hand sliding up my bare thigh, exposed by sitting. "If this were a coma dream, I would ravish you on this table and no one would bat an eye. But I promise you that this is real and my father would have some very strong opinions about any ravishing. To answer your question, yes, a trust fund. It's how I bought the apartment. It's set up and making some very smart investments to sustain me. It's why I didn't bat an eye at your quarter of a million hospital bill."

I choke on my champagne. "Now you're just bragging."

He kisses the spot below my ear, pulling me up to dance. "Maybe, but I like to think it impresses you when I do."

We don't dance the same way we did on New Year's Eve, but our bodies are just as close, his hands never leaving me. The celebrity DJ, who used to be on some trashy reality show, keeps screaming to do it for the deer and keeps trying to get more donations. I don't know how much it would cost to relocate deer, but I imagine the over one million dollars raised just in tables is enough. A slow song starts and couples pull their significant other closer to sway with the music. Charlie dips his head so that he can get closer to me. I turn and press a kiss to his lips.

"I love you," I say, giving his hand a gentle squeeze.

He spins me out on the floor before pulling me close to him. "I love you, too. There isn't anything that will change that."

I grin like a fool. The love between us is easy but it's the other voices around us that make it difficult. If his trust fund is as big as he likes to brag, maybe we should just move the kittens to Bora Bora and live the rest of our lives away from the detractors and naysayers.

We separate when I go to use the ladies room. I manage to get turned around, too tipsy and confused to know where in the museum I am. When I try to return, I wind up taking a wrong turn and catch sight of Charlie's back. I pause, hoping he might be talking to Ainsley like I suggested. It's wrong to eavesdrop, but I never claimed to be above it.

"I hope you're happy now. The Seaborns are withdrawing their investment. The Japanese social media company deal tanked because you were too busy thinking with your prick. You're missing meetings and you're being sloppy. Ashley keeps trying to cover for you but I know you're leaving work early to get soup dumplings or some other shit. If you want to keep your whore on hand, get her an apartment near the office so at least your time offline is reduced."

I can't see Charlie's face as his father says this, but I can see the rise and fall of his shoulders as his father dresses him down, shoving a finger in his face.

"Another thing: if you're incapable of actually doing your job, Brad emailed looking for an internship. Maybe I can have one son who isn't a total fucking failure. I was apparently wrong about all the business acumen I thought you had. Your brother might be better suited for taking over the company. Fuck, even Jack is doing a better job than you. You're an embarrassment to me and my company."

I'm sure they can both hear my heart hammering in my chest as I step just out of sight when I hear footsteps.

"Either you ditch the girl or you can find a new job. You can say goodbye to the cushy corporate card and doorman building and all your other luxuries. I will blacklist you in this industry, boy."

I watch as Charlie's father storms past me, not even noticing where I'm pressed against the wall. A moment later, Charlie's footfalls follow his father's out of the hallway, hands buried deep in his pockets. He doesn't notice me either.

I can't imagine how Charlie feels if I need to take a steadying breath from that encounter. I knew things weren't good, that being offered a payoff wasn't good, but fuck. Fuck. I can't think straight as I head back to the table. The light effervescent buzz I had going from dancing in Charlie's arms and the glasses of champagne is gone.

When I get to the table, Charlie is seated, laughing at something Jack has said. Jack is alone, I'm unsure where Vivian is, and it just makes my stomach turn seeing him. I don't want to face Jack, who will no doubt tell Charlie what a mistake staying with me would be. Who will reinforce that I'm the worst thing to happen to him, as if that wasn't already echoing in my mind.

Maybe, because of how much I love Charlie, I need to let him go. I have blown up his life in so many ways, I can't be the reason that he loses his job and his father. I can't imagine that would ease things with Jack either. My mind keeps jumping to that old adage, if you love someone let them go.

I shake off these thoughts, these worries, as I approach the table. I'm hobbling, thanks to my poorly broken-in heels, and I try to focus on the physical pain rather than the emotional pain I'm inflicting on myself. When Jack sees me approach, he nudges Charlie, gesturing to me before rising to leave us alone at the table. Charlie smiles at me, rising to pull out my chair, but the smile doesn't quite reach his eyes.

A waiter drops off plates of various desserts. The petit fours are gorgeous, looking like tiny presents, and I can't wait to dig in. I press my hand on top of Charlie's, wanting to say something, suggest we leave. For all the glamor that the night has brought, I just want us to go home. It feels like every time we take a step forward, we're shoved five steps back.

"Lia?"

I look up, recognizing a nickname that my parents used to call me. I take in the sight of the waiter, but I don't recognize him. He clearly recognizes me. He has piercing blue eyes and is a few inches shorter than Charlie, but still towers over me. His hair is jet black, slicked for this job, but it's trying to fight back; a few strands are pointing in the wrong directions.

"I'm sorry, have we met?" I ask, feeling Charlie's hand on my hip lending me strength. I can feel him move closer to me, curious and cautious about this man.

"You don't..." he hesitates, looking confused, "remember me?"

he barely chokes out. The stranger's eyes don't move from me, not even to look at Charlie.

"I'm sorry, I had an accident a few months ago, and have some related memory problems."

This crushes the man and he sits down in Vivian's vacant seat. I glance at Charlie and we both remain standing.

"I wondered," he sighs, looking at me. "You dyed your hair. But I would recognize you anywhere."

"How do you know her?" Charlie asks as he subtly puffs out his chest. His hand has moved to my shoulder and he gives me a little squeeze.

"I am, or, I guess, was, her fiancé." His words are a physical blow and I stumble back.

Charlie's hands catch me, steadying me. I ease down into the chair, finding my knees weak. He sits beside me, his hand staying on me.

"Fiancé?" I choke. "Can you elaborate?" I try to remember his face, his lips, anything about him, but I find nothing, emptiness. My soul doesn't reach for his, trying to reconnect us; he's as good as some random person on the street.

"What is there to elaborate on? We were engaged," this man says simply. I wish he were wearing a name tag.

"And you haven't looked for her in the five months since the accident?" Charlie asks incredulously. There is a hint of fury in his words. "She didn't have a ring on during the accident. Why is that? What was your name?" he demands.

"I'm sorry, but who are you? I'm Bryan. And no. She wouldn't have been wearing a ring. Our relationship was above such materialistic displays of ownership. We had a huge fight and I thought you were done with me. I tried to call you, but I got a message that the number was disconnected. I went to your apartment but no one answered when I knocked. I thought this was your way of cutting me out." He exhales sharply. "And now, to find out that you didn't leave me. That you don't even remember me. I should have been there." Bryan slams his fists on the table, seemingly angry with himself.

I flinch, leaning into Charlie. He pulls me to him, trying to tether me to him. I glance around to see if anyone else heard, but the party goes on around us as my whole world shifts on its axis.

"What was the fight about?" I ask, wondering what was so bad that he would think that I ghosted him for five months. That he thinks I would have walked out like that.

"I had been at a bachelor party and kissed a waitress. It was a stupid mistake that I was honest with you about. The last time I saw you, you were leaving in the middle of the night while it rained. I tried to plead with you to stay, but you said you needed space. I thought I was giving you space." His voice cracks again and he rubs furiously at his eyes as a tear escapes. I fight the urge to correct him that it was a hurricane but splitting hairs over that seems petty. I could see myself having that sort of reaction to a betrayal like that; leaving, needing space, but I would never leave for so long.

"Lia, I love you. I'm so sorry," he says, reaching out and taking my hands in his.

I am the one frozen this time, unsure what to do. I pull my hands back, just a little, but he holds tight to me, blue eyes boring into me. I don't want to believe this. I don't want to have, of all things, a fiancé hidden in the five years of lost memories. Maybe he's just an actor hired by Charlie's father or Jack to further sabotage us. But he called me Lia. It's a nickname I've had before, and it feels familiar somehow coming from this stranger. The lure of finally getting answers is too strong.

"This really isn't the place for this," Charlie says abruptly.

Bryan stands, not wanting to let go of me. "Can we talk after this is over? Please?" His voice is pleading. "Losing you once nearly ended me. I can't lose you again."

Charlie reaches into his pocket and pulls out a business card, always prepared. "Call me tomorrow and we can set up a time."

Charlie's voice is calm but I can feel him nearly shaking beside me.

"No, it needs to be tonight," Bryan insists, tightening his grip on my limp hands.

Charlie sighs, looking at me. I meet his eyes and I can't imagine what he sees reflected back at him. Fear, confusion, love. I know what I see in his: terror and steely resolve.

"Get back to work and you will have an answer before we leave." Charlie's voice is firm, his work voice that I've heard him use on calls.

Bryan doesn't seem to like being dismissed but finally lets go and walks off.

Charlie sits back down and pulls me close to him, turning so I'm looking at him.

"You don't have to talk to him," Charlie reassures me, voice soft.

I seem to come back into the moment. I'm no longer floating above myself, watching these events unfold and wondering what to do with this new information. Fate threw Charlie and I together, but was it just so Charlie could learn that there is more to life than work? Is this the universe's way of correcting our course? Sending me back into the life I don't remember so Charlie doesn't have to address the ultimatum?

"I think I have to. You don't?" I ask. I need guidance, someone to tell me what I should do.

"I am the first person who will support you in anything and everything you do." He lets out a breath and looks in my eyes, trying to read my mind.

I can't look at him, looking past him around the party, everyone in their glittering dresses and tuxedos. Of all the thoughts that cross my mind, the horrible little insecure voice in my head reminds me about what his father said and what Jack continues to say about our relationship. I trace a finger along Charlie's strong jaw, my thumb brushing his lips. He purses them, kisses my thumb, grabs my hand, and then kisses the inside of my palm. I have to hold onto the feel of his skin against mine.

If hearing Bryan out and letting Charlie go will save Charlie from having to choose between me and his closest friends and family, then I will do it. I have to do it. I love this man. I love everything about him, but I won't put him in the position where he has to choose between me and his father, me and his job, me and his friends.

"I think I owe it to the woman I was for the last five years to talk to him. He was my fiancé before the accident."

I watch as my words strike him the way I want them to. His eyes shutter, bringing back the guilt of the early days when all he would talk about was trying to make my life right again. The mention of what I lost is all it takes to stir those buried feelings of his. What he may have taken from me because of the accident or what I left behind. Neither one of us imagined a fiancé lurking.

"If this is what you want, then I'll set it up." Charlie presses a kiss to my forehead and I think we both feel that this is the beginning of the end. I try to savor the feel of his kiss on my skin but I know that it will fade. Even if nothing comes from talking to this Bryan guy, I've done enough to Charlie. Tonight made it clear why I don't fit in with his crowd. I wish we had never returned from Bora Bora because there our bliss was genuine, but here in New York, there is no bliss for us; just the harshness and cruelty of the real world.

He rises and goes back to find Bryan. I sit at the table and cover my mouth with my hand as I consider what I have just done.

Twenty-Three

CHARLIE, true to his word, set up a meeting with Bryan. We found a quiet, neutral place for us to talk the next day since Bryan was desperate to have this conversation. Charlie and I barely speak when we head home and then retire early due to the elephant in the room. There is no ravishing as promised earlier. I can't really sleep. I wonder what's on Charlie's mind, and if the restless movements next to me are any indication, Charlie doesn't sleep either.

I can barely handle looking Charlie in the eye as we head to the meeting. Is his father's ultimatum running through his mind? Is he wondering what he would do if he was fired and blacklisted? I don't know how much power his father has to make that happen. He seems like the sort of snake oil salesman who has a lot of chips to cash in and a lot of friends in powerful places. Would Charlie's trust fund keep him afloat? Would his friends still talk to him if he's so completely exiled?

Before we go into the restaurant, Charlie holds me back, his hands gently holding my upper arms. "Are you sure?" he asks, his eyes searching my face, looking for even a hint of hesitation.

I don't trust myself to speak, so I just nod. Charlie holds the door open for me and steps back to give me space. If he knew I was doing this for him, he wouldn't let me go. I wouldn't put it past him to throw me over his shoulder and march us home.

Bryan is already seated in a booth, playing with a pack of cigarettes on the table. When he sees me, his eyes don't leave me. I'm more bundled up than in the dress I was in last night. I feel safer in the wool sweater and boots than in the red dress and heels.

Charlie looks from me to Bryan before crossing to the bar and pulling up a stool. I wasn't sure I could talk to my fiancé while my boyfriend sat beside me.

I slide into the booth across from Bryan, studying his face, hoping for some sort of memory to be jogged. His hair is messier than it was last night and there is a fresh layer of stubble on his cheeks. He looks like he got just about as much sleep as the rest of us. There is no sudden flare in my chest. I try to reach out to him with my heart, looking for something hidden away, a reminder that this is the man that I wanted to build a life with.

"You look so different. I miss the blonde. You loved being blonde."

I touch my dark tresses, fingers tangling with my curls before tossing them over my shoulder and letting out a long, steadying breath. Maybe I had liked being blonde, but for the last four months, it hasn't felt like me.

"I didn't come here to talk about my hair. How did we meet?" I feel like I'm playing twenty-one questions as I ask Bryan about our relationship.

"I guess I have to fill you in on our whole lives together since you don't remember me at all. Amnesia, really? I thought that was just something that happened in books and movies or on soap operas." Bryan rubs his hands on his jeans, lifting his eyes to mine.

A waitress stops by and asks if we would like anything. We both just order coffee. I can't imagine keeping any food down.

"So, we met a few years ago at a bookshop. You looked so cute and I just wanted to get to know you, so I took a chance. I picked up a book you had looked at and then put down. I scribbled my number in it and I told you it was such a great book because the characters were so real, and you bought it. That night you texted and asked if I was the bookstore guy. The rest is kind of history."

He pauses when the waitress delivers our coffees. I glance at Charlie and see him nursing a glass with a clear amber liquid in it. I can't think about that so I focus back on Bryan.

"Getting married just seemed like the natural next step. You basically lived in my apartment. You only kept yours as an office during the day when you weren't temping. You said my apartment was too loud because of the fucktards across the hall in 6E. There wasn't a big engagement party or ring; you never were materialistic and you said our love was the only thing that mattered. We were in bed when I proposed. I pressed a kiss to your birthmark, and we spent the rest of the day making love."

My cheeks flush because the mention of my birthmark confirms that this man has most definitely seen me naked. I stay silent, willing him to fill the empty air with more information and he obliges.

"You were going to give up your apartment when we got married. We were planning on getting married on Valentine's Day. We were starting to try for a baby when, well, I guess when your accident happened. You were hesitant, you weren't sure, but I convinced you that we didn't need money or anything because our love was enough."

My hands, which rest in my lap, press to my lower stomach, a gesture I'm sure he can't see. This just doesn't jibe with me or anything I have known about myself the past few months. But is that because I was with Charlie and not Bryan? I just don't know. So, I decide it's time to find out about that fateful night.

"What about the fight? Why would I leave in the middle of a storm?"

"It was stupid. Some of my work buddies had invited me out for my bachelor party. With the fall coming, work was going to get busy so we did it then. They took me to a strip club and the waitress kissed me. One of the guys took a photo of it and sent it to me. I told you about it right away just to let you know it didn't mean anything."

He reaches out for where my hands are around the coffee I haven't touched. He squeezes my fingers and looks like it pains him to remember the day.

"This was at the end of September. The fight was unlike anything that we had ever had. You told me you needed space and to not call. You said that you would call me. I told you that you should just stay but you were stubborn and you grabbed your helmet and left in the middle of a thunderstorm. I tried to chase after you but you wouldn't listen. Watching you ride away from me broke my heart. When you blocked my number and didn't answer at your apartment, I thought that it was completely over and it broke my heart all over again. And...and now I get to see you again." He reaches out and touches my face, his fingertips rough on my cheek. There is no spark of familiarity there, but he knows things that only someone I have been intimate with would know.

"Come home to me," he says and my eyes lock on his, searching for that recognition.

I consider it, the words of Charlie's father echoing in my head. I think about letting Charlie free of constantly having to fight with his friends and family over my presence in his life. I think about how much easier it would be for him if he could talk to his best friend again without having to constantly jump to my defense. How he could save himself the battles with me over spending money and working late that haven't come yet, but still might. I tell myself that this is for Charlie, that I'm removing the thing that has him at odds with those he loves. Without me, his life can go back to normal, the way it was before I crashed into his life.

"I don't know," I whisper, but I already know the answer is yes. I need tonight to say goodbye to Charlie and to let him go. To say goodbye to the life I thought I was going to have with him.

"Come home with me," he pushes.

"I have things and kittens and..." My voice catches in my throat. Still, I hand him my phone for him to program his number into.

"Bring your stuff but I'm allergic to cats. Leave them where they are. Cats hate to be moved anyway."

I swallow the lump in my throat as I think of Bonsai and Mochi at home, probably sleeping and snuggled together. I think of how they have spent most nights curled in the crease of my hip.

Bryan hands me back my phone and then rises and then, without hesitation, presses a kiss to the top of my head. I can't miss how his eyes drop to my lips, though, and I'm glad when he doesn't pursue that.

"I still have all your stuff. Part of me was always hoping you would come back; that we would talk and be able to clear the air. You were my whole world. I quit smoking for you." He waves the pack at me. "Not that it stuck. I slipped back after you left. I've been a mess. I need you."

His hand cups my cheek and I hate myself for comparing him to Charlie. Bryan's hands are rough and calloused like a manual laborer. Charlie's hands are soft and smooth, made that way by sneaking moisturizer and working at a computer.

Bryan drops a few bucks on the table, enough for his coffee.

"Call me when you want to come home to me."

I watch Bryan leave, feeling more confused than before. I thought this was going to give me more answers, but instead I have more questions. Charlie turns and sees it written all over my face. This time he's the one who won't meet my eye. He turns back to his drink, knocking it back before dropping a fifty on the counter without a second thought. I leave money on my table for my coffee and the tip.

"Let's go home," Charlie says, holding his hand out to me. I slip my fingers in his hand, trying to commit the feel of him to memory.

As soon as we get home, I scoop up Bonsai and Mochi and snuggle their faces to mine. They bite at my hair but I don't care nor do I care that I woke them by doing this. Right now, I want to remember the warmth of their squirming bodies.

"You're leaving," Charlie states with an edge to his voice.

"I think I have to," I say, letting the kittens down on the floor and tossing my coat over one of the island stools.

"No, you don't. I can't believe you're just going to give up on us."

He rushes at me, kissing me on the mouth and trying to make me remember why I love him. I don't need the reminder because I know it in every look he gives me and every tender-hearted thing he has done since his car hit me. He stood there and let me rail against him as I screamed about how unfair this all was. He let me pound my fists on his chest in frustration as I tried to walk again. He helped me when I struggled with myself most, and he loved me before I was put back together again.

I kiss him, knowing that this is the last time that I will be with him, and that breaks my heart. I try to keep the tears from falling as he scoops me up and carries me to our bed, to his bed. We throw our clothes every which way and say goodbye with our bodies. It's tender and we both cry from the overwhelming emotions. When we're done, he holds me and I wonder if he will go back to Ainsley.

"You do not have to leave," he says again. It is then that I decide that I hope he does call her. They looked beautiful together, two magnets finally facing the right way.

"I do. For all the good in your life that you think I've brought, I've made things harder everywhere else. I never thought this could be permanent. I never thought I could be more. I'm never going to be an Ainsley Seaborn."

"I don't want you to be Ainsley." But he doesn't deny that I've made his life harder just by being in it.

"Charlie, I've caused enough of a disruption to your life. I don't fit in your world. I don't have the right pedigree or family. I'll never be able to compete with these women. It was so fun while it lasted." I start to cry again and he holds me close to him, my tears sliding off his skin onto the bed.

He lets me go abruptly, rolling out of the bed. I sit up and look at him, pulling the sheet up over my bare chest. I'm starting to rebuild the walls between us.

"You have brought meaning to my life. You are all that matters. But if you really think that. If you really think you should be with Bryan, then go. I won't sit here and watch you twist yourself into knots trying to justify leaving me." His anger is justified, even if it feels like it comes from nowhere.

"Charl – "

He is pulling on clothes, wrinkled pants and the shirt he wore earlier, and turns quickly to me.

"No, Elia, just don't. You got your last good fuck. You left here this morning with your mind already made up. I can't convince you that you're wrong. I don't know what has you so fucking spooked, but fine. I give up. I've spent the last four months fighting for you, but I'm not going to fight for someone who isn't going to fight for me. You can leave your key with the front desk. I'm going to the office."

He storms out and I try to reason that the anger is better. Anger means he won't be sitting here, drinking by himself. I want so badly to tell him that I'm doing this so he doesn't have to make the hard choice, because I want to spare him from that pain. This heartache is easier; it's something he can get past. If he chose me, if he left all he knew behind, it would only lead to him resenting me, and this, this is at least better.

It has to be.

Twenty-Four

I SPEND a good hour sobbing after he leaves but soon my thoughts start to race. I wonder if he's asked Benji to let him know when I'm gone. I only have one suitcase so I have to be efficient about what I take. I'm going back to my old apartment, regardless of the pain that the stairs will bring. I'll just have to make sure I get good at buzzing people up because I may never leave again.

I try to get as much as I can into the one suitcase. I focus on clothes and things I'll need most urgently until I can come back for the rest. I collect my remaining things and tuck them away in the guest room. The last thing I want is to leave a painful reminder for Charlie. I draft a text to Vivian, asking her to collect the stuff for me at some later time, and make a mental note to send it later.

I am dismayed to realize that my two blankets won't fit into the case. Maybe it's childish, but the heartbreak of having to leave them behind, even if only for a little while, is what almost does me in. I swipe at the tears in my eyes, knowing Charlie wouldn't do anything to damage them, no matter how hurt he might be. I move them to the guest room as well, laying them in the drawers of the dresser I had known so well. I take down the Christmas lights and tend to the other décor, trying to erase every sign of myself .

282

I write out how and when to feed the cats since I've been their primary caregiver. It's yet another thing that breaks my heart. I'm devastated to leave them behind since I have bonded with them so much already. I feel like it's incredibly unfair that I must leave them but it's also the only thing that can be done. I can't take them from Charlie; they are his as much as they are mine, but I just love them so much. It's as if I am leaving my children behind.

The last thing I do is write my goodbye to Charlie. I glance at the bed we have shared for the last two months. It's almost too much to bear. Already, tears are falling from my eyes and the pen is shaking in my hand. I have to keep telling myself that I'm doing this for Charlie. He may think we're happy now, but we won't always be if he has to keep making sacrifices for me.

Charlie,

I never meant to fall in love with you but you made it so easy. From your deep belly laughs to the warmth of your touch, there was no way around it. You took me in when you didn't have to. You went above and beyond simple responsibility to right the wrong caused by the accident.

You were never at fault. It was an act of fate that brought us together and I know that I am better for knowing you. I don't say it lightly: these last few months by your side have meant everything to me. I didn't know who I was, but I know who you have made me.

I am stronger and more confident for knowing you. You have made me a better woman by loving me.

I will forever cherish the time we spent together, knowing that even if you were only mine for a little while, I was so blessed in that time.

I'm taking the coward's way out with this note, and I know it. I would never be able to leave if I had to see you face to face. I would have toppled empires if it meant I got to love you, but I cannot let my love for you deprive you of your friends and family. As much as we hate to admit it, I don't belong in your world.

Thank you for letting me be a part of your life, however briefly, and for letting me love you always.

Forever,

Elia

By the time I sign my name, I can't contain the deep hiccupping sobs that rack my body. I sit at the island with tears streaming down my face as I fold the letter. I press my lips against it, lean it up against a mug, and then close the door on us forever.

The tears don't stop once I'm out of the apartment. I send a text to Bryan to let him know that I'm going back to my own apartment. I'm not running back into his arms, though. I believe what he said about us being together, but I don't know him. And I can't leave Charlie and run into someone else's arms. I might let Charlie think that, though. I hope someday Charlie will forgive me, even though I don't deserve it, and see that this was for him.

Bryan offers to meet at my apartment but I ignore his text and call Vivian instead. I must look like a crazy person to my cab driver, but I don't care. When Vivian doesn't answer, I'm an odd combination of crushed and relieved. This way, I can just text her what is happening, adding on to the one I already started about my things. It's a lengthy text but is better than leaving a voicemail.

Before I can hit send, Vivian texts me, saying that she's in a meeting with the florist and will call me back later. I don't respond. Instead, I delete the entire wall of text I had been writing. I can't adequately convey what is happening via text.

I'm surprised to find Bryan waiting for me outside my building. He's dressed the same as he was at breakfast. I've changed and showered, even though I was sad to wash off the feel of Charlie's hands on my body. Bryan pushes off of the wall he was leaning on and walks over to me, taking my suitcase from the trunk. Once I'm free of the cab, he wraps his arms around me and pulls me to his chest. I'm stiff and awkward but he hugs me close anyway.

I push him away, the keys tight in my hands. "I told you that I didn't need you to come," I say, reaching for my suitcase.

He keeps my suitcase at arm's length and then grabs the keys from my hand and pockets them. "I know but I was close by. I wanted to be here for you and have a better conversation than this morning, without Mr. Megabucks looking over your shoulder. I figured that was why you were so tense." His hand settles on my shoulder, digging his thumb into my tense muscles. It only serves to make me clam up more.

I hate that I wind up feeling thankful for him being there when my leg starts to hurt on the fourth-floor landing. Dancing last night in heels had done my leg no favors and it's honestly easier that he is carrying my suitcase up the flights of stairs. When I get to the top of the stairs, I notice that he not only has my suitcase, but a bag of his own.

I'm too winded to ask him where the bag came from. He turns my key in the door and pushes it open, letting us both into the space. The musty smell still hasn't faded. It's January but I walk over and pop open the window over the kitchen sink. I need fresh air in this stifling space.

"We were going to be married in two weeks," Bryan says wistfully, looking around the room. There are no photos of us in here, I realize, and I frown at the thought.

"I don't know what I'm supposed to say to that."

"Nothing, you don't have to say anything. I just thought I should acknowledge it."

I set my phone down on the small kitchen table. I put my hand out for my keys but Bryan ignores my hand as he walks into the bedroom and then strides back out into the kitchen. He is walking with the authority of someone who has been here before.

"Where did that come from?" I ask, gesturing at his bag.

"My friend, Des, lives in this building too. He actually got his apartment thanks to you. I packed up a bag and left it with him since I figured I would come stay with you until the stairs aren't such a trial."

I don't like it, but he has a point. It was a lot for me to climb the stairs, almost too much. Although I'm not sure what he can do to help me with them.

"You're out of beer," he comments with a laugh, holding the door wider for me to see that the fridge is very empty.

"I'm out of everything. I haven't exactly been here." It's a struggle to keep the bite out of my voice.

Bryan crosses to me, twining a finger around a lock of my damp hair, and giving it a tug. It straddles the line of too much but I turn and look up at him. "I'll go get us some groceries so I can make dinner tonight. You always were useless in the kitchen." Before I can stop him, he strides out the door, my keys still in his hand.

Embracing the solitude, I use the time to unpack and tidy up. I try to rearrange the space, removing things that don't feel like they're mine and setting them aside to either sell or trash. I had only come here with Charlie once, but all I can think of is us being here together. These thoughts make me want to bang my head against the wall. I need Charlie in all the best ways, but thinking about him and what I'm missing...it hurts. It's going to be hard for both of us, for now, but he'll see: in the long run, this is the right thing. I think about what I want to text Vivian or Taryn, but don't even know where to start to explain what I've done or why.

When Bryan returns, he has much more than just groceries. He apparently has more of his things as well.

"What's all this?" I ask, crossing my arms, then immediately uncrossing them. It's a defensive position and I don't want him to feel like I'm attacking him.

"I figured I would just move in while you get settled. I know, I know, this is your 'work space,'" he says, with finger quotes, "but I saw how you struggled with the stairs. It's for your own good."

He has a point but I refuse to cede to him.

"I really wish you would have asked me first." I take the food bags, though, and start unloading them into the fridge and cabinets.

Bryan puts some of the things aside for dinner, I assume. "I'm sorry. I'm just so used to us working as a unit. I didn't think you would have a problem with it. Besides, I brought my game system, so I'll stay out of your hair while you 'work.'" He uses the finger quotes again and I narrow my eyes.

"Don't *you* have work?" I point out.

"No, I took off for the next two weeks so we could spend time together and get reacquainted." He presses a kiss to my temple, before slapping my ass. "Go sit down, put your feet up, and relax while I make dinner."

My leg is sore, so I tell myself I'm only sitting down because I want to, not because he ordered me to. Bryan chatters as he cooks, telling me about people he says we know and what's going on in their lives. I try to listen to him, but I really just want a night where

I can eat my feelings and watch sad, old romances like *Titanic* or *The Notebook*.

I realize that all those horror pornos were actually Bryan's when, without asking, he pops one into the DVD player while we eat.

"Oh, you owe me $200 for the groceries and my cab. You can send me the money on EfUPayMe."

Charlie has been out of my life for a week and I've been miserable every day of it. It's like a hangover, only there is no remedy for it. Every moment is spent just trying to get through it and forget how his mouth felt on mine and how hard it was to win a laugh from him...and how he started to laugh easier the longer we were together. I start to doubt that I've made the right call.

On day seven, I get a text message from a number I don't recognize. It's a photo of Charlie and Ainsley sitting in a restaurant next to a window with a bottle of wine between them. The text with the picture makes me grit my teeth.

> Are C and A back together now that E has crawled back to the hole she came from? My money is on yes, but only time will tell!
>
> XOXO Gossip Girl.

I fight the urge to throw my phone at the wall. I know that the text is from Jack, intent on torturing me even though I'm not a problem. He wants to make sure it stays that way. I've texted Vivian, too, with no response. Is she mad at me for leaving Charlie? I turn my attention to Bryan, trying to distract myself.

"Tell me more about our life together. What sorts of things did we like to do?" I ask over dinner that night. He's been grouchy since being relegated to the couch. I pointed out that he can just go to his own apartment if he wants to sleep in a bed, but he insists on staying here while I 'convalesce,' in his words.

"I don't know. I played video games and you watched a lot of movies. You would draw some pictures every so often. We would hang out with my friends a lot and get baked. You used to make these wicked weed brownies, but I'm guessing you don't remember how to make those now."

Weed brownies sounded great but not like something I would know how to make. I open my mouth again but Bryan holds up a hand to stop me.

"I'm pretty tired of the constant questions. But I got you a surprise!"

I sit up straighter, wondering if it's something that will help me remember. His movements seem excited as he gets up, running to a bag he had dropped by the door this morning. When Bryan whips out a box of blonde hair dye, I have to keep my whole body from deflating.

"I thought maybe if you dyed your hair you would feel more like yourself."

I smile weakly, trying to appreciate the gesture. I'm happy with my hair as it is. I had gone through so much and had just gotten it back.

"Thank you," I say, trying to mean it, "but I just dyed it back and the stylist said that my hair needs a break. It's kind of brittle." I look down, lifting the fork to my mouth.

Bryan had come home with ingredients and told me to make dinner. He'd offered me no instructions, so the chicken is burned and dried out from having been cooked too long. The broccoli is bland and difficult to eat. I'm only a few bites in when he takes the plate and dumps the rest of it into the trash.

"Hey!" I object, "I wasn't done with that." I scowl. I'm starting to get tired of the constant cutting short of my meals. Each time he goes out, he takes my keys with him, which essentially leaves me stuck in the apartment. Even if I did want to test my knee and get out, I can't.

"You looked done." He shrugs. "Well, come on, let's get started." He takes my hand and drags me to the bathroom.

"We used to hang out with only your friends? What about my friends, like Vivian?" I know he said no more questions but I have to know if he knows what happened.

"That stuck up bitch ghosted you. She moved in with her boyfriend and forgot all about you. You didn't really have anyone else." He kisses me, catching me off guard. It's not the soft, gentle exploration of a first kiss; it's swift and brutal like it's owed to him. "God, I've been dying to do that since we got back together again."

"We're *not* back together," I say and he looks like I hit him.

"I've given up so much to be here with you, to help you. How could you say that? Do my sacrifices mean nothing because I haven't whisked you off to some penthouse?" Bryan pins me to the wall with his body and proceeds to kiss my neck.

I push him back. "I didn't ask for any of that," I point out, crossing my arms over my chest.

"Yeah, you probably didn't ask for any of the *pearl necklaces* that rich fucker gave you either but I bet you took those willingly." He reaches up to touch my neck.

I feel anger surge and I bat his hand away. "I think you should go, Bryan." I hear the quaver in my voice when I say it.

He immediately looks repentant. "I'm sorry, that was over the line. It's just hard for me to think about you being with him. For me, you were still my fiancée. My feelings for you haven't changed." He strokes the back of a finger down my cheek and tucks my hair behind my ear.

"You have to realize that things for me *have* changed. I don't remember you. This, you staying here, that's weird for me. I appreciate you staying and trying to help me with groceries and stuff but...I don't need you around."

"I'm sorry. I promise I'll be better. I want to try to make this work between us. I love you." He takes a step away from me, making a show of giving me space. All it really shows me is that I can't forcibly move him.

"You need to do better than just give me physical space. This is really confusing for me."

"I will, I promise. You get started on your hair and I'll go wash the dinner dishes." He thrusts the box of hair dye into my hand and crosses back to the kitchen sink.

I'm looking at the box in my hands when I hear him fill the sink with water. I refuse to dye my hair and go into the bathroom to tuck the box away in hopes that he will forget the whole idea. I'm finding a good hiding spot when I hear the sound of a splash.

"Fuck!" I hear Bryan shout so I turn and go back to the kitchen. After a few moments of him digging around in the sink, his hand emerges with my phone. My heart sinks. So much for texting Vivian about getting my stuff or ever responding to Taryn.

"Did you get any rice?" I ask as I rush over to him. I've never drowned my phone like this before but I know rice is the best way to fix it. I regret not letting Charlie get me the newest, most water-resistant phone on the market. The thought of Charlie sends a pang through my chest, and I try to focus on the situation at hand: the man in front of me and the ruined phone.

"I'm sorry, I didn't... I'm so sorry." He sets the phone aside and turns off the tap. He doesn't offer me a reason for why my phone was anywhere near the water in the first place. Bryan dries his hands and starts to pull out all the insides of my phone, separating out the battery. It couldn't have been underwater for more than a minute, but the inside is dripping like it was under for way longer. He lays it out on a paper towel, patting the components dry.

"If we don't have rice, I can go to the store and get a new one." I'm dismayed at not being able to use my phone, but it was an accident. I have to let it go. In the week he's been here, I've learned that it's easier to let things go with Bryan. He is not that easy to be around. I've been picking up after him because asking him to pick up after himself has gotten me nowhere. Yet another reminder for why I didn't want children: picking up after someone for the rest of my life is not something I'm interested in. So, the thought of Bryan and me trying to have children is just perplexing.

I felt like my life was finally on track before Bryan emerged and jumbled things back up again. I was happy with Charlie. I was whole. I try to tell myself that I *had* wanted this, but maybe my time with Charlie made me outgrow Bryan and our relationship. I had thought if this man was my fiancé, I had to give it a chance. But I'm not enjoying having him in my space. I don't know how to get him out. I have no way of getting help, either. My laptop charger has gone missing in the mess of things he's brought here, and now, my phone is dead too.

"No rice. And it's too late to go get a new one. I'll pick up some rice tomorrow and we can go from there. It's supposed to sit in the rice for a few days anyway." He does seem genuinely sorry about what happened.

I feel sad for my phone, sitting there with all the meaty bits exposed and on display. I take care to move it to somewhere safer, to my nightstand drawer, where hopefully nothing else can go wrong.

Twenty-Five

"HAVE YOU SEEN MY WALLET?" I ask in the morning as I move a pile of Bryan's clothes. I want to get out of the apartment, out of what was supposed to be my safe space, but I can't find my keys or my wallet. All it takes is waking up an amnesiac once to make sure you always have identification on you.

My apartment reeks of weed and cigarette smoke and I need to get out of here or I might hit Bryan. I'm not a violent person, but I feel like a caged bird, stuck in here with a cat waiting for its next meal.

"No, but what do you even need it for?" He doesn't even look up from the video game he's playing. It's Valentine's Day and I've been stuck here with him for too long. I'm at the end of my rope and I will sooner walk out this door and sleep at Vivian and Jack's before I spend another minute cooped up here.

"Bryan, I need to go get a new phone. I get it, you're too busy to get it, but my phone has been dead for over a week and I still need to get the last of my stuff from Charlie's." I put my hands on my hips, standing in front of him as he ignores me in favor of whatever stupid game he's playing with his friends. This is a usual scene around the small apartment: he plays video games and I work on my physical therapy. Standing in front of the TV while he plays Halo online with his buddies is sure to get his attention. He moves so fast that I don't see him coming as he backhands me. With my tongue, I feel that my lip split. I lift my hand to my cheek. The pain is a dull roar in my mind compared to the surprise that he hit me, compared to the feeling that this isn't the first time.

"God, why did you do that? You just make me so mad when you talk about him. I'm sorry... I just...you need to forget him. He took you away from me, from us."

I don't have time to express my shock before he looks immediately apologetic. He kisses my head and my lips before grabbing my chin. His fingers dig into my skin and forces me to look into his eyes. I stare with doe-eyed confusion, even though I feel anger surging.

"Don't ever say his name again, you ungrateful whore." He lets go of my face before sitting back down and unpausing his game. I'm too stunned to move and way too angry to say anything. Things start to slide into place as I think over this time we have been together. Things he has said and done, and now, I'm angry with myself for being back in this situation. I did this to myself.

"Get your fat ass out of my way so I can play my game. Better yet, blow me. I used to love when you would do that thing with your tongue." When I don't move, his eyes flick to me.

"You owe me." There is a challenge in his eyes, a dare to not do what he wants, and I take him up on it.

I walk into the bathroom without saying a word.

I hope that his game is enough to keep him distracted and forget about me so I can think. I lean against the door and force myself to look in the mirror at someone I no longer recognize. Gone is the confident woman who would take things into her own hands with her lover. I've been reduced to a coward by this tiny man.

I look at the bruise blossoming on my cheek and trace the contours of it with my finger. I remember flinching when Charlie threw a shirt in my direction. Things that didn't click before are now making sense. Déjà vu overwhelms me as I use wet toilet paper to clean the blood from my lip. My stomach turns and I can't stop myself from dropping to my knees and throwing up, cursing my gullibility and naivety.

I want to scream and throw things and get the fuck out. But I don't have a phone or a wallet. He has reduced me to a prisoner in my own home. I'm sure he's been squirreling away all of my things. My phone going in the sink was no accident. I wipe at an errant tear and resolve to clean today, keeping an eye out for my shit. I need to leave and it has to be tonight when he's asleep. I don't doubt that he will prevent me from leaving if he's aware.

I go to the kitchen to make breakfast, pointedly ignoring Bryan on the couch. I've gotten better in these two weeks at making eggs but my skills don't go much further than that. Bryan comes up behind me and slaps my ass as he grinds against me. My hands tighten around the spatula and the pan. He's been getting frustrated that I refuse to sleep with him and even to kiss him. Does he think that hitting me will make me horny for him? Make me forget that I already didn't want to kiss him and now my swollen lip means I want to do it even less? His hand starts to slide from my hip and it doesn't take a genius to guess where it's headed. I move my elbow, blocking him, swiveling so I can dump the eggs on a plate.

"Remind me to call that guy, Jack, and thank him for putting us in touch again," he says sweetly as he kisses my neck.

His hand wanders to my hip but I barely notice since I'm rigid, feeling as if he's dumped ice water over me. I shouldn't be surprised that Jack was involved somehow. I wonder if Jack and Charlie's dad coordinated this: drop the comments that I'm not good enough, make me feel inferior, and bring my ex-boyfriend out of the woodwork.

I feel like such a fool to have fallen for it. I have serious doubts that Bryan and I were ever engaged. Suddenly, leaving him in the middle of a hurricane doesn't feel so far-fetched. I had enough autonomy before, since I was able to get out from under his thumb. I was able to escape to my apartment but since he has ensconced himself here, I am at his mercy. I look out the kitchen window and see snow starting to come down. I've forgotten to care about the weather, but now that I've going to leave, I need to worry about it.

"Did you know it was supposed to snow?" I comment. Now I have to find my winter coat in addition to everything else.

"Yeah, apparently we name winter storms now. This one is Winter Storm Ellie." Bryan laughs at this, mopping up his eggs with toast.

"We should go out and make snow angels!" I suggest, wondering if I can get him to bite. Then he would have to reveal where my keys are. I can make due without my wallet for now, though leaving in a snowstorm without ID feels like asking for trouble.

"Babe, no. Don't you remember? You donated your winter coat and all those clothes."

I go still. "What are you talking about? And don't call me 'babe.'"

His eyes lift to mine. "Yeah, you were all like, 'God, New York City apartments are so small. What am I supposed to do with all this winter gear? It's not like I'll be able to leave any time soon.' Then you started to talk about those clothes you wanted to donate so I took the clothes and your coats and got rid of them. You can get a new one next year."

"You had no right," I snap, seething.

Bryan lifts his plate and throws it across the room, narrowly missing my head.

I flinch and duck.

"I was doing you a favor! Try being grateful for once!"

I don't respond. I set about cleaning up the mess he made. I slice my finger on the plate, but don't react. I'm not going to make a big deal right now. I don't care if I can't find my stuff; I'm leaving tonight no matter what.

I offer to go get the ingredients for dinner that night but he insists on getting them himself to ensure that they're right. The snow that started light in the morning is really coming down now. The wind howls outside the window and makes it look like I'm trapped in a snow globe. A fleeting thought of how it must look outside Charlie's windows has me wishing I could see Bonsai and Mochi's first interaction with snow. As these thoughts flit through my mind, I actually feel a shooting pang through my heart.

The steak is too well done, the mashed potatoes are too mealy, and the asparagus is bland. With every bite of food, Bryan sighs heavily, obviously frustrated that I screwed up the entire meal. There are a lot of frustrated sighs lately; seemingly over everything that I do or don't do. It really doesn't make much sense why he wants to be with me. I never seem to do anything right. Bryan only brought home one steak; just enough for him. With every bite, there's a comment that it's too chewy or not red enough for such a red-blooded man. My eyes nearly roll back into my head.

I wasn't successful in finding anything I was looking for. I tried to put my phone back together but it never powered on. It just looks sad and lifeless instead.

My plate is sparse with just asparagus and a small helping of mashed potatoes. Even then, he reaches to my place for forkfuls of the starch, as if mine is somehow better than his.

"What is your problem, Bryan?" I ask, already flinching away from him as I clear the plates. I never realized I had developed that reflex, to do it before I've even finished pissing him off. I should be keeping calm, thereby keeping him calm. But I can't be meek and keep myself from standing up to him. He's a bully and my parents raised me to stand up to bullies. Maybe I forgot about that somewhere along the way, but Charlie helped me find that again.

Every word tonight has grated on me like a raw nerve and I can't take it any longer. I can't listen to his incessant whining. I'm better than that, and that's why I lose my patience.

"My problem?" He grabs my wrist and squeezes until I drop the plates, shattering the ceramic. I can feel the bones grinding together but I grit my teeth, refusing to react. Naturally it's the wrist that was broken in the accident that he's crushing in his grip.

"My problem is that you expected me to take you back after you whored around with that prick. You are disgusting." He points to the mess on the floor. "Clean it up."

I try to twist my wrist away from him. "I can't until you let me go," I say, causing him to tug me towards him, so we are nose to nose.

"It seems you not only forgot how to cook but also your common sense. You should know better than to speak back to your betters. You disgust me." He releases my wrist and pushes me away. I bend over to pick up the broken pieces, setting them on the largest piece. Being on my hands and knees in front of him makes my head spin with anger. I do lose all common sense but not because he's my better in any way.

"I apparently also forgot you're a misogynistic dick but we all have to make due," I mutter. I'm distracted by wiping the abundant steak sauce, the only thing that could salvage my meal, off the floor, so I don't see the kick coming until it lands on my ribs.

The air whooshes from my lungs. I curl up in a fetal position, and some of my memories kick in. I remember the first time he kicked me, immediately dropping to his knees to apologize and saying he loved me.

I get back on my hands and knees as I fight to suck in air. The memory and this kick has left me spiraling. I need to get out of here and away from him.

I choose to ignore him and go back to cleaning. This is the wrong move and he kicks me again. This time I cry out. I have no frame of reference if this is good or bad for how he behaves.

I think that Charlie is what changed things. My relationship with him made me better, and Bryan sees he can't control me as easily as before. It's why my ID and credit cards are out of reach. It's why he gave away my winter coat and made me reliant on him. I'm trapped in this hell of my own making.

"I'm sorry," Bryan says as he gets on his knees to help me clean up. "This was supposed to be a nice Valentine's Day dinner and it's been ruined. We should just skip dessert. You don't need the extra weight anyway, since it would just go straight to your hips."

He stays beside me as I wheeze, trying to get a deep breath in and finish cleaning the mess on the floor. I give him a weak smile and ask him to set up the movie while I do the dishes. When I stand up, his hand curls in my hair and he grabs a fistful of it. I'm too aware that the steak knife is still sitting on the table where he left it. I don't think he would kill me but I just don't know.

He kisses me instead. His chapped lips are rough against mine but I relax a little.

I turn to put the broken dish in the trash. "Why don't you..."

My words are cut off when he cracks my head into the doorway to the living room. The blow glances too close to my eye for comfort. It makes my knees weak but I don't drop down again. I won't let myself be so vulnerable. He grabs my throat, not enough to restrict airflow, but enough to remind me that he is in control.

"You shouldn't worry about suggesting things. You've made it clear that you're not great at thinking for yourself. Your mouth is better suited to other activities." He grabs his crotch as if his meaning wasn't clear enough.

With his hands still on me, I start to remember why I was on my bike in the rain in the middle of the night. I remember bruises that became too hard to explain in an office so I quit and started to work freelance. I remember begging Vivian to delete all the photos of us on Pictogram because Bryan hated seeing me with Vivian, even if they were taken before we met. I remember the friends who were uncomfortable with how he treated me, slowly distancing themselves after their concerns fell on deaf ears.

My fight with Bryan that drove me from him at two in the morning was not over some kiss with a cocktail waitress at a bachelor party. I was done after a series of indiscretions, bruises, and belittingings. He wanted me to give up my apartment, my only safe haven away from him, to move into his studio. We were arguing over him wanting a baby and me never wanting one.

The night of the accident, I was finally freeing myself from the trap I was stuck in.

But because of my insecurities, I was a stupid bird who flew willingly back into the cage. I am back to being a prisoner. The accident was both my saving grace and now my downfall. I had never understood why Bryan was desperate to have a baby, but I remembered having to keep my birth control in a different pill bottle to avoid his tampering with it. I was lucky he never questioned that I needed allergy medication every day.

I try to look away from him now, not wanting him to see the tears in my eyes, but he won't break his gaze on me. He releases my throat, grabbing my jaw instead to force me to look at him, blue eyes boring into mine.

"Remember that I'm the one in charge, not that rich prick. It's me. You're lucky I took you back after you whored yourself out to that asshole. Did you go down on him? Did you let him cum all over your face?" He is relentless in belittling me until he brings a hand across my face again. This time it's not my lip, but a second hit for the eye that hit the wall.

I don't say anything. I just follow him silently to the couch. I follow him because that's what he wants and I want to stop getting hurt. I sit as far away from him as I can. He keeps trying to reach for me and I fold in on myself smaller and smaller, trying to prevent skin to skin contact. I get up and go to the bathroom to hide out for a while.

I'm in there longer than I expect looking at the marks on my face and neck. Just seeing the bruises there, remembering the way he held my throat, makes my heart slam against my chest. I need out and I need out yesterday. I'm careful cleaning the wounds. If I remove myself from this space mentally, I can make it through this without crying. It takes several deep breaths in through my nose before I feel calm enough to start.

I begin with the dried blood near my eye. The skin is tender and starting to swell around my eye. It's vain but I start to apply some cover-up, just to make myself feel better and to send a message. He may hurt me but the marks he leaves are not permanent.

When I emerge, I see he's already had three beers, so maybe my grand-planned escape will work if he's boozed up.

"See? That's better. I'm so sorry about what happened before but you're resilient. It's going to take some getting used to, but you'll remember your place."

I plaster on a smile, as much as I can before grabbing him another beer and handing it to him. "Of course," I murmur, sinking into the couch.

"Oh, I wanted to tell you the good news. I've been emailing with a lawyer; we have a good case against that prick and can take him for a nice ride. I'm talking, quit my job nice ride." He slaps a hand on my thigh, rubbing it.

I don't point out that Charlie wasn't driving. I don't point out that PickMeUp! has lawyers and insurance for just this. I don't say anything. I just nod and agree because tomorrow it's not going to matter. Tomorrow I will be anywhere but here.

My options are limited. Vivian has frozen me out. Even before my phone went for a swim, Vivian wasn't answering my messages. She picked a side and it wasn't mine. I don't know where Taryn lives or even what her number is. I have one place to go, even if it's only temporary.

Charlie's.

It's selfish of me to go there when I know I did this. I tried to create this space so he could get his life back on track to where it was before I crashed into it. I don't know what else to do or where else to go. I just need to get there for tonight. Tomorrow I'll do the thing I never thought I would do again.

I'll go home.

I don't know if I've been back to my parents' house since it was rebuilt with insurance money. I don't know if New York City is for me. The city I loved took me in, chewed me up, and is spitting me back out. Maybe I need a fresh start: away from the man I love and my broken heart and away from this asshole who thinks he can lay hands on me.

Before bed, I change into leggings and a sweater, feigning chilliness. Bryan doesn't seem to notice because he's already three sheets to the wind and I don't stop bringing him beer until we're out. Thankfully, he doesn't pick up on the fact that I'm forcing beer down his throat. He passes out at nine, and by ten, I'm waving a hand in front of his face to see if he's awake. When he doesn't move, I don't waste another second. I grab the sweatshirt he uses when he comes and goes. It's not warm enough by far but it's going to have to do.

I quietly shuffle things around, looking for my wallet and credit cards but when Bryan stirs, I still. I'm quiet for a few minutes as I listen to the even sounds of his breathing. I can deal with getting that stuff later. I'm done being a prisoner in my own apartment.

I step outside the apartment, shoes in hand. I'm quick to throw them on before running down the stairs, regardless of the pain in my ribs and leg.

I had forgotten about the snow until I step into the cold February air. The fresh air helps to drown out the reek of weed and beer on the sweatshirt. The essence of Bryan is something that makes me sick.

The last time I left Bryan in a flurry in the middle of the night, it was pouring. I stopped long enough outside his apartment to block him on everything, utterly and completely done with his brand of bullshit. This time, it's snowing during my escape and I have nothing: no money, no bike, and no phone. If I get hit by another car, there will be no way to know who I am. The snow is heavy and thick as it falls. There has already been quite a bit of accumulation.

I'm on the wrong side of town from Charlie and I don't know how I'm going to make the trek there. A quick glance around shows the streets mostly deserted. So, I have to start with one step at a time. Getting from Washington Heights to Charlie's place on the Upper East Side isn't the easiest of things to do even in the best of conditions. The subway doesn't run crosstown this high up.

With no cabs in sight, I start walking. I need to put as much distance as I can between Bryan and me in case he wakes up. I don't know if he would follow me and track me down, but I'm not willing to risk it. I'll make my way toward the subway and even if it takes me an hour to get there, it's better than standing here and crying about the situation.

I regret not taking his phone and calling for help but in the dark of the apartment, I didn't know where it was and it wasn't worth the risk to look for it. A few cabs speed past me, their lights off, either occupied or done for the night. I still try to flag them down, hoping one will take pity on me. I had given up hope when it finally happens: a cab pulls up beside me. The driver leans over and calls out through the rolled-down passenger window. I try to open the back door but it's locked.

"Do you have any money?" he asks and I realize I must look like a crazy person. I'm in a ratty hoodie and leggings in the middle of a snow storm. It's a terrible thought, but I probably wouldn't help me.

"Well, not exactly, but..." I never get to finish before he drives away. I rub my arms, desperate to warm up, and I keep walking. After another ten minutes, my hope drops further.

I am a New Yorker, not a survivalist. How long will it take to get frostbite? I can't walk much further. My body is trying to do what it can to conserve energy. I need to push on but my fight is fading. I start to cry, dropping my head into my hands. It's not helping, but I don't know what else I can do. I hear the sound of a car coming and I turn, waving my arms frantically. My heart soars when the cab stops. The backdoor is open and I climb in, thankful for the heat. A shiver shakes my body as it warms up.

"You crazy or homeless?" the driver asks, looking at me before turning on the meter.

"Neither. I need you to take me to 102 and 5th," I order, and the cabbie whistles. The driver's eyes glance at me in the rearview mirror and I catch him turning up the heat for me, even if it means he's sweating. I anxiously stare out the window and watch the streets fly by. There are others outside, better dressed and better prepared for the weather. They are throwing snowballs and enjoying the white wonderland perfection before the snow plows and salt make it a slushy mess. We turn down the 97th Street Transverse and I almost laugh at how life can take you full circle. When the driver makes the turn and stops in front of Charlie's building, a feeling of safety settles in my bones, and I know I'm breathing easier.

"Thank you. I can't pay you right now, but if you wait, I promise it will be worth your time." I watch as one of the door-men, Benji, runs out with an umbrella to greet the cab, opening the door.

The cabbie lets out a disgruntled sigh. "Yeah, sure," he says, doubting me.

"Just wait. Please." I say as I climb out and huddle under the umbrella. If Benji is surprised to see me, he's too much of a profes-sional to show it. The lighting under the awning is terrible and I hope he can't see how much of a mess I am. I hold my head high, refusing to reduce myself any more than I already have.

"Benji, is Charlie home?" I ask, hoping that he's here and not somewhere else for the night. I don't know what I would do if he's not here. I would have to go to Vivian and Jack's as a last resort. The thought that maybe Charlie is with Ainsley crosses my mind and for a second, my heart seizes. I wouldn't come between them if he were. I just need somewhere safe to be so I can collect my thoughts and my stuff. I don't think Charlie would turn me away.

"Miss Elia," Benji greets me in a neutral tone. He's been trained to face situations that are difficult and complicated with the high paying tenants. I know he won't let me up. He will play gatekeeper, and I can't blame him for it.

"Can you please call up to him? Or just call him? I need to pay this guy," I say, glancing at the cab and wishing I was back in its warmth. Benji relents, leading me inside under the umbrella. My shoes squeak on the marble floor as he goes to the lobby phone. His eyes stay on me and mine stay on the cabbie, my lips repeating his license number so even if he does drive off, I can send him money later.

I'm surprised when Jack is the one who comes down to the lobby. It takes a minute for it to register that Charlie has not come to my rescue. Jack is casually dressed and I'm not sure I've ever seen him look so informal.

"You need to go back to your fiancé, Elia," his voice is hard and harsh. I'm tired of people talking down to me. Surely, Vivian told him what Bryan was really like.

But does she even really know? I downplayed it at every turn: why the pictures needed to be deleted, where the bruises were from, why I couldn't hang out. I never placed the blame on Bryan, only on my own shortcomings. I was trying to lose weight so the pictures made me self-conscious; I was bruising easier because of a change in my diet. I didn't feel like going out to the bars again to be hit on by strangers.

I back up until my back hits the wall and I slide down it, my head in my hands.

"I'm serious Elia. You've done enough damage. Vivian is heartbroken and so is my best friend. You need to go. You're a tornado, not caring who you take out."

I feel the tears well in my eyes, hopelessness dragging me down like a rock. I will drown under this feeling.

"Can you..." My voice cracks and I clear my throat. "Can you pay the cabbie? I don't have any money," I whisper.

Jack sighs and squats down to my level. He's able to get a really good look at me and he hesitates. The bruising and swelling around my eye and mouth are obvious. But he hardens his gaze due to some inward conclusion, and he doesn't bother to ask about my injuries.

"Looking for another handout?"

I look up at him and I truly hate him. I hate admitting it to myself, but I'm sure I look like I'm in distress. And yet he still has to make me feel like a gold-digging bitch.

"I just need fare for a cab." I can figure out the rest after this man has been paid. I could see if Benji can look up a women's shelter that I can go to until the morning.

"I'd rather not involve him," Jack says, but the elevator doors open and Charlie is there.

I've never seen a more perfect sight in my life: his arms are braced on either side of the elevator doors, eyes closed as he steadies himself. If I were standing, I know my knees would have given out at the sight of him. He's wearing dark green sweatpants and an old crew t-shirt, looking every part the glorious man he is. I want to run to him, but I hold myself back.

"Do you know how fast this elevator is? It's actually nauseating," he mumbles before looking for Jack. "Where did you go, man? Trouble with the stripper?" he says, and my heart sinks.

It's Valentine's Day; of course his best friend is here with him after I stomped on his heart. Charlie's eyes find Jack and no stripper, but then they land on me. For a moment, I don't move, not even able to take in a breath. He looks like he's been drinking, his movements lacking their usual grace.

"Elia?" he asks, confused.

I look away from him, wiping my eyes. I stand up, my back to him, and I look at Jack. I try to keep my face turned away from Charlie.

"I just need cash to pay the cabbie." I need to get out of there; I don't want Charlie to see me like this. Jack was right; I've done irreparable damage and Charlie never deserved that. Jack reaches for his pocket but I feel a hand on my shoulder. Charlie turns me around, and I wipe my tears away before facing him.

He has a stubble along his cheeks but it's more uneven and careless than while we were in Bora Bora. He always took pride in being clean-shaven and smooth. He looks more haggard than before, and I have to fight fresh tears. I clench and unclench my fists as his eyes rove over all of me, from my knotted hair to the healing cut on my lip and the bruises near my eye and neck. My bowed head had blocked Jack's view of the bruises on my neck, but now I can hear the sharp intake of breath from his direction. Charlie says nothing, but his eyes flash angrily and he pulls me tight against him.

"You're safe," he whispers. His whole body is tense, full of tight energy that needs to be released, but right now his focus is on me. I feel him press his lips to the top of my head. Maybe I'm projecting or imagining it, but I think I feel something wet on my scalp. I reason that it's not Charlie, just the long-since melted snow from the beginning of this journey.

I hesitate a moment before wrapping my arms around him as I start to cry. Behind me, the cabbie honks his horn and Charlie looks out the door at him.

I pull back, wiping at my tears. "I didn't have any money to pay him," I say, clenching my teeth and looking down because I don't want to see pity on Charlie's face.

Charlie reaches into his pocket, pulls out cash, and hands it to Jack.

"Dude, this is $200," Jack objects.

"I don't care. Pay him and go home to Viv," he says, pulling me back against him. Charlie turns his back on Jack to lead me to the elevator. I can feel him itching to pick me up and carry me, but I'm determined to take these shaky steps myself.

"Can I at least grab my jacket?!" Jack calls after us.

"You can get it tomorrow," Charlie calls without looking back. The elevator doors slide closed quietly and I'm able to get the first glimpse of myself in the gold doors. There are shadows on my cheeks that I think are bruises. My hair is a mess, brittle and frizzy after drying in the warmth of the cab. My fingers come up to my lip, feeling the scab there. My attempt at applying cover-up was just that, an attempt, and a poor one at that. Charlie is watching me, standing back and giving me space. His hands grip the railing behind him.

We're quiet as the elevator goes express to his floor. Once we reach the apartment, I stand just inside the threshold, unsure of what to do. How do I begin to explain to Charlie what happened? How do I explain that I made a huge mistake? I'm not sure how to begin to explain or make up for what I did. Charlie locks up behind me and walks deeper into the apartment.

"Can I get you anything?" His voice is soft, as if he is trying not to startle a frightened bird. I realize that's exactly what I am: this small, frightened thing that startles at any noise.

"Water?" My voice sounds foreign to my ears. "And I just really need a bath or a shower or something."

I could get the water myself but it feels like something I shouldn't do. This stopped being my home the minute I chose to do what I thought was best for Charlie. Bonsai and Mochi approach me, weaving between my legs. I bend down, scoop them up, and take comfort in their tiny warm bodies. They got bigger in the time I was gone, and tears escape my eyes, landing on their fur.

I hate the look of pity in Charlie's eyes as he regards the state of me. I set the cats back on the island before pulling off the shoes that Ashley had picked for me so long ago. I hesitate, unsure of which bathroom to use. Opting for the easiest choice, I move toward the guest bathroom, the one I used for months before our relationship became so much more.

"I'll draw you a bath," he says, placing a glass of water on the island for me before heading to the bathroom. I take a sip of water and immediately regret not asking for something to warm my insides. I follow him into the bathroom, where we both stand in silence watching the tub fill, steam rising out of it. I know it's going to burn my skin and I want it to. I want to shed all the skin that Bryan has touched.

"Can you turn around?" I ask, not wanting him to see the bruises.

He looks like he wants to object, but doesn't. I catch him watching me in the mirror, his eyes stuck on the bruises on my side from when Bryan kicked me. To his credit, he does not react to me, but I catch how his hands clench and unclench. I slip into the water, gasping at the heat, letting it envelope me. I sink down so only my eyes are above the water. I cross my arms over my breasts. It's not that he hasn't seen them, but I don't want him to see me like this. I want him to remember me when I was strong and powerful, riding him, not this breakable thing that feels out of sorts in her own body. Charlie pulls a chair in and sits beside me, handing me a bar of soap, keeping his eyes averted. I hold it in my hands before letting it slip into the water and sink to the bottom of the tub.

"You can look," I whisper, curling in on myself. I see the muscle in his jaw tick as Charlie slowly brings his eyes from the ceiling to meet my gaze. I can see the effort he's expending to not let his eyes drift lower.

"You don't have to tell me anything," Charlie says as he watches me. He clears his throat. The entire time I've known him it was all about going at my pace. It's clear that he wants to ask questions, wants answers for what I went through, and even though he doesn't say it, it is also clear that he wants blood for what happened. "I can also call Vivian."

I shake my head.

"I'm okay. I just..." I pause. "I can breathe again."

We sit there in silence, the water going cold before I grab the bar of soap and start scrubbing at my skin. Charlie offers to get my back and I let him, drawing my knees up to my chest and hugging them close. He gently scrubs at my back and it's while he's distracted that I tell him what happened.

"I started to remember a few days ago. I don't remember the whole five years, but being around Bryan again..." I screw my face up in disgust and wrinkle my nose. "The smell of him: stale beer and cigarettes. It wasn't specific memories, but being in his company brought back a lot of uneasiness at first. When he hit me this morning, I remembered that same shame. That I had done something wrong." My fingers go to the fresh scab on my lip. "I got out as soon as I could."

I swipe at the tears springing to my eyes. Charlie has stopped using the soap but his hand is on my shoulder and he squeezes gently as he listens to me.

"He donated my winter coat and boots. My wallet with my ID and credit cards is missing, somewhere in my apartment where he has taken up residence. He made some excuse about accidentally submerging my phone in water so it was useless.. He took over my space and made it so I couldn't leave."

I turn to look at Charlie. "I'm so sorry." My voice cracks.

Charlie shushes me as he brushes my crazed hair out of my face. His palm rests against my cheek, his thumb rubbing a stray tear. "I'm the one who is sorry. I never should have pushed you toward him. I said what I said because I was angry. I never should have let you leave."

I lean into his hand, knowing that I am safe with him. "It

wasn't... I just..." I swallow deeply, remembering that I didn't leave Charlie for me; I left so he could get his life back. Bryan was just a convenient excuse. "I'm sorry for barging in. I just needed to get out of there and I couldn't think of anywhere else to go. I just need to stay here a night while I figure out how to leave town." I consider that Charlie may not want to be with me after everything.

"Where would you go?" he says with alarm in his voice.

I don't want to make a mountain out of a molehill, but I think the only reason he would react like this is because he doesn't want me to go.

"My parents' house. I had it repaired with the insurance money but I couldn't bring myself to sell it. It's been vacant all this time, with neighbors telling me they keep an eye on it."

"Is that what you want?" he says carefully. "To go back to your hometown?"

How do I tell him I never wanted to leave here in the first place? How do I tell him that I only left because I thought I was doing what was right for him? That I belong to him and him alone?

"I don't want to impose." I swallow, not sure what to expect from him.

Charlie's hand slides into the water to take mine, wetting the sleeve of his shirt. He brings my hand to his mouth, and he presses a kiss to each knuckle and then the palm of my hand before laying it in his cheek. Charlie holds it there, leaning into my touch and I don't dare let him go until he does.

"Baby, I'm going to stop dancing around this because we don't have the same time we did in the beginning of our relationship. If you want to stay, I want you to stay. If you're worried that I won't want you after you left, you're way off-base. I still and always will want you. Nothing is going to change that. Nothing that has happened since you've been gone will change that." His brown eyes stay on me, his tone fierce.

"I kissed him." I don't know what else to say to him.

"I told you, there is nothing that will change my mind." Charlie reaches for me, turning my face so I can look only at him. I can see the anger burning through him, but I know when he's looking at me now, he's not seeing the bruises. He's seeing me. Gently, his thumb rubs over my cheek with a pressure that shows me he's not afraid of me. He let's go of me when I look down and away from him, overwhelmed by the intensity in his gaze.

I suck on my top lip, half-expecting him to push me away. I expect the worst, even though I know that would not be something Charlie would do, but I am lost again. I don't know my worth. I doubt I deserve someone like Charlie.

He continues, "If I were ten years younger, I would beat him to hell for putting his hands on you. As it is, I am considered a respectable member of society and would serve time if I did that now. Knowing that you are here with me, safe and away from him, is good enough for me. Jack and I will take care of getting your stuff back. Rest assured that I love you. I will always *love* you and that isn't going to change."

"I'm sorry." I'm not sure what I'm apologizing for, disrupting his life the first time, for all of it, for leaving, but I feel like I have to say it. Charlie's entire body seems to collapse in on itself at my words.

"You have nothing to apologize for. *Nothing.* I want to make that very, *very* clear. Not for leaving, not for coming back, and not for his actions. You did nothing wrong. I was the asshole that let you walk away. I was the asshole that didn't fight for you. I wish I had followed you and chased you and not walked out like a damn coward, but I was a coward. I didn't think I deserved to be loved back, and rather than face what I was feeling head on, I just accepted that and made the biggest mistake of my life by letting you go. I'm not making that mistake again. Not ever."

I pull the drain out and just sit, letting his words wrap around me like a protective shield. He grabs a towel and stands there, holding it out for me when I'm ready.

"Do you want me to turn around?" he asks.

I shake my head and I stand, looking at myself in the mirror. I barely recognize myself. There are bruises on my jaw, neck, and along my side where Bryan kicked me.

Was I so desperate for love before that I convinced myself that this was it? I always prided myself on being strong and independent. Knowing when to say no, but somehow, I let Bryan manipulate me and pull me away from my friends.

"It was never this bad before. He never hit me so much. We were together for three years. I just don't understand how..." I trail off and then continue in a low voice, "tonight was the worst it's ever been." I don't remember the specifics but I'm confident in this statement. I wasn't as under his thumb before as I was this time. Before, I was able to confidently leave.

Charlie wraps the towel around me and envelopes me in a hug, holding me tight against his chest. I feel him press his cheek to the top of my head, the tension leaving his own body. Just holding me serves as the reassurance we both need that I'm here and I can get through this.

He helps me out of the tub and gives me clothes to wear. They're his clothes: one of his favorite shirts that I would steal often and a pair of shorts. I feel comfortable, like his clothes are a type of armor. We head over to the bed and Charlie doesn't push anything. He leaves the option open to me to curl against him, and I do. I keep my back to his chest, leaving a spot for the kittens, like we used to do. His arms fold around me, tentatively at first. He seems to be testing the waters to make sure I'm comfortable with the contact before tightening his arms, which lets me know I'm safe as I fall asleep.

Twenty-Six

WHEN I WAKE in the morning I'm alone and confused, but the vicious memory of the night before comes back immediately. From behind the closed door of the bedroom, I hear two men arguing.

"So, that's it? You're taking her back? After everything, including the dramatics last night? What even happened?" Jack's voice is sour.

"I swear, Jack, you're my oldest friend but if you say one more fucking word about her, I am going to kick your ass." Charlie's voice is deadly. I can't imagine he'll take kindly to it when I tell him about all the shit that Jack has been pulling the past several months. We never got around to that conversation, and I wish we had.

"What happened?" Jack asks again.

I hear the sound of one of the stools from the island scraping against the floor as one of them settles into it. Mochi starts to nibble at my hair and I pull her away, settling her back on my chest.

"Open your fucking eyes. She has bruises all over her face and neck. She has bruises on her ribs. She didn't give me details but from what I can see, he kicked her. I know you've never liked her, but man, you're heartless if you expect me to just throw her out. I told you I love her and that should be the end of it." Charlie lets out a shaky breath. "If I ever get my hands on him, I hope Vivian will take on a murder case, because I will put him in the ground."

The bed creaks as I get out of it and go into the bathroom, taking my time and moving a little slowly. When I emerge into the kitchen, holding my head high, I find Jack is still there. His eyes linger on the bruises on my neck.

"Vivian is on her way," he says awkwardly, unable to meet my eyes as he focuses on the bruises on my face and neck.

"He wasn't trying to kill me, if that's what you're thinking."

Jack flinches and it gives me satisfaction in a way I hadn't expected.

"I'm..." Jack can't find any words.

"Save it, Jack. I didn't realize you hated me that much."

Charlie's eyes flick to me. "What do you mean by that?" he asks, slowly.

I cross my arms over my chest, nostrils flaring. "Ask your 'best friend' what I mean by that." I let my anger fuel me and keep me upright, knowing that if I run out of adrenaline and allow myself to stop and think about last night, I will collapse. If I think about the damage to my psyche, let alone my body, all that is fueling me to stand will just disappear and I will be a puddle on the floor.

Charlie looks at Jack. He's starting to make connections that he doesn't want to see. Charlie's jaw clenches while he studies his friend's face. "Jack?" he asks, uncertain.

But then Vivian bursts in, rushing to me in her winter jacket, and crushing me in a bearhug. "Are you okay? Don't answer that, it's a stupid question." She squeezes me too tightly and I cry out, the pain igniting in my side. Charlie takes a step toward me as Vivian lets me go. She looks to see where I'm hurting and I feel the inhalation of breath as she takes in my state.

"I'll survive. I'm pissed as hell. Why didn't you ever text me back?" I can't keep the wounded tone from my voice. I rub my side.

Jack seems to relax now that the focus is off him, but I haven't let it go. I don't say that I'm okay, because I'm not.

"What texts? You totally disappeared off the face of the planet. I only found out you were gone because Charlie asked if I had heard from you." Vivian sounds so confused and hurt.

One look at Jack and I see he looks defiant. "Why do you hate me so much?" I ask him, trying to keep my composure.

Charlie and Vivian look at Jack.

"What is she talking about?" Charlie pushes.

"Oh, hell." Jack runs his hand through his dark locks before putting his hands in his pockets. "I was talking to your dad, and he told me about the offer he made to Elia."

Charlie looks at me and asks, "What offer?" His composure is slipping. That muscle in his cheek tightens as he clenches his teeth.

I shake my head. "Later."

I gesture at Jack to continue. He turns away from us so he doesn't have to face us when he admits to his crimes.

"Your dad had a private investigator dig into Elia's background, so I asked for the PI's info. I had him dig a little deeper and he found Bryan."

I close my eyes and clench my jaw, listening. I open my eyes to find Jack looking directly at me. He is not explaining his actions to his best friend or his fiancée. He is trying to justify what he has done to me.

"So, I went to meet the guy. When I asked him about you, he told me that you were engaged and he hadn't heard from you in months. So, I offered to help you two reconnect."

"*Reconnect.*" I venomously spit my words out. "How does this look for reconnecting?" I ask, tilting my head up so he can see the bruises on my neck. "Or this?" I lift my shirt to show him the bruises on my side. "Did we *reconnect* to your satisfaction, Jack?" I can't take my anger out on Bryan, but I can take it out on Jack. I can make sure Jack sees the extent of what he's caused. All while I'm making Jack see the impact of his meddling, Charlie is watching too, devastation tearing him apart. I understand the look on his face because I've seen it on my own. It's a look that has you pulled in two directions, earth-shattering anger or crumbling self destruction.

I can barely contain my fury but Charlie doesn't even try to contain his. I don't even see him move. Suddenly, he's on the other side of the island and his fist is connecting with Jack's jaw. The force of it, and the surprise, sends Jack stumbling into Vivian. She catches him, but it's only out of reflex, stopping his motion so she doesn't fall backward herself. She pushes him away.

"I can't believe you," Vivian says as Charlie shakes out his hand, clenching and unclenching it.

Charlie doesn't even look sorry he's thrown the punch; he just looks sorry that Jack is still standing after it. I've never had to see this side of Charlie. As he rolls his shoulders back, his eyes flick to me, apology written in them as he catches the marks on my face. His mouth opens in surprise. I want to rush to him and tell him I'm not afraid of him; I never will be. Instead, I move closer to him, wanting to bridge the gap between us, but Jack distracts me with his pathetic excuses.

"How was I supposed to know?!" he shouts, holding his jaw. The bruise blossoming on his cheek isn't satisfying enough to me.

"You were supposed to leave well enough alone, Jack. I was free of him, of his manipulations, of his hands on my body, and you drove me back to him. I had no idea what I was going back to. With no memory of our time together and with no defenses. I was so low after Charlie's dad tried to buy me off, Ainsley showing up constantly, and then Charlie's dad's ultimatum to him. I was made to feel worthless and inferior to Charlie and his world. Then you pushed me back into Bryan's trap." I can't even give those feelings words, but a sudden thought stops me from trying. "Did you delete my texts to Vivian?"

"I didn't. I blocked your number on her phone." Jack sounds genuinely apologetic.

"You should't have fucking meddled. It wasn't good enough that you drove me away? You just *had* to rub my face in it when Charlie started to see Ainsley again, too? It wasn't good enough until you kicked me while I was down. You're no better than Bryan! At least it became obvious he was a snake. You're just some wolf in sheep's clothing, pretending you don't know exactly the harm you're doing." I shove Jack as hard as I can and he stumbles again, but Vivian doesn't catch him this time.

"Fuck you, Jack," I snarl, walking away from him and deeper into the kitchen, where Bonsai and Mochi are circling their food bowls.

I grab a bag of peas from the freezer and gently place them over Charlie's knuckles. For a moment, Jack looks surprised, as if he'd expected them to be for him. There's a light knock on the door and Charlie looks at the clock and curses as it opens.

"I brought bagels," Ainsley singsongs as she walks in. She looks too tidy for this scene: her hair is bundled into a neat bun on top of her head, and her winter coat matches her pristine snow boots and her tight yoga pants. She looks around the room, clearly surprised by the congregation. "But clearly not enough," she says, setting them down. I turn away from her, trying to take a calming breath and brush away the angry tears that have started to fall. I hold my breath for a second to center myself, then release it on a count of three. I pick up the cats' bowls and go to fill them.

"Am I interrupting something?" Ainsley asks, cutting into the tension with her words.

"Yes," Charlie bites out, barely able to look at Jack.

"No," I snap.

"Abso-fucking-lutely," Vivian says.

All of us speak at once. I fall quiet and try to focus on feeding the kittens; who, to be fair, are screaming in outrage at the delay in their meal.

"Well, that was specific." Ainsley sits at the island, waiting for an explanation. Charlie continues to murderously glare at Jack. When no one clarifies, she looks at me. "Nice to see you again, Elia," she says, politely.

"Hi, Ainsley," I reply, wanting to get out of this space and put something on to cover my neck. I tuck my head and hunch my shoulders, wondering if I still have a scarf in the guest room. Vivian is twisting her engagement ring. She turns to Jack as she takes it off.

"I can't fucking believe you," she says as she puts it in his hand.

We all freeze.

"Vivian," he pleads, reaching for her but she pulls away from him.

It's almost as if there are consequences for his actions, I think wryly.

"I'm not kidding, Jack. You were told how many times by both me and Charlie to let. It. Go. And you couldn't. You couldn't trust me. You couldn't listen. You had to be right. If Elia wasn't going to prove you wrong, you were going to make her prove you right. You and his father with your Machiavellian schemes. I'm not interested in marrying someone who won't listen to me. And I'm *definitely* not interested in marrying someone who would manipulate my friends and lead them into danger for no good reason other than your petty little ego."

Charlie sets the bag of peas on the counter as I put the food down for the kittens, petting them both.

"I think you should go," Charlie says to Ainsley.

She looks up at him, pausing mid bite. "I really stepped into the middle of it, didn't I?"

No one answers her. Jack is trying to reach for Vivian, who is staying out of his grasp.

"Can I offer my services as a *literal* mediator?" Ainsley asks, putting her bagel down. She sounds glib but she looks genuinely concerned.

"No, Ainsley, now really isn't a good time," I say, placing my hands on the island, looking at her straight on. I watch her eyes flick along my bruises, then back up to my eyes. She doesn't react to the bruises like I'd expected her to, but her brow furrows slightly as she tries to calculate what has happened. Behind me, Charlie places his hands on my shoulders gently, nearly withdrawing them when I flinch. He holds steady, sliding them down my arms, and I look at him out of the corner of my eye.

"Can we talk, privately, for a minute?" I ask, and he nods, letting me lead him to his bedroom. We leave everyone in the kitchen as we close the door behind us. Charlie sits on the bed, his brown eyes sad as they follow me.

"I don't want to fuck everything up for you, again," I start. He opens his mouth to object and I put my finger on his lips, silencing him. Even that feels like too much, so I drop my hand and start to pace. Last night, I shouldn't have stayed in his bed, but I had needed that security, that safety. I'd needed to know that if by some bizarre happenstance, Bryan came looking for me there, I would still be safe and protected.

"I didn't come here to fuck everything up for you again. I don't want you to think I'm this broken bird you need to keep fixing. I'm not here to break you and Ainsley up. I just needed to be somewhere safe and I knew I would be safe here." I stop pacing and stand in front of him, watching his reaction.

He takes my hands and pulls me close to him, slowly.

"Is this okay?" he asks, and I nod. He brushes my hair out of my face. I love him for keeping himself smaller than me. He could stand and engulf me with his size, but he doesn't. He lets me tower over him, letting me have all the power between us. I never realized until this moment how much power Charlie gave me over him and how badly I need it, how badly I need to feel in control of something. "I'm not back with Ainsley. I told you I love you and I meant it. I meant it yesterday. I'll mean it tomorrow. I'll mean it in ten, twenty, fifty, a hundred years. There is no moving on from you, and certainly not in two weeks. If you want to push me away, you're going to have to try harder."

My resolve breaks, and my body falls into his. I won't be broken by the things that Bryan said and did. I won't let him take anything more from me. Some part of me, that part that doesn't believe Charlie could ever love me, shuts up for good at his declaration. My self-worth isn't something that I can measure against another person and their success. My upbringing doesn't make me any less worthy of Charlie and it's going to take time for that to sink in, but I'm not ready to give up on him, not again. I want to be with him, I want this. I don't ever want to let him go.

He kisses me tenderly as he cradles my face, remaining wary of my bruises. I open my mouth to him as he kisses me: all love and no pressure. I pull away from him, press my head to his chest, and start to cry.

When we emerge, my eyes finally dry, it's just Vivian and Ainsley talking softly in the living room. Ainsley is comforting Vivian as she cries, but once she sees us, she stops.

"I got the cliffnotes," Ainsley says, rubbing Vivian's back.

I scoop up Bonsai and place her in Vivian's lap. "Kittens help."

Vivian cuddles Bonsai while she loudly protests. "I'm so sorry," she begins.

"You have nothing to be sorry for," I say, putting my hand on hers.

"My fiancé almost got you killed." Her voice cracks as she looks at my throat. My fingers absently touch the bruises. "Ex-fiancé."

"It was more scare tactic then attempted murder," I say.

Out of the corner of my eye, I see Charlie tense up as he loiters in the kitchen, unsure of what to do. He lets out a breath and his eyes lock with mine as he makes a move towards the door.

"I'm going to take a walk. Are you okay here?"

I feel my hair raise as I think about him being gone. I nod, knowing I can't stay glued to his side forever. I'm safe here and I'm not alone. He keeps watching me, giving me a chance to object, as he pulls on his jacket and shoes. I don't stop him as I let out a deep breath and pick up Mochi to snuggle her. Charlie shuts the door quietly behind him, turning the lock so we don't have to get up.

"Do you want to talk about it?" Vivian offers and I shake my head.

I know I should talk this out because not talking about it before is how I got into this situation to begin with. "I just feel so angry and powerless and frustrated. I want to take the time with Bryan, all of it but especially this last time, and throw it in the trash. I don't feel like me; I don't remember being that girl."

"I'm so sorry, Elia. Anything you need, just tell me," Vivian offers.

I set the kitten down on the table, watching her delight in having something new to explore.

"A spa day should help everyone start to feel a little better. I can even call Taryn," Ainsley says decisively, and I look over at her, surprised. I appreciate her staying to comfort Vivian, but her continued presence doesn't make sense to me. I don't think we talked much past the apology she'd issued at the gala, so what is she still doing here?

"Taryn has been missing you too," Vivian points out.

As much as I would like to see Taryn, I'm not ready to see her yet and have to rehash this entire story. Later, next week, when I've had some time to sort out my feelings and thoughts, I'd like to. But right now, they're all a jumble, caught in how mad I am at myself and Jack. The desire to have a time machine has never been as strong as it is now.

"Why are you here?" I ask, my voice harsher than I'd intended, but Ainsley seems unaffected by my tone.

"I was supposed to have breakfast with Charlie but...everyone was here." I wait for her to elaborate. "What, are you asking why I didn't turn tail the minute I saw you here? Because Charlie and I were friends long before we were lovers."

My stomach turns at her choice of words. When she sees that her answers are not satisfactory, she lets out a sigh.

"Elia. I'm not afraid of you, I'm not threatened by you, and I don't want Charlie back."

My entire body relaxes.

"I'm sorry for my behavior on New Year's Eve and at the gala. I've been getting a lot of mixed signals from family and friends since you showed up. Charlie and I finally cleared the air after you left him. He managed to not be belligerent for one night and we were able to have a good talk. Jack and I were splitting Charlie-watching duty to make sure he didn't do anything stupid, like text you, which he did, or hire a PI to find you when you never texted him back, which he was considering.

"So, to answer your question, I'm still here because you looked like you could use some good people around you. I also thought Jack had it coming." She looks at Vivian then. "I'm sorry, but he's been a grade-A asshole since freshman year of college. You deserve better." She takes a bite of her bagel.

"Then why is Charlie even friends with him?" I snag a wandering kitten, who immediately dives into my hair, clawing at it.

"Jack is all about the microaggressions, like pointing someone in the direction of their ex when neither are even looking for that particular door to be open. Because Dartmouth is a very bro-centric environment and he was never *directly* shitty in a big way to Chuck himself. And then when he got Jack the internship with his dad's company, Charlie overlooked a lot of his shittyness for the sake of the business. For all of Jack's faults, he *is* good at his job."

"But he's super fucking toxic," I say, my fingers tracing the bruises on my neck. He may not have inflicted them himself but it was still his fault they were there.

"Hi, who do you think told me I should give Charlie a lap dance on New Year's? Which, I haven't really apologized to your face for, but I *am* sorry. I should have put two and two together after seeing you with Charlie at the engagement party. That was also Jack's doing. He told me that you were Charlie's flavor of the week, and that Charlie just didn't want to risk being single at the engagement party if I was going to be there. The signs were there but I ignored them, and for that, I'm sorry."

I nod, realizing that she'd been as much of a pawn as I had been. Now that the tension is broken, Ainsley gets up and begins rummaging around the kitchen. She makes us mimosas and the three of us sit on the couch to have an actual conversation.

"I was serious before. You have nothing to worry about with Charlie and me. He's a good guy but he's just not good for me. I've decided to start exploring the buffet of men that New York City has to offer and I'm enjoying the *hell* out of it." Ainsley clinks her glass with Vivian.

"Good for you. I'm swearing off men for now. First Connor, then Jack. I'm miserable at picking winners."

"Sounds like you and I will be having a lot of casual sex for the foreseeable future. Not together, unless you're into that." Ainsley raises her glass and winks at Vivian, who tosses her head back with a laugh. She's forcing it a little, but I love her for it. She just ended her engagement, and like it or not, it did have a significant amount to do with me. But she's not home wallowing, though her eyes are still red-rimmed and watery; she's here with me, making sure I know I am loved and safe. Sometimes, I don't think I deserve her as a friend.

Charlie walks in and dusts snow off his shoulders.

"Don't you three look cozy," he says, placing a bag on the island before taking his jacket off. I realize that when he left the house he'd only had on a shirt, a light jacket, and his old sweatpants.

"Where did you disappear to?" Ainsley asks.

"Oh, nowhere in particular. I just needed a walk," He's vague as he disappears into his bedroom.

"That's convincing," Ainsley mutters, getting up to refill our glasses. I hand her mine and follow Charlie into the bathroom, where he's washing his hands. When he winces, I move closer and examine his hands. His knuckles are bruised and bleeding. I worriedly look up at him.

"I didn't hit him, if that's what you're worried about," Charlie says, locking eyes with me in the mirror. I grab the disinfectant and some bandages, setting them on the counter.

"Not that I didn't want to." He winces as I clean up his hands. "God, I wanted to. But I just told him that if he so much as thinks of you, I'm going to bury him in legal problems until the day he dies." His hands are still shaking. "I wanted to fucking end him." Charlie's rage is palpable. "It was cathartic, hitting Jack, but I didn't like it. I would have enjoyed hitting Bryan."

When I finish cleaning and bandaging his hands, I let them go and step back. "What did you do? If you want to tell me," I say, hoping he will. We never resolved what we are now. Charlie was clear that he's here to stay, but I feel more broken than I did after the accident. Before, I was free of emotional baggage. Now if we take a trip, I have so much I'm going to have to check it.

"Of course it's your business. That is, if you want to be in a relationship with me again after I fucked up so supremely. All I want is to know is why you really ran. Ellie, you're so much more than I could have ever dreamed of deserving. After the shit I pulled, I wouldn't be surprised if you made me work for it, but if you still want me, if you still want this, I will work for it with my every breath. I should have told you I didn't want you to leave. I should have said a lot of things to make you stay, but I didn't want you to feel like you had to. I didn't want you to feel like I was your only choice."

"I don't fit in your world, though. I'm just Elia." My words are so soft that a passing siren could carry them away. There is something so intimate about bearing your insecurities to someone. My heart slams against my ribcage, rattling within me. I can barely meet his eyes, expecting there to be pity written on his face. When I do finally look up from the counter, all I see is love in his eyes. Love and anger and a touch of determination. The muscle on his jaw ticks as he grinds his teeth, and I have to wonder how they're not just ground to dust after this morning. Looking at his face now gives me hope.

"I swear to God, I'm going to kill this motherfucker for everything he put you through. You're everything to me. This apartment, my job, it all means nothing without you. I told you, there is no circumstance in which I wouldn't want you. I will love you until the earth is ash. I will never stop loving you or wanting you. I'm not going to give you another reason to doubt me, to doubt us." He reaches out and takes my elbows, pulling me to him. His touch is light, trying to be gentle with my feelings as well as with my bruises.

"I will go at whatever speed you want right now but I'm not going away. You're safe here and you're welcome as long as you want to stay, even if you don't want to be with me."

I swallow hard. "I do want to stay with you, to be with you." I give him a tender kiss on his hands. "So, if you didn't hit him, how did this happen?" I ask, holding up his hands.

"I went to your place to get your things. The asshole was still passed out on your couch. He had no idea you were even gone. I may have punched the door frame and he woke up. He told me I had no right to be there and I told him he could report me to my friend, who's a cop. I offered to make the call for him. I reminded him that I'm wealthy enough to make any problem disappear, including people."

"I wish I could have seen his face." I laugh.

Charlie kisses my forehead. "I can neither confirm nor deny that he pissed himself." He pauses and smirks. "Who am I kidding? I absolutely am confirming that."

We walk back out to our guests, who are still chatting.

"I'm happy to play intermediary between you and Jack so you can get some stuff," Charlie says to Vivian. He sits on the couch and pulls me onto his lap. I wrap my arms around his neck and nestle into his embrace, already comforted just by being with him.

"You spoke with him?" Vivian asks, looking up. She is holding her champagne glass so tightly that I'm afraid she might break it.

"I did. I told him it would be best if he started to look for another job. I did actually go for a walk, by the way," he reassures us. We've all been wronged by Jack in ways that will leave a lasting mark.

"Before or after you beat the shit out of this guy?" Ainsley asks, pouring a fresh mimosa for Charlie.

"That is slander. I have two lawyers in the room; can't one of you provide a legal defense?" Charlie's hands are clasped at my hip, tugging me close every so often to remind himself that I'm here.

"Pass. I'm a mediator and she's a litigator. We don't do criminal law." Ainsley sets her empty glass on the table, her eyes playful. "Let's go," she says, holding her hand out to Vivian, who takes it and stands.

"Where are you going to stay?" I ask, my heart hurting for Viv. "Charlie has the guest room if you need."

"*We* have a guest room. For as long as you need," Charlie amends, tugging me closer.

"She's actually going to crash with me," Ainsley says, and Vivian nods. "I have an empty guest room with her name on it."

I wish that Jack hadn't pitted me and Ainsley against each other all this time. I think I would have really liked her and it would have prevented so many problems. But I'm glad I have the chance to get to know her now.

"Let's go get boozy," she says, just to Vivian. "I have a case of Prosecco waiting for us."

I stand and hug Vivian tightly. "I'm so sorry about Jack." For all his faults, I didn't intend to break them up.

"It's for the best," Vivian says, obviously trying to make herself feel better. I can tell this is going to take some time. This is the second fiancé she won't be making it down the aisle with.

"Honestly, you saved me from needing a divorce lawyer," she says with a thin smile.

"Now *that* I could have helped with," Ainsley volunteers as they pull on their jackets.

I hug Vivian again. "I love you," I tell her, my voice stern.

Vivian bites her lip, tears springing to her eyes. She spent the day comforting me when her heart was broken. I don't know what I did to deserve such a friend.

Charlie and I spend the rest of the day in bed, just cuddling and playing with the kittens. His hand never strays far from me, needing reassurance that I am not going anywhere. All day, his fingers trail along my arms and legs, stroking me just to have skin to skin contact. His phone rings and his eyes darken when he sees his dad's name on the screen. He sends it to voicemail, sitting up and looking at me.

"Before I answer that call, I need an explanation. What was the offer from my father that Jack was talking about?"

I sit up, crushing the kittens' crinkle ball in my hand, not looking at him at first. When I do, his eyes are patient, but hard, expecting the worst.

"Your father offered me a blank check to get out of your life. This was, oh, about a week before the gala. We just never had a chance to talk about it. I never would have taken it. But I had his words already echoing in my head when I overheard your argument about losing Ainsley's family as investors. Then Bryan showed up and it felt like a sign. Like, I just didn't belong in your life. My insecurities took hold."

Charlie pulls me onto his lap and I drop another cat toy. Bonsai, ready to pounce, stands up and meows angrily at the now-unmoving mouse.

Charlie's hand braces behind my neck, pulling me closer to him so our foreheads are touching. Our eye contact doesn't break so there will be no mistaking his meaning over what he is about to say.

"I am your partner. You have absolutely nothing to be insecure about with me. I love everything about you, and I will love everything about you. Want to dye your hair orange? Cool. Put on a hundred pounds? Great, more of you to love. You want to, I don't know, open a farm upstate for rescue animals, where do I send the check? I will love and support you at all times. My love for you is boundless and I will never stop showing you that." His phone rings again and he sends it to voicemail a second time. My heart slams in my chest, likely to break out from the anxiety I feel. Just seeing his father on the caller ID makes me want to crawl out of my skin. Every insecurity I told myself I would let go of comes roaring back. I told myself I want Charlie, I want to be with him, so that means trying to rein in my reaction. I clench my hands in my lap, trying hard to meet Charlie's eye.

"You could tell me that we're never having sex again, and I won't lie, the disappointment will be real, but I respect you and your body, so that just means I'll need to get creative. There are *genuinely* no limits. If you decide you don't want me to love you anymore, I will fight you to make sure that is what you really want, and that you're not making that decision from a place of fear, like you did before.

"I learned an important fucking lesson in the last month, and that is just how important communication is. I can't expect you..." The phone rings again and he just turns it off with a huff of frustration. "I can't expect you to understand what I'm not saying. Someday we may get to the Vulcan mind meld point of a relationship, but right now I'll just tell you and keep telling you. At all times, unequivocally, I want you here. I want you in my life. No more of this 'am I a burden?' bullshit. No more of these concerns about power roles. If I'm exerting undue pressure on you, I want you to tell me. I am laying myself bare for you.

"You are and never were *not* good enough for me. Your upbringing and your family are not a disappointment or a shame or something you need to hide. You feel like you don't fit in my world? Great, neither do I..."

He'll keep going if I let him, but I put him out of his misery by kissing him. His arms slide up my back, holding me to him as I straddle him. There is nothing sexual about how we hold each other in this moment: it is about being as close to one another as we can get. I pull away and he looks up at me, brushing the tendrils of hair from my face.

His words and his actions keep wearing down my vulnerability. Charlie has proven time and time again that he's here for *me.* I was stupid to let his father and Jack get into my head and convince me otherwise. I needed to listen to my gut and to myself. Fuck all the white noise telling me that this is wrong. My heart is the only thing I need to listen to. Charlie is the only person I need to listen to. Both are telling me that this is the right thing. I blink away tears.

"I love you, too. I *will* be more open and honest with you. I'm sorry I wasn't before." I slide off his lap as he gets up, reluctantly powering his phone back up.

"Anything goes down that you are upset about? Call me at work, I don't care. You matter and that's all." He watches as the missed calls tally up, his phone rings again and this time he answers it.

"H--" Charlie isn't able to get a word in before the screaming on the other end of the phone begins. I can hear it from where I sit on the bed. He braces his hand on the door frame, his eyes nearly rolling to the back of his head.

"Are you finished?" he asks.

Silence.

"Good. I fucking quit." He hangs up the phone, powers it down, and tosses it on the bed. "My God, that felt so good. I should have done that ages ago." He climbs into bed with me and gets back under the covers. He kisses Mochi on the head, which earns a tiny adorable hiss at the abrupt affection.

"Let's get away," his eyes are bright and clear.

I laugh, unsurprised by this. Remembering how happy he was during most of our trip away, I want to bring him that peace again. I never want to be the thing that causes him pain. "Get away where?"

"Anywhere. I can get hired somewhere else tomorrow and even if I don't, I have enough stashed away to take a sabbatical. Let's travel, see world for a few months, anything. Vivian can come stay here with the cats until she knows what she wants to do. Let's do it."

I laugh, kiss him, and snuggle close, our future lying open ahead of us.

Epilogue

TEN MONTHS LATER

IT'S hard to think that I was on this same beach just one year ago, my relationship with Charlie just starting to blossom. Today, we are going to promise our love in front of our closest friends and family.

After abruptly quitting his job, Charlie and I took off to see the world, taking it two weeks at a time so he could actually look for a job. We started east and worked our way west; no real limits on what we saw or did. It was brutal for jet lag, but we adjusted.

While sitting on a balcony in Paris eating dinner, Charlie slid a box across the table and got down on one knee.

Our romance was a whirlwind but it kept us on our toes at all times. I was delighted to say yes. He was my everything and once we started to talk, to really be open about the things going on in our heads, all of our problems seemed to fade. Without his father and Jack spreading poison between us, we were happier in every way.

Returning to New York meant settling into a new norm. I found a graphic design job that I love, and Charlie is happier at his new job. His late nights no longer end in the early morning hours, when he might hit a girl riding a bike during a hurricane on his way home. Those nights now mean a late, *late* dinner at home with our cats.

"Are you ready?" Vivian asks, handing me my bouquet.

I take it and shake my head, smiling. "I don't really have a choice, considering you all flew down to Bora Bora to watch me get married."

Ainsley laughs. "Worst case scenario, I got a killer vacation out of it," she jokes.

I grin, glad that she and I have been able to move past my insecurities. She's become a good friend, as I'd hoped she would.

Ainsley, Taryn, and Vivian walk out ahead of me and I wait for my cue.

My hair is pulled back into a braided updo, adorned with tiny flowers, and my dress is light, a tulle skirt with floral appliqués on the bodice and around the waist. I'm barefoot, with a rhinestone over-the-top 'sandal' that hooks on my toes, and Charlie, waiting at the altar, is barefoot as well.

I hear my cue and I step forward into the next chapter of my life.

As I walk down the aisle, I reflect on our journey, unable to take my eyes off him, looking dapper in his black tuxedo against the backdrop of the clear blue water. I'd told him he didn't need to go so formal but he said he loved that it made me hot for him when he dressed up, so he had to do it. At the sight of me, Charlie breaks out into a grin, reaching up to wipe his eyes.

I never imagined when I woke up in the hospital that the stranger sitting beside me would become my whole world. I never imagined that I could become whole again or that he would be the one to make me that way.

Looking at him, I barely see the faces of our friends and family that have joined us here, but their presence warms me all the same. Charlie's mother, stepfather, and brother were delighted to be invited, fences slowly but surely being mended. I'm thankful that he has reconnected with them. Vivian, Ainsley, and Taryn stand to my side, here for the love of both of us.

I barely manage to look back at Vivian as I hand her my bouquet, unable to tear my eyes away from Charlie.

My "Something Old" is a bow woven into my hair, a scrap from my mother's wedding dress that had survived the fire. We found it during a trip we took to my parents' house so I could introduce him to them, even if it just meant showing him the place I grew up and going through the boxes of memories that were spared from the flames. The family quilt is resting over a chair in the front row, a photo of my parents sitting on it so I can have them here with me today.

I place my shaky hands in his. Another tear slides down his cheek and I reach up to catch it. He stops me, pressing my hand to his lips.

Our officiant, Walt who is a friend of Charlie's from high school who helped Charlie get his new job, starts talking but I can barely hear his words. I get lost in Charlie's eyes, thinking only of how much I can't wait to be his wife. He gives my hand a squeeze and I hear my name repeated.

"I'm sorry!" I laugh and wipe at a stray tear, taking the vows handed to me by Vivian and clearing my throat.

"Some people have said that we moved too fast, that we needed more time to get to know each other, but to those people I say, 'You don't know us.' A freak circumstance brought us together, a circumstance that has changed my life in so many ways, most importantly, by bringing you into my life.

"Before I met you, and I can say this with confidence now," I joke, "I was adrift, barely treading water, unable to keep my head up. It was the blinding light of your car's headlights that hit the reset button. Because of you, I was able to rediscover myself and I was able to rediscover what it meant to be truly loved and cherished. Every day, I think about how lucky I am to have fallen in love with you. I knew it the first time we kissed. There is no place in the world I would rather be than by your side. There is no adventure too big for us to tackle together. I love you, Charlie Breckenridge. From now until infinity, I bind my life to yours." I wipe my tears and Charlie takes the vows, sliding them into his pocket.

"Elia Daniels, I love you. I wasted all my best flowery words begging you to take me back, and again when I asked you to marry me, so I apologize if these aren't the vows you've dreamed of."

We laugh and I can't help myself. I reach out and cup his face again, his hands closing over mine, holding them there.

"I was asleep in my life before we met. I was going through the motions that I thought I had to go through. Checking boxes I didn't want to, just for the sake of checking them. The night we met," he smirks as he says this, as if no one around us knows that his car hit me, "the night we met changed me. It woke me up and I welcomed the challenge of being able to help you heal. So you know I'm already there for the 'in sickness' part. You taught me things about myself that I didn't know: that I like to cook, that I'm a cat guy, and that there is no force great enough to stop me from loving you. I told you once: fate bound us to each other and I wasn't going to turn my back on something that powerful. Not then, and not now, and not ever," Charlie clears his throat and wipes at his eyes. I hear his mother start to blubber somewhere off to one side.

"Asking you to be my wife was one of the scariest and most enriching moments of my life. I knew that we had already faced so much together and come out stronger for it and I know that we will face any and all challenges that come our way. I will love you for unlimited lifetimes, as from this day on, I am bound to you."

Charlie puts his vows in his pocket as well, and we both lean in to kiss, forgetting where we are, but Walt stops us.

"There is still one more step! Hold on, you two."

We laugh with him as he asks for the rings. We slide them onto each other's fingers, the waves crashing behind us.

"I now pronounce you partners for life. Now, *now* you can kiss."

We don't hesitate. His hand finds the nape of my neck as I stand on my toes to reach his lips. His other hand settles on my side as he dips me backward, instinctively steadying me and holding me so nothing will hurt. Ainsley, Taryn, and Vivian hoot and holler, while my new mother-in-law bawls and cheers. I hope her tears are happy ones, but for the moment, I find I don't much care if they aren't.

Charlie and I turn from each other and face those who are standing with us. Our loved ones watch us as we walk back down the aisle, hand in hand, into the rest of our lives.

Acknowledgments

Shit. I feel like at every step of this process, I found a new harder thing, but this is going to be the hardest. Like it takes a village to raise a baby, it takes a village to write a book.

I think the first person I absolutely need to thank is Hannah. Without Hannah, this book wouldn't be in your hands, it would still be sitting on my computer never to see the light of day. You've been my cheerleader, my sounding board, my motivation. I never thought I would need to write a dedication and I wouldn't be doing this without you. I love you, you're the best friend and officiant I could have asked for.

I want to thank next, the people who beta read for me. Thank you to Angie and Sabrina for jumping on the chance to read a baby version of Central Park Collision and give me feedback and the love that I needed. It's different for friends and family to tell you you're great, it's another thing entirely when it's random internet strangers.

Thank you, Jenn and Sam who have put up with me forcing my books into their hands, who have never said no to me. You've helped me morph my books into something more, into something better. I truly can't thank you enough for that guidance. Thank you for reading and for being our Disney running buddies! I can't wait to hit the parks with you again.

To Andi and Bailey, for taking the plunge and reading a friend's book! I know that it's not the easiest thing and I appreciate you so much for doing it. I'm so glad you have the final version with your comments incorporated!

Katie Land! Who will always be Katie Land to me, thank you

for making sure that I am representing my injuries and treatments accurately.

To Chris and Ish, for getting married and giving me a five hour car ride that gave me the chance to get Charlie and Elia's story on the pages. The love we felt the weekend of your wedding helped to shape their story.

My big sister, Jennifer talking me through things and helping me learn, not just in this process but with life. Life couldn't have given me a better sister. I know you asked for a baby brother, but hopefully this acknowledgement makes up for that disappointment.

For my Annie, there aren't enough words for everything I need to thank you for, but stepping in when you did...Thank you.

I have to thank my Angel Squadron - Katie, Tracy and Mel. When I was low, you make me soar with your feedback and support. Your guidance and confidence when I had none left in myself meant that this book got to see the light of day.

Amanda, my fairy godmother, my Mariano Rivera. You took the impossible and made it happen, you never once let me doubt myself and you helped strengthen this story in so many ways. You made me laugh and cry (in a good way, I promise!) with your feedback, and you kept me going in the darkest days I had with this book. Truly, thank you. Charlie and Elia thank you for your hard work and dedication to making sure their story was told right.

To my parents for showing me that I can do anything and everything. I'm able to put a book in people's hands because you taught me to never doubt myself.

I can't forget Chip and Harvey, the best butt-lickers in town. They have walked over my keyboard and deleted more passages then I care to admit, but I love those cats all the same. The comfort they bring is everything.

I saved the best for last, my husband Michael, who never doubted me once. Who told me that I can and I should do this. Who showed me what love really and truly was. For being my sounding board for what type of job Charlie should have. I really never would have done this without your continued silence and accepting when I shushed you because I was trying to write. For telling me at every point that I'm amazing, you're pretty fucking stellar yourself.

Okay, I lied, he wasn't last, because I have to thank you, my readers. For taking a chance on Charlie and Elia and their love story.

Follow the story

Thing's are about to get bach shit crazy.

See what the girls get up to when they plan an unforgettable bachelorette weekend for Elia in...

Available now!

Which love story is next?

Catch the girls in the next Love in the Big Apple book...

Madison Avenue Mediator

After seeing her ex-fiancé get married, can divorce mediator, Ainsley Seaborn find her own happily ever after?

Available now!

Interested in Romantasy?

Check out the Game of God's series - a Hades and Persephone re-imagining. Start Daphne Hale's story with The King's Game - available now!

THE
KING'S
GAME

About the Author

Nicole Sanchez has been writing stories on any scrap of paper she could get her hands since before middle school. She lives in New Jersey with her high school sweetheart and love of her life along with their two quirky cats. When she isn't writing or wielding the Force, she can be found traveling the world with her husband or training for her next RunDisney Event.

For more books and updates:

Newsletter

Website

Facebook Reader Group

Also by Nicole Sanchez

Love in the Big Apple Series:

Central Park Collision

Las Vegas Luck

Madison Avenue Mediator

Game of Gods Series:

The King's Game

The Queen's Gamble

The Royal Gauntlet

Anthologies:

Billionaires and Babes Charity Anthology

Getting Witchy With It Charity Anthology

No Going Back: Sultry in the City Anthology

Made in the USA
Monee, IL
16 May 2024

58353027R00197